D1282183

THE TRAIN FROM KATANGA

Also by Wilbur Smith

WHEN THE LION FEEDS

a novel by Wilbur Smith THE
TRAIN
FROM
KATANGA

NEW YORK · THE VIKING PRESS

THE TRAIN FROM KATANGA

"I don't like the idea," announced Wally Hendry and belched. He moved his tongue around his mouth getting the taste of it before he went on. "I think the whole idea stinks like a ten-day corpse." He lay sprawled on one of the beds with a glass balanced on his naked chest and he was sweating heavily in the Congo heat.

"Unfortunately your opinion doesn't alter the fact that we are going." Bruce Curry went on laying out his shaving tackle without looking up.

"You shoulda told them to keep it, told them we were staying here in Elisabethville—why didn't you tell them that, hey?" Hendry picked up his glass and swallowed the contents.

"Because they pay me not to argue." Bruce spoke without interest and looked at himself in the fly-spotted mirror above the wash basin. The face that looked back was sun-darkened with a cap of close-cropped black hair, soft hair that would be unruly and inclined to curl if it were longer; black eyebrows slanting upwards at the corners, green eyes with a heavy fringe of lashes, and a mouth that could smile as readily as it could sulk. Bruce regarded his good looks without pleasure. It was a long time since he had felt that emotion, a long time since his mouth had either smiled or sulked. He did not feel the old tolerant affection for his nose, the large slightly hooked nose that rescued his face from prettiness and gave him the air of a genteel pirate.

"Jesus!" growled Wally Hendry from the bed. "I've had just about a gutsful of this nigger army. I don't mind fighting— but I don't fancy going hundreds of miles out into the bush to play nursemaid to a bunch of bloody refugees."

"It's a hell of a life," agreed Bruce absently and spread shaving soap on his face. The lather was very white against his

1

tan. Under a skin that glowed so healthily that it appeared to have been freshly oiled, the muscles of his shoulders and chest changed shape as he moved. He was in good condition, fitter than he had been for many years, but this fact gave him no more pleasure than had his face.

"Get me another drink, André." Wally Hendry thrust his empty glass into the hand of the man who sat on the edge of the bed.

The Belgian stood up and went across to the table obediently.

"More whisky and less beer in this one," Wally instructed, turned once more to Bruce, and belched again. "That's what I think of the idea."

As André poured Scotch whisky into the glass and filled it with beer Wally hitched around the pistol in its webbing holster until it hung between his legs.

"When are we leaving?" he asked.

"There'll be an engine and five coaches at the goods yard first thing tomorrow morning. We'll load up and get going as soon as possible." Bruce started to shave, drawing the razor down from temple to chin and leaving the skin smooth and brown behind it.

"After three months of fighting a bunch of greasy little Gurkhas I was looking forward to a bit of fun—I haven't even had a pretty in all that time—now the second day after the cease-fire and they ship us out again."

"C'est la guerre," muttered Bruce, his face twisted in the act of shaving.

"What's that mean?" demanded Wally suspiciously.

"That's war," Bruce translated.

"Talk English, bucko."

It was the measure of Wally Hendry that after six months in the Belgian Congo he could neither speak nor understand a single word of French.

There was silence again, broken only by the scraping of Bruce's razor and the small metallic sounds as the fourth man in the hotel room stripped and cleaned his FN rifle.

"Have a drink, Haigh," Wally invited him.

"No, thanks." Michael Haigh glanced up, not trying to conceal his distaste as he looked at Wally.

"You're another snotty bastard—don't you want to drink with me, hey? Even the high-class Captain Curry is drinking with me. What makes you so goddam special?"

"You know that I don't drink." Haigh turned his attention back to his weapon, handling it with easy familiarity. For all of them the ugly automatic rifles had become an extension of their own bodies. Even while shaving, Bruce had only to drop his hand to reach the rifle propped against the wall, and the two men on the bed had theirs on the floor beside them.

"You don't drink!" Wally chuckled. "Then how did you get that complexion, bucko? How come your nose looks like a ripe plum?"

Haigh's mouth tightened and the hands on his rifle stilled.

"Cut it out, Wally," said Bruce without heat.

"Haigh don't drink," crowed Wally and dug the little Belgian in the ribs with his thumb. "Get that, André! He's a tee-bloody-total! My old man was a teetotal also; sometimes for two, three months at a time he was a teetotal, and then he'd come home one night and sock the old lady in the clock so you could hear her teeth rattle from across the street."

His laughter choked him and he had to wait for it to clear before he went on. "My bet is that you're that kind of teetotal, Haigh. One drink and you wake up ten days later—that's it, isn't it? One drink and—pow!—the old girl gets it in the chops and the kids don't eat for a couple of weeks."

Haigh laid the rifle down carefully on the bed and looked at Wally with his jaws clenched, but Wally had not noticed. He went on happily.

"André, take the whisky bottle and hold it under Old Tee-total Haigh's nose. Let's watch him slobber at the mouth."

Haigh stood up. He was twice the age of Wally—a man in his middle forties, with grey in his hair and the refinement of his features not completely obliterated by the marks that life had left upon them. He had arms like a boxer and a powerful set to his shoulders. "It's about time you learned a few manners, Hendry. Get on your feet."

"You wanta dance or something? I don't waltz—ask André. He'll dance with you—won't you, André?"

Haigh was balanced on the balls of his feet, his hands closed and raised slightly. Bruce Curry placed his razor on the shelf above the basin and moved quietly around the table, soap still on his face, to take up a position from which he could intervene. There he waited, watching the two men.

"Get up, you filthy guttersnipe!"

"Hey, André, get that. He talks pretty, hey? He talks real pretty."

"I'm going to smash that ugly face of yours right into the middle of the place where your brain should have been."

"Jokes! This boy is a natural comic." Wally laughed, but there was something wrong with the sound of it. Bruce knew then that Wally was not going to fight. Big arms and swollen chest covered with ginger hair, belly flat and hard looking, thicknecked below the wide flat-featured face with its little Mongolian eyes; but Wally wasn't going to fight. Bruce was puzzled: he remembered the night at the road bridge and he knew that Hendry was no coward, and yet now Hendry was not going to take up Haigh's challenge.

Mike Haigh moved towards the bed.

"Leave him, Mike." André spoke for the first time, his voice soft as a girl's. "He was only joking. He didn't mean it."

"Hendry, don't think I'm too much of a gentleman to hit you because you're on your back. Don't make that mistake."

"Big deal," muttered Wally. "This boy's not only a comic, he's a bloody hero too."

Haigh stood over him and lifted his right hand with the fist, bunched like a hammer, aimed at Wally's face.

"Haigh!" Bruce hadn't raised his voice but its tone checked the older man.

"That's enough," said Bruce.

"But this filthy little—"

"Yes, I know," said Bruce. "Leave him!"

With his fist still up Mike Haigh hesitated, and there was no movement in the room. Above them the corrugated iron roof popped loudly as it expanded in the heat of the Congo midday, and the only other sound was Haigh's breathing. He was panting and his face was congested with blood.

"Please, Mike," whispered André. "He didn't mean it."

Slowly Haigh's anger changed to disgust and he dropped his hand, turned away, and picked up his rifle from the other bed.

"I can't stand the smell in this room another minute. I'll wait for you in the truck downstairs, Bruce."

"I won't be long," agreed Bruce as Mike went to the door.

"Don't push your luck, Haigh," Wally called after him. "Next time you won't get off so easily."

In the doorway Mike Haigh swung quickly, but, with a hand on his shoulder, Bruce turned him again.

"Forget it, Mike," he said and closed the door after him.

"He's just bloody lucky that he's an old man," growled Wally. "Otherwise I'd have fixed him good."

"Sure," said Bruce. "It was decent of you to let him go." The soap had dried on his face and he wet his brush to lather again.

"Yeah, I couldn't hit an old bloke like that, could I?"

"No." Bruce smiled a little. "But don't worry, you frightened the hell out of him. He won't try it again."

"He'd better not!" warned Hendry. "Next time I'll kill the old bugger."

No, you won't, thought Bruce, you'll back down again as you have just done, as you've done a dozen times before. Mike and I are the only ones who can make you do it; in the same way as an animal will growl at its trainer but cringe away when he cracks the whip. He began shaving again.

The heat in the room was unpleasant to breathe; it drew the perspiration out of them, and the smell of their bodies blended sourly with stale cigarette smoke and liquor fumes.

"Where are you and Mike going?" André ended the long silence.

"We're going to see if we can draw the supplies for this trip.

If we have any luck we'll take them down to the goods yard and have Ruffy put an armed guard on them overnight," Bruce answered him, leaning over the basin and splashing water up on his face.

"How long will we be away?"

Bruce shrugged. "A week—ten days." He sat on his bed and pulled on one of his jungle boots. "That is, if we don't have any trouble."

"Trouble, Bruce?" asked André.

"From Msapa Junction we'll have to go two hundred miles through country crawling with Baluba."

"But we'll be in a train," protested André. "They've only got bows and arrows, they can't touch us."

"André, there are seven rivers to cross—one big one—and bridges are easily destroyed. Rails can be torn up." Bruce began to lace the boot. "I don't think it's going to be a Sunday school picnic."

"Christ. I think the whole thing stinks," said Wally moodily. "Why are we going anyway?"

"Because," Bruce began patiently, "for the last three months the entire population of Port Reprieve has been cut off from the rest of the world. There are women and children among them. They are fast running out of food and the other necessities of life." Bruce paused to light a cigarette and then went on talking as he exhaled. "All around them the Baluba tribe is in open revolt, burning, raping, and killing indiscriminately. As yet they haven't attacked the town, but it won't be very long until they do. Added to which there are rumours that rebel groups of Central Congolese troops and of our own forces have formed themselves into bands of heavily armed *shufta*. They also are running amok through the northern part of the territory. Nobody knows for certain what is happening out there, but whatever it is you can be sure it's not very pretty. We are going to fetch those people in to safety."

"Why don't the U.N. people send out a plane?" asked André.

"No landing field."

"Helicopters?"

"Out of range."

"For my money the bastards can stay there," grunted Wally. "If the Balubas fancy a little man steak, who are we to do them out of a meal? Every man's entitled to eat, and as long as it's not me they're eating, more power to their teeth, say I." He placed his foot against André's back and straightened his leg suddenly, throwing the Belgian off the bed onto his knees.

"Go and get me a pretty."

"There aren't any, Wally. I'll get you another drink." André scrambled to his feet and reached for Wally's empty glass, but Wally's hand dropped onto his wrist.

"I said 'pretty,' André, not 'drink.' "

"I don't know where to find them, Wally," André's voice was desperate. "I don't know what to say to them even."

"You're being stupid, bucko. I might have to break your arm." Wally twisted the wrist slowly. "You know as well as I do that the bar downstairs is full of them. You know that, don't you?"

"But what do I say to them?" André's face was contorted with the pain of his twisted wrist.

"Oh, for Christ's sake, you stupid bloody frog-eater—just go down and flash a banknote. You don't have to say a dicky bird."

"You're hurting me, Wally."

"No? You're kidding!" Wally smiled at him, twisting harder, his slitty eyes smoky from the liquor, and Bruce could see he was enjoying it. "Are you going, bucko? Make up your mind— get me a pretty or get yourself a broken arm."

"All right, if that's what you want. I'll go. Please leave me, I'll go," mumbled André.

"That's what I want." Wally released him.

André straightened up, massaging his wrist.

"See that she's clean and not too old. You hear me?"

"Yes, Wally. I'll get one." André went to the door, and Bruce noticed his expression. It was stricken beyond the pain of a bruised wrist. *What lovely creatures they are,* thought Bruce, *and I am one of them and yet apart from them. I am the watcher, stirred by them as much as I would be by a bad play.*

André went out.

"Another drink, bucko?" said Wally expansively. "I'll even pour you one."

"Thanks," said Bruce and started on the other boot. Wally brought the glass to him and he tasted it. It was strong, and the mustiness of the whisky was ill matched with the sweetness of the beer, but he drank it.

"You and me," said Wally, "we're the shrewd ones. We drink 'cause we want to, not 'cause we have to. We live like we want to live, not like other people think we should. You and I got a lot in common, Bruce. We should be friends, you and me. I mean us being so much alike." The drink was working in him now, blurring his speech a little.

"Of course we are friends—I count you as one of my very dearest, Wally." Bruce spoke solemnly, no trace of sarcasm showing.

"No kidding?" Wally asked earnestly. "How's that, hey? Christ, I always thought you didn't like me. Christ, you never can tell, isn't that right? You just never can tell,"—shaking his head in wonder, suddenly sentimental with the whisky. "That's really true? You like me. Yeah, we could be buddies. How's that, Bruce? Every guy needs a buddy. Every guy needs a back stop."

"Sure," said Bruce. "We're buddies. How's that, hey?"

"That's on, bucko!" agreed Wally with deep feeling.

And I feel nothing, thought Bruce, *no disgust, no pity— nothing. That way you are secure; they cannot disappoint you, they cannot disgust you, they cannot sicken you, they cannot smash you up again.*

They both looked up as André ushered the girl into the room. She had a sexy little pug face, painted lips—ruby on amber.

"Well done, André," applauded Wally, looking at the girl's body. She wore high heels and a pink dress that flared into a skirt from her waist but did not cover her knees.

"Come here, cookie." Wally held out his hand to her, and she crossed the room without hesitation, smiling a bright professional smile. Wally drew her down beside him on the bed.

André went on standing in the doorway. Bruce got up and shrugged into his camouflage battle jacket, buckled on his webbing belt and adjusted the holstered pistol until it hung comfortably on his outer thigh.

"Are you going?" Wally was feeding the girl from his glass.

"Yes." Bruce put his slouch hat on his head; the red, green, and white Katangese sideflash gave him an air of artificial gaiety.

"Stay a little—come on, Bruce."

"Mike is waiting for me." Bruce picked up his rifle.

"Muck him. Stay a little, we'll have some fun."

"No, thanks." Bruce went to the door.

"Hey, Bruce, take a look at this." Wally tipped the girl backwards over the bed; he pinned her with one arm across her chest while she struggled playfully, and with the other hand he swept her skirt up above her waist. "Take a good look at this and tell me you still want to go!"

The girl was naked under the skirt, her lower body shaven so that her plump little sex pouted sulkily.

"Come on, Bruce," said Wally, laughing. "You first. Don't say I'm not your buddy."

Bruce glanced at the girl; her legs scissored and her body wriggled as she fought with Wally. She was giggling.

"Mike and I will be back before curfew. I want this woman out of here by then," said Bruce.

There is no desire, he thought as he looked at her, *that is all finished.* He opened the door.

"Curry," shouted Wally, "you're a bloody nut also! Christ, I thought you were a man. Jesus Christ! You're as bad as the others. André, the doll boy. Haigh, the rummy. What's with you, bucko? It's women with you, isn't it? You're a bloody nut-case also!"

Bruce closed the door and stood alone in the passage. The taunt had gone through a chink in his armour, and he clamped his mind down on the sting of it, smothering it. *It's all over.*

She can't hurt me any more, he thought with determination, remembering her, the woman, not the one in the room he had just left but the other one who had been his wife.

"The bitch," he whispered, and then quickly, almost guiltily, "I do not hate her. There is no hatred and there is no desire."

2

The lobby of the Grand Hotel Leopold II was crowded. There were gendarmes carrying their weapons ostentatiously, talking loudly, lolling against walls and over the bar; women with them, varying in colour from black through to pastel brown, some already drunk; a few Belgians still with the stunned disbelieving eyes of the refugee, one of the women crying as she rocked her child on her lap; other white men in civilian clothes but with the alertness about them and the quick, restless eyes of the adventurer, talking quietly with Africans in business suits; a group of journalists at one table in damp shirtsleeves, waiting and watching with the patience of vultures. And everybody sweated in the heat.

Two South African charter pilots hailed Bruce from across the room. "Hi, Bruce. How about a snort?"

"Dave. Carl." Bruce waved. "Big hurry now—tonight perhaps."

"We're flying out this afternoon." Carl Engelbrecht shook his head. "Back next week."

"We'll make it then," Bruce agreed and went out of the front door into the Avenue du Kasai. As he stopped on the sidewalk the whitewashed buildings bounced the glare into his face. The naked heat made him wince, and he felt fresh sweat start out of his body beneath his battle suit. He took the dark glasses from his top pocket and put them on as he crossed the street to the Chev three-tonner in which Mike Haigh waited.

"I'll drive, Mike."

"Okay." Mike slid across the seat and Bruce stepped up into the cab. He started the truck north down the Avenue du Kasai.

"Sorry about that scene, Bruce."

"No harm done."

"I shouldn't have lost my temper like that."

Bruce did not answer; he was looking at the deserted buildings on either side. Most of them had been looted and all of them were pockmarked with shrapnel from the mortar bursts. At intervals along the sidewalk were parked the burned-out bodies of automobiles, looking like the carapaces of long-dead beetles.

"I shouldn't have let him get through to me, and yet the truth hurts like hell."

Bruce was silent but he trod down harder on the accelerator and the truck picked up speed. *I don't want to hear*, he thought, *I am not your confessor—I just don't want to hear.* He turned into the Avenue l'Etoile, headed towards the zoo.

"He was right, he had me measured to the inch," persisted Mike.

"We've all got troubles, otherwise we wouldn't be here." And then, to change Mike's mood, "We few, we happy few. We band of brothers."

Mike grinned, and his face was suddenly boyish. "At least we have the distinction of following the second oldest profession— we, the mercenaries."

"The oldest profession is better paid and much more fun," said Bruce and swung the truck into the driveway of a double-storied residence, parked outside the front door, and switched off the engine.

Not long ago the house had been the home of the chief accountant of Union Minière du Haut; now it was the billet of "D" section, Special Striker Force, commanded by Captain Bruce Curry.

Half a dozen of his black gendarmes were sitting on the low wall of the veranda, and as Bruce came up the front steps they shouted the greeting that had become traditional since the United Nations intervention.

"U.N.—*merde!*"

"Ah!" Bruce grinned at them in the feeling of companionship that had grown up between them in the past months. "The cream of the Army of Katanga!"

He offered his cigarettes around and stood chatting idly for a few minutes before asking, "Where's the sergeant major?" One of the gendarmes jerked a thumb at the glass doors that led into the lounge, and Bruce went through with Mike behind him.

Equipment was piled haphazardly on the expensive furniture; the stone fireplace was half filled with empty bottles; a gendarme lay snoring on the Persian carpet; one of the oil paintings on the wall had been ripped by a bayonet and the frame hung askew; the imbuia-wood coffee table tilted drunkenly towards its broken leg, and the whole lounge smelled of men and cheap tobacco.

"Hello, Ruffy," said Bruce.

"Just in time, boss." Sergeant Major Ruffararo grinned delightedly from the armchair which he was overflowing. "These goddam Arabs have run fresh out of folding stuff." He gestured at the gendarmes that crowded about the table in front of him. "Arab" was Ruffy's word of censure or contempt and bore no relation to a man's nationality.

Ruffy's accent was always a shock to Bruce. You never expected to hear pure Americanese come rumbling out of that huge black frame. But three years previously Ruffy had returned from a scholarship tour of the United States with a command of the idiom, a diploma in land husbandry, a prodigious thirst for bottled beer (preferably Schlitz, but any other was acceptable), and a raving dose of the Old Joe.

The memory of this last, which had been a farewell gift from a high-yellow coed at U.C.L.A., returned painfully to Ruffy when he was in his cups; so painfully that it could be assuaged only by throwing the nearest citizen of the United States.

Fortunately, it was only on rare occasions that an American and the necessary five or six gallons of beer were assembled in the same vicinity so that Ruffy's latent race antipathy could find expression. A throwing by Ruffy was an unforgettable experience, both for the victim and the spectators. Bruce vividly recalled that night at the Hotel Lido when he had been a witness at one of Ruffy's most spectacular throwings.

The victims, three of them, were journalists representing publications of repute. As the evening wore on they talked louder; an American accent has a carry like a well-hit golf ball, and Ruffy recognized it from across the terrace. He became silent, and in his silence drank the last gallon which was necessary to tip the balance. He wiped the froth from his upper lip and stood up with his eyes fastened on the party of Americans.

"Ruffy, hold it. Hey!" Bruce might not have spoken.

Ruffy started across the terrace. They saw him coming and fell into an uneasy silence.

The first was in the nature of a practice throw; besides, the man was not aerodynamically constructed and his stomach had too much wind resistance: a middling distance of twenty feet.

"Ruffy, leave them!" shouted Bruce.

On the next throw Ruffy was getting warmed up but he put excessive loft into it: thirty feet. The journalist cleared the terrace and landed on the lawn below with his empty glass still clutched in his hand.

"Run, you fool!" Bruce warned the third victim, but the man was paralyzed.

And this was Ruffy's best ever; he took a good grip—neck and seat of the pants—and put his whole weight into it. Ruffy must have known that he had executed the perfect throw, for his shout of "Gonorrhoea!" as he launched his man had a ring of triumph to it.

Afterwards, when Bruce had soothed the three Americans, and they had recovered sufficiently to appreciate the fact that they were privileged by being party to a record throwing session, they all paced out the distances. The three journalists developed an almost proprietary affection for Ruffy and spent the rest of the evening buying him beers and boasting to every newcomer in the bar. One of them—he who had been thrown last and farthest—wanted to do an article on Ruffy, with pictures. Towards the end of the evening he was talking wildly of whipping up sufficient international enthusiasm to have a man-throwing event included in the Olympic Games.

Ruffy accepted both their praise and their beer with modest gratitude; and when the third American offered to let Ruffy throw him again, Ruffy declined the offer on the grounds that he never threw the same man twice. All in all, it had been a memorable evening.

Apart from these occasional lapses Ruffy had a more powerful body and happier mind than any man Bruce had ever known, and Bruce could not help liking him. He could not prevent himself smiling as he tried to reject Ruffy's invitation to play cards.

"We've got work to do now, Ruffy. Some other time."

"Sit down, boss. We'll play just a couple of tricks, then we talk about work." He shuffled the three cards back and forth in his hands.

"Sit down, boss," Ruffy repeated, and Bruce grimaced resignedly and took the chair opposite him.

"How much you going to bet?" Ruffy leaned forward.

"*Une mille.*" Bruce laid a thousand-franc note on the table. "When that's gone, then we go."

"No hurry," Ruffy soothed him. "We got all day." He dealt the three cards face down. "The old Christian monarch is in there somewhere; all you got to do is find him, and it's the easiest *mille* you ever made."

"In the middle," whispered the gendarme standing beside Bruce's chair. "That's him in the middle."

"Take no notice of that mad Arab—he's lost five *mille* already this morning," Ruffy advised.

Bruce turned over the right-hand card.

"Mis-luck," crowed Ruffy. "You got yourself the queen of hearts." He picked up the banknote and stuffed it into his breast pocket. "She'll see you wrong every time, that sweet-faced little bitch." Grinning, he turned over the middle card to expose the jack of spades with his sly eyes and curly little mustache. "She's been shacked up there with the jack right under the old king's nose." He turned the king face up. "Look you at that dozy old guy—he's not even facing in the right direction."

Bruce stared at the three cards and he felt that sickness in his stomach again. The whole story was there; even the man's name was right, but the jack should have worn a beard and driven a red Jaguar and his queen of hearts never had such innocent eyes.

Bruce spoke abruptly. "That's it, Ruffy. I want you and ten men to come with me."

"Where we going?"

"Down to Ordnance—we're drawing special supplies."

Ruffy nodded and buttoned the playing cards into his top pocket while he selected the gendarmes to accompany them; then he asked Bruce, "We might need some oil—what you think, boss?"

Bruce hesitated; they had only two cases of whisky left of the dozen they had looted in August. The purchasing power of a bottle of genuine Scotch was enormous, and Bruce was loath to use them except in extraordinary circumstances. But now he realized that his chances of getting the supplies he needed were remote unless he took along a substantial bribe for the quarter-master.

"Okay, Ruffy. Bring a case."

Ruffy came up out of the chair and clapped his steel helmet on his head. The chin straps hung down on each side of his round black face. "A full case?" He grinned at Bruce. "You want to buy a battleship?"

"Almost," agreed Bruce. "Go and get it."

Ruffy disappeared into the back area of the house and returned almost immediately with a case of Grant's Standfast under one arm and half a dozen bottles of Simba beer held by their necks between the fingers of his other hand. "We might get thirsty," he explained.

The gendarmes climbed into the back of the truck with a clatter of weapons and shouted cheerful abuse at their fellows on the veranda. Bruce, Mike, and Ruffy crowded into the cab, and Ruffy set the whisky on the floor and placed two large booted feet upon it.

"What's this all about, boss?" he asked as Bruce trundled the truck down the drive and turned into the Avenue l'Etoile. Bruce told him, and when he had finished Ruffy grunted non-committally and opened a bottle of beer with his big white chisel-blade teeth; the gas hissed softly and a little froth ran down the bottle and dripped onto his lap.

"My boys aren't going to like it," he commented as he offered the open bottle to Mike Haigh. Mike shook his head, and Ruffy passed the bottle to Bruce.

Ruffy opened a bottle for himself and spoke again. "They going to hate it like hell." He shook his head. "And there'll be even bigger trouble when we get to Port Reprieve and pick up the diamonds."

Bruce glanced sideways at him, startled. "What diamonds?"

"From the dredgers," said Ruffy. "You don't think they're sending us all that way just to bring in these other guys. They're worried about the diamonds, that's for sure!"

Suddenly, for Bruce, much that had puzzled him was explained. A half-forgotten conversation that he had held earlier in the year with an engineer from Union Minière jumped back into his memory. They had discussed the three diamond dredgers that worked the gravel from the bed of the Lufira swamps. The boats were based at Port Reprieve and clearly they would have returned there at the beginning of the emergency; they must still be there with three or four months' recovery of diamonds on board—something like half a million sterling in uncut stones. That was the reason the Katangese government placed such priority on this expedition, the reason such a powerful force was being used, the reason no approaches had been made to the U.N. authorities to conduct the rescue.

Bruce smiled sardonically as he remembered the humanitarian arguments that had been given to him by the Minister of the Interior.

"It is our duty, Captain Curry. We cannot leave these people to the not-so-tender mercy of the tribesmen. It is our duty as civilized human beings."

There were others cut off in remote mission stations and government outposts throughout southern Kasai and Katanga; nothing had been heard of them for months, but their welfare was secondary to that of the settlement at Port Reprieve.

Bruce lifted the bottle to his lips again, steering with one hand and squinting ahead through the windscreen as he drank. All right, we'll fetch them in and afterwards an ammunition box will be loaded onto a chartered aircraft, and later still there will be another deposit to a numbered account in Zurich. Why should I worry? They're paying me for it.

"I don't think we should mention the diamonds to my boys." Ruffy spoke sadly. "I don't think that would be a good idea at all."

Bruce slowed the truck as they ran into the industrial area beyond the railway line. He watched the buildings as they passed, until he recognized the one he wanted and swung off the road to stop in front of the gate. He blew a blast on the hooter and a gendarme came out and inspected his pass minutely. Satisfied, he shouted out to someone beyond the gate, and it swung open. Bruce drove the truck through into the yard and switched off the engine.

There were half a dozen other trucks parked in the yard, all emblazoned with the Katangese shield and surrounded by gendarmes in uniforms patchy with sweat.

A white lieutenant leaned from the cab of one of the trucks and shouted, "*Ciao*, Bruce!"

"How are things, Sergio?" Bruce called back.

"Crazy! Crazy!"

Bruce smiled. For the Italian everything was crazy. Bruce remembered that in July, during the fighting at the road bridge, he had bent him over the bonnet of a Land Rover and with a bayonet dug a piece of shrapnel out of his hairy buttocks—that also had been crazy.

"See you around," Bruce dismissed him and led Mike and Ruffy across the yard to the warehouse. There was a sign on the large double doors, *Dépôt Ordnance—Armée du Katanga*, and beyond them at a desk in a glass cubicle sat a major with a pair of Gandhi-type steel-rimmed spectacles perched on a face like that of a jovial black toad.

He looked up at Bruce. "*Non*," he said with finality. "*Non, non.*"

Bruce produced his requisition form and laid it before him.

The major brushed it aside contemptuously. "We have not got these items, we are destitute. I cannot do it. No! I cannot do it. There are priorities. There are circumstances to consider. No, I am sorry."

He snatched a sheaf of papers from the side of his desk and turned his whole attention to them, ignoring Bruce.

"This requisition is signed by Monsieur le Président," Bruce pointed out mildly, and the major laid down his papers and came round from behind the desk. He stood close to Bruce with the top of his head on a level with Bruce's chin.

"Had it been signed by the Almighty himself, it would be of no use. I am sorry, I am truly sorry."

Bruce lifted his eyes and for a second allowed them to wander over the mountains of stores that packed the interior of the warehouse. From where he stood he could identify at least twenty items that he needed. The major noticed the gesture and his French became so excited that Bruce could make out only the repeated use of the word *non*. He glanced significantly at Ruffy and the sergeant major stepped forward and placed an arm soothingly about the major's shoulders; then very gently he led him, still protesting, out into the yard and across to the truck. He opened the door of the cab and the major saw the case of whisky.

A few minutes later, after Ruffy had prised open the lid with his bayonet and allowed the major to inspect the seals on the caps, they returned to the office with Ruffy carrying the case.

"Captain," said the major as he picked up the requisition from the desk, "I see now that I was mistaken. This is indeed signed by Monsieur le Président. It is my duty to afford you the most urgent priority."

Bruce murmured his thanks and the major beamed at him. "I will give you men to help you."

"You are too kind. It would disrupt your routine. I have my own men."

"Excellent," agreed the major and waved a podgy hand around the warehouse. "Take what you need."

3

Again Bruce glanced at his wrist watch. It was still twenty minutes before the curfew ended at 6 o'clock. Until then he must fret away the time watching Wally Hendry finishing his breakfast. This was a spectacle without much appeal, for Hendry was a methodical but untidy eater.

"Why don't you keep your mouth closed?" snapped Bruce irritably, unable to stand it any longer.

"Do I ask you your business?" Hendry looked up from his plate. His jowls were covered with a ginger stubble of beard, and his eyes were inflamed and puffy from the previous evening's debauchery. Bruce looked away from him and checked his watch again.

The suicidal temptation to ignore the curfew and set off immediately for the railway station was very strong. It required an effort to resist it. The least he could expect if he followed that course was an arrest by one of the patrols and a delay of twelve hours while he cleared himself; the worst would be a shooting incident.

He poured himself another cup of coffee and sipped it slowly. *Impatience has always been one of my weaknesses*, he reflected; *nearly every mistake I have ever made stems from that cause. But I have improved a little over the years—at twenty I wanted to live my whole life in a week. Now I'll settle for a year.*

He finished his coffee and checked the time again. Five minutes before six, he could risk it now. It would take almost that long to get out to the truck.

"If you are ready, gentlemen." He pushed back his chair and picked up his pack, slung it over his shoulder, and led the way out.

Ruffy was waiting for them, sitting on a pile of stores in one of the corrugated-iron goods sheds. His men squatted around a dozen small fires on the concrete floor, cooking breakfast.

"Where's the train?"

"That's a good question, boss," Ruffy congratulated him.

Bruce groaned.

"It should have been here long ago," Bruce protested, and Ruffy shrugged.

" 'Should have been' is a lot different from 'is.' "

"Goddammit! We've still got to load up. We'll be lucky if we get away before noon," snapped Bruce. "I'll go up to the station master."

"You'd better take him a present, boss. We've still got a case left."

"No, hell!" Bruce growled. "Come with me, Mike."

With Mike beside him they crossed the tracks to the main platform and clambered up onto it. At the far end a group of railway officials stood chatting, and Bruce fell upon them furiously.

Two hours later Bruce stood beside the coloured engine driver on the footplate and they puffed slowly down towards the goods yard.

The driver was a roly-poly little man with a skin too dark for mere sunburn and a set of teeth with bright red plastic gums.

"Monsieur, you do not wish to proceed to Port Reprieve?" he asked anxiously.

"Yes."

"There is no way of telling the condition of the permanent way. No traffic has used it these last four months."

"I know. You'll have to proceed with caution."

"There is a United Nations barrier across the lines near the old airfield," protested the man.

"We have a pass." Bruce smiled to soothe him; his bad temper was abating now that he had his transport. "Stop next to the first shed."

With a hiss of steam brakes the train pulled up beside the concrete platform and Bruce jumped down. "All right, Ruffy," he shouted, "let's get cracking."

Bruce had placed the three steel-sided open railway cars in the van, for they were the easiest to defend. From behind the breast-high sides the Bren guns could sweep ahead and on both flanks. Then followed the two passenger coaches, to be used as storerooms and officers' quarters; also for the accommodation of the refugees on the return journey; finally, the locomotive in the rear, where it would be least vulnerable and would not spew smoke and soot back over the train.

The stores were loaded into four of the compartments, the windows shuttered and the doors locked. Then Bruce set about laying out his defenses. In a low circle of sandbags on the roof of the first coach he sited one of the Brens and made this his own post. From here he could look down over the open cars, back at the locomotive, and also command an excellent view of the surrounding country.

The other Brens he placed in the leading car and put Hendry in command there. He had obtained from the major at Ordnance three of the new walkie-talkie sets; one he gave to the engine driver, another to Hendry up front, and the third he retained in his emplacement; and his system of communication was satisfactory.

It was almost twelve o'clock before these preparations were complete and Bruce turned to Ruffy who sat on the sandbags beside him. "All set?"

"All set, boss."

"How many missing?" Bruce had learned from experience never to expect his entire command to be in any one place at any one time.

"Eight, boss."

"That's three more than yesterday; leaves us only fifty-two men. Do you think they've taken off into the bush also?" Five of his men had deserted with their weapons on the day of the cease-fire. Obviously they had gone out into the bush to join one of the bands of *shufta* that were already playing havoc along the main roads: ambushing all unprotected traffic, beating up lucky travellers and murdering those less fortunate, raping when they had the opportunity, and generally enjoying themselves.

"No, boss. I don't think so, those three are good boys. They'll be down in the *cité indigène* having themselves some fun; guess they just forgot the time." Ruffy shook his head. "Take us about half an hour to find them; all we do is go down and visit all the knock-shops. You want to try?"

"No, we haven't time to mess around if we are going to make Msapa Junction before dark. We'll pick them up again when we get back." Was there ever an army since the Boer War that treated desertion so lightly, Bruce wondered.

He turned to the radio set beside him and depressed the transmit button. "Driver."

"*Oui, monsieur.*"

"Proceed—very slowly until we approach the United Nations barrier. Stop well this side of it."

"*Oui, monsieur.*"

They rolled out of the goods yard, clicking over the points; leaving the industrial quarter on their right with the Katangese guard posts on the Avenue du Cimetière intersection; out through the suburbs until ahead of them Bruce saw the U.N. positions and felt the first stirring of anxiety. The pass he carried in the breast pocket of his jacket was signed by General Rhee Singh, but before in this war the orders of an Indian general had not been passed by a Sudanese captain to an Irish sergeant. The reception that awaited them could be exciting.

"I hope they know about us." Mike Haigh lit his cigarette with a show of nonchalance, but he peered over it anxiously at the piles of fresh earth on each side of the tracks that marked the position of the emplacements.

"These boys have got bazookas, and they're Irish Arabs," muttered Ruffy. "I reckon that's the maddest kind of Arab there is—Irish. How would you like a bazooka bomb up the throat, boss?"

"No, thanks, Ruffy," Bruce declined and pressed the button on the radio. "Hendry!"

In the leading car Wally Hendry picked up his set and, holding it against his chest, looked back at Bruce. "Curry?"

"Tell your gunners to stand away from the Brens, and the rest of them to lay down their rifles."

"Right."

Bruce watched him relaying the order, pushing them back, moving among the gendarmes that crowded the forward cars. Bruce could sense the air of tension that had fallen over the whole train, watched as his gendarmes reluctantly laid down their weapons and stood empty-handed, staring sullenly ahead at the U.N. barrier.

"Driver!" Bruce spoke again into the radio. "Slow down. Stop fifty metres this side of the barrier. But if there is any shooting, open the throttle and take us straight through."

"*Oui, monsieur.*"

Ahead of them there was no sign of a reception committee, only the hostile barrier of poles and petrol drums across the line.

Bruce stood up on the roof and lifted his arms above his head in a gesture of neutrality. It was a mistake; the movement changed the passive mood of the gendarmes in the cars below him. One of them lifted his arms also, but his fists were clenched.

"U.N.—*merde!*" he shouted, and immediately the cry was taken up.

"U.N.—*merde!* U.N.—*merde!*" They chanted the war cry—laughing at first, but then no longer laughing, their voices rising sharply.

"Shut up, damn you!" Bruce roared and swung his open hand against the head of the gendarme beside him, but the man hardly noticed it. His eyes were glazing with the infectious hysteria to which the African is so susceptible; he had snatched up his rifle and was holding it across his chest; already his body was beginning to jerk convulsively as he chanted.

Bruce hooked his fingers under the rim of the man's steel helmet and yanked it forward over his eyes so that the back of his neck was exposed; he chopped him with a judo blow, and the gendarme slumped forward over the sandbags, his rifle slipping from his hands.

Bruce looked up desperately; in the cars below him the hysteria was spreading.

"Stop them—Hendry, de Surrier! Stop them, for God's sake!" But his voice was lost in the chanting.

A gendarme snatched up his rifle from where it lay at his feet; Bruce saw him elbow his way towards the side of the car to begin firing; he was working the slide to lever a round into the breach.

"Mwembe!" Bruce shouted the gendarme's name, but his voice could not penetrate the uproar.

In two seconds the whole situation would dissolve into a pandemonium of tracer and bazooka fire.

Poised on the forward edge of the roof, Bruce checked for an instant to judge the distance, and then he jumped. He landed squarely on the gendarme's shoulders, his weight throwing the man forward so his face hit the steel edge of the car, and they went down together on the floor.

The gendarme's finger was resting on the trigger, and the rifle fired as it spun from his hands. A complete hush followed the roar of the rifle, and in it Bruce scrambled to his feet, drawing his pistol from the canvas holster on his hip.

"All right," he said panting, menacing the men around him. "Come on, give me a chance to use this!" He picked out one of his sergeants and held his eyes. "You! I'm waiting for you—start shooting!"

At the sight of the revolver the man relaxed slowly and the madness faded from his face. He dropped his eyes and shuffled awkwardly.

Bruce glanced up at Ruffy and Haigh on the roof and raised his voice. "Watch them. Shoot the first one who starts it again."

"Okay, boss." Ruffy thrust forward the automatic rifle in his hands. "Who's it going to be?" he asked cheerfully, looking down at them. But the mood had changed. Their attitudes of defiance gave way to sheepish embarrassment, and a small buzz of conversation filled the silence.

"Mike," Bruce yelled, urgent again, "call the driver, he's trying to take us through!"

The noise of their passage had risen, the driver accelerating at the sound of the shot, and now they were racing down towards the U.N. barrier.

Mike Haigh grabbed the set, shouted an order into it, and immediately the brakes swooshed and the train jolted to a halt not a hundred yards short of the barrier.

Slowly Bruce clambered back onto the roof of the coach. "Close?" asked Mike.

"My God!" Bruce shook his head and lit a cigarette with slightly unsteady hands. "Another fifty yards—!" Then he turned and stared coldly down at his gendarmes.

"*Canaille*! Next time you try to commit suicide, don't take me with you." The gendarme he had knocked down was now sitting up, fingering the ugly black swelling above his eye. "My friend," Bruce turned on him, "later I will have something for your further discomfort!" Then to the other man in the emplacement beside him who was massaging his neck, "And for you also! Take their names, Sergeant Major."

"Sir!" growled Ruffy.

"Mike"—Bruce's voice changed, soft again—"I'm going ahead to toss the blarney with our friends behind the bazookas. When I give you the signal, bring the train through."

"You don't want me to come with you?" asked Mike.

"No, stay here." Bruce picked up his rifle, slung it over his shoulder, dropped down the ladder onto the path beside the tracks, and walked forward with the gravel crunching beneath his boots.

An auspicious beginning to the expedition, he decided grimly —tragedy averted by the wink of an eye before they had even passed the outskirts of the city.

At least the Mickies hadn't added a few bazooka bombs to the altercation. Bruce peered ahead and could make out the shape of helmets behind the earthworks.

Without the breeze of the train's passage it was hot again, and Bruce felt himself starting to sweat.

"Stay where you are, mister"—a deep brogue from the emplacement nearest the tracks. Bruce stopped, standing on the wooden crossties in the sun. Now he could see the faces of the men beneath the helmets: unfriendly, not smiling.

"What was the shooting for?" the voice questioned.

"We had an accident."

"Don't have any more or we might have one also."

"I'd not be wanting that, Paddy." Bruce smiled thinly, and the Irishman's voice had an edge to it as he went on. "What's your mission?"

"I have a pass—do you want to see it?" Bruce took the folded sheet of paper from his breast pocket.

"What's your mission?" repeated the Irishman.

"Proceed to Port Reprieve and relieve the town."

"We know about you." The Irishman nodded. "Let me see the pass."

Bruce left the tracks, climbed the earth wall, and handed the pink slip to the Irishman. He wore the three pips of a captain, and he glanced briefly at the pass before speaking to the man beside him.

"Very well, Sergeant, you can be clearing the barrier now."

"I'll call the train through?" Bruce asked, and the captain nodded again.

"But make sure there are no more accidents—we don't like hired killers."

"Sure and begorrah now, Paddy, it's not your war you're a-fighting either," snapped Bruce and abruptly turned his back on the man, jumped down to the tracks, and waved to Mike Haigh on the roof of the coach.

The Irish sergeant and his party had cleared the tracks, and while the train rumbled slowly down to him Bruce struggled to control his irritation—the Irish captain's taunt had reached him. Hired killer, and of course that was what he was. Could a man sink any lower?

As the coach drew level with where he stood, Bruce caught the hand rail and swung himself aboard, waved an ironical farewell to the Irish captain and climbed up onto the roof.

"No trouble?" asked Mike.

"A bit of lip delivered in music-hall brogue," Bruce answered, "but nothing serious." He picked up the radio set. "Driver."

"Monsieur?"

"Do not forget my instructions."

"I will not exceed forty kilometres the hour, and I shall at all times be prepared for an emergency stop."

"Good!" Bruce switched off the set and sat down on the sandbags between Ruffy and Mike.

Well, he thought, here we go at last. Six hours' run to Msapa Junction. That should be easy. And then—God knows, God alone knows.

The tracks curved, and Bruce looked back to see the last whitewashed buildings of Elisabethville disappear among the trees. They were out in the open savannah forest.

Behind them the black smoke from the loco rolled sideways into the trees; beneath them the crossties clattered in strict rhythm; and ahead the line ran arrow-straight for miles, dwindling with perspective until it merged into the olive-green mass of the forest.

Bruce lifted his eyes. Half the sky was clear and tropical blue, but in the north it was bruised with cloud, and beneath the cloud grey rain drifted down to meet the earth. The sunlight through the rain spun a rainbow, and the cloud shadow moved across the land as slowly and as darkly as a herd of grazing buffalo.

He loosened the chin strap of his helmet and laid his rifle on the roof beside him.

"You'd like a beer, boss?"

"Have you any?"

"Sure." Ruffy called to one of the gendarmes, and the man climbed down into the coach and came back with half a dozen bottles. Ruffy opened two with his teeth. Each time half the contents frothed out and splattered back along the wooden side of the coach.

"This beer's as wild as an angry woman," he grunted as he passed a bottle to Bruce.

"It's wet anyway." Bruce tasted it, warm and gassy and too sweet.

"Here's how!" said Ruffy.

Bruce looked down into the open cars at the gendarmes who were settling in for the journey. Apart from the gunners at the Brens, they were lying or squatting in attitudes of complete relaxation, and most of them had stripped down to their underwear. One skinny little fellow was already asleep on his back with his helmet as a pillow and the tropical sun beating full into his face.

Bruce finished his beer and threw the bottle overboard.

Ruffy opened another and placed it in Bruce's hand without comment. "Why we going so slowly, boss?"

"I told the driver to keep the speed down—give us a chance to stop if the tracks have been torn up."

"Yeah. Them Balubas might have done that—they're mad Arabs all of them."

The warm beer drunk in the sun was having a soothing effect on Bruce. He felt at peace now, withdrawn from the need to make decisions, to participate in the life around him.

"Listen to that train-talk," said Ruffy, and Bruce focused his hearing on the clickety-clack of the crossties.

"Yes, I know. You can make it say anything you want it to," agreed Bruce.

"And it can sing," Ruffy went on. "It's got real music in it, like this." He inflated the great barrel of his chest, lifted his head and let it come.

His voice was deep, with a resonance that caught the attention of the men in the open cars below them. Those who had been sprawled in the amorphous shapes of sleep stirred and sat up. Another voice joined in, humming the tune, hesitantly at first, then more confidently. Then others took it up; the words were unimportant—it was the rhythm that they could not resist. They had sung together many times before, and like a well-trained choir each voice found its place, the star performers leading, changing the pace, improvising, quickening, until the original tune lost its identity and became one of the tribal chants. Bruce recognized it as a planting song. It was one of his favourites, and he sat drinking his lukewarm beer and letting the singing wash around him, build up into the chorus like storm waves, then fall back into a tenor solo before rising once more. And the train ran on through the sunlight towards the rain clouds in the north.

Presently André came out of the coach below him and picked his way forward through the men in the cars until he reached Hendry. The two of them stood together, André's face turned up towards the taller man and deadly earnest as he talked.

Doll boy, Hendry had called him, and it was an accurate description of the effeminately pretty face with the big toffee eyes; the steel helmet he wore seemed too large for his shoulders to carry.

I wonder how old he is; Bruce watched him laugh suddenly, his face still turned upwards to Hendry; not much over twenty, and I have never seen anything less like a hired killer.

"How the hell did anyone like de Surrier get mixed up in this?" His voice echoed the thought, and beside him Mike answered.

"He was working in Elisabethville when it started, and he couldn't return to Belgium. I don't know the reason but I guess it was something personal. When it started his firm closed down. I suppose this was the only employment he could find."

"That Irishman, the one at the barrier, he called me a hired killer." Thinking of André's position in the scheme of things had turned Bruce's thoughts back to his own status. "I hadn't thought about it that way before but I suppose he's right. That is what we are."

Mike Haigh was silent for a moment; when he spoke there was a stark quality in his voice. "Look at these hands!"

Involuntarily Bruce glanced down at them and for the first time noticed that they were narrow, with long, moulded fingers, possessed of a functional beauty, the hands of an artist.

"Look at them," Mike repeated, flexing them slightly. "They were fashioned for a purpose, they were made to hold a scalpel, they were made to save life." Then he relaxed them and let them drop onto the rifle across his lap, the long, delicate fingers incongruous upon the blue metal. "But look what they hold now!"

Bruce stirred irritably. He had not wanted to provoke another bout of Mike Haigh's soul-searching. Damn the old fool—why must he always start this, he knew as well as anyone that in the mercenary army of Katanga there was a taboo upon the past. It did not exist.

"Ruffy," Bruce snapped, "aren't you going to feed your boys?"

"Right now, boss." Ruffy opened another beer and handed it to Bruce. "Hold that—it will keep your mind off food while I rustle it up." He lumbered off along the roof of the coach, still singing.

"Three years ago—it seems like all eternity," Mike went on as though Bruce had not interrupted. "Three years ago I was a surgeon, and now this—" The desolation had spread to his eyes, and Bruce felt his pity for the man deep down where he kept it imprisoned with all his other emotions. "I was good. I was one of the best. Royal College. Harley Street. Guy's." Mike laughed without humour, with bitterness. "Can you imagine me being driven in my Rolls to address the College on my advanced technique of cholecystectomy?"

"What happened?" The question was out before Bruce could stop it, and he realized how near to the surface he had let his pity rise. "No, don't tell me. It's your business. I don't want to know."

"But I'll tell you, Bruce. I want to. It helps somehow, talking about it."

At first, thought Bruce, *I wanted to talk also, to try and wash the pain away with words.*

Mike was silent for a few seconds. Below them the singing rose and fell, and the train ran on through the forest.

"It had taken me ten hard years to get there, but at last I had done it. A fine practice, doing the work I loved with skill, earning the rewards I deserved. A wife that any man would have been proud of, a lovely home, many friends, too many friends perhaps; for success breeds friends the way a dirty kitchen breeds cockroaches."

Mike pulled out a handkerchief and dried the back of his neck where the wind could not reach.

"Those sort of friends mean parties," he went on. "Parties when you've worked all day and you're tired; when you need the lift that you can get so easily from a bottle. You don't know if you have the weakness for the stuff until it's too late; until you have a bottle in the drawer of your desk; until suddenly your practice isn't so good any more."

Mike twisted the handkerchief around his fingers as he plowed doggedly on. "Then you know it suddenly. You know it when your hands dance in the morning and all you want for breakfast is *that*; when you can't wait until lunch time because you have to operate and that's the only way you can keep your hands steady. But you know it finally and utterly when the knife turns in your hand and the artery starts to spurt and you watch it, paralyzed—you watch it hosing red over your gown and forming pools on the operating room floor." Mike's voice dried up then, and he tapped a cigarette from his pack and lit it. His shoulders were hunched forward and his eyes were full of the shadows of his guilt. Then he straightened up, and his voice was stronger.

"You must have read about it. I was headlines for a few days, all the papers. But my name wasn't Haigh in those days. I changed it to sound like the name on a barroom bottle.

"Gladys stayed with me, of course, she was that type. We came out to Africa. I had enough saved from the wreck for a down payment on a tobacco farm in the Centenary block outside Salisbury. Two good seasons, and I was off the bottle. Gladys was having our first baby—we had both wanted one so badly. It was all coming right again."

Mike stuffed the handkerchief back in his pocket, and his voice lost its strength again, turned dry and husky.

"Then one day I took the truck into the village, and on the way home I stopped at the club. I had been there often before, but this time it was different. Instead of half an hour I stayed there until they threw me out at closing time, and when I got back to the farm I had a case of Scotch on the seat beside me."

Bruce wanted to stop him; he knew what was coming and he didn't want to hear it.

"The first rains started that night and the rivers came down in flood. The telephone lines were knocked out and we were cut off. In the morning—" Mike stopped again and turned to Bruce. "I suppose it was the shock of seeing me like that again, but in the morning Gladys went into labour. It was her first and she wasn't so young any more. She was still in labour the next day, but by then she was too weak to scream. I remember how peaceful it was without her screaming and pleading with me to help. You see, she knew I had all the instruments I needed. She begged me to help. I can remember that—her voice through the fog of whisky. I think I hated her then. I think I remember hating her—it was all so confused, so mixed up with the screaming and the liquor. But at last she was quiet. I don't think I realized she was dead. I was simply glad she was quiet and I could have peace."

He dropped his eyes from Bruce's face.

"I was too drunk to go to the funeral. Then I met a man in a barroom—I can't remember how long after it was, I can't even remember where. It must have been on the Copperbelt. He was recruiting for Tshombe's army and I signed up; there didn't seem anything else to do."

Neither of them spoke again until a gendarme brought food to them, hunks of brown bread spread with tinned butter and filled with bully beef and pickled onions. They ate in silence, listening to the singing, and Bruce said at last, "You needn't have told me."

"I know."

"Mike—" Bruce paused.

"Yes?"

"I'm sorry, if that's any comfort."

"It is," Mike said. "It helps to have—not to be completely alone. I like you, Bruce." He blurted out the last sentence, and Bruce recoiled as though Mike had spat in his face.

You fool, he rebuked himself savagely, *you were wide open then. You nearly let one of them in again.* Remorselessly he crushed down his sympathy, shocked at the effort it required, and when he picked up the radio the gentleness had gone from his eyes.

"Hendry," he spoke into the set, "don't talk so much. I put you up front to watch the tracks."

From the leading truck Wally Hendry looked around and forked two fingers at Bruce in a casual obscenity, but he turned back and faced ahead.

"You'd better go and take over from Hendry," Bruce told Mike. "Send him back here."

Mike Haigh stood up and looked down at Bruce. "What are you afraid of?" His voice was softly puzzled.

"I gave you an order, Haigh."

"Yes, I'm on my way."

4

The aircraft found them in the late afternoon. It was a Vampire jet of the Indian Air Force and it came from the north.

They heard the soft rumble of it across the sky and then saw it glint like a speck of mica in the sunlight above the storm clouds ahead of them.

"I bet you a thousand francs to a handful of dung that this bucko don't know about us," said Hendry with anticipation, watching the jet turn off its course towards them.

"Well, he does now," said Bruce.

Swiftly he surveyed the rain clouds in front of them. They were close; another ten minutes' run and they would be under them, and once there they were safe from air attack, for the belly of the clouds pressed close against the earth and the rain was a thick blue-grey mist that would reduce visibility to a few hundred feet.

He switched on the radio. "Driver, give us all the speed you have—get us into that rain."

"Oui, monsieur," came the acknowledgment, and almost immediately the puffing of the loco quickened and the clatter of the crossties changed its rhythm.

"Look at him come," growled Hendry. The jet fell fast against the backdrop of cloud, still in sunlight, still a silver point of light, but growing.

Bruce clicked over the band selector of the radio, searching the ether for the pilot's voice. He tried four wave lengths and each time found only the crackle and drone of static, but with the fifth came the gentle singsong of Hindustani. Bruce could not understand it, but he could hear that the tone was puzzled. There was a short silence on the radio while the pilot listened to an instruction from the Kamina base, which was beyond the power of their small set to receive, then a curt affirmative.

"He's coming in for a closer look," said Bruce; then, raising his voice, "Everybody under cover—and stay there." He was not prepared to risk another demonstration of friendship.

The jet came cruising in towards them under half power, yet incredibly fast, leaving the sound of its engine far behind it, sharklike above the forest. Then Bruce could see the pilot's head through the canopy; now he could make out his features. His face was very brown beneath the silver crash helmet and he had a little mustache, the same as the jack of spades. He was so close that Bruce saw the exact moment that he recognized them as Katangese; his eyes showed white and his mouth puckered as he swore. Beside Bruce the radio relayed the oath with metallic harshness, and then the jet was banking away steeply, its engine howling in full throttle, rising, showing its swollen silver belly and the racks of rockets beneath its wings.

"That frightened seven years' growth out of him," said Hendry, laughing. "You should have let me blast him. He was close enough for me to hit him in the left eyeball."

"You'll get another chance in a moment," Bruce assured him grimly. The radio was gabbling with consternation as the jet dwindled back into the sky. Bruce switched quickly to their own channel. "Driver, can't you get this thing moving?"

"Monsieur, never before has she moved as she does now."

Once more Bruce switched back to the jet's frequency and listened to the pilot's excited voice. The jet was turning in a wide circle, perhaps fifteen miles away. Bruce glanced at the piled mass of cloud and rain ahead of them; it was moving down to meet them, but with ponderous dignity.

"If he comes back," Bruce shouted down at his gendarmes, "we can be sure that it's not just to look at us again. Open fire as soon as he's in range. Give him everything you've got— we must try and spoil his aim."

Their faces were turned up towards him, subdued by the awful inferiority of the earthbound to the hunter in the sky. Only André did not look at Bruce; he was staring at the aircraft with his jaws clenching nervously and his eyes too large for his face.

Again there was silence on the radio, and every head turned back to watch the jet.

"Come on, bucko, come on!" grunted Hendry impatiently. He spat into the palm of his right hand and then wiped it down the front of his jacket. "Come on, we want you." With his thumb he flicked the safety catch on his rifle on and off, on and off.

Suddenly the radio spoke again. Two words, obviously acknowledging an order, and one of the words Bruce recognized. He had heard it before in circumstances that had burned it into his memory. The Hindustani word *attack*!

"All right," he said and stood up. "He's coming!" He settled his helmet firmly and pumped a round into the chamber of his FN.

"Get down into the car, Hendry," he ordered.

"I can see better from here." Hendry was standing beside him, legs planted wide to brace himself against the violent motion of the train.

"As you like," said Bruce. "Ruffy, you get under cover."

"Too damn hot down there in the box." The huge Negro grinned.

"You're a mad Arab too," said Bruce.

"Sure, we're all mad Arabs."

The jet wheeled sharply and swooped towards the forest, levelling, still miles out on their flank.

"This bucko is a real apprentice. He's going to take us from the side, so we can all shoot at him. If he was half awake he'd give it to us up the bum, hit the loco, and make sure that we were all shooting over the top of each other," gloated Hendry.

Silently, swiftly, it closed with them, almost touching the tops of the trees. Then suddenly the cannon fire sparkled lemon-pale on its nose, and all around them the air was filled with the sound of a thousand whips. Immediately every gun on the train opened up in reply. The tracers from the Brens chased each other out to meet the plane, and the rifles joined their voices in a clamour that drowned the cannon fire.

Bruce aimed carefully, the jet unsteady in his sights from the lurching of the coach; then he pressed the trigger and the rifle juddered against his shoulder. From the corners of his eyes he saw the empty cartridge cases spray from the breech in a bright bronze stream, and the stench of cordite stung his nostrils.

The aircraft slewed slightly, flinching from the torrent of fire.

"He's yellow!" howled Hendry. "The bastard's yellow!"

"Hit him!" roared Ruffy. "Keep hitting him!"

The jet twisted, lifted its nose so that the fire from its cannons passed harmlessly over their heads. Then its nose dropped again and it fired its rockets, two from under each wing. The gunfire from the train stopped abruptly as everybody ducked for safety; only the three of them on the roof kept shooting.

Shrieking like four demons in harness, leaving parallel lines of white smoke behind them, the rockets came from about four hundred yards out and they covered the distance in the time it takes to draw a deep breath, but the pilot had dropped the nose too sharply and fired too late. The rockets exploded in the embankment of the tracks below them.

The blast threw Bruce over backwards. He fell and rolled, clutching desperately at the smooth roof, but as he went over the edge his fingers caught in the guttering and he hung there. He was dazed with the concussion, the guttering cutting into his fingers, the shoulder strap of the rifle around his neck strangling him, and the gravel of the embankment rushing past beneath him.

Ruffy reached over, caught him by the front of his jacket, and lifted him back like a child. "You going somewhere, boss?" The great round face was coated with dust from the explosions, but he was grinning happily. Bruce had a confused conviction that it would take at least a case of dynamite to make any impression on that mountain of black flesh.

Kneeling on the roof, Bruce tried to rally himself. He saw

that the wooden side of the coach nearest the explosions was splintered and torn and the roof was covered with earth and pebbles. Hendry was sitting beside him, shaking his head slowly from side to side; a small trickle of blood ran down from a scratch on his cheek and dripped from his chin. In the open cars the men stood or sat with stunned expressions on their faces, but the train still raced on towards the rainstorm and the dust of the explosions hung in a dense brown cloud above the forest far behind them.

Bruce scrambled to his feet, searched frantically for the aircraft, and found its tiny shape far off above the mass of cloud.

The radio was undamaged, protected by the sandbags from the blast. Bruce reached for it and pressed the transmit button. "Driver, are you all right?"

"Monsieur, I am greatly perturbed. Is there—"

"Not you alone," Bruce assured him. "Keep this train going."

"*Oui, monsieur.*"

Then Bruce switched to the aircraft's frequency. Although his ears were singing shrilly from the explosions, he could hear that the voice of the pilot had changed its tone. There was a slowness in it, a breathless catch on some of the words. He's frightened or he's hurt, thought Bruce, but he still has time to make another pass at us before we reach the storm front.

His mind was clearing fast now, and he became aware of the complete lack of readiness in his men. "Ruffy!" he shouted. "Get them on their feet. Get them ready. That plane will be back any second now."

Ruffy jumped down into the car, and Bruce heard his palm slap against flesh as he began to bully them into activity. Bruce followed him down, then climbed over into the second car and began the same process there.

"Haigh, give me a hand, help me get the lead out of them."

Further removed from the shock of the explosion, the men in this car reacted readily and crowded to the side, starting to reload, checking their weapons, swearing, faces losing the dull, dazed expressions.

Bruce turned and shouted back, "Ruffy, are any of your lot hurt?"

"Couple of scratches, nothing bad."

On the roof of the coach Hendry was standing again, watching the aircraft, blood on his face, his rifle in his hands.

"Where's André?" Bruce asked Haigh as they met in the middle of the car.

"Up front. I think he's been hit."

Bruce went forward and found André doubled up, crouching in a corner of the car, his rifle lying beside him and both hands covering his face. His shoulders heaved as though he were in pain.

Eyes, thought Bruce, he's been hit in the eyes. He reached André and stooped over him, pulling his hands from his face, expecting to see blood.

André was crying, his cheeks wet with tears and his eyelashes gummed together. For a second Bruce stared at him, and then he caught the front of his jacket and pulled him to his feet. He picked up André's rifle and the barrel was cold, not a single shot had been fired out of it. He dragged the Belgian to the side and thrust the rifle into his hands.

"De Surrier," he snarled, "I'm going to be standing beside you. If you do that again I'll shoot you. Do you understand?"

"I'm sorry, Bruce." André's lips were swollen where he had bitten them; his face was smeared with tears and slack with fear. "I'm sorry. I couldn't help it."

Bruce ignored him and turned his attention back to the aircraft. It was turning in for its next run.

He's going to come from the side again, Bruce thought; this time he'll get us. He can't miss twice in a row.

In silence once more they watched the jet slide down the valley between two vast white mountains of cloud and level off above the forest. Small and dainty and deadly, it raced in towards them.

One of the Bren guns opened up, rattling raucously, sending out tracers like bright beads on a string.

"Too soon," muttered Bruce. "Much too soon; he must be all of a mile out of range."

But the effect was instantaneous. The jet swerved, almost hit the treetops, and then over-corrected, losing its line of approach.

A howl of derision went up from the train and was immediately lost in the roar as every gun opened fire. The jet loosed its remaining rockets, blindly, hopelessly, without a chance of a hit. Then it climbed steeply, turning away into the cloud ahead of them. The sound of its engines receded, was muted by the cloud, and then was gone.

Ruffy was performing a dance of triumph, waving his rifle over his head. Hendry on the roof was shouting abuse at the clouds into which the jet had vanished. One of the Brens was still firing short, ecstatic bursts; someone else was chanting the Katangese war cry and others were taking it up. And then the driver in the locomotive came in with his whistle, spurting steam with each shriek.

Bruce slung his rifle over his shoulder, pushed his helmet onto the back of his head, took out a cigarette and lit it, then stood watching them sing and laugh and chatter with the relief from danger.

Next to him André leaned out and vomited over the side; a little of it came out of his nose and dribbled down the front of his battle jacket. He wiped his mouth with the back of his hand. "I'm sorry, Bruce. I'm sorry, truly I am sorry," he whispered.

And they were under the cloud; its coolness slumped over them like air from an open refrigerator. The first drops stung Bruce's cheek and then rodded down heavily, washing away the smell of cordite, melting the dust from Ruffy's face until it shone again like washed coal.

Bruce felt his jacket cling wetly to his back.

"Ruffy, two men at each Bren. The rest of them can get back into the covered coaches. We'll relieve every hour." He reversed his rifle so the muzzle pointed downwards. "De Surrier, you can go, and you as well, Haigh."

"I'll stay with you, Bruce."

"All right then."

The gendarmes clambered back into the covered coaches, still laughing and chattering, and Ruffy came forward with a ground sheet and handed it to Bruce.

"The radios are all covered. If you don't need me, boss, I got some business with one of those Arabs in the coach. He's got near twenty thousand francs on him, so I'd better go and give him a couple of tricks with the cards."

"One of these days I'm going to explain your Christian monarchs to the boys. Show them that the odds are three to one against them," Bruce threatened.

"I wouldn't do that, boss," Ruffy advised seriously. "All that money isn't good for them, just gets them into trouble."

"Off you go then. I'll call you later," said Bruce. "Tell them I said 'well done,' I'm proud of them."

"Yeah. I'll tell them," promised Ruffy.

Bruce lifted the tarpaulin that covered the set. "Driver, desist before you burst the boiler!"

The abandoned flight of the train steadied to a more sedate pace, and Bruce tilted his helmet over his eyes and pulled the ground sheet up around his mouth before he leaned out over the side of the car to inspect the rocket damage.

"All the windows blown out on this side and the woodwork torn a little," he muttered. "But a lucky escape all the same."

"What a miserable comic-opera war this is," grunted Mike Haigh. "That pilot had the right idea: why risk your life when it's none of your business."

"He was wounded," Bruce guessed. "I think we hit him on his first run."

Then they were silent, with the rain driving into their faces, their eyes slitting to peer ahead along the tracks. The men at the Brens huddled into their brown and green camouflage ground sheets, all their jubilation of ten minutes earlier completely gone. They are like cats, thought Bruce as he noticed their dejection, they can't stand being wet.

"It's half-past five already." Mike spoke at last. "Do you think we'll make Msapa Junction before nightfall?"

"With this weather it will be dark by six." Bruce looked up at the low cloud that was prematurely bringing on the night. "I'm not going to risk travelling in the dark. This is the edge of Baluba country, and we can't use the headlight of the loco."

"You going to stop then?"

Bruce nodded. What a stupid bloody question, he thought irritably. Then he recognized his irritation as reaction from the danger they had just experienced, and he spoke to make amends.

"We can't be far now. If we start again at first light we'll reach Msapa before sun-up."

"My God, it's cold," complained Mike, and he shivered briefly.

"Either too hot or too cold," Bruce agreed; he knew that it was also the reaction that was making him garrulous. But he did not attempt to stop himself. "That's one of the things about this happy little planet of ours: nothing is in moderation. Too hot or too cold, either you are hungry or you've over-eaten, you are in love or you hate the world—"

"Like you?" asked Mike.

"Dammit, Mike, you're as bad as a woman. Can't you conduct an objective discussion without introducing personalities?" Bruce demanded. He could feel his temper rising to the surface; he was cold and edgy.

"Objective theories must have subjective application to prove their worth," Mike pointed out. There was just a trace of an amused smile on his broad, ravaged face.

"Let's forget it then. I don't want to talk personalities," snapped Bruce, then immediately went on to do so. "Humanity sickens me if I think about it too much. De Surrier puking his heart out with fear, that animal Hendry, you trying to keep off the liquor, Joan—" He stopped himself abruptly.

"Who is Joan?"

"Do I ask you your business?" Bruce flashed the standard reply to all personal questions in the mercenary army of Katanga.

"No. But I'm asking you yours—who is Joan?"

All right, I'll tell him. If he wants to know, I'll tell him.
Anger had made Bruce reckless.

"Joan was the bitch I married."

"So that's it then!"

"Yes—that's it! Now you know. So you can leave me alone."

"Kids?"

"Two—a boy and a girl." The anger was gone from Bruce's
voice and the raw naked pain was back for an instant. Then he
rallied and his voice was neutral once more. "And none of it
matters a damn. As far as I'm concerned, the whole human
race—all of it—can go and lose itself. I don't want any part of
it."

"How old are you, Bruce?"

"Leave me alone, damn you!"

"How old are you?"

"I'm thirty."

"You talk like a teenager."

"And I feel like an old, old man."

The amusement was no longer on Mike's face as he asked,
"What did you do before this?"

"I slept and breathed and ate—and got trodden on."

"What did you do for a living?"

"Law."

"Were you successful?"

"How do you measure success? If you mean, did I make
money, the answer is yes."

I made enough to pay off the house and the car, he thought
bitterly, *and to contest custody of my children, and finally to
meet the divorce settlement. I had enough for that, but, of
course, I had to sell my partnership.*

"Then you'll be all right," Mike told him. "If you've succeeded once you'll be able to do it again when you've recovered from the shock; when you've rearranged your life and
taken other people into it to make you strong again."

"I'm strong now, Haigh. I'm strong *because* there is no one
in my life. That's the only way you can be secure, on your own.
Completely free and on your own."

"Strong!" Anger flared in Mike's voice for the first time. "On your own you're *nothing,* Curry. On your own you're so weak I could piss on you and wash you away!" Then the anger evaporated and Mike went on softly, "But you'll find out— you're one of the lucky ones. You attract people to you. You don't have to be alone."

"Well, that's the way I'm going to be from now on."

"We'll see," murmured Mike.

"Yes, we'll see," Bruce agreed and lifted the tarpaulin covering the radio. "Driver, we are going to halt for the night. It's too dark to proceed with safety."

5

Brazzaville Radio came through weakly on the set and the static was bad, for outside the rain still fell and thunder rolled around the sky like an unsecured cargo in a high sea.

"—our Elisabethville correspondent reports that elements of the Katangese army in the South Kasai province today violated the cease-fire agreement by firing upon a low-flying aircraft of the United Nations command. The aircraft, a Vampire jet fighter of the Indian Air Force, returned safely to its base at Kamina airfield. The pilot, however, was wounded by small-arms fire. His condition is reported as satisfactory.

"The United Nations commander in Katanga, General Rhee, has lodged a strong protest with the Katangese government—" The announcer's voice was overlaid by the electric crackle of static.

"We winged him!" rejoiced Wally Hendry. The scab on his cheek had dried black, with angry red edges.

"Shut up," snapped Bruce, "we're trying to hear what's happening."

"You can't hear a bloody thing now. André, there's a bottle in my pack. Get it! I'm going to drink to that coolie with a bullet up his—"

Then the radio cleared and the announcer's voice came through loudly.

"—at Senwati Mission fifty miles from the river harbour of Port Reprieve. A spokesman for the Central Congolese government denied that Congolese troops were operating in this area, and it is feared that a large body of armed bandits is taking advantage of the unsettled conditions to—" Again the static drowned it out.

"Damn this set," muttered Bruce as he tried to tune it.

"—stated today that the removal of missile equipment from

47

the Russian bases in Cuba had been confirmed by aerial re-connaissance—"

"That's all that we are interested in." Bruce switched off the radio. "What a shambles! Ruffy, where is Senwati Mission?"

"Top end of the swamp, near the Rhodesian border."

"Fifty miles from Port Reprieve," muttered Bruce, not at-tempting to conceal his anxiety.

"It's more than that by road, boss, more like a hundred."

"That should take them three or four days in this weather, with time off for looting along the way," Bruce calculated. "It will be cutting it fairly fine. We must get through to Port Re-prieve by tomorrow evening and pull out again at dawn the next day."

"Why not keep going tonight?" Hendry removed the bottle from his lips to ask. "Better than sitting here being eaten by mosquitoes."

"We'll stay," Bruce answered. "It won't do anybody much good to derail this lot in the dark." He turned back to Ruffy. "Three-hour watches tonight, Sergeant Major. Lieutenant Haigh will take the first, then Lieutenant Hendry, then Lieutenant de Surrier, and I'll do the dawn spell."

"Okay, boss. I'd better make sure my boys aren't sleeping." He left the compartment, and the broken glass from the cor-ridor windows crunched under his boots.

"I'll be on my way also." Mike stood up and pulled the ground sheet over his shoulders.

"Don't waste the batteries of the searchlights, Mike. Sweep every ten minutes or so."

"Okay, Bruce." Mike looked across at Hendry. "I'll call you at nine o'clock."

"Jolly good show, old fruit." Wally exaggerated Mike's ac-cent. "Good hunting, what!" And then as Mike left the com-partment, "Silly old bugger, why does he have to talk like that?"

No one answered him, and he pulled up his shirt behind. "André, what's this on my back?"

"It's a pimple."

"Well, squeeze it then."

Bruce woke in the night, sweating, with the mosquitoes whining about his face. Outside it was still raining, and occasionally the reflected light from the searchlight on the roof of the coach lit the interior dimly.

On one of the bottom bunks Mike Haigh lay on his back. His face was shining with sweat and he rolled his head from side to side on the pillow. He was grinding his teeth—a sound to which Bruce had become accustomed and which he preferred to Hendry's snores.

"You poor old bugger," whispered Bruce.

From the bunk opposite, André de Surrier whimpered. In sleep he looked like a child with dark soft hair falling over his forehead.

6

The rain petered out in the dawn, and the sun was hot before it cleared the horizon. It lifted a warm mist from the dripping forest. As they ran north the forest thickened; the trees grew closer together and the undergrowth beneath them was coarser than it had been around Elisabethville.

Through the warm misty dawn Bruce saw the water tower at Msapa Junction rising like a lighthouse above the forest, its silver paint streaked with brown rust. Then they came around the last curve in the tracks, and the little settlement huddled before them.

It was small, half a dozen buildings in all, and there was about it the desolate aspect of human habitation reverting to jungle.

Beside the tracks stood the water tower and the raised concrete coal bins; then the station buildings of wood and iron, with the large sign above the veranda:

MSAPA JUNCTION. Elevation 963m.

then an avenue of cassia flora trees with very dark green foliage and orange flowers; and beyond that, on the edge of the forest, a row of cottages.

One of the cottages had been burned, its ruins were fire-blackened and tumbled; and the gardens had lost all sense of discipline with three months' neglect.

"Driver, stop beside the water tower. You have fifteen minutes to fill your boiler."

"Thank you, monsieur."

With a heavy sigh of steam the loco pulled up beside the tower.

"Haigh, take four men and go back to give the driver a hand."

"Okay, Bruce."

Bruce turned once more to the radio. "Hendry."

"Hello there."

"Get a patrol together, six men, and search those cottages. Then take a look at the edge of the bush—we don't want any unexpected visitors."

Wally Hendry waved an acknowledgement from the leading car, and Bruce went on, "Put de Surrier on." He watched Hendry pass the set to André. "De Surrier, you are in charge of the leading cars in Hendry's absence. Keep Hendry covered, but watch the bush behind you also. They could come from there."

Bruce switched off the set and turned to Ruffy. "Stay up here on the roof, Ruffy. I'm going to chase them up with the watering. If you see anything, don't write me a postcard, start pooping off."

Ruffy nodded. "Have some breakfast to take with you." He proffered an open bottle of beer.

"Better than bacon and eggs." Bruce accepted the bottle and climbed down onto the platform. Sipping the beer, he walked back along the train and looked up at Mike and the engine driver in the tower.

"Is it empty?" he called up at them.

"Half full, enough for a bath if you want one," answered Mike.

"Don't tempt me." The idea was suddenly very attractive, for he could smell his own stale body odour and his eyelids were itchy and swollen from mosquito bites. "My kingdom for a bath." He ran his fingers over his jowls and they rasped over stiff beard.

He watched them swing the canvas hose out over the loco. The chubby little engine driver clambered up and sat astride the boiler as he fitted the hose.

A shout behind him made Bruce turn quickly, and he saw Hendry's patrol coming back from the cottages. They were dragging two small prisoners with them.

"Hiding in the first cottage," shouted Hendry. "They tried to leg it into the bush." He prodded one of them with his bayonet.

The child cried out and twisted in the hands of the gendarme.

"Enough of that." Bruce stopped him from using the bayonet again and went to meet them. He looked at the two children.

The girl was close to puberty with breasts like insect bites just starting to show, thin legged with enlarged knee caps out of proportion to her thighs and calves. She wore only a dirty piece of trade cloth drawn up between her legs and secured round her waist by a length of bark string, and the tribal tattoo marks across her chest and cheeks and forehead stood proud in ridges of scar tissue.

"Ruffy." Bruce called him down from the coach. "Can you speak to them?"

Ruffy picked up the boy and held him on his hip. He was younger than the girl—seven, perhaps eight years old—very dark skinned and completely naked, as naked as the terror on his face.

Ruffy grunted sharply and the gendarme released the girl. She stood trembling, making no attempt to escape.

Then in a soothing rumble Ruffy began talking to the boy on his hip; he smiled as he spoke and stroked the child's head. Slowly a little of the fear melted and the boy answered in a piping treble that Bruce could not understand.

"What does he say?" urged Bruce.

"He thinks we're going to eat them." Ruffy laughed. "Not enough here for a decent breakfast." He patted the skinny little arm, grey with crushed filth, then he gave an order to one of the gendarmes. The man disappeared into the coach and came back with a handful of chocolate bars. Still talking, Ruffy peeled one of them and placed it in the boy's mouth. The child's eyes widened appreciatively at the taste and he chewed quickly, his eyes on Ruffy's face, his answers now muffled with chocolate.

At last Ruffy turned to Bruce.

"No trouble here, boss. They come from a small village about an hour's walk away. Just five or six families, and no war party. These kids sneaked across to have a look at the houses, pinch what they could perhaps, but that's all."

"How many men at this village?" asked Bruce, and Ruffy turned back to the boy. In reply to the question he held up the fingers of both hands, without interrupting his chewing.

"Does he know if the line is clear through to Port Reprieve? Have they burned the bridges or torn up the tracks?" Both children were dumb to this question. The boy swallowed the last of his chocolate and looked hungrily at Ruffy, who filled his mouth again.

"Jesus," muttered Hendry with deep disgust. "Is this a nursery or something? Let's all play ring around the roses."

"Shut up," snapped Bruce, and then to Ruffy, "Have they seen any soldiers?"

Two heads were shaken in solemn unison.

"Have they seen any war parties of their own people?"

Again solemn negative.

"All right, give them the rest of the chocolate," instructed Bruce. That was all he could get out of them, and time was wasting. He glanced back at the tower and saw that Haigh and the engine driver had finished watering. For a further second he studied the boy. His own son would be about the same age now; it was twelve months since—Bruce stopped himself hurriedly. That way lay madness.

"Hendry, take them back to the edge of the bush and turn them loose. Hurry up. We've wasted long enough."

"You're telling me!" grunted Hendry and beckoned to the two children. With Hendry leading and a gendarme on each side they trotted away obediently and disappeared behind the station building.

"Driver, are your preparations complete?"

"Yes, monsieur, we are ready to depart."

"Shovel all the coal in, we've got to keep her rolling." Bruce smiled at him; he liked the little man, and their stilted exchanges gave him pleasure.

"Pardon, monsieur?"

"It was an imbecility, a joke—forgive me."

"Ah, a joke!" The roly-poly stomach wobbled merrily.

"Okay, Mike," Bruce shouted, "get your men aboard. We are—"

A burst of automatic gunfire cut his voice short. It came from behind the station buildings, and it battered into the heat-muted morning with such startling violence that for an instant Bruce stood paralyzed.

"Haigh," he yelled, "get up front and take over from de Surrier." That was the weak point, and Mike's party ran down the train.

"You men"—Bruce stopped the six gendarmes—"come with me." They fell in behind him, and with a quick glance Bruce assured himself that the train was safe. All along its length rifle barrels were poking out protectively, while on the roof Ruffy was dragging the Bren around to cover the flank. A charge by even a thousand Baluba must fail before the fire power that was ready now to receive it.

"Come on," said Bruce and ran, with the gendarmes behind him, to the sheltering wall of the station building. There had been no shot fired since that initial burst, which could mean either that it was a false alarm or that Hendry's party had been overwhelmed by the first rush.

The door of the station master's office was locked. Bruce kicked, and it crashed open with the weight of his booted foot behind it.

I've always wanted to do that, he thought happily in his excitement, ever since I saw Gable do it in *San Francisco*.

"You four—inside! Cover us from the windows." They crowded into the room with their rifles held ready. Through the open door Bruce saw the telegraph equipment on a table by the far wall; it was clattering metallically from traffic on the Elisabethville–Jadotville line. *Why is it that under the stimulus of excitement my mind always registers irrelevancies? Which thought is another irrelevancy,* he decided.

"Come on, you two, stay with me." He led them down the outside wall, keeping in close to its sheltering bulk, pausing at the corner to check the load of his rifle and slip the selector on to rapid fire.

A further moment he hesitated. What will I find around this corner? A hundred naked savages crowded around the mutilated bodies of Hendry and his gendarmes, or—?

Crouching, ready to jump back behind the wall, rifle held at high port across his chest, every muscle and nerve of his body cocked like a hair-trigger, Bruce stepped sideways into the open.

Hendry and the two gendarmes stood in the dusty road beyond the first cottage. They were relaxed, talking together, Hendry reloading his rifle, cramming the magazine with big red hands on which the gingery hair caught the sunlight. A cigarette dangled from his lower lip, and he laughed suddenly, throwing his head back as he did so, and the cigarette ash dropped down his jacket front. Bruce noticed the long, dark sweat stain across his shoulders.

The two children lay in the road fifty yards farther on.

Bruce was suddenly cold; it came from inside, a cramping coldness of the guts and chest. Slowly he straightened up and began to walk towards the children. His feet fell silently in the powder dust, and the only sound was his own breathing, hoarse, as though a wounded beast followed close behind him. He walked past Hendry and the two gendarmes without looking at them; they stopped talking, watching him uneasily.

He reached the girl first and went down on one knee beside her, laying his rifle aside and turning her gently onto her back.

"This isn't true," he whispered. "This can't be true."

The bullet had taken half her chest out with it, a hole the size of a coffee cup, with the blood still moving in it, but slowly, oozing, welling up into it with the viscosity of new honey.

Bruce moved across to the boy; he felt an almost dreamlike sense of unreality. "No, this isn't true." He spoke louder, trying to undo it with words.

Three bullets had hit the boy; one had torn his arm loose at the shoulder and the sharp white end of the bone pointed accusingly out of the wound. The other bullets had severed his trunk almost in two.

It came from far away, like the rising roar of a train along a tunnel. Bruce could feel his whole being shaken by the strength of it; he shut his eyes and listened to the roaring in his head, and with his eyes tight closed his vision was filled with the colour of blood.

"Hold on!" a tiny voice screamed in his roaring head. "Don't let go, fight it. Fight it as you've fought before."

And he clung like a flood victim to the straw of his sanity while the great roaring was all around him. Then the roar was muted, rumbling away, gone past, a whisper, now nothing.

The coldness came back to him, a coldness more vast than the flood had been.

He opened his eyes and breathed again, stood up and walked back to where Hendry stood with the two gendarmes.

"Corporal," Bruce addressed one of the men beside Hendry, and with a shock he heard that his own voice was calm, without any trace of the fury that had so nearly carried him away on its flood.

"Corporal, go back to the train. Tell Lieutenant Haigh and Sergeant Major Ruffararo that I want them here."

Thankfully the man went, and Bruce spoke to Wally Hendry in the same dispassionate tone. "I told you to turn them loose," he said.

"So they could run home and call the whole pack down on us—is that what you wanted, bucko?" Hendry had recovered now; he was defiant, grinning.

"So instead you murdered them?"

"Murdered! You crazy or something, Bruce? They're Balubes, aren't they? Bloody man-eating Balubes!" shouted Hendry angrily, no longer grinning. "What's wrong with you, man? This is war, bucko, war. *C'est la guerre*, like the man said, *c'est la guerre*!" Then suddenly his voice moderated again. "Let's forget it. I did what was right, now let's forget it. What's two more bloody Balubes after all the killing that's been going on? Let's forget it."

Bruce did not answer. He lit a cigarette and looked beyond Hendry for the others to come.

"How's that, Bruce? You willing we just forget it?" persisted Hendry.

"On the contrary, Hendry, I make you a sacred oath, and I call upon God to witness it." Bruce was not looking at him—he couldn't trust himself to look at Hendry without killing him. "This is my promise to you: I will have you hanged for this—not shot—hanged on good hemp rope. I have sent for Haigh and Ruffararo so we'll have plenty of witnesses. The first thing I do once we get back to Elisabethville will be to turn you over to the proper authorities."

"You don't mean that!"

"I have never meant anything so seriously in my life."

"Jesus, Bruce—!"

Then Haigh and Ruffy came; they came running until they saw, and then they stopped suddenly and stood uncertainly in the bright sun, looking from Bruce to the two frail little corpses lying in the road.

"What happened?" asked Mike.

"Hendry shot them," answered Bruce.

"What for?"

"Only he knows."

"You mean he—he just killed them, just shot them down?"

"Yes."

"My God," said Mike, and then again, his voice dull with shock, "My God."

"Go and look at them, Haigh. I want you to look closely so you remember."

Haigh walked across to the children.

"You too, Ruffy. You'll be a witness at the trial."

Mike Haigh and Ruffy walked side by side to where the children lay and stood staring down at them.

Hendry shuffled his feet in the dust awkwardly and then went on loading the magazine of his rifle. "Oh, for Chrissake!" he blustered. "What's all the fuss? They're just a couple of Balubes."

Wheeling slowly to face him, Mike Haigh's face was a yellowish colour with his cheeks and his nose still flushed with the tiny burst veins beneath the surface of the skin, but there was no colour in his lips. Each breath he drew sobbed in his throat. He started back towards Hendry, still breathing that way, and his mouth was working as he tried to force it to speak. As he came on he unslung the rifle from his shoulder.

"Haigh!" said Bruce sharply.

"This time—you—you bloody—this is the last—" mouthed Haigh.

"Watch it, bucko!" Hendry warned him. He stepped back, clumsily trying to fit the loaded magazine onto his rifle.

Haigh dropped the point of his bayonet to the level of Hendry's stomach.

"Haigh!" shouted Bruce.

Haigh charged surprisingly quickly for a man of his age, leaning forward, leading with the bayonet at Hendry's stomach, the incoherent mouthings reaching their climax in a formless bellow.

"Come on then!" Hendry answered him and stepped forward.

As they came together Hendry swept the bayonet to one side with the butt of his own rifle. The point went under his armpit, and they collided chest to chest, staggering as Haigh's weight carried them backwards. Hendry dropped his rifle and locked both arms around Haigh's neck, forcing Haigh's head back so that his face was tilted up at the right angle.

"Look out, Mike, he's going to butt!" Bruce had recognized the move, but his warning came too late. Hendry's head jerked forward, and Mike gasped as the front of Hendry's steel helmet caught him across the bridge of the nose. The rifle slipped from Mike's grip and fell into the road; he lifted his hands and covered his face with spread fingers, and the redness oozed out between them.

Again Hendry's head jerked forward like a hammer, and again Mike gasped as the steel smashed into his face and fingers.

"Knee him, Mike!" Bruce yelled as he tried to take up a position from which to intervene, but they were staggering in a circle, turning like a wheel, and Bruce could not get in.

Hendry's legs were braced apart as he drew his head back to strike again, and Mike's knee went up between them, all the way up with power into the fork of Hendry's crotch.

Breaking from the clinch, his mouth open in a silent scream of agony, Hendry doubled up, with both hands holding his stomach, and sagged slowly onto his knees in the dust.

Dazed, with blood running into his mouth, Mike fumbled with the canvas flap of his holster. "I'll kill you, you murdering swine!" The pistol came out into his right hand; short-barrelled, blue, and ugly.

Bruce stepped up behind him, his thumb found the nerve centre below the elbow, and as he dug in the pistol dropped from Mike's paralyzed hand and dangled on its lanyard against his knee.

"Ruffy, stop him!" Bruce shouted, for Hendry was clawing painfully at the rifle that lay in the dust beside him.

"Got it, boss!" Ruffy's huge boot trod down heavily on the rifle, and Hendry struggled ineffectually to pull it out from under him.

"Take his pistol," Bruce ordered.

"Got that too!" Ruffy stooped quickly over the crawling body at his feet, in one swift movement opened the flap of the holster, drew the revolver, and the lanyard snapped like cotton as he jerked on it.

They stood like that: Bruce holding Haigh from behind and Hendry crouched at Ruffy's feet. The only sound for several seconds was the hoarse rasping of breath.

Bruce felt Mike relaxing in his grip as the madness left him; he unclipped the pistol from its lanyard and let it drop.

"Leave me, Bruce. I'm all right now."

"Are you sure? I don't want to shoot you."

"No, I'm all right."

"If you start it again, I'll have to shoot you. Do you understand?"

"Yes, I'll be all right now. I lost my senses for a moment."

"You certainly did," Bruce agreed and released him.

They formed a circle around the kneeling Hendry, and

Bruce spoke. "If either you or Haigh start it again, you'll an-swer to me, do you hear me?"

Hendry looked up, his small eyes slitted with pain. He did not answer.

"Do you hear me?" Bruce repeated the question, and Hendry nodded.

"Good! From now on, Hendry, you are under open arrest. I can't spare men to guard you, and you're welcome to escape if you'd like to try. The local gentry would certainly entertain you most handsomely; they'd probably arrange a special ban-quet in your honour."

Hendry's lips drew back in a snarl that exposed teeth with green slimy stains on them.

"But remember my promise, Hendry. As soon as we get back to—"

"Wally, Wally, are you hurt?" André came running from the direction of the station. He knelt beside Hendry.

"Get away, leave me alone." Hendry struck out at him im-patiently, and André recoiled.

"De Surrier, who gave you permission to leave your post? Get back to the train."

André looked up uncertainly, then back to Hendry.

"De Surrier, you heard me. Get going. And you also, Haigh."

He watched them disappear behind the station building be-fore he glanced once more at the two children. There was a smear of blood and melted chocolate across the boy's cheek and his eyes were wide open in an expression of surprise. Already the flies were settling, crawling delightedly over the two small corpses.

"Ruffy, get spades. Bury them under those trees." He pointed at the avenue of cassia flora. "But do it quickly." He spoke brusquely so that how he felt would not show in his voice.

"Okay, boss. I'll fix it."

"Come on, Hendry," Bruce snapped, and Wally Hendry heaved to his feet and followed him meekly back to the train.

7

Slowly from Maspa Junction they travelled northwards through the forest. Each tree seemed to have been cast from the same mould, tall and graceful in itself, but when multiplied a countless million times the effect was that of numbing monotony. Above them was a lane of open sky with the clouds scattered, but slowly regrouping for the next assault, and the forest shut in the moist heat so they sweated even in the wind of the train's movement.

"How is your face?" asked Bruce, and Mike Haigh touched the parallel swellings across his forehead where the skin was broken and discoloured.

"It will do," Haigh decided; then he lifted his eyes and looked across the open cars at Wally Hendry. "You shouldn't have stopped me, Bruce."

Bruce did not answer, but he also watched as Hendry leaned uncomfortably against the side of the leading car, obviously favoring his injuries, his face turned half away from them, talking to André.

"You should have let me kill him," Mike went on. "A man who can shoot down two small children in cold blood and then laugh about it afterwards—!" Mike left the rest unsaid, but his hands were opening and closing in his lap.

"It's none of your business," said Bruce, sensitive to the implied rebuke. "What are you? One of God's avenging angels?"

"None of my business, you say?" Mike turned quickly to face Bruce. "My God, what kind of man are you? I hope for your sake that you don't mean that!"

"I'll tell you in words of one syllable what kind of man I am, Haigh," Bruce answered flatly. "I'm the kind that minds my own bloody business, that lets other people lead their own lives. I am ready to take reasonable measures to prevent others from

61

flouting the code which society has drawn up for us, but that's all. Hendry has committed murder; this I agree is a bad thing, and when we get back to Elisabethville I will bring it to the attention of the people whose business it is. But I am not going to wave banners and quote from the Bible and froth at the mouth."

"That's all?"

"That's all."

"You don't feel sorry for those two kids?"

"Yes, I do. But pity doesn't heal bullet wounds; all it does is distress me. So I switch off the pity—they can't use it."

"You don't feel anger or disgust or horror at Hendry?"

"The same thing applies," explained Bruce, starting to lose patience again. "I could work up a sweat about it if I let myself loose on an emotional orgy, as you are doing."

"So instead you treat something as evil as Hendry with an indifferent tolerance?" asked Mike.

"Jesus Christ!" grated Bruce. "What the hell do you want me to do?"

"I want you to stop playing dead. I want you to be able to recognize evil and to destroy it." Mike was starting to lose his temper also; his nerves were taut.

"That's great! Do you know where I can buy a secondhand crusader outfit and a white horse? Then singlehanded I will ride out to wage war on cruelty and ignorance, lust and greed and hatred and poverty—"

"That's not what I—" Mike tried to interrupt, but Bruce overrode him, his handsome face flushed darkly with anger and the sun. "You want me to destroy evil wherever I find it. You old fool, don't you know that it has a hundred heads and that for each one you cut off another hundred grow in its place? Don't you know that it's in you also, so to destroy it you have to destroy yourself?"

"You're a coward, Curry! The first time you burn a finger you run away and build yourself an asbestos shelter—"

"I don't like being called names, Haigh. Put a leash on your tongue."

Mike paused and his expression changed, softening into a grin. "I'm sorry, Bruce. I was just trying to teach you—"

"Thank you," scoffed Bruce, his voice still harsh; he had not been placated by the apology. "You are going to teach me, thanks very much! But what are you going to teach me, Haigh? What are you qualified to teach? 'How to Find Success and Happiness' by Laughing Lad Haigh, who worked his way down to a lieutenancy in the black army of Katanga—how's that as a title for your lecture? Or do you prefer something more techni- cal, like 'The Applications of Alcohol to Spiritual Research—' "

"All right, Bruce, drop it. I'll shut up," and Bruce saw how deeply he had wounded Mike. He regretted it then; he would have liked to unsay it. But that's one thing you can never do.

Beside him Mike Haigh was suddenly much older and more tired looking, the pouched wrinkles below his eyes seemed to have deepened in the last few seconds, and a little more of the twinkle had gone from his eyes. His short laughter had a bitter, humourless ring to it. "When you put it that way, it's really quite funny."

"I punched a little low," admitted Bruce, and then, "perhaps I should let you shoot Hendry. A waste of ammunition really, but, seeing that you want to so badly"—Bruce drew his pistol and offered it to Mike butt first—"use mine." He grinned dis- armingly at Mike, and his grin was almost impossible to resist. Mike started to laugh. It wasn't a very good joke, but somehow it caught fire between them and suddenly they were laughing together.

Mike Haigh's battered features spread like warm butter and twenty years dropped from his face. Bruce leaned back against the sandbags with his mouth wide open, the pistol still in his hand, and his long, lean body throbbing uncontrollably with laughter.

There was something feverish in it, as though they were try- ing with laughter to gargle away the taste of blood and hatred. It was the laughter of despair.

Below them the men in the trucks turned to watch them,

puzzled at first, and then beginning to chuckle in sympathy, not recognizing the sickness of that sound.

"Hey, boss," called Ruffy, "first time I ever seen you laugh like you meant it."

And the epidemic spread; everyone was laughing, even André de Surrier was smiling.

Only Wally Hendry was untouched by it, silent and sullen, watching them with small, expressionless eyes.

They came to the bridge over the Cheke in midafternoon. The road and the railway line crossed it side by side, but after this brief meeting they diverged and the road twisted away to the left. The river was padded on each bank by dense dark green bush, three hundred yards thick; a matted tangle of thorn and tree fern with the big trees growing up through it and bursting into flower as they reached the sunlight.

"Good place for an ambush," muttered Mike Haigh, eying the solid green walls of vegetation on each side of the lines.

"Charming, isn't it," agreed Bruce, and by the uneasy air of alertness that had settled on his gendarmes it was clear that they agreed with him.

The train nosed its way carefully into the river bush like a steel snake along a rabbit run, and they came to the river. Bruce switched on the set. "Driver, stop this side of the bridge. I wish to inspect it before entrusting our precious cargo to it."

"*Oui, monsieur.*"

The Cheke River at this point was fifty yards wide, deep, quick flowing, and angry, with flood water which had almost covered the white sand beaches along each bank. Its bottle-green colour was smoked with mud and there were whirlpools around the stone columns of the bridge.

"Looks all right," Haigh gave his opinion. "How far are we from Port Reprieve now?"

Bruce spread his field map on the roof of the coach between his legs and found the brackets that straddled the convoluted ribbon of the river.

"Here we are." He touched the spot and then ran his finger

along the stitched line of the railway until it reached the red circle that marked Port Reprieve. "About thirty miles to go—another hour's run. We'll be there before dark."

"Those are the Lufira hills." Mike Haigh pointed to the blue smudge that only just showed above the forest ahead of them.

"We'll be able to see the town from the top," said Bruce. "The river runs parallel to them on the other side, and the swamp is off to the right—the swamp is the source of the river."

He rolled the map and passed it back to Ruffy, who slid it into the plastic map case.

"Ruffy, Lieutenant Haigh and I are going ahead to have a look at the bridge. Keep an eye on the bush."

"Okay, boss. You want a beer to take with you?"

"Thanks." Bruce was thirsty, and he emptied half the bottle before climbing down to join Mike on the gravel embankment. Rifles unslung, watching the bush on each side uneasily, they hurried forward and with relief reached the bridge and went out into the centre of it.

"Seems solid enough," commented Mike. "No one has tampered with it."

"It's wood." Bruce stamped on the heavy wild mahogany timbers. They were three feet thick and stained with a dark chemical to inhibit rotting.

"So, it's wood?" inquired Mike.

"Wood burns," explained Bruce. "It would be easy to burn the bridge down." He leaned his elbows on the guard rail, drained the beer bottle, and dropped it to the surface of the river twenty feet below. There was a thoughtful expression on his face.

"Very probably there are Baluba in the bush"—he pointed at the banks—"watching us at this moment. They might get the same idea. I wonder if I should leave a guard here?"

Mike leaned on the rail beside him, and they both stared out to where the river took a bend two hundred yards downstream; in the crook of the bend grew a tree twice as tall as any of its neighbours. The trunk was straight and covered with smooth silvery bark, and its foliage piled to a high green steeple against the clouds. It was the natural point of focus for their eyes as they weighed the problem.

"I wonder what kind of tree that is. I've never seen one like it before." Bruce was momentarily diverted by the grandeur of it. "It looks like a giant blue gum."

"It's quite a sight," Mike concurred. "I'd like to go down and have a closer—" Suddenly he stiffened, and there was an edge of alarm in his voice as he pointed. "Bruce, there! What's that in the lower branches?"

"Where?"

"Just above the first fork, on the left—" Mike was pointing, and suddenly Bruce saw it. For a second he thought it was a leopard; then he realized it was too dark and long.

"It's a man," exclaimed Mike.

"Baluba," snapped Bruce. He could see the shape now, and the sheen of naked black flesh, the kilt of animal tails, and the headdress of feathers. A long bow stood up behind the man's shoulder as he balanced on the branch and steadied himself with one hand against the trunk. He was watching them.

Bruce glanced around at the train. Hendry had noticed their agitation and, following the direction of Mike's raised arm, he had spotted the Baluba. Bruce realized what Hendry was going to do and he opened his mouth to shout, but before he could do so Hendry had snatched his rifle off his shoulder, swung it up, and fired a long, rushing, hammering burst.

"The trigger-happy idiot," snarled Bruce and looked back at the tree. Slabs of white bark were flying from the trunk, and the bullets reaped leaves that fluttered down like crippled insects, but the Baluba had disappeared.

The gunfire ceased abruptly and in its place Hendry was shouting with hoarse excitement. "I got him, I got the bastard."

"Hendry"—Bruce's voice was also hoarse, but with anger— "who ordered you to fire?"

"He was a bloody Baluba, a mucking big bloody Baluba. Didn't you see him, hey? Didn't you see him, man?"

"Come here, Hendry."

"I got the bastard," rejoiced Hendry.

"Are you deaf? Come here!"

While Hendry climbed down from the car and came towards them, Bruce asked Haigh, "Did he hit him?"

"I'm not sure. I don't think so. I think he jumped. If he had been hit he'd have been thrown backwards—you know how it knocks a man over."

"Yes," said Bruce, "I know." A .300 bullet from an FN struck with a force of well over a ton. When you hit a man there was no doubt about it. All right, so the Baluba was still in there.

Hendry came up, swaggering, laughing with excitement.

"So you killed, hey?" Bruce asked.

"Stone dead, stone bloody dead!"

"Can you see him?"

"No, he's down in the bush."

"Do you want to go and have a look at him, Hendry? Do you want to go and get his ears?"

Ears are the best trophy you can take from a man, not as good as the skin of a black-maned lion or the great bossed horns of a buffalo, but better than a scalp. The woolly cap of an African scalp is a drab thing, messy to take and difficult to cure. You have to salt it and stretch it inside out over a helmet; even then it smells bad. Ears are much less trouble, and Hendry was an avid collector. He was not the only one in the army of Katanga; the taking of ears was common practice.

"Yeah, I want them." Hendry detached the bayonet from the muzzle of his rifle. "I'll nip down and get them."

"You can't let anyone go in there, Bruce. Not even him," protested Haigh quietly.

"Why not? He deserves it; he worked hard for it."

"Only take a minute." Hendry ran his thumb along the bayonet to test the edge.

My God! he really means it, thought Bruce; he'd go into that tangled stuff for a pair of ears. He's not brave, he's just stupendously lacking in imagination.

"Wait for me, Bruce, it won't take long." Hendry started back.

"You're not serious, Bruce?" Mike asked.

"No," agreed Bruce, "I'm not serious," and his voice was cold and hard as he caught hold of Hendry's shoulder and stopped him. "Listen to me! You have no more chances—that was it. I'm waiting for you now, Hendry. Just once more, that's all. Just once more."

Hendry's face turned sullen again. "Don't push me, bucko."

"Get back to the train and bring it across," said Bruce contemptuously and turned to Haigh. "Now we'll have to leave a guard here. They know we've gone across and they'll burn it for a certainty, especially after that little fiasco."

"Whom are you going to leave?"

"Ten men, say, under a sergeant. We'll be back by nightfall or tomorrow morning at the latest. They should be safe enough. I doubt there is a big war party here, a few strays perhaps, but the main force will be closer to the town."

"I hope you're right."

"So do I," said Bruce absently, his mind busy with the problem of defending the bridge. "We'll strip all the sandbags off the coaches and build an emplacement here in the middle of the roadway, leave two of the battery-operated searchlights and a case of flares with them, one of the Brens and a couple of cases of grenades. Food and water for a week. No, they'll be all right."

The train was rolling down slowly towards them—and a single arrow rose from the edge of the jungle. Slowly it rose, curving in flight and falling towards the train, dropping faster now, silently, into the mass of men in the leading car.

So Hendry had missed and the Baluba had come upstream through the thick bush to launch his arrow in retaliation. Bruce sprang to the guard rail and, using it as a rest for his rifle, opened up in short bursts, searching the edge of the jungle blindly, firing into the green mass and seeing it tremble with his bullets. Haigh was shooting also, hunting the area from which the arrow had come.

The train was up to them now, and Bruce slung his rifle over his shoulder and scrambled up the side of the car. He pushed his way to the radio set. "Driver, stop the covered coaches in the middle of the bridge," he snapped, and then he switched it off and looked for Ruffy. "Sergeant Major, get all those sandbags off the roof into the roadway." While they worked, the gendarmes would be protected from further arrows by the body of the train.

"Okay, boss."

"Kanaki,"—Bruce picked his most reliable sergeant—"I am leaving you here with nine men to hold the bridge for us. Take one of the Brens, and two of the lights—" Quickly Bruce issued his orders, and then he had time to ask André, "What happened to that arrow? Was anyone hit?"

"No, missed by a few inches. Here it is."

"That was a bit of luck." Bruce took the arrow from André and inspected it quickly: a light reed, crudely fletched with green leaves and with the iron head bound into it with a strip of rawhide. It looked fragile and ineffectual, but the barbs of the head were smeared thickly with a dark paste that had dried like toffee.

"Pleasant," murmured Bruce, and then he shuddered slightly. He could imagine it embedded in his body with the poison purple-staining the flesh beneath the skin. He had heard that it was not a comfortable death, and the iron-tipped reed was suddenly malignant and repulsive. He snapped it in half and threw it out over the side of the bridge before he jumped down from the car to supervise the building of the guard post.

"Not enough sandbags, boss."

"Take the mattresses off all the bunks, Ruffy." Bruce solved that quickly. The leather-covered coir pallets would stop an arrow with ease.

Fifteen minutes later the post was completed, a shoulder-high ring of sandbags and mattresses large enough to accommodate ten men and their equipment, with embrasures sited to command both ends of the bridge.

"We'll be back early tomorrow, Kanaki. Let none of your men leave this post for any purpose; the gaps between the timbers are sufficient for purposes of sanitation."

"We shall enjoy enviable comfort, Captain, but we will lack that which soothes." Kanaki grinned meaningly at Bruce.

"Ruffy, leave them a case of beer."

"A whole case?" Ruffy made no attempt to hide his shocked disapproval of such a prodigal order.

"Is my credit not good?"

"Your credit is okay, boss," and then he changed to French to make his protest formal. "My concern is the replacement of such a valuable commodity."

"You're wasting time, Ruffy."

8

From the bridge it was thirty miles to Port Reprieve. They met the road again six miles outside the town; it crossed under them and disappeared into the forest again, to circle around the high ground, taking the easier route into Port Reprieve. But the railroad climbed up the hills in a series of traverses and came out at the top, six hundred feet above the town. On the stony slopes the forest found meagre purchase and the vegetation was sparser; it did not obscure the view.

Standing on the roof, Bruce looked out across the Lufira swamps to the north, a vastness of poisonous green swamp grass and open water, disappearing into the blue heat haze without any sign of ending. From its southern extremity it was drained by the Lufira river. The river was half a mile wide, deep olive-green, ruffled darker by eddies of wind across its surface, fenced to the very edge of the water by a solid barrier of dense river bush. In the angle formed by the swamp and the river was a headland that protected the natural harbour of Port Reprieve. The town was on a spit of land, the harbour on one side and a smaller swamp on the other. The road came around the right-hand side of the hills, crossed a causeway over the swamp, and entered the single street of the town from the far side.

There were three large buildings in the centre of the town opposite the railway yard, their iron roofs bright beacons in the sunlight; and clustered around them were perhaps fifty smaller thatched dwellings.

Down on the edge of the harbour was a long shed, obviously a workshop, and two jetties ran out into the water. The diamond dredgers were moored alongside, three of them, ungainly black hulks with high superstructures and blunt ends.

It was a place of heat and fever and swamp smells, an ugly little village by a green reptilian river.

"Nice place to retire," Mike Haigh grunted.

"Or to open a health resort," said Bruce.

Beyond the causeway, on the main headland, there was another cluster of buildings, just the tops showing above the forest. Among them rose the copper-clad spire of a church.

"Mission station," guessed Bruce.

"St. Augustine's," agreed Ruffy. "My first wife's little brother got himself educated there. He's an attaché to the ministry or something or other in Elisabethville now, doing damn good for himself." Boasting a little.

"Bully for him," said Bruce.

The train had started angling down the hills towards the town.

"Well, I reckon we've made it, boss."

"I reckon also. All we have to do is get back again."

"Yessir, I reckon that's all."

And they ran into the town.

There were more than forty people in the crowd that lined the platform to welcome them.

"We'll have a heavy load on the way home," thought Bruce as he ran his eye over them. He saw the bright spots of women's dresses in the throng. Bruce counted four of them. That's another complication; one day I hope I find something in this life that turns out exactly as expected, something that will run smoothly and evenly through to its right and logical conclusion. Some hope, he decided, some bloody hope.

The joy and relief of the men and women on the platform were pathetically apparent in their greetings. Most of the women were crying, and the men ran beside the train like small boys as it slid in along the raised concrete platform. All of them were of mixed blood, Bruce noted. They varied in colour from creamy yellow to charcoal. The Belgians had certainly left much to be remembered by.

Standing back from the throng, a little aloof from the general jollification, was a half-blooded Belgian. There was an air of authority about him that was unmistakable. On one side of him stood a large bosomy woman of his own advanced age, darker skinned than he was; but Bruce saw immediately that she was his wife. At his other hand stood a figure dressed in a white open-necked shirt and blue jeans that Bruce at first thought was a boy, until the head turned and he saw the long plume of dark hair that hung down her back, and then the unmanly double pressure beneath the white shirt.

The train stopped. Bruce jumped down onto the platform and laughingly pushed his way through the crowd towards the Belgian. Despite a year in the Congo, Bruce had not grown accustomed to being kissed by someone who had not shaved for two or three days and who reeked of garlic and cheap tobacco. This atrocity was committed upon him a dozen times or more before he arrived before the Belgian.

"The good Lord bless you for coming to our aid, Monsieur Capitaine." The Belgian recognized the twin bars on the front of Bruce's helmet and held out his hand.

Bruce had expected another kiss, so he accepted the handshake with relief. "I am only glad that we are in time," he answered.

"May I introduce myself—Martin Boussier, district manager of Union Minière du Haut, and this is my wife, Madame Boussier."

He was a tall man but, unlike his wife, sparsely fleshed. His hair was completely silver and his skin folded, toughened, and browned by a life under the equatorial sun. Bruce took an instant liking to him. Madame Boussier pressed her bulk against Bruce and kissed him heartily. Her mustache was too soft to cause him discomfort, and she smelled of toilet soap, which was a distinct improvement, decided Bruce.

"May I also present Madame Cartier."

For the first time Bruce looked squarely at the girl. A number of things registered in his mind simultaneously: the paleness of her skin, which was not unhealthy but had an opaque coolness that he wanted to touch; the size of her eyes, which seemed to fill half her face; the unconscious provocation of her lips; and the use of the word "madame" before her name.

"Captain Curry—of the Army of Katanga," said Bruce. She's too young to be married, can't be more than seventeen. She's still got that little-girl freshness about her, and I bet she smells like an unweaned puppy.

"Thank you for coming, monsieur." She had a throatiness in her voice as though she were just about to laugh or to make love, and Bruce added three years to his estimate of her age. That was not a little girl's voice, nor were those little girl's legs in the jeans, and little girls had less under their shirt fronts.

His eyes came back to her face, and he saw colour in her cheeks now and sparks of annoyance in her eyes.

My God, he thought, I'm ogling her like a matelot on shore leave. He hurriedly transferred his attention back to Boussier, but his throat felt constricted as he asked, "How many are you?"

"There are forty-two of us, of whom five are women and two are children."

Bruce nodded, it was what he had expected. The women could ride in one of the covered coaches. He turned and surveyed the railway yard.

"Is there a turntable on which we can revolve the locomotive?" he asked Boussier.

"No, Captain."

They would have to reverse all the way back to Msapa Junction, another complication. It would be more difficult to keep a watch on the tracks ahead, and it would mean a sooty and uncomfortable journey.

"What precautions have you taken against attack, monsieur?"

"They are inadequate, Captain," Boussier admitted. "I have not sufficient men to defend the town—most of the population left before the emergency. Instead I have posted sentries on all the approaches and I have fortified the hotel to the best of my ability. It was there we intended to stand in the event of attack."

Bruce nodded again and glanced up at the sun. It was already reddening as it dropped towards the horizon—perhaps another hour or two of daylight.

"Monsieur, it is too late to entrain all your people and leave before nightfall. I intend to load their possessions this evening. We will stay overnight and leave in the early morning."

"We are all anxious to be away from this place. We have twice seen large parties of Baluba on the edge of the jungle."

"I understand," said Bruce. "But the dangers of travelling by night exceed those of waiting another twelve hours."

"The decision is yours," Boussier agreed. "What do you wish us to do now?"

"Please see to the entrainment of your people. I regret that only the most essential possessions may be taken. We will be almost a hundred persons."

"I shall see to that myself," Boussier assured him. "And then?"

"Is that the hotel?" Bruce pointed across the street at one of the large double-storied buildings. It was only two hundred yards from where they stood.

"Yes, Captain."

"Good," said Bruce. "It is close enough. Your people can spend the night there in more comfort than aboard the train."

He looked at the girl again; she was watching him with a small smile on her face. It was a smile of almost maternal amusement, as though she were watching a little boy playing at soldiers. Now it was Bruce's turn to feel annoyed. He was suddenly embarrassed by his uniform and epaulettes, by the pistol at his hip, the automatic rifle across his shoulder, and the heavy helmet on his head.

"I will require someone who is familiar with the area to accompany me. I want to inspect your defenses," he said to Boussier.

"Madame Cartier could show you," suggested Boussier's wife artlessly.

I wonder if she noticed our little exchange, thought Bruce. Of course she did. All women have a most sensitive nose for that sort of thing.

"Will you go with the captain, Shermaine?" asked Madame Boussier.

"As the captain wishes." She was still smiling.

"That is settled then," said Bruce gruffly. "I will meet you at the hotel in ten minutes, after I have made arrangements here." He turned back to Boussier. "You may proceed with the boarding, monsieur." Bruce left them and went back to the train.

"Hendry," he shouted, "you and de Surrier will stay on board. We are not leaving until the morning, but these people are going to load their stuff now. In the meantime rig the searchlights to sweep both sides of the track, and make sure the Brens are properly sited."

Hendry grunted an acknowledgement without looking at Bruce.

"Mike, take ten men with you and go to the hotel. I want you there in case of trouble during the night."

"Okay, Bruce."

"Ruffy."

"Boss!"

"Take a gang and help the driver refuel."

"Okay, boss. Hey, boss?"

"Yes?" Bruce turned to him.

"When you go to the hotel, have a look-see—maybe they got some beer up there."

"I'll keep it in mind."

"Thanks, boss." Ruffy looked relieved. "I'd hate like hell to die of thirst in this hole."

The townsfolk were streaming back towards the hotel. The girl Shermaine walked with the Boussiers, and Bruce heard Hendry's voice above him.

"Jesus, look what that pretty has got in her pants. Whatever it is, one thing is sure: it's round and it's in two pieces, and those pieces move like they don't belong to each other."

"You haven't any work to do, Hendry?" Bruce asked harshly.

"What's wrong, Curry?" Hendry jeered down at him. "You got plans yourself—is that it, bucko?"

"She's married," said Bruce and immediately was surprised that he had said it.

"Sure"—Hendry laughed—"all the best ones are married; that don't mean a thing, not a bloody thing."

"Get on with your work," snapped Bruce, and then to Haigh, "Are you ready? Come with me then."

9

When they reached the hotel Boussier was waiting for them on the open veranda. He led Bruce aside and spoke quietly.

"Monsieur, I don't wish to be an alarmist but I have received some most disturbing news. There are brigands armed with modern weapons raiding down from the north. The last reports state that they have sacked Senwati Mission about a hundred miles by road north of here. They are travelling in a convoy of stolen vehicles, and at Senwati they captured a gasoline tanker belonging to the commercial oil companies."

Bruce nodded. "Yes, I know about them. We heard on the radio."

"Then you will have realized that they can be expected to arrive here very soon."

"I still don't see them arriving before tomorrow afternoon; by then we should be well on our way to Msapa Junction."

"I hope you are right, monsieur. The atrocities committed by this General Moses at Senwati are beyond the conception of any normal mind. He appears to bear an almost pathological hatred for all people of European descent." Boussier hesitated before going on. "There were a dozen white nuns at Senwati. I have heard that they—"

"Yes," Bruce interrupted him quickly; he did not want to listen to it. "I can imagine. Try and prevent these stories circulating among your people. I don't want to have them panic."

"Of course." Boussier nodded.

"Do you know what force this General Moses commands?"

"It is not more than a hundred men, but, as I have said, they are all armed with modern weapons. I have even heard that they have with them a cannon of some description, though I think this unlikely."

"I see," mused Bruce. "But it doesn't alter my decision to

remain here overnight. However, we must leave at first light tomorrow."

"As you wish, Captain."

"Now, monsieur—" Bruce changed the subject. "I require some form of transport. Is that car in running order?" He pointed at a pale green Ford Ranchero station wagon parked beside the veranda wall.

"It is. It belongs to my company." Boussier took a key ring from his pocket and handed it to Bruce. "Here are the keys. The tank is full of gasoline."

"Good," said Bruce. "Now if we can find Madame Cartier—"

She was waiting in the hotel lounge and she stood up as Bruce and Boussier came in.

"Are you ready, madame?"

"I await your pleasure," she answered, and Bruce looked at her sharply. Just a trace of a twinkle in her dark blue eyes suggested that she was aware of the double meaning.

They walked out to the Ford and Bruce opened the door for her.

"You are gracious, monsieur." She thanked him and slid into the seat. Bruce went around to the driver's side and climbed in beside her.

"It's nearly dark," he said.

"Turn right onto the Msapa Junction road—there is one post there."

Bruce drove out along the dirt road through the town until they came to the last house before the causeway. "Here," said the girl, and Bruce stopped the car. There were two men there, both armed with sporting rifles. Bruce spoke to them. They had seen no sign of Baluba, but they were both very nervous. Bruce made a decision.

"I want you to go back to the hotel. The Baluba will have seen the train arrive. They won't attack in force—we'll be safe tonight—but they may try and cut a few throats if we leave you out here."

The two men gathered together their belongings and set off towards the centre of town, obviously with lighter hearts.

"Where are the others?" Bruce asked the girl.

"The next post is at the pumping station down by the river. There are three men there."

Bruce followed her directions. Once or twice as he drove he glanced surreptitiously at her. She sat in her corner of the seat with her legs drawn up sideways under her. She sat very still, Bruce noticed. *I like a woman who doesn't fidget; it's soothing.* Then she smiled. *This one isn't soothing. She is as disturbing as hell!* She turned suddenly and caught him looking again, but this time she smiled.

"You are English, aren't you, Captain?"

"No, I am a Rhodesian," Bruce answered.

"It's the same," said the girl. "You speak French so very badly that you had to be English."

Bruce laughed. "Perhaps your English is better than my French," he challenged her.

"It couldn't be much worse." She answered him in his own language. "You are different when you laugh, not so grim, not so heroic. Take the next road to your right."

Bruce turned the Ford down towards the harbour.

"You are very frank," he said. "Also your English is excellent."

"Do you smoke?" she asked, and when he nodded she lit two cigarettes and passed one to him.

"You are also very young to smoke, and very young to be married."

She stopped smiling and swung her legs off the seat. "Here is the pumping station," she said.

"I beg your pardon. I shouldn't have said that."

"It's of no importance."

"It was an impertinence," Bruce demurred.

"It doesn't matter."

Bruce stopped the car and opened his door. He walked out onto the wooden jetty towards the pump house, and the boards rang dully under his boots. There was a mist coming up out of the reeds around the harbour, and the frogs were piping in fifty different keys. He spoke to the men in the single room of the pump station.

"You can get back to the hotel by dark if you hurry."

"Oui, monsieur," they agreed.

Bruce watched them set off up the road before he went to the car. He spun the starter motor, and above the noise of it the girl asked, "What is your given name, Captain Curry?"

"Bruce."

She repeated it, pronouncing it "Bruise," and then asked, "Why are you a soldier?"

"For many reasons." His tone was flippant.

"You do not look like a soldier, for all your badges and your guns, for all the grimness and the frequent giving of orders."

"Perhaps I am not a very good soldier." He smiled at her.

"You are very efficient and very grim except when you laugh. But I am glad you do not look like one," she said.

"Where is the next post?"

"On the railway line. There are two men there. Turn to your right again at the top, Bruce."

"You are also very efficient, Shermaine." They were silent again, having used each other's name. Bruce could feel it between them, a good feeling, warm, like new bread. But what of her husband? he thought. I wonder where he is, and what he is like. Why isn't he here with her?

"He is dead," she said quietly. "He died four months ago of malaria."

With the shock of it—Shermaine answering his unspoken question and also the answer itself—Bruce could say nothing for a moment; then, "I'm sorry."

"There is the post," she said, "in the cottage with the thatched roof."

Bruce stopped the car and switched off the engine.

In the silence she spoke again. "He was a good man, so very gentle. I only knew him for a few months but he was a good man."

She looked very small sitting beside him in the gathering

dark, with the sadness on her, and Bruce felt a great wave of tenderness wash over him. He wanted to put his arm around her and hold her, to shield her from the sadness. He searched for the words, but before he found them she roused herself and spoke in a matter-of-fact tone.

"We must hurry, it's dark already."

At the hotel the lounge was filled with Boussier's employees. Haigh had mounted a Bren in one of the upstairs windows to cover the main street and posted two men in the kitchens to cover the back. The civilians were in little groups, talking quietly, and their expressions of complete doglike trust as they looked at Bruce disconcerted him.

"Everything under control, Mike?" he asked brusquely.

"Yes, Bruce. We should be able to hold this building against a sneak attack. De Surrier and Hendry, down at the station yard, shouldn't have any trouble either."

"Have these people"—Bruce pointed at the civilians—"loaded their luggage?"

"Yes, it's all aboard. I have told Ruffy to issue them food from our stores."

"Good." Bruce felt relief; no further complications so far.

"Where is old man Boussier?"

"He is across at his office."

"I'm going to have a chat with him."

Unbidden, Shermaine fell in beside Bruce as he walked out into the street, but he liked having her there.

Boussier looked up as Bruce and Shermaine walked into his office. The merciless glare of the petromax lamp accentuated the lines at the corners of his eyes and mouth and showed up the streaks of pink scalp beneath his neatly combed hair.

"Martin, you are not still working!" exclaimed Shermaine, and he smiled at her, the calm smile of his years.

"Not really, my dear, just tidying up a few things. Please be seated, Captain."

He came around and cleared a pile of heavy leather-bound ledgers off the chair and packed them into a wooden case on the floor, went back to his own chair, opened a drawer in the desk, brought out a box of cheroots and offered one to Bruce.

"I cannot tell you how relieved I am that you are here, Captain. These last few months have been very trying—the doubt, the anxiety." He struck a match and held it out to Bruce, who leaned forward across the desk and lit his cheroot. "But now it is all at an end. I feel as though a great weight has been lifted from my shoulders." Then his voice sharpened. "But you were not too soon. I have heard within the last hour that this General Moses and his column have already left Senwati and are on the road south less than a hundred miles north of here. They will arrive tomorrow at their present rate of advance."

"Where did you hear this?" Bruce demanded.

"From one of my men, and do not ask me how he knows. There is a system of communication in this country which even after all these years I do not understand. Perhaps it is the drums—I heard them this evening—I do not know. However, their information is usually reliable."

"I had not placed them so close," muttered Bruce. "Had I known this I might have risked travelling tonight, at least as far as the bridge."

"I think your decision to stay overnight was correct. General Moses will not travel during darkness—none of his men would risk that—and the condition of the road from Senwati after three months' neglect is such that he will need ten or twelve hours to cover the distance."

"I hope you're right." Bruce was worried. "I'm not sure that we shouldn't pull out now."

"That involves a risk also, Captain," Boussier pointed out. "We know there are tribesmen in close proximity to the town. They have been seen. They must be aware of your arrival and might easily have wrecked the lines to prevent our departure. I think your original decision is still good."

"I know." Bruce was hunched forward in his chair, frowning, sucking on the cheroot. At last he sat back, and the frown evaporated. "I can't risk it. I'll place a guard on the causeway, and if this Moses gentleman arrives we can hold him there long enough to entrain your people."

"That is probably the best course," agreed Boussier. He paused, glanced towards the open windows, and lowered his voice. "There is another point, Captain, which I wish to bring to your attention."

"Yes?"

"As you know, the activity of my company in Port Reprieve is centred on the recovery of diamonds from the Lufira swamps."

Bruce nodded.

"I have in my safe"—Boussier jerked his thumb at the heavy steel door built into the wall behind his desk—"nine-and-a-half-thousand carats of gem-quality diamonds and some twenty-six thousand carats of industrial diamonds."

"I had expected that." Bruce kept his tone noncommittal.

"It may be as well if we could agree on the disposition and handling of these stones."

"How are they packaged?" asked Bruce.

"A single wooden case."

"Of what size and weight?"

"I will show you."

Boussier went to the safe, turned his back to them, and they heard the tumblers whir and click. While he waited Bruce realized suddenly that Shermaine had not spoken since her initial greeting to Boussier. He glanced at her now, and she smiled at him. *I like a woman who knows when to keep her mouth shut.*

Boussier swung the door of the safe open and carried a small wooden case across to the desk.

"There," he said.

Bruce examined it. Eighteen inches long, nine deep, and twelve wide. He lifted it experimentally.

"About twenty pounds weight," he decided. "The lid is sealed."

"Yes," agreed Boussier, touching the four wax imprints.

"Good." Bruce nodded. "I don't want to draw unnecessary attention to it by placing a guard upon it."

"No, I agree."

Bruce studied the case a few seconds longer and then he asked, "What is the value of these stones?"

Boussier shrugged. "Possibly five hundred million francs."

Bruce was impressed: half a million sterling. Worth stealing, worth killing for.

"I suggest, monsieur, that you secrete this case in your luggage. In your blankets, say. I doubt there will be any danger of theft until we reach Msapa Junction. A thief will have no avenue of escape. Once we reach Msapa Junction I will make other arrangements for its safety."

"Very well, Captain."

Bruce stood up and glanced at his watch. "Seven o'clock, as near as dammit. I will leave you and see to the guard on the causeway. Please make sure that your people are ready to entrain before dawn tomorrow morning."

"Of course."

Bruce looked at Shermaine, and she stood up quickly. Bruce held the door open for her and was just about to follow her when a thought struck him.

"That mission station—St. Augustine's, is it? I suppose it's deserted now?"

"No, it's not." Boussier looked a little shamefaced. "Father Ignatius is still there, and of course the patients at the hospital."

"Thanks for telling me." Bruce was bitter.

"I'm sorry, Captain. It slipped my mind. There are so many things to think of."

"Do you know the road out to the mission?" Bruce snapped at Shermaine. *She* should have told him.

"Yes, Bruce."

"Well, perhaps you'd be good enough to direct me."

"Of course." She also looked guilty.

Bruce slammed the door of Boussier's office and strode off towards the hotel with Shermaine trotting to keep pace with him. You can't rely on anyone, he thought, not anybody!

And then he saw Ruffy coming up from the station, looking like a big bear in the dusk. With a few exceptions, Bruce corrected himself.

"Sergeant Major."

"Hello, boss."

"This General Moses is closer to us than we reckoned. He's reported less than a hundred miles north of here on the Senwati road."

Ruffy whistled through his teeth. "Are you going to take off now, boss?"

"No. I want a machine-gun post on this end of the causeway. If they come we can hold them there long enough to get away. I want you to take command."

"I'll see to it now."

"I'm going out to the mission—there's a white priest there. Lieutenant Haigh is in command while I'm away."

"Okay, boss."

10

"I'm sorry, Bruce. I should have told you." Shermaine sat small and repentant at her end of the Ranchero.

"Don't worry about it," said Bruce, not meaning it.

"We have tried to make Father Ignatius come in to town. Martin has spoken to him many times, but he refuses to move."

Bruce did not answer. He took the car down onto the causeway, driving carefully. There were shreds of mist lifting out of the swamp and drifting across the concrete ramp. Small insects, bright as tracer in the headlights, zoomed in to squash against the windscreen. The froggy chorus from the swamp honked and clinked and boomed deafeningly.

"I have apologized," she murmured.

"Yes, I heard you," said Bruce. "You don't have to do it again."

She was silent, and then, "Are you always so bad tempered?" she asked in English.

"Always," snapped Bruce, "is one of the words which should be eliminated from the language."

"Since it has not been, I will continue to use it. You haven't answered my question: are you always so bad tempered?"

"I just don't like balls-ups."

"What is *balls-up*, please?"

"What has just happened: a mistake, a situation precipitated by inefficiency, or by somebody not using his head."

"You never make balls-up, Bruce?"

"It is not a polite expression, Shermaine. Young ladies of refinement do not use it." Bruce changed into French.

"You never make mistakes?" she corrected herself.

Bruce did not answer. *That's quite funny,* he thought—*never make mistakes! Bruce Curry, the original balls-up.*

Shermaine held one hand across her middle and sat up straight.

"Bonaparte," she said. "Cold, silent, efficient."

"I didn't say that—" Bruce started to defend himself. Then in the glow from the dash light he saw her impish expression and he could not stop himself; he had to grin.

"All right, I'm acting like a child."

"You would like a cigarette?" she asked.

"Yes, please."

She lit it and passed it to him. "You do not like"—she hesitated—"mistakes. Is there anything you do like?"

"Many things," said Bruce.

"Tell me some."

They bumped off the end of the causeway and Bruce accelerated up the far bank.

"I like being on a mountain when the wind blows, and the taste of the sea. I like Sinatra, crayfish thermidor, the weight and balance of a Purdey Royal, and the sound of a little girl's laughter. I like the first draw of a cigarette lit from a wood fire, the scent of jasmine, the feel of silk; I also enjoy sleeping late in the morning, and the thrill of forking a queen with my knight. Shadows on the floor of a forest please me. And, of course, money. But especially I like women who do not ask too many questions."

"Is that all?"

"No, but it's a start."

"And apart from—mistakes, what are the things you do not like."

"Women who ask too many questions," and he saw her smile. "Selfishness except my own, turnip soup, politics, blond pubic hairs, Scotch whisky, classical music, and hangovers."

"I'm sure that is not all."

"No, not nearly."

"You are very sensual. All these things are of the senses."

"Agreed."

"You do not mention other people. Why?"

"Is this the turn off to the mission?"

"Yes, go slowly, the road is bad. Why do you not mention your relationship to other people?"

"Why do you ask so many questions? Perhaps I'll tell you someday."

She was silent a while, and then softly, "And what do you want from life—just those things you have spoken of? Is that all you want?"

"No. Not even them. I want nothing, expect nothing; that way I cannot be disappointed."

Suddenly she was angry. "You not only act like a child, you talk like one."

"Another thing I don't like: criticism."

"You are young. You have brains, good looks—"

"Thank you, that's better."

"—and you are a fool."

"That's not so good. But don't fret about it."

"I won't, don't worry," she flamed at him. "You can"— she searched for something devastating—"You can go jump out of the lake."

"Don't you mean into?"

"Into, out of, backwards, sideways, I don't care!"

"Good, I'm glad we've got that settled. There's the mission. I can see a light."

She did not answer but sat in her corner, breathing heavily, drawing so hard on her cigarette that the glowing tip lit the interior of the Ford.

The church was in darkness, but beyond it and to one side was a long low building. Bruce saw a shadow move across one of the windows.

"Is that the hospital?"

"Yes."—abruptly.

Bruce stopped the Ford beside the small front veranda and switched off the headlights and the ignition.

"Are you coming in?"

"No."

"I'd like you to present me to Father Ignatius."

For a moment she did not move, then she threw open her

door and marched up the steps of the veranda without looking back at Bruce.

He followed her through the front office, down the passage, past the clinic and small operating theatre, into the ward.

"Ah, Madame Cartier." Father Ignatius left the bed over which he was stooping and came towards her.

"I heard that the relief train had arrived at Port Reprieve. I thought you would have left by now."

"Not yet, Father. Tomorrow morning."

Father Ignatius was tall, six foot three or four, Bruce estimated, and thin. The sleeves of his brown cassock had been cut short as a concession to the climate, and his exposed arms appeared to be all bone, hairless, with the veins blue and prominent. Big bony hands, and big bony feet in brown open sandals.

Like most tall, thin men he was round-shouldered. His face was not one that you would remember, an ordinary face with steel-rimmed spectacles perched on a rather shapeless nose, neither young nor old, nondescript hair without grey in it, but there was about him that unhurried serenity you often find in a man of God. He turned his attention to Bruce, scrutinizing him gently through his spectacles.

"Good evening, my son."

"Good evening, Father." Bruce felt uncomfortable; they always made him feel that way. If only, he wished with envy, I could be as certain of one thing in my life as this man is certain of everything in his.

"Father, this is Captain Curry." Shermaine's tone was cold, and then suddenly she smiled again. "He does not care for people—that is why he has come to take you to safety."

Father Ignatius held out his hand, and Bruce found the skin was cool and dry, making him conscious of the moistness of his own.

"That is most thoughtful of you," he said, smiling, sensing the tension between his visitors. "I don't want to seem ungrateful, but I regret I cannot accept your offer."

"We have received reports that a column of armed bandits

is less than a hundred miles north of here. They will arrive tomorrow. You are in great danger—these people are completely merciless," Bruce urged him.

"Yes," Father Ignatius nodded. "I have also heard, and I am taking the steps I consider necessary. I shall take all my staff and patients into the bush."

"They'll follow you," said Bruce.

"I think not." Father Ignatius shook his head. "They will not waste their time. They are after loot, not sick people."

"They'll burn your mission."

"If they do, then we shall have to rebuild it when they leave."

"The bush is crawling with Baluba—you'll end up in the cooking pot." Bruce tried another approach.

"No." Father Ignatius shook his head. "Nearly every member of the tribe has at one time or another been a patient in this hospital. I have nothing to fear there, they are my friends."

"Look here, Father. Don't let us argue. My orders are to bring you back to Elisabethville. I must insist."

"And my orders are to stay here. You do agree that mine come from a higher authority than yours?" He smiled mildly.

Bruce opened his mouth to argue further; then, instead, he laughed. "No, I won't dispute that. Is there anything you need that I might be able to supply?"

"Medicines?" asked Father Ignatius.

"Acriflavine, morphine, field dressings, not much I'm afraid."

"They would help. And food?"

"Yes. I will let you have as much as I can spare," promised Bruce.

One of the patients, a woman at the end of the ward, screamed so suddenly that Bruce started.

"She will be dead before morning," Father Ignatius explained softly. "There is nothing I can do."

"What's wrong with her?"

"She has been in labour these past two days; there is some complication."

"Can't you operate?"

"I am not a doctor, my son. We had one here before the

trouble began, but he is here no longer—he has gone back to Elisabethville. No"—his voice seemed to carry helpless regret for all the suffering of mankind—"No, she will die."

"Haigh!" said Bruce.

"Pardon?"

"Father, you have an operating room here. Is it fully equipped?"

"Yes, I believe so."

"Anaesthetic?"

"We have chloroform and pentathol."

"Good," said Bruce. "I'll get you a doctor. Come on, Shermaine."

11

"This heat, this stinking heat!" Wally Hendry mopped at his face with a grubby handkerchief and threw himself down on the green leather bunk. "You notice how Curry leaves me and you here on the train while he puts Haigh up at the hotel and he goes off with that little French bit? It doesn't matter that me and you must cook in this box, long as he and his buddy Haigh are all right. You notice that, hey?"

"Somebody's got to stay aboard, Wally," André said.

"Yeah, but you notice who it is? Always you and me—those high society boys stick together, you've got to give them that, they look after each other." He transferred his attention back to the open window of the compartment. "Sun's down already and still hot enough to boil eggs. I could use a drink." He unlaced his jungle boots, peeled off his socks, and regarded his large white feet with distaste. "This stinking heat got my athlete's foot going again."

He separated two of his toes and picked at the loose scaly skin between. "You got any of that ointment left, André?"

"Yes, I'll get it for you." André opened a flap of his pack, took out the tube, and crossed to Wally's bunk.

"Put it on," instructed Wally and lay back, offering his feet. André took them in his lap as he sat down on the bunk and went to work. Wally lit a cigarette and blew smoke towards the roof, watching it disperse.

"Hell, I could use a drink. A beer with dew on the glass and a head that thick." He held up four fingers, then he lifted himself on one elbow and studied André as he spread ointment between the long prehensile toes.

"How's it going?"

"Nearly finished, Wally."

"Is it bad?"

"Not as bad as last time—it hasn't started weeping yet."

"It itches like you wouldn't believe it," said Wally.

André did not answer, and Wally kicked him in the ribs with the flat of his free foot. "Did you hear what I said?"

"Yes, you said it itches."

"Well, answer me when I talk to you. I ain't talking to myself."

"I'm sorry, Wally."

Wally grunted and was silent a while; then, "Do you like me, André?"

"You know I do, Wally."

"We're friends, aren't we, André?"

"Of course, you know that, Wally."

An expression of cunning had replaced Wally's boredom.

"You don't mind when I ask you to do things for me, like putting stuff on my feet?"

"I don't mind—it's a pleasure, Wally."

"It's a pleasure, is it?" There was an edge in Wally's voice now. "You like doing it?"

André looked up at him apprehensively. "I don't mind it." His molten toffee eyes clung to the narrow Mongolian ones in Wally's face.

"You like touching me, André?"

André stopped working with the ointment and nervously wiped his fingers on his towel.

"I said, do you like touching me, André? Do you sometimes wish I'd touch you?"

André tried to stand up, but Wally's right arm shot out and his hand fastened on André's neck, forcing him down onto the bunk.

"Answer me, damn you, do you like it?"

"You're hurting me, Wally," whispered André.

"Shame, now ain't that a shame!"

Wally was grinning. He shifted his grip to the ridge of muscle above André's collarbone and dug his fingers in until they almost met through the flesh.

"Please, Wally, please," whimpered André, wriggling face down on the bunk.

"You love it, don't you? Come on, answer me."

"Yes, all right, yes. Please don't hurt me, Wally."

"Now, tell me truly, doll boy, have you ever had it before? I mean for real." Wally put his knee in the small of André's back, bearing down with all his weight.

"No!" shrieked André. "I haven't. Please, Wally, don't hurt me."

"You're lying to me, André. Don't do it."

"All right. I was lying." André tried to twist his head around, but Wally pushed his face into the bunk.

"Tell me all about it—come on, doll boy."

"It was only once, in Brussels."

"Who was this beef bandit?"

"My employer—I worked for him. He had an export agency."

"Did he throw you out, doll boy? Did he throw you out when he was tired of you?"

"No, you don't understand!" André denied with sudden vehemence. "You don't understand. He looked after me. I had my own apartment, my own car, everything. He wouldn't have abandoned me if it hadn't been for—for what happened. He couldn't help it, he was true to me. I swear to you—he loved me!"

Wally snorted with laughter; he was enjoying himself now.

"Loved you! Jesus wept!" He threw his head back, for the laughter was almost strangling him, and it was ten seconds before he could ask, "Then what happened between you and your true-blue lover? Why didn't you get married and settle down to raise a family, hey?" At the improbability of his own joke Wally convulsed with laughter once more.

"There was an investigation. The police—ooh! you're hurting me, Wally."

"Keep talking, mamselle!"

"The police—he had no alternative. He was a man of position, he couldn't afford the scandal. There was no other way out—there never is for us. It's hopeless, there is no happiness."

"Cut the crap, doll boy. Just give me the story."

"He arranged employment for me in Elisabethville, gave me money, paid for my air fare, everything. He did everything, he looked after me, he still writes to me."

"That's beautiful, real true love. You make me want to cry."

Then Wally's laughter changed its tone, harsher now. "Well, get this, doll boy, and get it good. I don't like queers!" He dug his fingers in again and André squealed.

"I'll tell you a story. When I was in reform school there was a queer there that tried to touch me up. One day I got him in the shower rooms with a razor, just an ordinary Gillette razor. There were twenty guys singing and shouting in the other cubicles. He screamed just like they were all screaming when the cold water hit them. No one took any notice of him. He wanted to be a woman, so I helped him." Hendry's voice went hoarse and gloating with the memory. "Jesus!" he whispered. "Jesus, the blood!"

André was sobbing now, his whole body shaking. "I won't— please, Wally. I can't help it. It was just that one time. Please leave me."

"How would you like me to help you, André?"

"No," shrieked André. And Hendry lost interest; he released him, left him lying on the bunk, and reached for his socks.

"I'm going to find me a beer." He laced on his boots and stood up. "Just you remember," he said darkly, standing over the boy on the bunk. "Don't get any ideas with me, bucko." He picked up his rifle and went out into the corridor.

Wally found Boussier on the veranda of the hotel, talking with a group of his men.

"Where's Captain Curry?" he demanded.

"He has gone out to the mission station."

"When did he leave?"

"About ten minutes ago."

"Good," said Wally. "Who's got the key to the bar?"

Boussier hesitated. "The captain has ordered that the bar is to remain locked."

Wally unslung his rifle. "Don't give me a hard time, friend."

"I regret, monsieur, that I must obey the captain's instructions."

For a minute they stared at each other, and there was no sign of weakening in the older man.

"Have it your way then," said Wally and swaggered through the lounge to the barroom door. He put his foot against the lock, and the flimsy mechanism yielded to the pressure. The door flew open, and Wally marched across to the counter, laid his rifle on it, and reached underneath to the shelves loaded with Simba beer.

The first bottle he emptied without taking it from his lips. He belched luxuriously and reached for the second, hooked the cap off with the opener and inspected the bubble of froth that appeared at its mouth.

"Hendry!" Wally looked up at Mike Haigh in the doorway.

"Hello, Mike." He grinned.

"What do you think you're doing?" Mike demanded.

"What does it look like?" Wally raised the bottle in salutation and then sipped delicately at the froth.

"Bruce has given strict orders that no one is allowed in here."

"Oh, for Chrissake, Haigh. Stop acting like an old woman."

"Out you get, Hendry. I'm in charge here."

"Mike"—Wally grinned at him—"you want me to die of thirst or something?" He leaned his elbows on the counter. "Give me a couple more minutes. Let me finish my drink."

Mike Haigh glanced behind him into the lounge and saw the interested group of civilians who were craning to see into the barroom. He closed the door and walked across to stand opposite Hendry.

"Two minutes, Hendry," he agreed in an unfriendly tone, "then out with you."

"You're not a bad guy, Mike. You and I rubbed each other up wrong. I tell you something, I'm sorry about us."

"Drink up!" said Mike. Without turning, Wally reached backwards and took a bottle of Rémy Martin cognac off the shelf. He pulled the cork with his teeth, selected a brandy balloon with his free hand, and poured a little of the oily amber fluid into it.

"Keep me company, Mike," he said and slid the glass across the counter towards Haigh. First without expression, and then with his face seeming to crumble, Mike Haigh stared at the glass, again older and tired looking. He moistened his lips. With a physical wrench he pulled his eyes away from the glass.

"Damn you, Hendry." His voice was unnaturally low. "God damn you to hell." He hit out at the glass, spinning it off the counter to shatter against the far wall.

"Did I do something wrong, Mike?" asked Hendry softly. "Just offered you a drink, that's all."

The smell of spilled brandy, sharp, fruity with the warmth of the grape—and Mike moistened his lips again. The saliva jetted from under his tongue, and the deep, yearning, aching want in his stomach spread outwards slowly, numbing him.

"Damn you," he whispered. "Oh, damn you, damn you"—pleading now as Hendry filled another glass.

"How long has it been, Mike? A year, two years? Try a little, just a mouthful. Remember the lift it gives you. Come on, boy. You're tired, you've worked hard. Just one—there you are. Just have this one with me."

Mike wiped his mouth with the back of his hand, sweating now across the forehead and on his upper lip, tiny jewels of sweat squeezed out of the skin by the craving of his body.

"Come on, boy." Wally's voice was hoarse with excitement, teasing, wheedling, tempting.

Mike's hand closed round the tumbler, moving of its own volition, lifting it towards lips that were suddenly slack and trembling, his eyes filled with mingled loathing and desire.

"Just this one," whispered Hendry. "Just this one."

Mike gulped it with a sudden savage flick of his arm—one

swallow and the glass was empty. He held it with both hands, his head bowed over it.

"I hate you. My God, I hate you." He spoke to Hendry, and to himself, and to the empty glass.

"That's my boy!" crowed Wally. "That's the lad! Come on, let me fill you up."

12

Bruce went in through the front door of the hotel with Shermaine trying to keep pace with him. There were a dozen or so people in the lobby, and an air of tension among them. Boussier was one of them, and he came quickly to Bruce.

"I'm sorry, Captain, I could not stop them. That one, that one with the red hair, he was violent. He had his gun and I think he was ready to use it."

"What are you talking about?" Bruce asked him, but before Boussier could answer there was the bellow of Hendry's laughter from behind the door at the far end of the lobby, the door to the barroom.

"They are in there," Boussier told him. "They have been there for the past hour."

"Goddammit to hell," swore Bruce. "Now of all times. Oh, goddam that bloody animal."

He almost ran across the room and threw open the double doors. Hendry was standing against the far wall with a tumbler in one hand and his rifle in the other. He was holding the rifle by the pistol grip and waving vague circles in the air with it.

Mike Haigh was building a pyramid of glasses on the bar counter. He was just placing the final glass on the pile.

"Hello, Bruce, old cock, old man, old fruit," he greeted and waved in an exaggerated manner. "Just in time. You can have a couple of shots as well. But Wally's first, he gets first shot. Must abide by the rules, no cheating, strictly democratic affair, everyone has equal rights. Rank doesn't count. That's right, isn't it, Wally?" Haigh's features had blurred; it was as though he were melting, losing his shape. His lips were loose and flabby, his jowls hung pendulously as an old woman's breasts, and his eyes were moist.

He picked up a glass from beside the pyramid, but this glass was nearly full and a bottle of cognac stood beside it.

"A very fine old brandy, absolutely exquisite." The last two words didn't come out right, so he repeated them carefully. Then he grinned loosely at Bruce, and his eyes weren't quite in focus.

"Get out of the way, Mike," said Hendry and raised the rifle, one-handed, aiming at the pile of glasses.

"Every time she bucks, she bounces," hooted Haigh, "and every time she bounces you win a coconut. Let her rip, old fruit."

"Hendry, stop that!" snapped Bruce.

"Go and get mucked," answered Hendry and fired. The rifle kicked back over his shoulder and he fell against the wall. The pyramid of glasses exploded in a shower of fragments and the room was filled with the roar of the rifle.

"Give the gentleman a coconut!" crowed Mike.

Bruce crossed the room with three quick strides and pulled the rifle out of Hendry's hand. "All right, you drunken ape. That's enough."

"Go and muck yourself," growled Hendry. He was massaging his wrist; the rifle had twisted it.

"Captain Curry," said Haigh from behind the bar, "you heard what my friend said. You go and muck yourself sideways to sleep."

"Shut up, Haigh."

"This time I'll fix you, Curry," Hendry growled. "You've been on my back too long—now I'm going to shake you off!"

"Kindly descend from my friend's back, Captain Curry," chimed in Mike Haigh. "He's not a howdah elephant, he's my blood brother. I will not allow you to persecute him."

"Come on, Curry. Come on then!" said Wally.

"That's it, Wally. Muck him up." Haigh filled his glass again as he spoke. "Don't let him ride you."

"Come on then, Curry."

"You're drunk," said Bruce.

"Come on then; don't talk, man. Or do I have to start it?"

"No, you don't have to start it," Bruce assured him and lifted the rifle, butt first under his chin, swinging it up hard. Hendry's head jerked and he staggered back against the wall. Bruce looked at his eyes; they were glazed over. That will hold him, he decided; that's taken the fight out of him. He caught Hendry by the shoulder and threw him into one of the chairs. I must get to Haigh before he absorbs any more of that liquor, he thought, I can't waste time sending for Ruffy and I can't leave this thing behind me while I work on Haigh.

"Shermaine," he called. She was standing in the doorway and she came to his side. "Can you use a pistol?"

She nodded. Bruce unclipped his Smith & Wesson from its lanyard and handed it to her. "Shoot this man if he tries to leave that chair. Stand here where he cannot reach you."

"Bruce—" she started.

"He is a dangerous animal. Yesterday he murdered two small children and, if you let him, he'll do the same to you. You must keep him here while I get the other one."

She lifted the pistol, holding it with both hands, and her face was even paler than was usual.

"Can you do it?" Bruce asked.

"Now I can," she said and cocked the action.

"Hear me, Hendry." Bruce took a handful of his hair and twisted his face up. "She'll kill you if you leave this chair. Do you understand? She'll shoot you."

"Muck you and your little French whore, muck you both. I bet that's what you two have been doing all evening in that car —playing 'hide the sausage' down by the riverside."

Anger flashed through Bruce so violently that it startled him. He twisted Hendry's hair until he could feel it coming away in his hand. Hendry squirmed with pain.

"Shut that foul mouth or I'll kill you."

He meant it, and suddenly Hendry knew he meant it.

"Okay, for Chrissake, okay. Just leave me."

Bruce loosened his grip and straightened up. "I'm sorry, Shermaine," he said.

"That's all right—go to the other one."

Bruce went to the bar counter, and Haigh watched him come.

"What do you want, Bruce? Have a drink." He was nervous. "Have a drink, we are all having a little drink. All good clean fun, Bruce. Don't get excited."

"You're not having any more; in fact, just the opposite," Bruce told him as he came around the counter.

Haigh backed away in front of him. "What are you going to do?"

"I'll show you," said Bruce and caught him by the wrist, turning him quickly and lifting his arm up between his shoulder-blades.

"Hey, Bruce, cut it out! You've made me spill my drink."

"Good," said Bruce and slapped the empty glass out of Haigh's hand.

Haigh started to struggle. He was still a powerful man but the liquor had weakened him, and Bruce lifted his wrist higher, forcing him onto his toes.

"Come along, buddy boy," instructed Bruce and marched him towards the back door of the barroom. He reached around Haigh with his free hand, turned the key in the lock, and opened the door.

"Through here," he said and pushed Mike into the kitchen. He kicked the door shut behind him and went to the sink, dragging Haigh with him.

"All right, Haigh, let's have it up," he said and changed his grip quickly, thrusting Haigh's head down over the sink. There was a dish towel hanging beside it, which Bruce screwed into a ball; then he used his thumbs to open Haigh's jaws and wedged the towel between his back teeth.

"Let's have all of it." He probed his finger down into Haigh's throat. It came up hot and gushing over his hand, and he fought down his own nausea as he worked. When he had finished he turned on the cold tap and held Haigh's head under it, washing Haigh's face and his own hand.

"Now I've got a little job for you, Haigh."

"Leave me alone, damn you," groaned Haigh, his voice indistinct beneath the rushing tap. Bruce pulled him up and held him against the wall.

"There's a woman in childbirth at the mission. She's going to die, Haigh. She's going to die if you don't do something about it."

"No," whispered Haigh. "No, not that. Not that again."

"I'm taking you there."

"No, please, not that. I can't—don't you see that I can't?" The little red and purple veins in his nose and cheeks stood out in vivid contrast to his pallor. Bruce hit him open-handed across the face and the water flew in drops from his hair at the shock.

"No," he mumbled, "please, Bruce, please."

Bruce hit him twice more, hard, watching him carefully, and at last he saw the first flickering of anger.

"Damn you, Bruce Curry, damn you to hell!"

"You'll do," rejoiced Bruce. "Thank God for that."

He hustled Haigh back through the barroom. Shermaine still stood over Hendry, holding the pistol.

"Come on, Shermaine. You can leave that thing now. I'll attend to him when we get back."

As they crossed the lobby Bruce asked Shermaine, "Can you drive the Ford?"

"Yes."

"Good," said Bruce. "Here are the keys. I'll sit with Haigh in the back. Take us out to the mission."

Haigh lost his balance on the front steps of the hotel and nearly fell, but Bruce caught him and half carried him to the car. He pushed him into the back seat and climbed in beside him. Shermaine slid in behind the wheel, started the engine, and U-turned neatly across the street.

"You can't force me to do this, Bruce. I can't, I just can't," Haigh pleaded.

"We'll see," said Bruce.

"You don't know what it's like. You can't know. She'll die on the table." He held out his hands palms down. "Look at that, look at them. How can I do it with these?" His hands were trembling violently.

"She's going to die anyway," said Bruce, his voice hard. "So you might as well do it for her quickly and get it over with."

Haigh brought his hands up to his mouth and wiped his lips.

"Can I have a drink, Bruce? That'll help. I'll try then, if you give me a drink."

"No," said Bruce, and Haigh began to swear. The filth poured from his lips and his face twisted with the effort. He cursed Bruce, he cursed himself and God in a torrent of the most obscene language that Bruce had ever heard. Then suddenly he snatched at the door handle and tried to twist it open. Bruce had been waiting for this and he caught the back of Haigh's collar, pulled him backwards across the seat, and held him there. Haigh's struggles ceased abruptly and he began to sob softly.

Shermaine drove fast, across the causeway, up the slope, and into the side road. The headlights cut into the darkness and the wind drummed softly round the car. Haigh was still sobbing on the back seat.

Then the lights of the mission were ahead of them through the trees, and Shermaine slowed the car, turned in past the church, and pulled up next to the hospital block.

Bruce helped Haigh out of the car, and while he was doing so the side door of the building opened and Father Ignatius came out with a petromax lantern in his hand. The harsh white glare of the lantern lit them all and threw grotesque shadows behind them. It fell with special cruelty on Haigh's face.

"Here's your doctor, Father," Bruce announced.

Father Ignatius lifted the lantern and peered through his spectacles at Haigh. "Is he sick?"

"No, Father," said Bruce, "he's drunk."

"Drunk? Then he can't operate?"

"Yes, he damn well can!"

Bruce took Haigh through the door and along the passage to the little operating room. Father Ignatius and Shermaine followed them.

"Shermaine, go with the Father and help him bring the woman," Bruce ordered, and they went; then he turned his attention back to Haigh.

"Are you so far down there in the slime that you can't understand me?"

"I can't do it, Bruce. It's no good."

"Then she'll die. But this much is certain: you are going to make the attempt."

"I've got to have a drink, Bruce." Haigh licked his lips. "It's burning me up inside, you've got to give me one."

"Finish the job and I'll give you a whole case."

"I've got to have one now."

"No." Bruce spoke with finality. "Have a look at what they've got here in the way of instruments. Can you do it with these?" Bruce crossed to the sterilizer and lifted the lid; the steam came up out of it in a cloud.

Haigh looked in also. "That's all I need, but there's not enough light in here, and I need a drink."

"I'll get you more light. Start cleaning up."

"Bruce, please let me—"

"Shut up," snarled Bruce. "There's the basin. Start getting ready."

Haigh crossed to the hand basin; he was more steady on his feet and his features had firmed a little. You poor old bastard, thought Bruce, I hope you can do it. My God, how much I hope you can!

"Get a move on, Haigh, we haven't got all night."

Bruce left the room and went quickly down the passage to the ward. The windows of the operating room were fixed, and Haigh could escape only into the passage. Bruce knew that he could catch him if Haigh tried to run for it.

He looked into the ward. Shermaine and Father Ignatius, with the help of an African orderly, had lifted the woman onto the wheeled stretcher.

"Father, we need more light."

"I can get you another lantern, that's all."

"Good, do that then. I'll take the woman through."

Father Ignatius disappeared with the orderly, and Bruce helped Shermaine manoeuvre the stretcher down the length of the ward and into the passage. The woman was whimpering with pain, and her face was grey, waxy grey. *They only go like that when they are very frightened, or when they are dying.*

"She hasn't much longer," he said.

"I know," agreed Shermaine. "We must hurry."

The woman moved restlessly on the stretcher and gabbled a few words; then she sighed so that the great blanket-covered mound of her belly rose and fell, and she started to whimper again.

Haigh was still in the room. He had stripped off his battle-jacket and, in his vest, was stooped over the basin, washing. He did not look around as they wheeled the woman in.

"Get her on the table," he said, working the soap into suds up to his elbows.

The stretcher was of a height with the table and, using the blanket to lift her, it was easy to slide the woman across.

"She's ready, Haigh," said Bruce.

Haigh dried his arms on a clean towel and turned. He came to the woman and stood over her. She did not know he was there; her eyes were open but unseeing. Haigh drew a deep breath; he was sweating a little across his forehead, and the stubble of beard on the lower part of his face was stippled with grey.

He pulled back the blanket. The woman wore a short white jacket, open-fronted, that did not cover her stomach. Her stomach was swollen, hard looking, with the navel inverted; knees raised slightly, and the thick peasant's thighs spread wide in the act of labour. As Bruce watched, her whole body arched in another contraction. He saw the stress of the muscles beneath the dark skin as they struggled to expel the trapped fetus.

"Hurry, Mike!" Bruce was appalled by the anguish of birth. *I didn't know it was like this*; *in sorrow thou shalt bring forth children—but this*! Through the woman's dry grey swollen lips burst another of those moaning little cries, and Bruce swung towards Mike Haigh.

"Hurry, goddam you!"

And Mike Haigh began his examination, his hands very pale as they groped over the dark skin. At last he was satisfied and he stood back from the table.

Father Ignatius and the orderly came in with two more lanterns. Father Ignatius started to say something, but instantly he sensed the tension in the room and he fell silent. They all watched Mike Haigh's face.

His eyes were tight closed, and his face was hard angles and harsh planes in the lantern light. His breathing was shallow and laboured.

I must not push him now, Bruce knew instinctively. I have dragged him to the lip of the precipice and now I must let him go over the edge on his own.

Mike opened his eyes again, and he spoke. "Caesarean section," he said, as though he had pronounced his own death sentence. Then his breathing stopped. They waited, and at last the breath came out of him in a sigh.

"I'll do it," he said.

"Gowns and gloves?" Bruce fired the question at Father Ignatius.

"In the cupboard."

"Get them!"

"You'll have to help me, Bruce. And you also, Shermaine."

"Yes, show me."

Quickly they scrubbed and dressed. Father Ignatius held the pale green operating gowns while they dived into them and flapped and struggled through.

"That tray, bring it here," Mike ordered as he opened the sterilizer. With a pair of long-nosed forceps he lifted the instruments out of the steaming box and laid them on the tray, naming each one as he did so.

"Scalpel, retractors, clamps."

In the meantime the orderly was swabbing the woman's belly with alcohol and arranging the sheets.

Mike filled the syringe with pentathol and held it up to the light. He was an unfamiliar figure now—his face masked, the green skull cap covering his hair, and the flowing gown falling to his ankles. He pressed the plunger, and a few drops of the pale fluid dribbled down the needle.

He looked at Bruce, only his haunted eyes showing above the mask. "Ready?"

"Yes." Bruce nodded.

Mike stooped over the woman, took her arm, and sent the needle searching under the soft black skin on the inside of her elbow. The fluid in the syringe was suddenly discoloured with drawn blood as Mike tested for the vein, and then the plunger slid slowly down the glass barrel.

The woman stopped whimpering, the tension went out of her body, and her breathing slowed and became deep and unhurried.

"Come here." Mike ordered Shermaine to the head of the table, and she took up the chloroform mask and soaked the gauze that filled the cone.

"Wait until I tell you."

She nodded.

Christ, what lovely eyes she has, thought Bruce, before he turned back to the job in hand.

"Scalpel," said Mike from across the table, pointing to it on the tray, and Bruce handed it to him.

Afterwards the details were confused and lacking reality in Bruce's mind.

The wound opening behind the knife, the tight, stretched skin parting, and the tiny blood vessels starting to squirt.

Pink muscle laced with white; butter-yellow layers of subcutaneous fat; and then through to the massed bluish coils of the gut. Human tissue, soft and pulsing, glistening in the flat glare of the petromax.

Clamps and retractors, like silver insects crowding into the wound as though it were a flower.

Mike's hands, inhuman in yellow rubber, moving in the open pit of the belly. Swabbing, cutting, clamping, tying off.

Then the swollen purple bag of the womb, suddenly unzipped by the knife.

And at last, unbelievably, the child curled in a dark grey ball of legs and tiny arms, head too big for its size, and the fat pink snake of the placenta enfolding it.

Lifted out, the infant hung by its heels from Mike's hand like a small grey bat, still joined to its mother.

Scissors snipped, and it was free. Mike worked a little longer, and the infant cried.

It cried with minute fury, indignant and alive. From the head of the table Shermaine laughed with spontaneous delight and clapped her hands like a child at a Punch and Judy show. Suddenly Bruce was laughing also. It was a laugh from long ago, coming out from deep inside him.

"Take it," said Haigh, and Shermaine cradled it, wet and feebly wriggling in her arms. She stood with it while Haigh sewed up. Watching her face and the way she stood, Bruce suddenly and unaccountably felt the laughter snag his throat, and he wanted to cry.

Haigh closed the womb, stitching the complicated pattern of knots like a skilled seamstress, then the external sutures laid neatly across the fat lips of the wound, and at last the white tape hiding it all. He covered the woman, jerked the mask from his face, and looked up at Shermaine.

"You can help me clean it up," he said, and his voice was strong again and proud. The two of them crossed to the basin.

Bruce threw off his gown and left the room, went down the passage and out into the night. He leaned against the bonnet of the Ford and lit a cigarette.

Tonight I laughed again, he told himself with wonder, *and then I nearly cried. And all because of a woman and a child. It is finished now, the pretense. The withdrawal. The big act. There was more than one birth in there tonight. I laughed again, I had the need to laugh again, and the desire to cry. A woman and a child, the whole meaning of life.* The abscess had burst, the poison drained, and he was ready to heal.

"Bruce, Bruce, where are you?" She came out through the

door; he did not answer her, for she had seen the glow of his cigarette and she came to him, standing close in the darkness.

"Shermaine—" Bruce said, then he stopped himself. He wanted to hold her, just hold her tightly.

"Yes, Bruce." Her face was a pale round in the darkness, very close to him.

"Shermaine, I want—" said Bruce and stopped again.

"Yes, me too," she whispered, and then, drawing away, "Come, let's go and see what your doctor is doing now." She took his hand and led him back into the building. Her hand was cool and dry, with long tapered fingers in his.

Mike Haigh and Father Ignatius were leaning over the cradle that now stood next to the table on which lay the blanket-covered body of the Baluba woman. The woman was breathing softly, and the expression on her face was of deep peace.

"Bruce, come and have a look. It's a beauty," called Haigh.

Still holding hands, Bruce and Shermaine crossed to the cradle.

"He'll go all of eight pounds," announced Haigh proudly.

Bruce looked at the infant: newborn black babies are more handsome than ours—they have not got that half-boiled look.

"Pity he's not a trout," murmured Bruce. "That would be a national record." Haigh stared blankly at him for a second, then he threw back his head and laughed. It was a good sound. There was a different quality in Haigh now, a new confidence in the way he held his head, a feeling of completeness about him.

"How about that drink I promised you, Mike?" Bruce tested him.

"You have it for me, Bruce. I'll duck this one."

He isn't just saying it either, thought Bruce, looking at Haigh's face; he really doesn't need it now. "I'll make it a double as soon as we get back to town." Bruce glanced at his watch. "It's past ten. We'd better get going."

"I'll have to stay until she comes out from the anaesthetic," demurred Haigh. "You can come back for me in the morning."

Bruce hesitated. "All right then. Come on, Shermaine."

They drove back to Port Reprieve, sitting close together in the intimate darkness of the car. They did not speak until after they had reached the causeway, then Shermaine said, "He is a good man, your doctor. He is like Paul."

"Who is Paul?"

"Paul was my husband."

"Oh," Bruce was embarrassed. The mention of that name snapped the silken thread of his mood.

Shermaine went on, speaking softly and staring down the path of the headlights. "Paul was of the same age. Old enough to have learned understanding—young men are so cruel."

"You loved him." Bruce spoke flatly, trying to keep any trace of jealousy from his voice.

"Love has many shapes," she answered; then, "Yes, I had begun to love him. Very soon I would have loved him enough to—" She stopped.

"To what?" Bruce's voice had gone rough as a wood rasp. *Now it starts*, he thought, *once again I am vulnerable*.

"We were married only four months before he—before the fever."

"So?" Still harsh, his eyes on the road ahead.

"I want you to know something. I must explain it all to you. It is very important. Will you be patient with me while I tell you?"

There was a pleading in her voice that he could not resist, and his expression softened. "Shermaine, you don't have to tell me."

"I must. I want you to know." She hesitated a moment, and when she spoke again her voice had steadied. "I am an orphan, Bruce. Both my Mama and Papa were killed by the Germans, in the bombing. I was only a few months old when it happened, so I do not remember them. I do not know anything, not one little thing, about them; there is not even a photograph." For a second her voice had gone shaky, but again it firmed. "The nuns took me, and they were my family. But somehow that is different, not really your own. I have never had anything that has truly belonged to me, something of my very own."

Bruce reached out and took her hand; it lay very still in his grasp. *You have now*, he thought, *you have me for your very own*.

"Then when the time came the nuns made the arrangements with Paul Cartier. He was an engineer with Union Minière du Haut here in the Congo, a man of position, a suitable man for one of their girls.

"He flew to Brussels and we were married. I was not unhappy, for although he was old—as old as Doctor Mike—yet he was very gentle and kind, of great understanding. He did not—" She stopped and turned suddenly to Bruce, gripping his hand with both of hers, leaning towards him with her face serious and pale in the half darkness, the plume of dark hair falling forward over her shoulder, and her voice full of appeal. "Bruce, do you understand what I am trying to tell you?"

Bruce stopped the car in front of the hotel; deliberately he switched off the ignition and deliberately he spoke. "Yes, I think so."

"Thank you." She flung the door open and went out of it and up the steps of the hotel with her long, jeaned legs flying and her hair bouncing on her back.

Bruce watched her go through the double doors. Then he pressed the lighter on the dashboard and fished a cigarette from his pack. He lit it, exhaled a jet of smoke against the windscreen, and suddenly he was happy. He wanted to laugh again.

He threw the cigarette away only a quarter finished and climbed out of the Ford. He looked at his wrist watch; it was after midnight. *My God, I'm tired. Too much has happened today; rebirth is a severe emotional strain.* And he laughed out loud, savouring the sensation, letting it come slowly up his throat from his chest.

Boussier was waiting for him in the lounge. He wore a terry dressing-gown, and the creases of sleep were on his face.

"Are all your preparations complete, monsieur?"

"Yes," the old man answered. "The women and the two children are asleep upstairs. Madame Cartier has just gone up."

"I know," said Bruce, and Boussier went on, "As you see, I have all the men here." He gestured at the sleeping bodies that covered the floor of the lounge and barroom.

"Good," said Bruce. "We'll leave as soon as it's light tomorrow." He yawned, then rubbed his eyes, massaging them with his finger tips. "Where is my officer, the one with the red hair?"

"He has gone back to the train, very drunk. We had more trouble with him after you left." Boussier hesitated delicately. "He wanted to go upstairs, to the women."

"Damn him." Bruce felt his anger coming again. "What happened?"

"Your sergeant major, the big one, dissuaded him and took him away."

"Thank God for Ruffy."

"I have reserved a place for you to sleep." Boussier pointed to a comfortable leather armchair. "You must be exhausted."

"That is kind of you," Bruce thanked him. "But first I must inspect our defenses."

13

Bruce woke with Shermaine leaning over the chair and tickling his nose. He was fully dressed, with his helmet and rifle on the floor beside him, and only his boots unlaced.

"You do not snore, Bruce," she congratulated him, laughing her small husky laugh. "That is a good thing."

He struggled up, dopey with sleep. "What time is it?"

"Nearly five o'clock. I have breakfast for you in the kitchen."

"Where is Boussier?"

"He is dressing; then he will start moving them down to the train."

"My mouth tastes as though a goat slept in it." Bruce moved his tongue across his teeth, feeling the fur on them.

"Then I shall not kiss you good morning, mon capitaine." She straightened up with the laughter still in her eyes. "But your toilet requisites are in the kitchen. I sent one of your gendarmes to fetch them from the train. You can wash in the sink."

Bruce laced up his boots and followed her through into the kitchen, stepping over sleeping bodies on the way.

"There is no hot water," Shermaine apologized.

"That is the least of my worries." Bruce crossed to the table and opened his small personal pack, taking out his razor and soap and comb.

"I raided the chickencoop for you," Shermaine confessed. "There were only two eggs. How shall I cook them?"

"Soft boiled, one minute." Bruce stripped off his jacket and shirt, went to the sink and filled it. He sluiced his face and lifted handfuls of water over his head, snorting with pleasure.

Then he propped his shaving mirror above the taps and spread soap on his face. Shermaine came to sit on the drainboard beside him and watched with frank interest.

"I will be sorry to see the beard go," she said. "It looked like the pelt of an otter. I liked it."

"Perhaps I will grow it for you one day." Bruce smiled at her. "Your eyes are blue, Shermaine."

"It has taken you a long time to find that out," she said and pouted dramatically. Her skin was silky and cool looking, lips pale pink without make-up. Her dark hair, drawn back, emphasized the high cheekbones and the size of her eyes.

"In India 'sher' means 'tiger,' " Bruce told her, watching her from the corner of his eye. Immediately she abandoned the pout and drew her lips up into a snarl. Her teeth were small and very white and only slightly uneven. Her eyes rolled wide and then crossed at an alarming angle. She growled. Taken by surprise, Bruce laughed and nearly cut himself.

"I cannot abide a woman who clowns before breakfast. It ruins my digestion." He laughed at her.

"Breakfast!" said Shermaine and uncrossed her eyes, jumped off the drainboard, and ran to the stove.

"Only just in time." She checked her watch. "One minute and twenty seconds, will you forgive me?"

"This once only, never again." Bruce washed the soap off his face, dried and combed his hair, and came to the table. She had a chair ready for him.

"How much sugar in your coffee?"

"Three, please." Bruce chopped the top off his egg, and she brought the mug and placed it in front of him.

"I like making breakfast for you."

Bruce didn't answer her. This was dangerous talk.

She sat down opposite him, leaned forward on her elbows with her chin in her hands. "You eat too fast," she announced, and Bruce raised an eyebrow. "But at least you keep your mouth closed."

Bruce started on his second egg.

"How old are you?"

"Thirty," said Bruce.

"I'm twenty—nearly twenty-one."

"A ripe old age."

"What do you do?"

"I'm a soldier," he answered.

"No, you're not."

"All right, I'm a lawyer."

"You must be clever," she said solemnly.

"A genius—that's why I'm here."

"Are you married?"

"No—I was. What is this, a formal interrogation?"

"Is she dead?"

"No." He prevented the hurt from showing in his face; it was easier to do now.

"Oh!" said Shermaine. She picked up the teaspoon and concentrated on stirring his coffee.

"Is she pretty?"

"No—yes, I suppose so."

"Where is she?" Then quickly, "I'm sorry, it's none of my business."

Bruce took the coffee from her and drank it. Then he looked at his watch. "It's nearly five-fifteen. I must go out and get Mike Haigh."

Shermaine stood up quickly. "I'm ready."

"I know the way. You had better get down to the station."

"I want to come with you."

"Why?"

"Just because, that's why." Searching for a reason. "I want to see the baby again."

"You win." Bruce picked up his pack, and they went through into the lounge. Boussier was there, dressed and efficient. His men were nearly ready to move.

"Madame Cartier and I are going out to the mission to fetch the doctor. We will be back in half an hour or so. I want all your people aboard by then."

"Very well, Captain."

Bruce called to Ruffy, who was standing on the veranda. "Did you load those supplies for the mission?"

"They're in the back of the Ford, boss."

"Good. Bring all your sentries in and take them down to

the station. Tell the engine driver to get steam up and keep his hand on the throttle. We'll shove off as soon as I get back with Lieutenant Haigh."

"Okay, boss."

Bruce handed him the pack. "Take this down for me, Ruffy." Then his eyes fell on a large heap of cardboard cartons at Ruffy's feet. "What's that?"

Ruffy looked a little embarrassed. "Coupla bottles of beer, boss. Thought we might get thirsty going home."

"Good for you!" Bruce grinned. "Put them in a safe place and don't drink them all before I get back."

"I'll save you one or two," promised Ruffy.

"Come along, tiger girl," and Bruce led Shermaine out to the Ford. She sat closer to him than the previous day, but with her legs curled up under her, as before. As they crossed the causeway she lit two cigarettes and passed one to him.

"I'll be glad to leave this place," she said, looking out across the swamp with the mist lifting sluggishly off in the dawn, hanging in grey shreds from the fluffy tops of the papyrus grass.

"I've hated it here since Paul died. I hate the swamp and the mosquitoes and the jungle all around. I'm glad we're going."

"Where will you go?" Bruce asked.

"I haven't thought about it. Back to Belgium, I suppose. Anywhere away from the Congo. Away from this heat to a country where you can breathe. Away from the disease and the fear. Somewhere so that I know tomorrow I will not have to run. Where human life has meaning, away from the killing and the burning and the rape." She drew on her cigarette almost fiercely, staring ahead at the green wall of the forest.

"I was born in Africa," said Bruce. "In the time when the judge's gavel was not the butt of an FN rifle, before you registered your vote with a burst of gunfire." He spoke softly, with regret. "In the time before the hatred. But now I don't know. I haven't thought much about the future either."

He was silent for a while. They reached the turn-off to the mission, and he swung the Ford into it.

"It has all changed so quickly; I hadn't realized how quickly until I came here to the Congo."

"Are you going to stay here, Bruce? I mean, stay here in the Congo?"

"No," he said, "I've had enough. I don't even know what I'm fighting for." He threw the butt of his cigarette out of the window.

Ahead of them were the mission buildings.

Bruce parked the car outside the hospital buildings, and they sat together quietly. "There must be some other land," he whispered, "and if there is I'll find it."

He opened the door and stepped out. Shermaine slid across the seat under the wheel and joined him. They walked side by side to the hospital; her hand brushed his, and he caught it, held it, and felt the pressure of his fingers returned by hers. She was taller than his shoulder, but not much.

Mike Haigh and Father Ignatius were together in the women's ward, too engrossed to hear the Ford arrive.

"Good morning, Michael," called Bruce. "What's the fancy dress for?"

Haigh looked up and grinned. "Morning, Bruce. Hello, Shermaine." Then he looked down at the faded brown cassock he wore. "Borrowed it from Father Ignatius. A bit long in the leg and tight around the waist, but less out of place in a sick ward than the accoutrements of war."

"It suits you, Doctor Mike," said Shermaine.

"Nice to hear someone call me that again." The smile spread all over Haigh's face. "I suppose you want to see your baby, Shermaine?"

"Is he well?"

"Mother and child both doing fine," he assured her and led her down between the row of beds, each with a black woolly head on the pillow and big curious eyes following their progress.

"May I pick him up?"

"He's asleep, Shermaine."

"Oh, please!"

"I doubt it will kill him. Very well, then."

"Bruce, come and look. Isn't he a darling?" She held the tiny black body to her chest and the child snuffled, its mouth automatically starting to search. Bruce leaned forward to peer at it.

"Very nice," he said and turned to Father Ignatius. "I have those supplies I promised you. Will you send an orderly to get them out of the car?" Then to Haigh, "You'd better get changed, Mike. We're all ready to leave."

Not looking at Bruce, fiddling with the stethoscope around his neck, Mike shook his head. "I don't think I'll be going with you, Bruce."

Surprised, Bruce faced him. "What?"

"I think I'll stay on here with Father Ignatius. He has offered me a job."

"You must be mad, Mike."

"Perhaps," agreed Haigh and took the infant from Shermaine, placed it back in the cradle beside its mother, and tucked the sheet in round its tiny body. "And then again, perhaps not." He straightened up and waved a hand down the rows of occupied beds. "There's plenty to do here, that you must admit."

Bruce stared helplessly at him and then appealed to Shermaine. "Talk him out of it. Perhaps you can make him see the futility of it."

Shermaine shook her head. "No, Bruce, I will not."

"Mike, listen to reason, for God's sake. You can't stay here in this disease-ridden backwater. You can't—"

"I'll walk out to the car with you, Bruce. I know you're in a hurry—"

He led them out through the side door and stood by the driver's window of the Ford while they climbed in. Bruce extended his hand, and Mike took it, gripping hard.

"Cheerio, Bruce. Thanks for everything."

"Cheerio, Mike. I suppose you'll be taking orders and having yourself made into a fully licensed dispenser of salvation?"

"I don't know about that, Bruce. I doubt it. I just want another chance to do the only work I know. I just want a last-minute rally to reduce the formidable score that's been chalked up against me so far."

"I'll report you 'missing, believed killed'—throw your uniform in the river," said Bruce.

"I'll do that." Mike stepped back. "Look after each other, you two."

"I don't know what you mean," Shermaine informed him primly, trying not to smile.

"I'm an old dog, not easy to fool," said Mike. "Go to it with a will."

Bruce let out the clutch and the Ford slid forward.

"God speed, my children." That smile spread all over Mike's face as he waved.

"*Au revoir,* Doctor Michael."

"So long, Mike."

Bruce watched him in the rear-view mirror, tall in his ill-fitting cassock, something proud and worth while in his stance. He waved once more and then turned and hurried back into the hospital.

Neither of them spoke until they had almost reached the main road. Shermaine nestled softly against Bruce, smiling to herself, looking ahead down the tree-lined passage of the road.

"He's a good man, Bruce."

"Light me a cigarette, please, Shermaine." He didn't want to talk about it. It was one of those things that can only be made grubby by words.

Slowing for the intersection, Bruce dropped into second gear, automatically glancing to his left to make sure the main road was clear before turning into it.

"Oh, my God!" he gasped.

"What is it, Bruce?" Shermaine looked up with alarm from the cigarette she was lighting.

"Look!"

A hundred yards up the road, parked close to the edge of the forest, was a convoy of six large vehicles. The first five were heavy canvas-canopied trucks painted dull military olive; the sixth was a gasoline tanker in bright yellow and red with the

Shell Company insignia on the barrel-shaped body. Hitched behind the leading truck was a squat, rubber-tired, 25-pounder anti-tank gun with its long barrel pointed jauntily skywards. Around the vehicles, dressed in an assortment of uniforms and different styled helmets, were at least sixty men. They were all armed, some with automatic weapons and others with obsolete bolt-action rifles. Most of them were urinating carelessly into the grass that lined the road, while the others were standing in small groups smoking and talking.

"General Moses!" said Shermaine, her voice small with the shock.

"Get down," ordered Bruce and with his free hand thrust her onto the floor. He rammed the accelerator flat and the Ford roared out into the main road, swerving violently, the back end floating free in the loose dust as he held the wheel over. Correcting the skid, meeting it and straightening out, Bruce glanced at the rear-view mirror. Behind them the men had dissolved into a confused pattern of movement; he heard their shouts high and thin above the racing engine of the Ford. Bruce looked ahead; it was another hundred yards to the bend in the road that would hide them and take them down to the causeway across the swamp.

Shermaine was on her knees, pulling herself up to look over the back of the seat.

"Keep on the floor, damn you!" shouted Bruce and pushed her head down roughly.

As he spoke the roadside next to them erupted in a rapid series of leaping dust fountains, and he heard the high hysterical beat of machine-gun fire.

The bend in the road rushed towards them, just a few more seconds. Then with a succession of jarring crashes that shook the whole body of the car a burst of fire hit them from behind. The windscreen starred into a sheet of opaque diamond lacework; the dashboard clock exploded, powdering Shermaine's hair with particles of glass; two bullets tore through the seat, ripping out the stuffing like the entrails of a wounded animal.

"Close your eyes," shouted Bruce and punched his fist

through the windscreen. Slitting his own eyes against the chips of flying glass, he could just see through the hole his fist had made. The corner was right on top of them, and he dragged the steering wheel over, skidding around, his off-side wheels bumping into the verge, grass and leaves brushing the side of the car.

Then they were through the corner and racing down towards the causeway.

"Are you all right, Shermaine?"

"Yes, are you?" She emerged from under the dashboard, a smear of blood across one cheek where the glass had scratched her, and her eyes bigger than ever with fright.

"I only pray that Boussier and Hendry are ready to pull out. Those bastards won't be five minutes behind us."

They went across the causeway with the needle of the speedometer touching eighty, up the far side and into the main street of Port Reprieve. Bruce thrust his hand down on the hooter ring, blowing urgent warning blasts.

"Please God, let them be ready," he muttered. With relief he saw that the street was empty and the hotel seemed deserted. He kept blowing the horn as they roared down towards the station, a great billowing cloud of dust rising behind them. Braking the Ford hard, he turned it in past the station buildings and onto the platform.

Most of Boussier's people were standing next to the train. Boussier himself was beside the last car with his wife and the small group of women around him. Bruce shouted at them through the open window.

"Get those women into the train! The *shufta* are right behind us. We're leaving immediately."

Without question or argument old Boussier gathered them together and hurried them up the steel ladder into the car. Bruce drove down the station platform, shouting as he went.

"Get in! For Chrissake, hurry up! They're coming!"

He braked to a standstill next to the cab of the locomotive and shouted up at the bald head of the driver.

"Get going. Don't waste a second. Give her everything she's got. There's a bunch of *shufta* not five minutes behind us."

The driver's head disappeared into the cab without even the usual polite *"Oui, monsieur."*

"Come on, Shermaine." Bruce grabbed her hand and dragged her from the car. Together they ran to one of the covered coaches, and Bruce pushed her halfway up the steel steps.

At that moment the train jerked forward so violently that she lost her grip on the hand rails and tumbled backwards on top of Bruce. He was caught off balance, and they fell together in a heap on the dusty platform. Above them the train gathered speed, pulling away. He remembered this nightmare from his childhood, running after a train and never catching it. He had to fight down his panic as he and Shermaine scrambled up, both of them panting, clinging to each other, the coaches clackety-clacking, the rhythm of the wheels mounting.

"Run!" he gasped. "Run!" And with panic weakening their legs he just managed to catch the hand rail of the second coach. He clung to it, stumbling along beside the train, one arm around Shermaine's waist. Sergeant Major Ruffararo leaned out, took Shermaine by the scruff of her neck, and lifted her in like a lost kitten. Then he reached down for Bruce.

"Boss, someday we going to lose you if you go on playing around like that."

"I'm sorry, Bruce," she said, panting, leaning against him.

"No damage done." He could grin at her. "Now I want you to get into that compartment and stay there until I tell you to come out. Do you understand?"

"Yes, Bruce."

"Off you go." He turned from her to Ruffy. "Up onto the roof, Sergeant Major! We're going to have fireworks. Those *shufta* have got a field gun with them, and we'll be in full view of the town right up to the top of the hills."

By the time they reached the roof, the train had pulled out of Port Reprieve and was making its first angling turn up the slope of the hills. The sun was up now, well clear of the horizon, and the mist from the swamp had lifted so that they could see the whole village spread out beneath them.

General Moses' column had crossed the causeway and was

into the main street. As Bruce watched, the leading truck swung sharply across the road and stopped. Men boiled out from under the canopy and swarmed over the field gun, unhitching it, man-handling it into position.

"I hope those Arabs haven't had any drill on that piece," grunted Ruffy.

"We'll soon find out," Bruce assured him grimly and looked back along the train. In the last car Boussier stood protectively over the small group of four women and their children, like an old white-haired collie with its sheep. Crouched against the steel side of the truck, André de Surrier and half a dozen gendarmes were swinging and sighting the two Bren guns. In the second car, too, the gendarmes were preparing to open fire.

"What are you waiting for?" roared Ruffy. "Get me that field gun—start shooting."

They fired a ragged volley, then the Bren guns joined in. With every burst André's helmet slipped forward over his eyes, and he had to stop and push it back. Lying on the roof of the leading coach, Wally Hendry was firing short businesslike bursts.

The *shufta* round the field gun scattered, leaving one of their number lying in the road, but there were men behind the armour shield—Bruce could see the tops of their helmets.

Suddenly there was a long gush of white smoke from the barrel, and the shell rushed over the top of the train with a noise like the wings of a giant pheasant.

"Over!" said Ruffy.

"Under!" to the next shot as it plowed into the trees below them.

"And the third one right up the throat," said Bruce. But it hit the rear of the train. They were using armour-piercing pro-jectiles, not high explosive, for there was not the burst of yellow cordite fumes but only the crash and jolt as it struck.

Anxiously Bruce tried to assess the damage. The men and women in the rear cars looked shaken but unharmed, and he started a sigh of relief, which changed quickly to a gasp of horror as he realized what had happened.

"They've hit the coupling," he said. "They've sheared the coupling on the last car."

Already the gap was widening as the rear car started to roll back down the hill, cut off like the tail of a lizard.

"Jump!" screamed Bruce, cupping his hands round his mouth. "Jump before you gather speed!"

Perhaps they did not hear him, perhaps they were too stunned to obey, but no one moved. The car rolled back, faster and faster as gravity took it, down the hill towards the village and the waiting army of General Moses.

"What can we do, boss?"

"Nothing," said Bruce.

The firing around Bruce had petered out into silence as every man, even Wally Hendry, stared down the slope at the receding car. With a constriction of his throat Bruce saw old Boussier stoop and lift his wife to her feet, hold her close to his side, and the two of them stood looking back at Bruce on the roof of the departing train. Boussier raised his right hand in a gesture of farewell and then he dropped it again and stood very still. Behind him, André de Surrier had left the Bren gun and removed his helmet. He also was looking back at Bruce but he did not wave.

At intervals the field gun in the village punctuated the still-ness with its deep boom and gush of smoke, but Bruce hardly heard it. He was watching the *shufta* running down towards the station yard to welcome the car. Losing speed, it ran into the platform and halted abruptly as it hit the buffers at the end of the line. The *shufta* swarmed over it like little black ants over the body of a beetle, and faintly Bruce heard the pop, pop, pop of their rifles, saw the low sun glint on their bayonets. He turned away.

They had almost reached the crest of the hills; he could feel the train increasing speed under him. But he felt no relief, only the prickling at the corners of his eyes and the ache of it trapped in his throat.

"The poor bastards," growled Ruffy beside him. "The poor

bastards." And then there was another crashing jolt against the train, another hit from the field gun. This time up forward, on the locomotive. Shriek of escaping steam, the train checking its pace, losing power. But they were over the crest of the hills, the village was out of sight, and gradually the train speeded up again as they started down the back slope. But steam spouted out of it, hissing white jets of it, and Bruce knew they had received a mortal wound. He switched on the radio.

"Driver, can you hear me? How bad is it?"

"I cannot see, Captain. There is too much steam. But the pressure on the gauge is dropping swiftly."

"Use all you can to take us down the hill. It is imperative that we pass the level crossing before we halt. It is absolutely imperative. If we stop this side of the level crossing they will be able to reach us with their trucks."

"I will try, Captain."

They rocketed down the hills, but as soon as they reached the level ground their speed began to fall off. Peering through the dwindling clouds of steam, Bruce saw the pale brown ribbon of road ahead of them, and they were still travelling at a healthy thirty miles an hour as they passed it. When finally the train trickled to a standstill Bruce estimated that they were three or four miles beyond the level crossing, safely walled in by the forest and hidden from the road by three bends.

"I doubt they'll find us here, but if they do they'll have to come down the line from the level crossing to get at us. We'll go back a mile and lay an ambush in the forest on each side of the line," said Bruce.

"Those Arabs won't be following us, boss. They've got themselves women and a whole barful of liquor. Be two or three days before old General Moses can sober them up enough to move them on."

"You're probably right, Ruffy. But we'll take no chances. Get that ambush laid and then we'll try and think up some idea for getting home."

Suddenly a thought occurred to him: Martin Boussier had

the diamonds with him. They would not be too pleased about that in Elisabethville.

Almost immediately Bruce was disgusted with himself. The diamonds were by far the least important thing that they had left behind in Port Reprieve.

14

André de Surrier held his steel helmet against his chest the way a man holds his hat at a funeral; the wind blew cool and caressing through his dark sweat-damp hair. His hearing was dulled by the strike of the shell that had cut the car loose from the rear of the train, but he could hear one of the children crying and the crooning, gentling voice of its mother. He stared back up the railway line at the train, saw the great bulk of Ruffy beside Bruce Curry on the roof of the second coach.

"They can't help us now." Boussier spoke softly. "There's nothing they can do." He lifted his hand stiffly in almost a military salute and then dropped it to his side. "Be brave, *ma chère*," he said to his wife. "Please be brave," and she clung to him.

André let the helmet drop from his hands. It clanged onto the metal floor of the truck. He wiped the sweat from his face with nervous fluttering hands and then turned slowly to look down at the village.

"I don't want to die," he whispered. "Not like this, not now, please not now." One of his gendarmes laughed, a sound without mirth, and stepped across to the Bren. He pushed André away from it and started firing at the tiny running figures of the men in the station yard.

"No," shrilled André. "Don't do that! No, don't antagonize them. They'll kill us if you do that—"

"They'll kill us anyway." The gendarme laughed and emptied the magazine in one long despairing burst. André started towards him, perhaps to pull him away from the gun, but his resolve did not carry him that far. His hands dropped to his sides, clenching and unclenching. His lips quivered and then opened to spill out his terror.

"No!" he screamed. "Please, no! No! Oh, God have mercy. Oh, save me, don't let this happen to me, please, God. Oh, my God."

He stumbled to the side of the car and clambered onto it. The car was slowing as it ran into the platform. He could see men coming with rifles in their hands, shouting as they ran, black men in dirty tattered uniforms, their faces working with excitement, pink shouting mouths, baying like hounds in a pack.

André jumped, and the dusty concrete of the platform grazed his cheek and knocked the wind out of him. He crawled to his knees, clutching his stomach and trying to scream. A rifle butt hit him between the shoulderblades and he collapsed. Above him a voice shouted in French, "He is white—keep him for the general. Don't kill him." And again the rifle butt hit him, this time across the side of the head. He lay in the dust, dazed, with the taste of blood in his mouth, and watched them drag the others from the car.

They shot the black gendarmes on the platform, without ceremony, laughing as they competed with each other to use their bayonets on the corpses. The two children died quickly, torn from their mothers, held by the feet and swung head first against the steel side of the car.

Old Boussier tried to prevent them from stripping his wife and was bayoneted from behind in anger and then shot twice with a pistol held to his head as he lay on the platform.

All this happened in the first few minutes before the officers arrived to control them; by that time André and the four women were the only occupants of the truck left alive.

André lay where he had fallen, watching in fascinated skin-crawling horror as they tore the clothing off the women and with a man to each arm and each leg held them down on the platform as though they were calves to be branded, hooting with laughter at their struggling naked bodies, bickering for position, already unbuckling belts, pushing each other, arguing, some of them with fresh blood on their clothing.

And then two men, who by their air of authority and the red sashes across their chests were clearly officers, joined the crowd. One of them fired his pistol in the air to gain their attention, and both of them started a harangue that slowly had effect. The women were dragged up and herded off towards the hotel.

One of the officers came across to where André lay, stooped over him, and lifted his head by taking a handful of hair.

"Welcome, *mon ami*. The general will be very pleased to see you. It is a pity that your other white friends have left us, but then, one is better than nothing."

He pulled André into a sitting position, peered into his face, and then spat into his eyes with sudden violence. "Bring him! The general will talk to him later."

They tied André to one of the columns on the front veranda of the hotel and left him there. He could have twisted his head and looked through the large windows into the lounge at what they were doing to the women, but he did not. He could hear what was happening: by noon the screams had become groans and sobbing; by midafternoon the women were making no sound at all. But the queue of *shufta* was still out of the front door of the lounge. Some of them had been to the head of the line and back to the tail three or four times.

All of them were drunk now. One jovial fellow carried a bottle of Parfait Amour liqueur in one hand and a bottle of Harper's whisky in the other. Every time he came back to join the queue again he stopped in front of André.

"Will you drink with me, little white boy?" he asked. "Certainly you will," he answered himself, filled his mouth from one of the bottles and spat it into André's face. Each time it got a big laugh from the others waiting in the line. Occasionally one of the other *shufta* would stop in front of André, unsling his rifle, back away a few paces, sight along the bayonet at André's face and then charge forward, at the last moment twisting the point aside so that it grazed his cheek. Each time André could not suppress his shriek of terror, and the waiting men nearly collapsed with merriment.

Towards evening they started to burn the houses on the outskirts of town. One group, sad with liquor and rape, sat together at the end of the veranda and started to sing. Their deep beautiful voices carrying all the melancholy savagery of Africa, they kept on singing while an argument between two *shufta* developed into a knife fight in the road outside the hotel.

The sweet bass lilt of singing covered the coarse breathing of the two circling, bare-chested knife fighters and the shuffle, shuffle, quick shuffle of their feet in the dust. When finally they locked together for the kill, the singing rose, still deep and strong but with a triumphant note to it. One man stepped back with his rigid right arm holding the knife buried deep in the other's belly, and as the loser sank down, sliding slowly off the knife, the singing sank with him, plaintive, regretful, and lamenting, into silence.

They came for André after dark, four of them, less drunk than the others. They led him down the street to the Union Minière offices. General Moses was there, sitting alone at the desk in the front office.

There was nothing sinister about him; he looked like an elderly clerk, a small man with the short woollen cap of hair grizzled to grey above the ears and a pair of horn-rimmed spectacles. On his chest he wore three rows of full-dress medals; each of his fingers was encased in rings to the second joint, diamonds, emeralds, and the occasional red glow of a ruby; most of them had been designed for women, but the metal had been cut to enlarge them for his stubby black fingers. The face was almost kindly, except the eyes. There was a blankness of expression in them, the lifeless eyes of a madman. On the desk in front of him was a small wooden case made of unvarnished deal which bore the seal of the Union Minière Company stencilled in black upon its side. The lid was open, and as André came in through the door with his escort General Moses lifted a white canvas bag from the case, loosened the drawstring, and poured a pile of dark grey industrial diamonds onto the blotter in front of him.

He prodded them thoughtfully with his finger, stirring them so they glittered dully in the harsh light of the petromax.

"Was this the only case in the truck?" he asked without looking up.

"*Oui, mon général*. There was only the one," answered one of André's escorts.

"You are certain?"

"*Oui, mon général*. I myself have searched thoroughly."

General Moses took another of the canvas bags from the case and emptied it onto the blotter. He grunted with disappointment as he saw the drab little stones. He reached for another bag, and another, his anger mounting steadily as each yielded only dirty grey and black industrial diamonds. Soon the pile on the blotter would have filled a pint jug.

"Did you open the case?" he snarled.

"*Non, mon général*. It was sealed. The seal was not broken, you saw that."

General Moses grunted again, his dark chocolate face set hard with frustration. Once more he dipped his hand into the wooden case, and suddenly he smiled.

"Ah!" he said pleasantly. "Yes! yes! what is this?" He brought out a cigar box, with the gaudy wrapper still on the cedar wood. A thumbnail prised the lid back, and he beamed happily. In a nest of cotton wool, sparkling, breaking the white light of the petromax into all the rainbow colours of the spectrum, were the gem stones. General Moses picked one up and held it between thumb and forefinger.

"Pretty," he murmured. "Pretty, so pretty." He swept the industrial stones to one side and laid the gem in the centre of the blotter. Then one by one he took the others from the cigar box, fondling each and laying it on the blotter, counting them, smiling, once chuckling softly, touching them, arranging them in patterns.

"Pretty," he kept whispering. "*Bon*—forty-one, forty-two. Pretty! My darlings! Forty-three."

Then suddenly he scooped them up and poured them into one

of the canvas bags, tightened the drawstring, dropped it into his breast pocket above the medals and buttoned the flap.

He laid his black, bejewelled hands on the desk in front of him and looked up at André.

His eyes were smoky yellow with black centres behind his spectacles. They had an opaque, dreamlike quality.

"Take off his clothes," he said in a voice that was expressionless as the eyes.

They stripped André with rough dispatch, and General Moses looked at his body.

"So white," he murmured. "Why so white?" Suddenly his jaws began chewing nervously and there was a faint shine of sweat on his forehead. He came round from behind the desk, a small man, yet with an intensity about him that doubled his size.

"White like the maggots that feed in the living body of the elephant." He brought his face close to André's. "You should be fatter, my maggot, having fed so long and so well. You should be much fatter."

He touched André's body, running his hands down his flanks in a caress.

"But now it is too late, little white maggot," he said, and André cringed from his touch and from his voice. "For the elephant has shaken you from the wound, shaken you out onto the ground, shaken you out beneath his feet—and will you pop when he crushes you?"

His voice was still soft, though the sweat oozed in oily lines down his cheeks and the dreaminess of his eyes had been replaced by a burning black brightness.

"We shall see," he said and drew back. "We shall see, my maggot," he repeated—and brought his knee up into André's crotch with a force that jerked his whole frame and flung his shoulders back.

The agony flared through André's lower body, fierce as the touch of heated steel. It clamped in on his stomach, contracting it in a spasm like childbirth; it rippled up across the muscles of his chest into his head and burst beneath the roof of his skull in a whiteness that blinded him.

"Hold him," commanded General Moses, his voice suddenly shrill. The two guards took André by the elbows and forced him to his knees, so that his genitals and lower belly were easily accessible to the general's boots. They had done this often.

"For the times you jailed me!" And General Moses swung his booted foot into André's body.

The pain blended with the other pain, and it was too strong for André to scream.

"This, for the insults!"

And André could feel his testicles crush beneath it. Still it was too strong—he could not use his voice.

"This, for the times I have grovelled!"

The pain had passed its zenith, this time he could scream with it. He opened his mouth and filled his empty lungs.

"This, for the times I have hungered."

Now he must scream. Now he must—the pain, oh, sweet Christ, I must, please let me scream.

"This, for your white man's justice."

Why can't I, please let me. Oh, no! No—please. Oh, God, oh, please.

"This, for your prisons and your Kiboko!"

The kicks so fast now, like the beat of an insane drummer, like rain on a tin roof. In his stomach he felt something tear.

"And this, and this, and this!"

The face before André filled the whole field of his vision. The voice and the sound of boot into him filled his ears.

"This, and this, and this!"

The voice high-pitched, and within him the sudden warm flood of internal bleeding.

The pain was fading now as his body closed it out in defense, and he had not screamed. The leap of elation as he knew it. This last thing I can do well, I can die now *without screaming.* He tried to stand up, but they held him down, and his legs were not his own, they were on the other side of the great numb warmth of his belly. He lifted his head and looked at the man who was killing him.

"This for the white filth that bore you, and this, and this—"

The blows were not a part of reality; he could feel the shock of them as though he stood close to a man who was cutting down a tree with an axe. And André smiled.

He was still smiling when they let him fall forward to the floor.

"I think he is dead," said one of the guards.

General Moses turned away and walked back to his seat at the desk. He was shaking as though he had run a long way, and his breathing was deep and fast. The jacket of his uniform was soaked with sweat. He sank into the chair and his body seemed to crumple; slowly the brightness faded from his eyes until once more they were filmed over, opaque and dreamy. The two guards squatted down quietly on each side of André's body; they knew it would be a long wait.

Through the open window there came an occasional shout of drunken laughter, and the red flicker and leap of flames.

15

Bruce stood in the centre of the tracks and searched the floor of the forest critically. At last he could make out the muzzle of the Bren protruding a few inches from the patch of elephant grass. Despite the fact that he knew exactly where to look for it, it had taken him a full two minutes to find it.

"That'll do, Ruffy," he decided. "We can't get it much better than that."

"I reckon not, boss."

Bruce raised his voice. "Can you hear me?" There were muffled affirmatives from the bush on each side, and Bruce continued.

"If they come, you must let them reach this spot before you open fire. I will mark it for you." He went to a small shrub beside the line, broke off a branch, and dropped it on the tracks.

"Can you see that?"

Again the affirmatives from the men in ambush.

"You will be relieved before darkness—until then stay where you are."

The train was hidden beyond a bend in the line, half a mile ahead, and Bruce walked back with Ruffy.

The engine driver was waiting for them, talking with Wally Hendry beside the rear car.

"Any luck?" Bruce asked him.

"I regret, Captain, that she is irreparably damaged. The boiler is punctured in two places and there is considerable disruption of the copper tubing."

"Thank you." Bruce nodded. He was neither surprised nor disappointed. It was precisely what his own judgement had told him after a brief examination of the locomotive.

"Where is Madame Cartier?" he asked Wally.

"*Madame* is preparing the luncheon, *monsir*," Wally told him with heavy sarcasm. "Why do you ask, bucko? Are you feeling randy again so soon, hey? You feel like a slice of veal for lunch, is that it?"

Bruce snuffed out the quick flare of his temper and walked past him. He found Shermaine with four gendarmes in the cab of the locomotive. They had scraped the coals from the furnace into a glowing heap on the steel floor and were chopping potatoes and onions into the five-gallon pots.

The gendarmes were all laughing at something Shermaine had said. Her usually pale cheeks were flushed with the heat; there was a sooty smudge on her forehead. She wielded the big knife with professional dexterity. She looked up and saw Bruce, her face lighting instantly and her lips parting.

"We're having a Hungarian goulash for lunch—bully beef, potatoes, and onions."

"As of now I am rating you acting second cook without pay."

"You are too kind," and she put her tongue out at him. It was a pink pointed little tongue like a cat's. Bruce felt the old familiar tightening of his legs and the dryness in this throat as he looked at it.

"Shermaine, the locomotive is damaged beyond repair. It is of no further use." He spoke in English.

"It makes a passable kitchen," she demurred.

"Be serious." Bruce's anxiety made him irritable. "We're stranded here until we think of something."

"But, Bruce, you are the genius. I have complete faith in you. I'm sure you'll think of some truly beautiful idea." Her face was solemn, but she couldn't keep the banter out of her eyes. "Why don't you go and ask General Moses to lend you his transportation?"

Bruce's eyes narrowed in thought and the black curves of his eyebrows nearly touched above the bridge of his nose.

"The food better be good or I'll break you to third cook," he warned, clambered down from the cab to the ground, and hurried back along the train.

"Hendry, Sergeant Major, come here, please. I want to discuss something with you."

They came to join him, and he led the way up the ladder into one of the covered coaches. Hendry dropped onto the bunk and placed his feet on the wash basin.

"That was a quick one," he grinned through the coppery stubble of his beard.

"You're the most uncouth, filthy-mouthed son-of-a-bitch I have ever met, Hendry," said Bruce coldly. "When I get you back to Elisabethville I'm going to beat you to pulp before I hand you over to the military authority for murder."

"My, my," Hendry laughed. "Big talker, hey? Curry, big, big talker."

"Don't make me kill you now—don't do that, please. I still need you."

"What's with you and that Frenchy, hey? You love it or something? You love it, or you just fancy a bit of that fat little arse? It can't be her titties—she ain't got much there, not even a handful each side."

Bruce started for him, then changed his mind and swung round to stare out of the window. His voice was strangled when he spoke.

"I'll make a bargain with you, Hendry. Until we get out of this, you keep off my back and I'll keep off yours. When we reach Msapa Junction the truce is off. You can do and say whatever you like and, if I don't kill you for it, I'll try my level best to see you hanged for murder."

"I'm making no bargain with you or nobody, Curry. I play along until it suits me, and I won't give you no warning when it doesn't suit me to play along any more. And let me tell you now, bucko, I don't need you and I don't need nobody. Not Haigh or you, with your fancy too-good-to-kiss-my-arse talk; when the time comes I'm going to trim you down to size—just remember that, Curry. And don't say I didn't warn you." Hendry was leaning forward, hands on his knees, body braced, and his whole face twisting with the vehemence of his speech.

"Let's make it now, Hendry." Bruce wheeled away from the window, crouching slightly, his hands stiffening into the flat hard blades of the judo fighter.

Sergeant Major Ruffararo stood up from the opposite bunk with surprising grace and speed for such a big man. He interposed his great body. "You wanted to tell us something, boss?"

Slowly Bruce straightened out of his crouch, his hands relaxing. Irritably he brushed at the damp lock of dark hair that had fallen onto his forehead, as if to brush Wally Hendry out of his mind with the same movement.

"Yes"—controlling his voice with an effort—"I wanted to discuss our next move." He fished the cigarette pack from his top pocket and lit one, sucking the smoke down deep. Then he perched on the bunk and studied the ash on the tip of the cigarette. When he spoke again his voice was normal.

"There is no hope of repairing this locomotive, so we have to find alternative transport out of here. Either we can walk two hundred miles back to Msapa Junction with our friends the Baluba ready to dispute our passage, or we can ride back in General Moses' trucks." He paused to let this sink in.

"You going to pinch those trucks off him?" asked Ruffy. "That's going to take some doing, boss."

"No, Ruffy, I don't think we have any chance of getting them out from under his nose. What we will have to do is attack the town and wipe him out."

"You're bloody crazy!" exclaimed Wally. "You're raving bloody mad!"

Bruce ignored him. "I estimate that Moses has about sixty men. With Kanaki and nine men on the bridge, Haigh and de Surrier and six others gone, we have thirty-four men left. Correct, Sergeant Major?"

"That's right, boss."

"Very well." Bruce nodded. "We'll have to leave at least ten men here to man that ambush in case Moses sends a patrol after us or in case of an attack by the Baluba. It's not enough, I know, but we will just have to risk it."

"Most of these civilians got arms with them, shotguns and sports rifles," said Ruffy.

"Yes," agreed Bruce. "They should be able to look after themselves. So that leaves twenty-four men to carry out the attack, something like three to one."

"Those *shufta* will be so full of liquor, half of them won't be able to stand up."

"That's what I am banking on: drunkenness and surprise. We'll hit them and try and finish it before they know what's happened. I don't think they will have realized how badly we were hit; they probably expect us to be a hundred miles away by now."

"When do you want to leave, boss?"

"We are about twelve miles from Port Reprieve—say, six hours' march in the dark. I want to attack in the early hours of tomorrow morning, but I'd like to be in position around midnight. We'll leave here at six o'clock, just before dark."

"I'd better go and start sorting the boys out."

"Okay, Ruffy. Issue an extra hundred rounds to each man and ten grenades. I'll want four extra haversacks of grenades also." Bruce turned to Hendry and looked at him for the first time. "Go with the sergeant major, Hendry, and give him a hand."

"Jesus, this is going to be a ball!" Wally grinned in anticipation. "With any luck I'll get me a sackful of ears." He disappeared down the corridor behind Ruffy, and Bruce lay back on the seat and took off his helmet. He closed his eyes and once again he saw Boussier and his wife standing together in the truck as it rolled back down the hill, he saw the huddle of frightened women, and André standing bareheaded, staring back at him with big brown gentle eyes. He groaned softly. "Why is it always the good ones, the harmless, the weak?"

A tap on the door roused him and he sat up quickly. "Yes?"

"Hello, Bruce." Shermaine came in with a multiple-decked metal canteen in one hand and two mugs in the other. "It's lunch time."

"Already!" Bruce checked his watch. "Good Lord, it's after one."

"Are you hungry?"

"Breakfast was a century ago."

"Good," she said, lowered the collapsible table, and began serving the food.

"Smells good."

"I am a chef Cordon Bleu. My bully beef goulash is demanded by the crowned heads of Europe."

They ate in silence for both of them were hungry. Once they looked at each other and smiled but returned to the food.

"That was good," said Bruce at last.

"Coffee, Bruce?"

"Please."

As she poured it she asked, "So, what happens now?"

"Do you mean what happens now we are alone?"

"You are forward, monsieur. I meant how do we get out of here."

"I am adopting your suggestion: borrowing General Moses' transportation."

"You make jokes, Bruce!"

"No," he said and explained briefly.

"It will be very dangerous, will it not? You may be hurt?"

"Only the good die young."

"That is why I worry. Please do not get hurt—I am starting to think I would not like that." Her face was very serious and pale.

Bruce crossed quickly and stooped over her, lifting her to her feet. "Shermaine, I—"

"No, Bruce. Don't talk. Don't say anything." Her eyes were closed, with thick black lashes interlaced, her chin lifted, exposing the long smooth swell of her neck. He touched it with his lips, and she made a soft noise in her throat so he could feel the skin vibrate. Her body flattened against his and her fingers closed in the hair at the back of his head.

"Oh, Bruce. My Bruce, please do not get hurt. Do not let them hurt you."

Wanting now, urgently, his mouth hunted upwards and hers came to meet it, willing prey. Her lips were pink and not greased with make-up, they parted to the pressure of his tongue, he felt the tip of her nose cool upon his cheek, and his hand moved up her back and closed round the nape of her neck, slender neck with silky down behind her ears.

"Oh, Bruce—" she said into his mouth.

His other hand went down to the proud, round, deeply divided thrust of her buttocks; he pulled her lower body against his, and she gasped as she felt him—the arrogant maleness through cloth.

"No!" She gasped and tried to pull away, but he held her until she relaxed against him once more. She shook her head, "*Non, non,*" but her mouth was open still and her tongue fluttered against his.

Down came his hand from her neck and twitched her shirt tails loose from under her belt, then up again along her back, touching the deep lateral depression of her spine so that she shuddered, clinging to him; stroking velvet skin stretched tight over rubber-hard flesh, finding the outline of her shoulderblades, tracing them upwards, then back to the armpits, silky haired armpits that maddened him with excitement, quickly past them to her breasts, small breasts with soft tips hardening to his touch.

Now she struggled in earnest, her fists beating on his shoulders and her mouth breaking from his, and he stopped himself, dropped the hand away to encircle her waist, holding her loosely within his arms.

"That was not good, Bruce. You get naughty very quick." Her cheeks flamed with colour, and her blue eyes had darkened to royal, her lips still wet from his, and her voice was unsteady, as unsteady as his when he answered.

"I'm sorry, Shermaine. I don't know what happened then. I did not mean to frighten you."

"You are very strong, Bruce. But you do not frighten me, only a little bit. Your eyes frighten me when they look at me but do not see."

You really made a hash of that one, he rebuked himself. *Bruce Curry, the gentle sophisticated lover. Bruce Curry, the heavyweight, catch-as-catch-can, two-fisted rape artist.*

He felt shaky, his legs wobbly, and there was something seriously wrong with his breathing.

"You do not wear a brassière," he said without thinking and immediately regretted it, but she chuckled, soft and husky.

"Do you think I need to, Bruce?"

"No, I didn't mean that," he protested quickly, remembering the saucy tilt of her small breasts. He was silent then, marshalling his words, trying to control his breathing, fighting down the madness of desire.

She studied his eyes. "You can see again now—perhaps I will let you kiss me."

"Please," he said, and she came back to him.

Gently now, Bruce me boy.

The door of the compartment flew back with a crash and they jumped apart.

Wally Hendry stood on the threshold. "Well, well, well." His shrewd little eyes took it all in. "That's nice!"

Shermaine was hurriedly tucking in her shirt tail and trying to smooth her hair at the same time.

Wally grinned. "Nothing like it after a meal, I always say. Gets the digestion going."

"What do you want?" snapped Bruce.

"There's no doubt what *you* want," said Wally. "Looks like you're getting it too." He let his eyes travel up from Shermaine's waist, slowly over her body to her face.

Bruce stepped out into the corridor, pushing Hendry back, and slammed the door.

"What do you want?" he repeated.

"Ruffy wants you to check his arrangements, but I'll tell him you're busy. We can put the attack off until tomorrow night if you like."

Bruce scowled at him. "Tell him I'll be with him in two minutes."

Wally leaned against the door. "Okay, I'll tell him."

"What are you waiting for?"

"Nothing, just nothing," Wally grinned.

"Well, bugger off then," snarled Bruce.

"Okay, okay, don't get your knickers in a knot, bucko." He sauntered off down the corridor.

Shermaine was standing where Bruce had left her, her eyes bright with tears of anger. "He is a pig, that one. A filthy, filthy pig."

"He's not worth worrying about." Bruce tried to take her in his arms again, but she shrugged him off.

"I hate him. He makes everything seem so cheap, so dirty."

"Nothing between you and me could be cheap and dirty," said Bruce, and instantly her fury abated.

"I know, my Bruce. But he can make it seem that way." They kissed, gently.

"I must go. They want me."

For a second she clung to him. "Be careful. Promise me you'll be careful."

"I promise," said Bruce, and she let him go.

16

They left before dark, but the clouds had come up during the afternoon and now they hung low over the forest, trapping the heat beneath them.

Bruce led, with Ruffy in the middle of the line and Hendry in the rear.

By the time they reached the level crossing the night was on them and it had started to rain, soft fat drops weeping like a woman exhausted with grief, warm rain in the darkness. And the darkness was complete. Once Bruce touched the top of his nose with his open palm, but he could not see his hand.

He used a staff to keep contact with the steel rail that ran beside him, tapping along it like a blind man, and at each step the gravel of the embankment crunched beneath his feet. The hand of the man behind him was on his shoulder, and he could sense the presence of the others that followed him like the body of a serpent, could hear the crunch of their steps and the muted squeak and rattle of their equipment. A man's voice was raised in protest and immediately quenched by Ruffy's deep rumble.

They crossed the road, and the gradient changed beneath Bruce's feet so that he had to lean forward against it. They were starting up the Lufira hills.

I will rest them at the top, he thought, and from there we will be able to see the lights of the town.

The rain stopped abruptly, and the quietness after it was surprising. Now he could distinctly hear the breathing of the men behind him above the small sounds of their advance, and in the forest nearby a tree-frog clinked as though steel pellets were being dropped into a crystal glass. It was a sound of great purity and beauty.

All Bruce's senses were enhanced to compensate for his lack of sight: his hearing; his sense of smell, so that he could catch the over-sweet perfume of a jungle flower and the heaviness of decaying wet vegetation; his sense of touch, so that he could feel the raindrops on his face and the texture of his clothing against his body; then the other animal sense of danger told him with sickening, stomach-tripping certainty that there was something ahead of him in the darkness.

He stopped, and the man following him bumped into him, throwing him off balance. All along the line there was a ripple of confusion and then silence. They all waited.

Bruce strained his hearing, half crouched, with his rifle held ready. There was something there, he could almost feel it.

Please, God, let them not have a machine-gun set up here, he thought; they could cut us into a shambles.

He turned cautiously and felt for the head of the man behind him, found it, and drew it towards him until his mouth was an inch from the ear.

"Lie down very quietly. Tell the one behind you that he may pass it back."

Bruce waited, poised, listening, and trying to see ahead into the utter blackness. He felt a gentle tap on his ankle from the gendarme at his feet. They were all down.

"All right, let's go take a look." Bruce detached one of the grenades from his webbing belt. He drew the pin and dropped it into the breast pocket of his jacket. Then, feeling for the cross-ties of the rails with each foot, he started forward. Ten paces and he stopped again. Then he heard it, the tiny click of two pebbles just ahead of him. His throat closed so he could not breathe and his stomach was very heavy.

I'm right on top of them. My God, if they open up now—

Inch by inch he drew back the hand that held the grenade.

I'll have to lob short and then get down fast. Five-second fuse —too long, they'll hear it and start shooting.

His hand was right back; he bent his legs and sank slowly onto his knees.

Here we go, he thought, and at that instant sheet lightning fluttered across the sky and Bruce could see. The hills were out-lined black below the pale grey belly of the clouds, and the steel rails glinted in the sudden light. The forest was dark and high at each hand, and—a leopard, a big golden and black leopard, stood facing Bruce. In that brief second they stared at each other and then the night closed down again.

The leopard coughed explosively in the darkness, and Bruce tried desperately to bring his rifle up, but it was in his left hand and his other arm was held back ready to throw.

This time for sure, he thought, this time they lower the boom on you.

It was with a feeling of disbelief that he heard the leopard crash sideways into the undergrowth and the scrambling rush of its run dwindle into the bush.

He subsided onto his backside, with the primed grenade in his hand, the hysterical laughter of relief coming up into his throat.

"You okay, boss?" Ruffy's voice lifted anxiously.

"It was a leopard," answered Bruce and was surprised at the squeakiness of his own voice.

There was a buzz of voices from the gendarmes and a rattle and clatter as they started to stand up. Someone laughed.

"That's enough noise," snapped Bruce and climbed to his feet; he found the pin in his pocket and fitted it back into the grenade. He groped his way back, picked up the staff from where he had dropped it, and took his position at the head of the column again.

"Let's go," he said.

His mouth was dry, his breathing too quick, and he could feel the heat beneath the skin of his cheeks from the shock of the leopard.

I truly squirted myself full of adrenalin that time. Bruce grinned precariously in the dark. *I'm as windy as hell. And before tonight is over I shall find fear again.*

They moved on up the incline of the hills, a serpent of twenty-four men, and the tension was in all of them. Bruce could hear it in the footsteps behind him, feel it in the grip of the hand upon his shoulder, and catch it in the occasional whiffs of body smell that came forward to him, the smell of nervous sweat like acid on metal.

Ahead of them the clouds that had crouched low upon the hills lifted slowly, and Bruce could see the silhouette of the crests. It was no longer utterly dark, for there was a glow on the belly of the clouds now—a faint orange glow of reflected light that grew in strength, then faded and grew again. It puzzled Bruce for a while, and thinking about it gave his nerves a chance to settle. He plodded steadily on, watching the fluctuations of the light. The ground tilted more sharply upwards beneath his feet, and he leaned forward against it, slogging up the last half mile to the pass between the peaks, and at last came out on the top.

"Good God," Bruce spoke aloud, for from here he could see the reason for that glow on the clouds. They were burning Port Reprieve. The flames were well established in the buildings along the wharf, and as Bruce watched one of the roofs collapsed slowly in upon itself in a storm of sparks, leaving the walls naked and erect, the wooden sills of the windows burning fiercely. The railway buildings were also on fire, and there was fire in the residential area beyond the Union Minière offices and the hotel. Quickly Bruce looked towards St. Augustine's. It was dark, no flames there, no light even, and he felt a small lift of relief.

"Perhaps they have overlooked it; perhaps they're too busy looting," and as he looked back at Port Reprieve, his mouth hardened. "The senseless wanton bastards!" His anger started as he watched the meaningless destruction of the town.

"What can they possibly hope to gain by this?" There were new fires nearer the hotel. Bruce turned to the man behind him.

"We will rest here, but there will be no smoking and no talking."

He heard the order passed back along the line and the careful sounds of equipment being lowered and men settling gratefully down upon the gravel embankment. Bruce unslung the case that contained his binoculars. He focused them on the burning town.

It was bright with the light of fires, and through the glasses he could almost discern the features of the men in the streets. They moved in packs, heavily armed and restless. Many carried bottles, and already the gait of some of them was unsteady. Bruce tried to estimate their numbers but it was impossible; men kept disappearing into buildings and reappearing, groups met and mingled and dispersed.

He dropped his glasses onto his chest to rest his eyes and heard movement beside him in the dark. He glanced sideways. It was Ruffy, his bulk exaggerated by the load he carried: his rifle across one shoulder, on the other a full case of ammunition, and round his neck half a dozen haversacks full of grenades.

"Looks like they're having fun, hey, boss?"

"Fifth of November," agreed Bruce. "Aren't you going to take a breather?"

"Why not?" Ruffy set down the ammunition case and lowered his great backside onto it. "Can you see any of those folks we left behind?" he asked.

Bruce lifted the glasses again and searched the area beyond the station buildings. It was darker there, but he made out the square shape of the car standing among the moving shadows.

"The car's still there," he murmured, "but I can't see—"

At that moment the thatched roof of one of the houses exploded upwards in a column of flame, lighting the railway yard, and the car stood out sharply.

"Yes," said Bruce, "I can see them now." They were littered untidily across the yard, still lying where they had died. Small and fragile, unwanted as broken toys.

"Dead?" asked Ruffy.

"Dead," confirmed Bruce.

"The women?"

"It's hard to tell." Bruce strained his eyes. "I don't think so."

"No." Ruffy's voice was soft and very deep. "They wouldn't waste the women. I'd guess they've got them up at the hotel, taking it in turn to give them the business. Four women only—they won't last till morning. Those bastards down there could shag an elephant to death." He spat thoughtfully into the gravel at his feet. "What you going to do, boss?"

Bruce did not answer for a minute; he swung the glasses slowly back across the town. The field gun was still standing where he had last seen it, its barrel pointing accusingly up towards him. The transports were parked before the Union Minière offices; he could see the brilliant yellow and red paint and the Shell sign on the tanker. I hope it's full, Bruce thought. We'll need plenty of gasoline to get us back to Elisabethville.

"Ruffy, you'd better tell your boys to keep their bullets away from that tanker, otherwise it'll be a long walk home."

"I'll tell them," grunted Ruffy. "But you know these mad Arabs—once they start shooting they don't stop till they're out of bullets, and they're not too fussy where those bullets go."

"We'll split into two groups when we get to the bottom of the hill. You and I will take our lot through the edge of the swamp and cross to the far side of the town. Tell Lieutenant Hendry to come here." Bruce waited until Wally came forward to join them, and when the three of them were crouched together he went on.

"Hendry, I want you to spread your men out at the top of the main street—there in the darkness on this side of the station. Ruffy and I are going to cross the edge of the swamp to the causeway and lay out on the far side. For God's sake, keep your boys quiet until Ruffy and I hit them—all we need is for your lot to start pooping off before we are ready and we won't need those trucks, we'll need coffins for the rest of our journey. Do you understand me?"

"Okay, okay, I know what I'm doing," muttered Wally.

"I hope so," said Bruce, and then went on. "We'll hit them at four o'clock tomorrow morning, just before first light. Ruffy and I will go into the town and bomb the hotel—that's where most of them will be sleeping. The grenades should force the survivors into the street, and as soon as that happens you can open up—but not before. Wait until you get them in the open. Is that clear?"

"Jesus," growled Hendry, "do you think I'm a bloody fool? Do you think I can't understand English?"

"The crossfire from the two groups should wipe most of them out." Bruce ignored Wally's outburst. "But we mustn't give the remainder a chance to organize. Hit them hard, and as soon as they take cover again you must follow them in—close with them and finish them off. If we can't get it over in five to ten minutes, then we are going to be in trouble. They outnumber us three to one, so we have to exploit the element of surprise to the full."

"Exploit the element of surprise to the full!" mimicked Wally. "What for all the fancy talk—why not just murder the bastards?"

Bruce grinned tightly in the dark. "All right, murder the bastards," he agreed. "But do it as quickly as bloody possible." He stood up and inclined the luminous dial of his wrist watch to catch the light. "It's half-past ten now—we'll move down on them. Come with me, Hendry, and we'll sort them into two groups."

Bruce and Wally moved back along the line and talked to each man in turn.

"You will go with Lieutenant Hendry."

"You come with me."

Making sure that the two English-speaking corporals were with Wally, they took ten minutes to divide the men into two units and to redistribute the haversacks of grenades. Then they moved on down the slope, still in Indian file.

"This is where we leave you, Hendry," whispered Bruce. "Don't go jumping the gun—wait until you hear my grenades."

"Yeah, okay—I know all about it."

"Good luck," said Bruce.

"Your bum in a barrel, Captain Curry," rejoined Wally and moved away.

"Come on, Ruffy." Bruce led his men off the embankment down into the swamp. Almost immediately the slimy mud was knee deep, and as they worked their way out to the right it rose to their waists and then to their armpits, sucking and gurgling sullenly as they stirred it with their passage, belching little evil-smelling gusts of swamp gas.

The mosquitoes closed round Bruce's face in a cloud so dense that he breathed them into his mouth and had to blink them out of his eyes. Sweat dribbled down from under his helmet and clung heavily to his eyebrows, and the matted stems of the papyrus grass dragged at his feet. Their progress was tortuously slow, and for fifteen minutes at a time Bruce lost sight of the lights of the village through the wall of papyrus; he steered by the glow of the fires and the occasional column of sparks.

It was an hour before they had half completed their circuit of Port Reprieve. Bruce stopped to rest, still waist deep in swamp ooze and with his arms aching, numb from holding his rifle above his head.

"I could use a smoke now, boss," grunted Ruffy.

"Me too," answered Bruce, and he wiped his face on the sleeve of his jacket. The mosquito bites on his forehead and around his eyes burned like fire.

"What a way to make a living," he whispered.

"You go on living and you'll be one of the lucky ones," answered Ruffy. "My guess is there'll be some dying before tomorrow."

But the fear of death was submerged by physical discomfort. Bruce had almost forgotten that they were going into battle; right now he was more worried that the leeches which had worked their way through the openings in his anklets and were busily boring into his lower legs might find their way up to his crotch. There was a lot to be said in favour of a zip fly, he decided

"Let's get out of this," he whispered. "Come on, Ruffy. Tell your boys to keep it quiet."

He worked in closer to the shore and the level fell to their knees once more. Progress was more noisy now as their legs broke the surface with each step and the papyrus rustled and brushed against them.

It was almost two o'clock when they reached the causeway. Bruce left his men crouched in the papyrus while he made a stealthy reconnaissance along the side of the concrete bridge, keeping in its shadow, moving doubled up until he came to dry land on the edge of the village. There were no sentries posted, and except for the crackle of the flames the town was quiet, sunk into a drunken stupor, satiated. Bruce went back to call his men up.

He spread them in pairs along the outskirts of the village. He had learned very early in this campaign not to let his men act singly; nothing drains an African of courage more than to be on his own, especially in the night, when the ghosts are on the walk-about.

To each couple he gave minute instructions.

"When you hear the grenades you shoot at anybody in the streets or at the windows. When the street is empty, move in close beside that building there. Use your own grenades on every house and watch out for Lieutenant Hendry's men coming through from the other side. Do you understand?"

"It is understood."

"Shoot carefully. Aim each shot—not the way you did at the road bridge, and in the name of God do not hit the gasoline tanker. We need that to get us home."

Now it was three o'clock, Bruce saw by the luminous figures on his wrist watch. Nine hours since they had left the train, and twenty-two hours since Bruce had last slept. But he was not tired; although his body ached and there was that gritty feeling under his eyelids, yet his mind was clear and bright as a flame.

He lay beside Ruffy under a low bush on the outskirts of Port Reprieve, and the night wind drifted the smoke from the burning town down upon them, and Bruce was not tired. *For I am going to another rendezvous with fear.*

Fear is a woman, he thought, *with all the myriad faces and voices of a woman. Because she is a woman and because I am a man I must keep going back to her. Only this time the appointment is one that I cannot avoid, this time I am not deliberately seeking her out.*

I know she is evil, I know that after I have possessed her I will feel sick and shaken. I will say, "That was the last time, never again."

But just as certainly I know I will go back to her again, hating her, dreading her, but also needing her.

I have gone to find her on a mountain—on Dutoits Kloof Frontal, on Turret Towers, on the Wailing Wall, and the Devil's Tooth.

And she was there, dressed in a flowing robe of rock, a robe that fell sheer two thousand feet to the scree slope below. And she shrieked with the voice of the wind along the exposed face. Then her voice was soft, tinkling like cooling glass in the berg ice underfoot, whispering like nylon rope running free, grating as the rotten rock moved in my hand.

I have followed her into the Jessie bush on the banks of the Sabi and the Luangwa, and she was there, waiting, wounded, in a robe of buffalo hide, with the blood dripping from her mouth. And her smell was the sour-acid smell of my own sweat, and her taste was like rotten tomatoes in the back of my throat.

I have looked for her beyond the reef in the deep water with the demand valve of a Scuba repeating my breathing with metallic hoarseness. And she was there with rows of white teeth in the semicircle of her mouth, a tall fin on her back, dressed this time in shagreen, and her touch was cold as the ocean, and her taste was salt and the taint of dying things.

I have looked for her on the highway with my foot pressed to the floorboards, and she was there with her cold arm draped round my shoulders, her voice the whine of rubber on tarmac and the throaty hum of the motor.

With Colin Butler at the helm, a man who treated fear not as a lover but with tolerant contempt, as though she were his little sister, I went to find her in a small boat. She was dressed in green with plumes of spray, and she wore a necklace of sharp black rock. And her voice was the roar of water breaking on water.

We met in darkness at the road bridge and her eyes glinted like bayonets. But that was an enforced meeting not of my choosing, as tonight will be.

I hate her, he thought, *but she is a woman and I am a man.*

Bruce lifted his arm and turned his wrist to catch the light of the fires. "Fifteen minutes to four, Ruffy. Let's go and take a look."

"That's a good idea, boss." Ruffy grinned with a show of white teeth in the darkness.

"Are you afraid, Ruffy?" he asked suddenly, wanting to

know, for his own heart beat like a war drum and there was no saliva in his mouth.

"Boss, some questions you don't ask a man!" Ruffy rose slowly into a crouch. "Let's go take a look around."

So they moved quickly together into the town, along the street, hugging the hedges and the buildings, trying to keep in shadow, their eyes moving everywhere, their breathing quick and shallow, nerves screwed up tight, until they reached the hotel.

There were no lights in the windows, and it seemed deserted until Bruce made out the untidy mass of humanity strewn in sleep upon the front veranda.

"How many there, Ruffy?"

"Dunno—perhaps ten, fifteen." Ruffy breathed an answer. "Rest of them will be inside."

"Where are the women—be careful of them."

"They're dead long ago, you can believe me."

"All right then, let's get round the back." Bruce took a deep breath and then moved quickly across the twenty yards of open firelit street to the corner of the hotel. He stopped in the shadow and felt Ruffy close beside him. "I want to take a look into the main lounge. My guess is that most of them will be in there," he whispered.

"There's only four bedrooms," agreed Ruffy. "Say the officers upstairs and the rest in the lounge."

Now Bruce moved quickly round the corner and stumbled over something soft. He felt it move against his foot.

"Ruffy!" he whispered urgently as he teetered off balance. He had trodden on a man, a man sleeping in the dust beside the wall. He could see the firelight on his bare torso and the glint of the bottle clutched in one outflung hand. The man sat up, muttering, and then began to cough, hacking painfully, swearing as he wiped his mouth with his free hand. Bruce regained his balance and swung his rifle up to use the bayonet, but Ruffy was quicker. He put one foot on the man's chest and trod him flat onto his back once more; then, standing over him, he used his bayoneted rifle the way a gardener uses a spade to lift potatoes, leaning his weight on it suddenly, and the blade vanished into the man's throat.

The body stiffened convulsively, legs thrust out straight and arms rigid; there was a puffing of breath from the severed windpipe and then the slow melting relaxation of death. Still with his foot on the chest, Ruffy withdrew the bayonet and stepped over the corpse.

That was very close, thought Bruce, stifling the qualm of horror he felt at the neat execution. The man's eyes were fixed open in almost comic surprise, the bottle still in his hand, his chest bare, the front of his trousers unbuttoned and stiff with dried blood—not his blood, guessed Bruce angrily.

They moved on past the kitchens. Bruce looked in and saw that they were empty, with the white enamel tiles reflecting the vague light and piles of used plates and pots cluttering the tables and the sink. Then they reached the barroom, and there was a hurricane lamp on the counter diffusing a yellow glow; the stench of liquor poured out through the half-open window, the shelves were bare of bottles, and men were asleep upon the counter, men lay curled together upon the floor like a pack of dogs, broken glass and rifles and shattered furniture littered about them. Someone had vomited out of the window, leaving a yellow streak down the whitewashed wall.

"Stand here," whispered Bruce into Ruffy's ear. "I will go around to the front where I can throw onto the veranda and also into the lounge. Wait until you hear my first grenade blow."

Ruffy nodded and leaned his rifle against the wall; he took a grenade in each fist and pulled the pins.

Bruce slipped quickly round the corner and along the side wall. He reached the windows of the lounge. They were tightly closed, and he peered in over the sill. A little of the light from the lamp in the barroom came through the open doors and showed up the interior. Here again there were men covering the floor and piled upon the sofas along the far wall. Twenty of them at least, he estimated by the volume of their snoring, and he grinned without humour. My God, what a shambles it is going to be!

Then something at the foot of the stairs caught his eye and the grin on his face became fixed, baring his teeth, and his eyes narrowed to slits. It was the mound of nude flesh formed by the bodies of the four women; they had been discarded once they had served their purpose, dragged to one side to clear the floor for sleeping space, lying upon each other in a jumble of naked arms and legs and cascading hair.

No mercy now, thought Bruce, with hatred replacing his fear as he looked at the women and saw by the attitudes in which they lay that there was no life left in them. *No mercy now!*

He slung his rifle over his left shoulder and filled his hands with grenades, pulled the pins, and moved quickly to the corner so that he could look down the length of the covered veranda. He rolled both grenades down among the sleeping figures, hearing clearly the click of the priming and the metallic rattle against the concrete floor. Quickly he ducked back to the lounge window, snatched two more grenades from his haversack, and, pulling the pins, he hurled them through the closed windows. The crash of breaking glass blended with the double thunder of the explosions on the veranda.

Someone shouted in the room, a cry of surprise and alarm. Then the windows above Bruce blew outwards, showering him with broken glass and the noise half deafening him as he tossed two more grenades through the gaping hole of the window. They were screaming and groaning in the lounge. Ruffy's grenades roared in the barroom, bursting through the double doors; then Bruce's grenades snuffed out the sounds of life in the lounge with violent white flame and thunder. Bruce tossed in two more grenades and ran back to the corner of the veranda, unslinging his rifle.

A man with his hands over his eyes and blood streaming through his fingers fell over the low veranda wall and crawled to his knees. Bruce shot him from so close that the shaft of gun flame joined the muzzle of his rifle and the man's chest, punching him over backwards, throwing him spreadeagled onto the earth.

He looked beyond and saw two more in the road, but before he could raise his rifle the fire from his own gendarmes found them, knocking them down amid spurts of dust.

Bruce hurdled the veranda wall. He shouted, a sound without form or meaning. Exultant, unafraid, eager to get into the building, to get among them. He stumbled over the dead men on the veranda. A burst of gunfire from down the street rushed past him, so close he could feel the wind on his face. Fire from his own men.

"You stupid bastards!" Shouting without anger, without fear, with only the need to shout, he burst into the lounge through the main doors. It was half dark but he could see through the darkness and the haze of plaster dust.

A man on the stairs, the bloom of gunfire and the sting of the bullet across Bruce's thigh, fire in return, without aiming from the hip, miss, and the man gone up and around the head of the stairs, yelling as he ran.

A grenade in Bruce's right hand, throw it high, watch it hit the wall and bounce sideways around the angle of the stairs. The explosion shocking in the confined space and the flash of it lighting the building and outlining the body of the man as it blew him back into the lounge, lifting him clear of the banisters, shredded and broken by the blast, falling heavily into the room below.

Up the stairs three at a time and into the bedroom passage, another man naked and bewildered staggering through a doorway still drunk or half asleep, chop him down with a single shot in the stomach, jump over him and throw a grenade through the glass skylight of the second bedroom, another through the third, and kick open the door of the last room in the bellow and flash of the explosions.

A man was waiting for Bruce across the room with a pistol in his hand, and both of them fired simultaneously, the clang of the bullet glancing off the steel of Bruce's helmet, jerking his head back savagely, throwing him sideways against the wall, but he fired again, rapid fire, hitting with every bullet, so that the man seemed to dance, a jerky grotesque, twitching jig, pinned against the far wall by the bullets.

On his knees now, Bruce was stunned, ears singing like a million mad mosquitoes, hands clumsy and slow on the reload, back on his feet, legs rubbery, but the loaded rifle in his hands making a man of him.

Out into the passage, another one right on top of him, a vast dark shape in the darkness—kill him! kill him!

"Don't shoot, boss!"

Ruffy, thank God, Ruffy.

"Are there any more?"

"All finished, boss—you cleaned them out good."

"How many?" Bruce shouted above the singing in his ears.

"Forty or so. Jesus, what a mess! There's blood all over the place. Those grenades—"

"There must be more."

"Yes, but not in here, boss. Let's go and give the boys outside a hand."

They ran back down the passage, down the stairs, and the floor of the lounge was sodden and sticky, dead men everywhere; it smelled like an abattoir—blood and ripped bowels. One still on his hands and knees, creepy-crawling towards the door. Ruffy shot him twice, flattening him.

"Not the front door, boss. Our boys will get you for sure. Go out the window."

Bruce dived through the window head first, rolled over behind the cover of the veranda wall, and came to his knees in one movement. He felt strong and invulnerable. Ruffy was beside him.

"Here come our boys," said Ruffy, and Bruce could see them coming down the street, running forward in short bursts, stopping to fire, to throw a grenade, then coming again.

"And there are Lieutenant Hendry's lot." They came from the opposite direction but with the same dodging, checking run. Bruce could see Wally with them. He was holding his rifle across his hip when he fired, his whole body shaking with the juddering of the gun.

Like a bird rising in front of the beaters, one of the *shufta* broke from the cover of the grocery store and ran into the street unarmed, his head down and his arms pumping in time with his legs. Bruce was close enough to see the panic in his face. He seemed to be moving in slow motion, and the flames lit him harshly, throwing a distorted shadow in front of him. When the bullets hit him he stayed on his feet, staggering in a circle, thrashing at the air with his hands as though he were beating off a swarm of bees, the bullets slapping loudly against his body and lifting little puffs of dust from his clothing. Beside Bruce, Ruffy aimed carefully and shot him in the head, ending it.

"There must be more," protested Bruce. "Where are they hiding?"

"In the offices, I'd say."

And Bruce turned his attention quickly to the block of Union Minière offices. The windows were in darkness, and as he stared he thought he saw movement. He glanced quickly back at Wally's men and saw that four of them had bunched up close behind Wally as they ran.

"Hendry, watch out!" he shouted with all his strength. "On your right, from the offices!"

But it was too late. Gunfire sparkled in the dark windows, and the little group of running men disintegrated.

Bruce and Ruffy fired together, raking the windows, emptying their automatic rifles into them. As he reloaded Bruce glanced back at where Wally's men had been hit. With disbelief he saw that Wally was the only one still on his feet; crossing the road, sprinting through an area of bullet-churned earth towards them, he reached the veranda and fell over the low wall.

"Are you wounded?" Bruce asked.

"Not a touch—those bastards couldn't shoot their way out of a French letter," Wally shouted defiantly, and his voice carried clearly in the sudden hush. He snatched the empty magazine off the bottom of his rifle, threw it aside, and clipped on a fresh one.

"Move over," he growled. "Let me get a crack at those bastards." He lifted his rifle and rested the stock on top of the wall, knelt behind it, cuddled the butt into his shoulder, and began firing short bursts into the windows of the office block.

"This is what I was afraid of." Bruce lifted his voice above the clamour of the guns. "Now we've got a pocket of resistance right in the centre of the town. There must be fifteen or twenty of them in there—it might take us days to winkle them out." He cast a longing look at the canvas-covered trucks lined up outside the station yard. "They can cover the trucks from there, and as soon as they guess what we're after, as soon as we try and move them they'll knock out that tanker and destroy the trucks."

The firelight flickered on the shiny yellow and red paint of the tanker. It looked so big and vulnerable standing there in the open. It needed just one bullet out of the many hundred that had already been fired to end its charmed existence.

We've got to rush them now, he decided. Beyond the office block the remains of Wally's group had taken cover and were keeping up a heated fire. Bruce's group straggled up to the hotel and found positions at the windows.

"Ruffy." Bruce caught him by the shoulder. "We'll take four men with us and go around the back of the offices. From that building there we've got only twenty yards or so of open ground to cover. Once we get up against the wall they won't be able to touch us, and we can toss grenades in among them."

"That twenty yards looks like twenty miles from here," rumbled Ruffy, but he picked up his sack of grenades and crawled back from the veranda wall.

"Go and pick four men to come with us," ordered Bruce.

"Okay, boss. We'll wait for you in the kitchen."

"Hendry. Listen to me."

"Yeah. What is it?"

"When I reach that corner over there I'll give you a wave. We'll be ready to go then. I want you to give us all the cover you can—keep their heads down."

"Okay," agreed Wally and fired another short burst.

"Try not to hit us when we close in."

Wally turned to look at Bruce and he grinned wickedly. "Mistakes happen, you know. I can't promise anything. You'd look real grand in my sights."

"Don't joke," said Bruce.

"Who's joking?" Wally grinned, and Bruce left him. He found Ruffy and four gendarmes waiting in the kitchen.

"Come on," he said and led them out across the kitchen yard, down the sanitary lane with the steel doors for the buckets, behind the outhouses and the smell of them thick and fetid, round the corner, and across the road to the buildings beyond the office block. They stopped there and crowded together, as though to draw courage and comfort from each other. Bruce measured the distance with his eyes.

"It's not far," he announced.

"Depends on how you look at it," grunted Ruffy.

"There are only two windows opening out onto this side."

"Two's enough—how many do you want?"

"Remember, Ruffy, you can only die once."

"Once is enough," said Ruffy. "Let's cut out the talking, boss. Too much talk gets you in the guts."

Bruce moved across to the corner of the building out of the shadows. He waved towards the hotel and imagined that he saw an acknowledgement from the end of the veranda.

"All together," he said, sucked in a deep breath, held it a second, and then launched himself into the open. He felt small now, no longer brave and invulnerable, and his legs moved so slowly that he seemed to be standing still. The black windows gaped at him.

Now, he thought, now you die.

Where? he thought. Not in the stomach, please, God, not in the stomach.

And his legs moved stiffly under him, carrying him halfway across.

Only ten more paces, he thought, one more river, just one more river to Jordan. But not in the stomach, please, God, not in my stomach. And his flesh cringed in anticipation, his stomach drawn in hard as he ran.

Suddenly the black windows were brightly lit, bright white ob-
longs in the dark buildings, and the glass sprayed out of them
like untidy spittle from an old man's mouth. Then they were
dark again, dark with smoke billowing from them and the memory of the explosion echoing in his ears.

"A grenade!" Bruce was bewildered. "Someone let off a
grenade in there!"

He reached the back door without stopping, and it burst open
before his rush. He was into the room, shooting, coughing in the
fumes, firing wildly at the small movements of dying men.

In the half darkness something long and white lay against the
far wall. A body, a white man's naked body. He crossed to it
and looked down.

"André," he said, "it's André—he threw the grenade." And
he knelt beside him.

17

Curled naked upon the concrete floor, André was alive but dying as the hemorrhage within him leaked his life away. His mind was alive, and he heard the crump, crump of grenades, then the gunfire in the street and the sound of running men. The shouts in the night, and then the guns very close, they were in the room in which he lay.

He opened his eyes. There were men at each of the windows, crouched below the sills, and the room was thick with cordite fumes and the clamour of the guns as they fired out into the night.

André was cold, the coldness was all through him. Even his hands drawn up against his chest were cold and heavy. His stomach only was warm, warm and immensely bloated.

It was an effort to think, for his mind also was cold and the noise of the guns confused him.

He watched the men at the windows with detached interest, and slowly his body lost its weight. He seemed to float clear of the floor and look down upon the room from the roof. His eyelids sagged, and he dragged them up again and struggled down towards his own body.

There was suddenly a rushing sound in the room and plaster sprayed from the wall above André's head, filling the air with pale floating dust. One of the men at the windows fell backwards, his weapon ringing loudly on the floor as it dropped from his hands; he flopped over twice and lay still, face down, within arm's length of André.

Ponderously André's mind analyzed the sights his eyes were recording. Someone was firing on the building from outside. The man beside him was dead and from his head wound the blood spread slowly across the floor towards him. André closed his eyes again; he was very tired and very cold.

There was a lull in the sound of gunfire, one of those freak silences in the midst of battle. And in the lull André heard a voice far off, shouting. He could not hear the words but he recognized the voice and his eyelids flew open. There was an excitement in him, a new force, for it was Wally's voice he had heard.

He moved slightly, clenching his hands, and his brain started to sing.

Wally has come back for me—he has come to save me. He rolled his head slowly, painfully, and the blood gurgled in his stomach.

I must help him, I must not let him endanger himself—these men are trying to kill him. I must stop them. I mustn't let them kill Wally.

And then he saw the grenades hanging on the belt of the man that lay beside him. He fastened his eyes on the round polished metal bulbs and he began to pray silently.

Hail, Mary, full of grace, the Lord is with thee . . .

He moved again, straightening his body.

Blessed art thou among women, and blessed is the fruit of thy womb, Jesus . . .

His hand crept out into the pool of blood, and the sound of the guns filled his head so he could not hear himself pray. Walking on its fingers, his hand crawled through the blood as slowly as a fly through a saucer of treacle.

Blessed is the fruit of thy womb, Jesus. Oh, Jesus. Pray for me now, and at the hour. Full of grace . . .

He touched the smooth, deeply segmented steel of the grenade.

Us sinners . . . at the day, at the hour. This day . . . this day our daily bread . . .

He fumbled at the clip, fingers stiff and cold.

Hallowed be thy . . . hallowed be thy . . .

The clip clicked open and he held the grenade, curling his fingers round it.

Hail, Mary, full of grace . . .

He drew the grenade to him and held it with both hands against his chest. He lifted it to his mouth and took the pin between his teeth.

Pray for us sinners . . . He pulled the pin.

Now and at the hour of our death . . .

And he tried to throw it. It rolled from his hand and bumped across the floor. The firing handle flew off and rattled against the wall. General Moses turned from the window and saw it. His lips opened and his spectacles glinted above the rose-pink cave of his mouth. The grenade lay at his feet. Then everything was gone in the flash and roar of the explosion.

Afterwards, in the acrid swirl of fumes, in the patter of falling plaster, in the tinkle and crunch of broken glass, in the small scrabbling noises and the murmur and moan of dying men, André was still alive. The body of the man beside him had shielded his head and chest from the full force of the blast.

There was still enough life in him to recognize Bruce Curry's face close to his, though he could not feel the hands that touched him.

"André!" said Bruce. "It's André—he threw the grenade!"

"Tell him—" whispered André and stopped.

"Yes, André?" said Bruce.

"I didn't, this day and at the hour. I had to—not this time." He could feel it going out in him like a candle in a high wind and he tried to cup his hands around it.

"What is it, André? What must I tell him?"

Bruce's voice, but so far away. "Because of him—this time—not of it, I didn't." André stopped again and gathered all of what was left. His lips quivered as he tried so hard to say it.

"Like a man!" he whispered, and the candle went out.

"Yes," said Bruce softly, holding him. "This time like a man."

He lowered André gently until his head touched the floor again; then he stood upright and looked down at the terribly mutilated body. He felt empty inside, a hollowness, the same feeling as after love.

He moved across to the desk near the far wall. Outside, the gunfire dwindled like half-hearted applause, flared up again, and then ceased. Around him Ruffy and the four gendarmes moved excitedly, inspecting the dead, exclaiming, laughing the awkward, embarrassed laughter of men freshly released from mortal danger.

Loosening the chin straps of his helmet with slow steady fingers, Bruce stared across the room at André's body.

"Yes," he whispered again. "This time like a man. All the other times are wiped out, the score is levelled."

His cigarettes were damp from the swamp, but he took one from the centre of the pack and straightened it with calm nerveless fingers. He found his lighter and flicked it open—then, without warning, his hands started to shake. The flame of the lighter fluttered and he had to hold it steady with both hands. There was blood on his hands, new sticky blood. He snapped the lighter closed and breathed in the smoke. It tasted bitter, and the saliva flooded into his mouth. He swallowed it down, nausea in his stomach, and his breathing quickened.

It was not like this before, he remembered, even that night at the road bridge when they broke through on the flank and we met them with bayonets in the dark. Before it had no meaning, but now I can feel again. Once more I'm alive.

Suddenly he had to be alone; he stood up.

"Ruffy."

"Yes, boss?"

"Clean up here. Get blankets from the hotel for de Surrier and the women, also those men down in the station yard." It was someone else speaking; he could hear the voice as though it were a long way off.

"You okay, boss?"

"Yes."

"Your head?"

Bruce lifted his hand and touched the long dent in his helmet. "It's nothing," he said.

"Your leg?"

"Just a touch, get on with it."

"Okay, boss. What shall we do with these others?"

"Throw them in the river," said Bruce and walked out into the street.

Hendry and his gendarmes were still on the veranda of the hotel; they had started on the corpses there, using their bayonets like butchers' knives, taking the ears, laughing also the strained nervous laughter.

Bruce crossed the street to the station yard. The dawn was coming, drawing out across the sky like a sheet of steel rolled from the mill, purple and lilac at first, then red as it spread above the forest.

The Ford Ranchero stood on the station platform where he had left it. He opened the door, slid in behind the wheel, and watched the dawn become day.

18

"Captain, the sergeant major asks you to come. There is something he wants to show you."

Bruce lifted his head from where it was resting on the steering wheel. He had not heard the gendarme approach.

"I'll come," he said, picked up his helmet and his rifle from the seat beside him, and followed the man back to the office block.

His gendarmes were loading a dead man into one of the trucks, swinging him by his arms and legs.

"*Une, deux, trois,*" and a shout of laughter as the limp body flew over the tailboard onto the gruesome pile already there.

Sergeant Jacque came out of the office dragging a man by his heels. The head bumped loosely down the steps, and there was a wet brown drag mark left on the cement veranda.

"Like pork," Jacque called cheerily. The corpse was that of a small grey-headed man, skinny, with the marks of spectacles on the bridge of his nose and a double row of decorations on his tunic. Bruce noted that one of them was the purple and white ribbon of the military cross—strange loot for the Congo. Jacque dropped the man's heels, drew his bayonet, and stooped over the man. He took one of the ears that lay flat against the grizzled skull, pulled it forward, and freed it with a single stroke of the knife. The opened flesh was pink with the dark hole of the eardrum in the centre.

Bruce walked on into the office and his nostrils flared at the abattoir stench.

"Have a look at this lot, boss." Ruffy stood by the desk.

"Enough to buy you a ranch in Hyde Park." Hendry grinned beside him. In his hand he held a pencil. Threaded onto it like a kebab were a dozen human ears.

"Yes," said Bruce as he looked at the pile of industrial and gem diamonds on the blotter. "I know about those. Better count them, Ruffy, then put them back in the bags."

"You're not going to turn them in?" protested Hendry. "Jesus, if we share this lot three ways—you, Ruffy, and I—there's enough to make us all rich."

"Or put us against a wall," said Bruce grimly. "What makes you think the gentlemen in Elisabethville don't know about them?" He turned his attention back to Ruffy. "Count them and pack them. You're in charge of them. Don't lose any."

Bruce looked across the room at the blanket-wrapped bundle that was André de Surrier. "Have you detailed a burial squad?"

"Yes, boss. Six of the boys are out back digging."

"Good." Bruce nodded. "Hendry, come with me. We'll go and have a look at the trucks."

Half an hour later Bruce closed the bonnet of the last vehicle.

"This is the only one that won't run. The carburetor's smashed. We'll take the tires off it for spares." He wiped his greasy hands on the sides of his trousers. "Thank God, the tanker is untouched. We've got six hundred gallons there, more than enough for the return trip."

"You going to take the Ford?" asked Hendry.

"Yes, it may come in useful."

"And it will be more comfortable for you and your little French thing." Heavy sarcasm in Hendry's voice.

"That's right," Bruce answered evenly. "Can you drive?"

"What you think? You think I'm a bloody fool?"

"Everyone is always trying to get at you, aren't they? You can't trust anyone, can you?" Bruce asked softly.

"You're so bloody right!" agreed Hendry.

Bruce changed the subject. "André had a message for you before he died."

"Old doll boy!"

"He threw that grenade. Did you know that?"

"Yeah. I knew it."

"Don't you want to hear what he said?"

"Once a queer, always a queer, and the only good queer is a dead queer."

"All right." Bruce frowned. "Get a couple of men to help you. Fill the trucks with gas. We've wasted enough time already."

They buried their dead in a communal grave, packing them in quickly and covering them just as quickly. Then they stood embarrassed and silent round the mound.

"You going to say anything, boss?" Ruffy asked, and they all looked at Bruce.

"No." Bruce turned away and started for the trucks.

What the hell can you say, he thought angrily. Death is not someone to make conversation with. All you can say is, "These were men, weak and strong, evil and good, and a lot in between. But now they're dead—like pork."

He looked back over his shoulder. "All right, let's move out."

The convoy ground slowly over the causeway. Bruce led in the Ford, and the air blowing in through the shattered windscreen was too humid and steamy to give relief from the rising heat.

The sun stood high above the forest as they passed the turn-off to the mission.

Bruce looked along it, and he wanted to signal the convoy to continue while he went up to St. Augustine's. He wanted to see Mike Haigh and Father Ignatius, make sure that they were safe.

Then he put aside the temptation. If there is more horror up there at St. Augustine's, if the *shufta* have found them and there are raped women and dead men there, then there is nothing I can do and I don't want to know about it.

It is better to believe that they are safely hidden in the jungle. It is better to believe that out of all this will remain something good.

He led the convoy resolutely past the turn-off and over the hills towards the level crossing.

Suddenly another idea came to him, and he thought about it, turning it over with pleasure.

.

Four men came to Port Reprieve, men without hope, men abandoned by God.

And they learned that it was not too late—perhaps it is never too late.

For one of them found the strength to die like a man, although he had lived his whole life with weakness.

Another rediscovered the self-respect he had lost along the way, and with it the chance to start again.

The third found—he hesitated—yes, the third found love.

And the fourth? Bruce's smile faded as he thought of Wally Hendry. It was a neat little parable, except for Wally Hendry. What had he found? A dozen human ears threaded on a pencil?

19

"Can't you get up enough steam to move us back to the crossing—only a few miles?"

"I am desolate, monsieur. She will not hold even a belch, to say nothing of a head of steam." The engine driver spread his pudgy little hands in a gesture of helplessness. Bruce studied the rent in the boiler. The metal was torn open like the petals of a flower. He knew it had been a forlorn request.

"Very well. Thank you." He turned to Ruffy. "We'll have to carry everything back to the convoy. Another day wasted."

"It's a long walk," Ruffy agreed. "Better get started."

"How much food have we?"

"Not too much. We've been feeding a lot of extra mouths, and we sent a lot out to the mission."

"How much?"

"About two more days."

"That should get us to Elisabethville."

"Boss, you want to carry everything to the trucks? Search-lights, ammunition, blankets—all of it?"

Bruce paused for a moment. "I think so. We may need it."

"It's going to take the rest of the day."

"Yes," agreed Bruce. Ruffy walked back along the train, but Bruce called after him.

"Ruffy!"

"Boss?"

"Don't forget the beer."

Ruffy's black moon of a face split laterally into a grin. "You think we should take it?"

"Why not?" Bruce laughed.

"Man, you talked me right into it!"

And the night was almost on them before the last of the

equipment had been carried back from the abandoned train to the convoy and loaded into the trucks.

Time is a slippery thing, even more so than wealth. No bank vault can hold it for you, this precious stuff which we spend in such prodigal fashion on the trivialities. By the time we have slept and eaten and moved from one place to the next there is such a small percentage left for the real business of living.

Bruce felt futile resentment, as he always did when he thought about it. And if you discount the time spent at an office desk, then how much is there left? Half of one day a week, that's how much the average man lives! That's how far short of our potential is the actuality of existence.

Take it further than that: we are capable of using only a fraction of our physical and mental strength. Only under hypnosis are we able to exert more than a tenth of what is in us. So divide that half of one day by a week by ten, and the rest is waste! Sickening waste!

"Ruffy, have you detailed sentries for tonight?" Bruce barked at him.

"Not yet. I was just—"

"Well, do it, and do it quickly."

Ruffy looked at Bruce in speculation, and through his anger Bruce felt a qualm of regret that he had selected that mountain of energy on which to vent his frustration.

"Where the hell is Hendry?" he snapped.

Without speaking Ruffy pointed to a group of men round one of the trucks at the rear of the convoy, and Bruce left him.

Suddenly consumed with impatience, Bruce fell upon his men, shouting at them, scattering them to a dozen different tasks. He walked along the convoy making sure that his instructions were being carried out to the letter; checking the siting of the Brens and the searchlights, making sure that the single small cooking fire was screened from Baluba eyes, stopping to watch the refuelling of the trucks and the running maintenance he had ordered. Men avoided catching his eye and bent to their tasks with studied application. There were no raised voices or sounds of laughter in the camp.

Again Bruce had decided against a night journey. The temptation itched within him, but the exhaustion of those gendarmes who had not slept since the previous morning and the danger of travelling in the dark he could not ignore.

"We'll leave as soon as it's light tomorrow," Bruce told Ruffy.

"Okay, boss." Ruffy nodded, and then soothingly, "You're tired. Food's nearly ready, then you get some sleep."

Bruce glared at him, opening his mouth to snarl a retort, and then closed it again. He turned and strode out of the camp into the forest.

He found a fallen log, sat down, and lit a cigarette. It was dark now, and there were only a few stars among the rain clouds that blackened the sky. He could hear the faint sounds from the camp but there were no lights—the way he had ordered it.

The fact that his anger had no focal point inflamed it rather than quenched it. It ranged restlessly until at last it found a target—himself.

He recognized the brooding, undirected depression that was descending upon him. It was a thing he had not experienced for a long time, nearly two years, not since the wreck of his marriage and the loss of his children; not since he had stifled all emotion and trained himself not to participate in the life around him.

But now his barrier was gone; there was no sheltered harbour from the storm surf, and he would have to ride it out—furl all canvas and rig a sea anchor.

The anger was gone now. At least anger had heat, but this other thing was cold; icy waves of it broke over him, and he was small and insignificant in the grip of it.

His mind turned to his children, and the loneliness howled round him like a winter wind from the south. He closed his eyes and pressed his fingers against the lids. Their faces formed in the eye of his mind.

Christine with pink fat legs under her frilly skirt, and the face of a thoughtful cherub below soft hair cropped like a page boy. "I love you best of all," said with much seriousness, hold-

ing his face with small hands only a little sticky with ice cream.

Simon, a miniature reproduction of Bruce even to the nose. Scabs on the knees and dirt on the face. No demonstrations of affection from him, but in its place something much better, a companionship far beyond his six years. Long discussions on everything from religion, "Why didn't Jesus used to shave?" to politics, "When are you going to be prime minister, Dad?"

And the loneliness was a tangible thing now, like the coils of a reptile squeezing his chest. Bruce ground out the cigarette beneath his heel and tried to find refuge in his hatred for the woman who had been his wife, the woman who had taken them from him. But his hatred was a cold thing also, dead ash with a stale taste. For he knew that the blame was not all hers.

It was another of his failures; perhaps if I had tried harder, perhaps if I had left some of the cruel things unsaid, perhaps— yes, it might have been, and perhaps and maybe. But it was not. It was over and finished and now I am alone. There is no worse condition; no state beyond loneliness. It is the waste land and the desolation.

Something moved near him in the night, a soft rustle of grass, a presence felt rather than seen. And Bruce stiffened. His right hand closed over his rifle. He brought it up slowly, his eyes straining into the darkness.

The movement again, closer now. A twig popped underfoot. Bruce slowly trained his rifle round to cover it, pressure on the trigger and his thumb on the safety. Stupid to have wandered away from the camp; asking for it, and now he had got it. Baluba tribesmen! He could see the figure now in the dimness of starlight, stealthily moving across his front. How many of them? he wondered. If I hit this one, there could be a dozen others with him. Have to take a chance. One quick burst and then run for it. A hundred yards to the camp, about an even chance. The figure was stationary now, standing listening. Bruce could see the outline of the head—no helmet, can't be one of us. He raised the rifle and pointed it. Too dark to see the sights, but at that range he couldn't miss. Bruce drew his breath softly, filling his lungs, ready to shoot and run.

"Bruce?" Shermaine's voice, frightened, almost a whisper. He threw up the rifle barrel. God, that was close. He had nearly killed her.

"Yes, I'm here." His own voice was scratchy with the shock of realization.

"Oh, there you are."

"What the hell are you doing out of the camp?" he demanded furiously as anger replaced his shock.

"I'm sorry, Bruce. I came to see if you were all right. You were gone such a long time."

"Well, get back to the camp, and don't try any more tricks like that."

There was a long silence, and then she spoke softly, unable to keep the hurt out of her tone.

"I brought you something to eat. I thought you'd be hungry. I'm sorry if I did wrong."

She came to him, stooped, and placed something on the ground in front of him. Then she turned and was gone.

"Shermaine." He wanted her back, but the only reply was the fading rustle of the grass and then silence. He was alone again.

He picked up the plate of food.

You fool! he thought. *You stupid, ignorant, thoughtless fool! You'll lose her, and you'll have deserved it. You deserve everything you've had, and more.*

You never learn, do you, Curry? You never learn that there is a penalty for selfishness and for thoughtlessness.

He looked down at the plate in his hands. Bully beef and sliced onion, bread and cheese.

Yes, I have learned, he answered himself with sudden determination. *I will not spoil this, this thing that is between this girl and me. That was the last time; now I am a man I will put away childish things, like temper and self-pity.*

He ate the food, suddenly aware of his hunger. He ate quickly, wolfing it. Then he stood up and walked back to the camp.

A sentry challenged him on the perimeter, and Bruce an-

swered with alacrity. At night his gendarmes were very quick
on the trigger; the challenge was an unusual courtesy.

"It is unwise to go alone into the forest in the darkness," the
sentry reprimanded him.

"Why?" Bruce felt his mood changing. The depression
evaporated.

"It is unwise," repeated the man vaguely.

"The spirits?" Bruce teased him delicately.

"An aunt of my sister's husband disappeared not a short
throw of a spear from my hut. There was no trace, no shout,
nothing. I was there. It is not a matter for doubt," said the man
with dignity.

"A lion perhaps?" Bruce prodded him.

"If you say so, then it is so. I know what I know. But I say
only that there is no wisdom in defying the custom of the
land."

Suddenly touched by the man's concern for him, Bruce
dropped a hand on his shoulder and gripped it in the old
expression of affection.

"I will remember. I did it without thinking."

He walked into the camp. The incident had confirmed something he had vaguely suspected but in which previously he had
felt no interest. The men liked him. A hundred similar indica-
tions of this fact he had only half noted, not caring one way or
the other. But now it gave him intense pleasure, fully com-
pensating for the loneliness he had just experienced.

He walked past the little group of men round the cooking
fire to where the Ford stood at the head of the convoy. Peering
through the side window, he could make out Shermaine's
blanket-wrapped form on the back seat. He tapped on the glass,
and she sat up and rolled down the window.

"Yes?" she asked coolly.

"Thank you for the food."

"It is nothing." The slightest hint of warmth in her voice.

"Shermaine, sometimes I say things I do not mean. You
startled me. I nearly shot you."

"It was my fault. I should not have followed you."

"I was rude," he persisted.

"Yes." She laughed now, that husky little chuckle. "You were rude but with good reason. We shall forget it." She placed her hand on his arm. "You must rest, you haven't slept for two days."

"Will you ride in the Ford with me tomorrow to show that I am forgiven?"

"Of course." She nodded.

"Good night, Shermaine."

"Good night, Bruce."

No, Bruce decided as he spread his blankets beside the fire, *I am not alone. Not any more.*

20

"What about breakfast, boss?"

"They can eat on the road. Give them a tin of bully each. We've wasted enough time on this trip."

The sky was paling and pinking above the forest. It was light enough to read the dial of his wrist watch—twenty minutes to five.

"Get them moving, Ruffy. If we make Msapa Junction before dark we can drive through the night. Home for breakfast to-morrow."

"Now you're talking, boss." Ruffy clapped his helmet onto his head and went off to rouse the men who lay in the road beside the trucks.

Shermaine was asleep. Bruce leaned into the window of the Ford and studied her face. A wisp of hair lay over her mouth, rising and falling with her breathing. It tickled her nose and in her sleep it twitched like a rabbit.

Bruce felt an almost unbearable pang of tenderness towards her. With one finger he lifted the hair off her face. Then he smiled at himself.

If you can feel like this before breakfast, then you've got it in a bad way, he told himself.

Do you know something, he retorted. *I like the feeling.*

"Hey, you lazy wench!" He pulled the lobe of her ear. "Time to wake up."

It was almost half-past five before the convoy got under way. It had taken that long to bully and cajole the sleep out of the men and get them into the trucks. This morning Bruce did not find the delay unbearable. He had managed to find time for four hours' sleep during the night. Four hours was not nearly enough to make up for the previous two days.

Now he felt light-headed, a certain unreal quality of gaiety overlaying his exhaustion, a carnival spirit. There was no longer the same urgency, for the road to Elisabethville was clear and not too long. Home for breakfast tomorrow!

"We'll be at the bridge in a little under an hour." He glanced sideways at Shermaine.

"You've left a guard on it?"

"Ten men," answered Bruce. "We'll pick them up almost without stopping, and then the next stop, room 201, Grand Hotel Leopold II, Avenue du Kasai." He grinned in anticipation. "A bath so deep it will slop over onto the floor, so hot it will take five minutes to get into it. Clean clothes. A steak that thick, with French salad and a bottle of Liebfraumilch."

"For breakfast?" protested Shermaine.

"For breakfast," Bruce agreed happily. He was silent for a while, savouring the idea. The road ahead of him was tiger-striped with the shadows of the trees thrown by the low sun. The air that blew in through the missing windscreen was cool and clean smelling. He felt good. The responsibility of command lay lightly on his shoulders this morning; a pretty girl beside him, a golden morning, the horror of the last few days half-forgotten—they might have been going on a picnic.

"What are you thinking?" he asked suddenly. She was very quiet beside him.

"I was wondering about the future," she answered softly. "There is no one I know in Elisabethville, and I do not wish to stay there."

"Will you return to Brussels?" he asked. The question was without significance, for Bruce Curry had very definite plans for the immediate future, and these included Shermaine.

"Yes, I think so. There is nowhere else."

"You have relatives there?"

"An aunt."

"Are you close?"

Shermaine laughed, but there was bitterness in the husky chuckle. "Oh, very close. She came to see me once at the orphanage. Once in all those years. She brought me a comic book of a religious nature and told me to clean my teeth and brush my hair a hundred strokes a day."

"There is no one else?" asked Bruce.

"No."

"Then why go back?"

"What else is there to do?" she asked. "Where else is there to go?"

"There's a life to live, and the rest of the world to visit."

"Is that what you are going to do?"

"That is exactly what I'm going to do, starting with a hot bath."

Bruce could feel it between them. They both knew it was there, but it was too soon to talk about it. *I have only kissed her once, but that was enough. So what will happen? Marriage?* His mind shied away from that word with startling violence, then came hesitantly back to examine it; stalking it as though it were a dangerous beast, ready to take flight again as soon as it showed its teeth.

For some people it is a good thing. It can stiffen the spineless; ease the lonely; give direction to the wanderers; spur those without ambition—and, of course, there was the final unassailable argument in its favour: children.

But there are some who can only sicken and shrivel in the colourless cell of matrimony. With no space to fly, your wings must weaken with disuse; turned inwards, your eyes become short-sighted; when all your communication with the rest of the world is through the glass windows of the cell, then your contact is limited.

And I already have children. I have a daughter and I have a son.

Bruce turned his eyes from the road and studied the girl beside him. *There is no fault I can find. She is beautiful in the delicate, almost fragile way that is so much better and longer lived than blond hair and big bosoms. She is unspoiled; hardship has long been her travelling companion and from it she has learned kindness and humility.*

She is mature, knowing the ways of this world; knowing death and fear, the evilness of men and their goodness. I do not believe she has ever lived in the fairy-tale cocoon that most young girls spin about themselves.

And yet she has not forgotten how to laugh.

Perhaps, he thought, *perhaps. But it is too soon to talk about it.*

"You are very grim." Shermaine broke the silence, but the laughter shivered just below the surface of her voice. "Again you are Bonaparte. And when you are grim your nose is too big and cruel. It is a nose of great brutality and it does not fit the rest of your face. I think that when they had finished you they had only one nose left in stock. 'It is too big,' they said, 'but it is the only one we have, and when he smiles it will not look too bad.' So they took a chance and stuck it on anyway."

"Were you never taught that it is bad manners to poke fun at a man's weakness?" Bruce fingered his nose ruefully.

"Your nose is many things, but not weak. Never weak." She laughed now and moved a little closer to him.

"You know you can attack me from behind your own perfect nose, and I cannot retaliate."

"Never trust a man who makes pretty speeches so easily, because he surely makes them to every girl he meets." She slid an inch further across the seat until they were almost touching. "You waste your talents, *mon capitaine*. I am immune to your charm."

"In just one minute I will stop this car and—"

"You cannot." Shermaine jerked her head to indicate the two gendarmes in the seat behind them. "What would they think, Bonaparte? It would be very bad for discipline."

"Discipline or no discipline, in just one minute I will stop this car and spank you soundly before I kiss you."

"One threat does not frighten me, but because of the other I will leave your poor nose." She moved away a little and once more Bruce studied her face. Beneath the frank scrutiny she fidgeted and started to blush.

"Do you mind! Were you never taught that it is bad manners to stare?"

So now I am in love again, thought Bruce. *This is only the third time, an average of once every ten years or so. It frightens me a little because there is always pain with it. The exquisite pain of loving and the agony of losing.*

It starts in the loins and it is very deceptive because you think it is only the old thing, the tightness and tension that any well-rounded stern or cheeky pair of breasts will give you. Scratch it, you think, it's just a small itch. Spread a little of the warm salve on it and it will be gone in no time.

But suddenly it spreads, upwards and downwards, all through you. The pit of your stomach feels hot, then the flutters round the heart. It's dangerous now; once it gets this far it's incurable and you can scratch and scratch but all you do is inflame it.

Then the last stages, when it attacks the brain. No pain there, that's the worst sign. A heightening of the senses: your eyes are sharper, your blood runs too fast, food tastes good, your mouth wants to shout and legs want to run. Then the delusions of grandeur: you are the cleverest, strongest, most masculine male in the universe, and you stand ten feet tall in your socks.

How tall are you now, Curry? he asked himself. *About nine feet six and I weigh twenty stone,* he answered and almost laughed aloud.

And how does it end? It ends with words. Words can kill anything. It ends with cold words; words like fire that stick in the structure and take hold and lick it up, blackening and charring it, bringing it down in smoking ruins.

It ends in suspicion of things not done, and in the certainty of things done and remembered. It ends with selfishness and carelessness, and words, always words.

It ends with pain and greyness, and it leaves scar tissue and damage that will never heal.

Or it ends without fuss and fury. It just crumbles and blows away like dust on the wind. But there is still the agony of loss.

Both these endings I know well, for I have loved twice, and now I love again.

Perhaps this time it does not have to be that way. Perhaps this time it will last. Nothing is for ever, he thought. *Nothing is for ever, not even life, and perhaps this time if I cherish it and tend it carefully it will last that long, as long as life.*

"We are nearly at the bridge," said Shermaine beside him, and Bruce started. The miles had dropped unseen behind them, and now the forest was thickening. It crouched closer to the earth, greener and darker along the river.

Bruce slowed the Ford, and the forest became dense bush around them, the road a tunnel through it. They came round one last bend in the track and out of the tunnel of green vegetation into the clearing where the road met the railway line and ran beside it onto the heavy timber platform of the bridge.

Bruce stopped the Ranchero, switched off the engine, and they all sat silently, staring out at the solid jungle on the far bank with its screen of creepers and monkey-ropes hanging down, trailing the surface of the deep green swift-flowing river. They stared at the stumps of the bridge thrusting out from each bank towards each other like the arms of parted lovers; at the wide gap between, with the timbers still smouldering and the smoke drifting away downstream over the green water.

"It's gone," said Shermaine. "It's been burned."

"Oh, no," groaned Bruce. "Oh, God, no!"

With an effort he pulled his eyes from the charred remains of the bridge and turned to the jungle about them, a hundred feet away, ringing them in, hostile, silent. "Don't get out of the car," he snapped as Shermaine reached for the door handle. "Roll your window up, quickly."

She obeyed.

"They're waiting in there." He pointed at the edge of the jungle.

Behind them the first of the convoy came round the bend into the clearing. Bruce jumped from the Ford and ran back towards the leading truck.

"Don't get out, stay inside," he shouted and ran on down the line, repeating the instruction to each of them as he passed. When he reached Ruffy's cab he jumped onto the running board, jerked the door open, slipped in onto the seat, and slammed the door.

"They've burned the bridge."

"What's happened to the boys we left to guard it?"

"I don't know but we'll find out. Pull up alongside the others so that I can talk to them."

Through the half-open window he issued his orders to each of the drivers, and within ten minutes all the vehicles had been manœuvred into the tight defensive circle of the laager, a formation Bruce's ancestors had used a hundred years before.

"Ruffy, get out those tarpaulins and spread them over the top to form a roof. We don't want them dropping arrows in among us."

Ruffy selected half a dozen gendarmes and they went to work, dragging out the heavy folded canvas.

"Hendry, put a couple of men under each truck. Set up the Brens in case they try to rush us."

In the infectious urgency of defense, Wally did not make his usual retort but gathered his men. They wriggled on their stomachs under the vehicles, rifles pointed out towards the silent jungle.

"I want the extinguishers here in the middle so we can get them in a hurry. They might use fire again."

Two gendarmes ran to each of the cabs and unclipped the fire extinguishers from the dashboards.

"What can I do?" Shermaine was standing beside Bruce.

"Keep quiet and stay out of the way," said Bruce as he turned and hurried across to help Ruffy's gang with the tarpaulins.

It took them half an hour of desperate endeavour before they completed the fortifications to Bruce's satisfaction.

"That should hold them." Bruce stood with Ruffy and Hendry in the centre of the laager and surveyed the green canvas roof above them and the closely packed vehicles around them. The

Ford was parked beside the tanker, not included in the outer ring, for its comparative size would have made it a weak point in the defense.

"It's going to be bloody hot and crowded in here," grumbled Hendry.

"Yes, I know." Bruce looked at him. "Would you like to relieve the congestion by waiting outside?"

"Funny boy, big laugh," answered Wally.

"What now, boss?" Ruffy put into words the question Bruce had been asking himself.

"You and I will go and take a look at the bridge," he said.

"You'll look a rare old sight with an arrow sticking out of your jack." Wally grinned. "Boy, that's going to kill me!"

"Ruffy, get us half a dozen gas capes each. I doubt their arrows will go through them at a range of a hundred feet, and of course we'll wear helmets."

"Okay, boss."

It was like being in a sauna bath beneath the six layers of rubberized canvas. Bruce could feel the sweat squirting from his pores with each pace and rivulets of it coursing down his back and flanks as he and Ruffy left the laager and walked up the road to the bridge.

Beside him Ruffy's bulk was so enhanced by the gas capes that he reminded Bruce of a prehistoric monster reaching the end of its gestation period.

"Warm enough, Ruffy?" he asked, feeling the need for humour. The ring of jungle made him nervous. Perhaps he had underestimated the carry of a Baluba arrow—despite the light reed shaft, they used iron heads, barbed viciously and ground to a needle point, and poison smeared thickly between the barbs.

"Man, look at me shiver," grunted Ruffy, and the sweat greased down his jowls and dripped from his chin.

Long before they reached the access to the bridge the stench of putrefaction crept out to meet them. In Bruce's mind every smell had its own colour, and this one was green, the same green as the sheen on rotting meat. The stench was so heavy he could almost feel it bearing down on them, choking in his throat and coating his tongue and the roof of his mouth with the oily over-sweetness.

"No doubt what that is!" Ruffy spat, trying to get the taste out of his mouth.

"Where are they?" Bruce gagged, starting to pant from the heat and the effort of breathing the fouled air.

They reached the bank, and Bruce's question was answered as they looked down onto the narrow beach.

There were the black remains of a dozen cooking fires along the water's edge, and closer to the high bank were two crude structures of poles. For a moment their purpose puzzled Bruce, and then he realized what they were. He had seen those cross-pieces suspended between two uprights often before in hunting camps throughout Africa. They were paunching racks! At intervals along the crosspieces were the bark ropes used to string up the game, heels first, with head and forelegs dangling and belly bulging forward so that at the long abdominal stroke of the knife the viscera would drop out easily.

But the game that had been butchered on *these* racks were men, his men. He counted the hanging ropes. There were ten of them, so no one had escaped.

"Cover me, Ruffy. I'm going down to have a look." It was a penance Bruce was imposing upon himself. They were his men, and he had left them here.

"Okay, boss."

Bruce clambered down the well-defined path to the beach. Now the smell was almost unbearable, and he found the source of it. Between the racks lay a dark shapeless mass. It moved with flies; its surface moved, trembled, crawled with flies. Suddenly, humming, they lifted in a cloud from the pile of human debris and then settled once more upon it.

A single fly buzzed round Bruce's head and then settled on his hand. Metallic blue body, wings cocked back, it crouched on his skin and gleefully rubbed its front legs together. Bruce's throat and stomach convulsed as he began to retch. He struck at the fly and it darted away.

There were bones scattered round the cooking fires and a skull lay near his feet, split open to yield its contents.

Another spasm took Bruce, and this time the vomit came up into his mouth, acid and warm. He swallowed it, turned away, and scrambled up the bank to where Ruffy waited. He stood there gasping, suppressing his nausea, until at last he could speak.

"All right, that's all I wanted to know," and he led the way back to the circle of vehicles.

Bruce sat on the bonnet of the Ranchero and sucked hard on his cigarette, trying to get the taste of death out of his mouth.

"They probably swam downstream during the night and climbed the supports of the bridge. Kanaki and his boys wouldn't have known anything about it until they came over the sides." He drew on the cigarette again and trickled the smoke out of his nostrils, fumigating the back of his throat and his nasal passages. "I should have thought of that. I should have warned Kanaki of that."

"You mean they ate all ten of them—Jesus!" Even Wally Hendry was impressed. "I'd like to have a look at that beach. It must be quite something."

"Good!" Bruce's voice was suddenly harsh. "I'll put you in charge of the burial squad. You can go down there and clean it up before we start work on the bridge."

And Wally did not argue. "You want me to do it now?" he asked.

"No," snapped Bruce. "You and Ruffy are going to take two of the trucks back to Port Reprieve and fetch the materials we need to repair the bridge."

They both looked at Bruce with rising delight.

"I never thought of that," said Wally.

"There's plenty of roofing timber in the hotel and the office block." Ruffy grinned.

"Nails," said Wally as though he were making a major contribution. "We'll need nails."

Bruce cut through their comments. "It's two o'clock now. You can get back to Port Reprieve by nightfall, collect the material tomorrow morning, and return here by the evening. Take those two trucks there—check to see they're full of gas, and you'll need about fifteen men. Say five gendarmes, in case of trouble, and ten of those civilians."

"That should be enough," agreed Ruffy.

"Bring a couple of dozen sheets of corrugated iron back with you. We'll use them to make a shield to protect us from arrows while we're working."

"Yeah, that's a good idea."

They settled the details, picked men to go back, loaded the trucks, worked them out of the laager, and Bruce watched them disappear down the road towards Port Reprieve. An ache started deep behind his eyes and suddenly he was very tired, drained of energy by too little sleep, by the heat, and by the emotional pace of the last four days. He made one last circuit of the laager, checking the defenses, chatting for a few minutes with his gendarmes, and then he stumbled to the Ford, slid onto the front seat, laid his helmet and rifle aside, lowered his head onto his arms, and was instantly asleep.

21

Shermaine woke him after dark with food unheated from the cans and a bottle of Ruffy's beer.

"I'm sorry, Bruce, we have no fire to cook upon. It is very unappetizing and the beer is warm."

Bruce sat up and rubbed his eyes. Six hours' sleep had helped; they were less swollen and inflamed. The headache was still there.

"I'm not really hungry, thank you. It's this heat."

"You must eat, Bruce. Try just a little," and then she smiled. "At least you are more gallant after having rested. It is 'Thank you' now, instead of 'Keep quiet and stay out of the way.' "

Ruefully Bruce grimaced. "You are one of those women with a built-in recording unit; every word remembered and used in evidence against a man later." Then he touched her hand. "I'm sorry."

"I'm sorry," she repeated. "I like your apologies, *mon capitaine*. They are like the rest of you, completely masculine. There is nothing about you which is not male, sometimes almost overpoweringly so." Impishly she watched his eyes; he knew she was talking about the little scene on the train that Wally Hendry had interrupted.

"Let's try this food," he said, and then a little later, "Not bad —you are an excellent cook."

"This time the credit must go to M. Heinz and his fifty-seven children. But one day I shall make for you one of my tournedos au Prince. It is my special."

"Specialty," Bruce corrected her automatically.

The murmur of voices within the laager was punctuated occasionally by a burst of laughter. There was a feeling of relaxation. The canvas roof and the wall of vehicles gave security to them all. Men lay in dark huddles of sleep or talked quietly in small groups.

Bruce scraped the metal plate and filled his mouth with the last of the food.

"Now I must check the defenses again."

"Oh, Bonaparte. It is always duty." Shermaine sighed with resignation.

"I will not be long."

"And I'll wait here for you."

Bruce picked up his rifle and helmet and was halfway out of the Ford when out in the jungle the drums started.

"Bruce!" whispered Shermaine and clutched his arm. The voices round them froze into a fearful silence, and the drum beat in the night. It had a depth and resonance that you could feel; the warm sluggish air quivered with it; not fixed in space but filling it, beating monotonously, insistently, like the pulse of all creation.

"Bruce!" whispered Shermaine again; she was trembling, and the fingers on his arm dug into his flesh with the strength of terror. It steadied his own leap of fear.

"Baby, baby," he soothed her, taking her to his chest and holding her there. "It's only the sound of two pieces of wood being knocked together by a naked savage. They can't touch us here, you know that."

"Oh, Bruce, it's horrible—it's like bells, funeral bells."

"That's silly talk." Bruce held her at arm's length. "Come with me. Help me calm down these others—they'll be terrified. You'll have to help me."

And he pulled her gently across the seat out of the Ford, and with one arm round her waist walked her into the centre of the laager.

What will counteract the stupefying influence of the drum, the hypnotic beat of it? he asked himself. Noise, our own noise.

"Joseph, M'pophu," he shouted cheerfully, picking out the two best singers among his men. "I regret the drumming is of a low standard, but the Baluba are monkeys with no understanding of music. Let us show them how a Bambala can sing."

They stirred; he could feel the tension diminish.

"Come, Joseph—" He filled his lungs and shouted the opening chorus of one of the planting songs, purposely off-key, singing so badly that it must sting them.

Someone laughed, then Joseph's voice hesitantly started the chorus, gathered strength. M'pophu came in with the bass to give a solid foundation to the vibrant, sweet-ringing tenor. Halfbeat to the drum, hands clapped in the dark; around him Bruce could feel the rhythmic swinging of bodies begin.

Shermaine was no longer trembling; he squeezed her waist and felt her body cling to him.

Now we need light, thought Bruce. A night lamp for my children who fear the darkness and the drum.

With Shermaine beside him he crossed the laager.

"Sergeant Jacque."

"Captain?"

"You can start sweeping with the searchlights."

"Yes, Captain." The answer was less subdued. There were two spare batteries for each light, Bruce knew. Eight hours' life in each, so they would last tonight and tomorrow night.

From each side of the laager the beams leaped out, solid white shafts through the darkness; they played along the edge of the jungle and reflected back, lighting the interior of the laager sufficiently to make out the features of each man. Bruce looked at their faces. They're all right now, he decided, the ghosts have gone away.

"Bravo, Bonaparte," said Shermaine, and Bruce became aware of the grins on the faces of his men as they saw him embracing her. He was about to drop his arm, then stopped himself. The hell with it, he decided, give them something else to think about. He led her back to the Ford.

"Tired?" he asked.

"A little." She nodded.

"I'll fold down the seat for you. A blanket over the windows will give you privacy."

"You'll stay close?" she asked quickly.

"I'll be right outside." He unbuckled the webbing belt that carried his pistol. "You'd better wear this from now on."

Even at its minimum adjustment the belt was too large for her and the pistol hung down almost to her knee.

"The Maid of Orleans," Bruce revenged himself. She pulled a face at him and crawled into the back of the station wagon.

A long while later she called softly above the singing and the throb of the drum. "Bruce?"

"Yes?"

"I wanted to make sure you were there. Good night."

"Good night, Shermaine."

Bruce lay on a single blanket and sweated. The singing had long ago ceased but the drum went on and on, never faltering, throb-throb-throbbing out of the jungle. The searchlights swept regularly back and forth, at times lighting the laager clearly and at others leaving it in shadow. Bruce could hear around him the soft sounds of sleep, the sawing of breath, a muted cough, a gabbled sentence, the stirring of dreamers.

But Bruce could not sleep. He lay on his back with one hand under his head, smoking, staring up at the canvas. The events of the preceding four days ran through his mind: snatches of conversation, André dying, Boussier standing with his wife, the bursting of grenades, blood sticky on his hands, the smell of the dead, the violence and the horror.

He moved restlessly, flicked away his cigarette, and covered his eyes with his hands as though to shut out the memories. But they went on flickering through his mind like the images of a gigantic movie projector, confused now, losing all meaning but retaining the horror.

He remembered the fly upon his arm, grinning at him, rubbing its legs together, gloating, repulsive. He rolled his head from side to side on the blanket.

I'm going mad, he thought, I must stop this.

He sat up quickly, hugging his knees to his chest, and the memories faded. But now he was sad, and alone—so terribly alone, so lost, so without purpose.

He sat alone on the blanket and he felt himself shrinking, becoming small and frightened.

I'm going to cry, he thought, I can feel it there heavy in my throat. And like a hurt child crawling into its mother's lap, Bruce Curry groped his way over the tailboard of the station wagon to Shermaine.

"Shermaine!" he whispered, blindly searching for her.

"Bruce, what is it?" She sat up quickly. She had not been sleeping either.

"Where are you?" There was panic in Bruce's voice.

"Here I am—what's the matter?"

And he found her; clumsily he caught her to him. "Hold me, Shermaine, please hold me."

"Darling." She was anxious. "What is it? Tell me, my darling."

"Just hold me, Shermaine. Don't talk." He clung to her, pressing his face into her neck. "I need you so much—oh, God! How I need you!"

"Bruce." She understood, and her fingers were at the nape of his neck, stroking, soothing.

"My Bruce," she said and held him. Instinctively her body began to rock, gentling him as though he were her child.

Slowly his body relaxed, and he sighed against her, a gusty broken sound.

"My Bruce, my Bruce." She lifted the thin cotton vest that was all she wore and instinctively, in the ageless ritual of comfort, she gave him her breast, holding his mouth to it with both her arms clasped around his neck, her head bowed protectively over his, her hair falling forward and covering them both.

With the hard length of his body against hers, with the soft tugging at her bosom, and in the knowledge that she was giving strength to the man she loved, she realized she had never known happiness before this moment. Then his body was no longer quiescent; she felt her own mood change, a new urgency.

"Oh, yes, Bruce, yes!" Speaking up into his mouth, his hungry hunting mouth, and he above her, no longer child, but full man again.

"So beautiful, so warm." His voice was strangely husky.

She shuddered with the intensity of her own need. "Quickly, Bruce, oh, Bruce." His cruel loving hands, seeking, finding.

"Oh, Bruce—quickly," and she reached up for him with her hips.

"I'll hurt you."

"No—yes, I want the pain." She felt the resistance to him within her and cried out impatiently against it. "Go through!" And then, "Ah! It burns."

"I'll stop."

"No, No!"

"Darling, it's too much."

"Yes—I can't—oh, Bruce. My heart—you've touched my heart."

Her clenched fists drumming on his back. And in to press against the taut, reluctantly yielding springiness, away, then back, away, and back to touch the core of all existence, leave it, and come long gliding back to it, nuzzle it, feel it tilt, then come away, then back once more. Welling slowly upwards, scalding, no longer to be contained, with pain almost—and gone, and gone, and gone.

"I'm falling. Oh, Bruce! Bruce! Bruce!"

Into the gulf together—gone, all gone. Nothing left, no time, no space, no bottom to the gulf.

Nothing and everything. Complete.

Out in the jungle the drum kept beating.

Afterwards, long afterwards, she slept with her head on his arm and her face against his chest. And he unsleeping listened to her sleep. The sound of it was soft, so gentle breathing soft that you could not hear it unless you listened very carefully—or unless you loved her, he thought.

Yes. I think I love this woman—but I must be certain. In fairness to her and to myself I must be entirely certain, for I cannot live through another time like the last, and because I love her I don't want her to take the terrible wounding of a bad marriage. Better, much better to leave it now, unless it has the strength to endure.

Bruce rolled his head slowly until his face was in her hair, and the girl nuzzled his chest in her sleep.

But it is so hard to tell, he thought. *It is so hard to tell at the beginning. It is so easy to confuse pity or loneliness with love, but I cannot afford to do that now. So I must try to think clearly about my marriage to Joan. It will be difficult, but I must try.*

Was it like this with Joan in the beginning? It was so long ago, seven years, that I do not know, he answered truthfully. *All I have left from those days are the pictures of places and the small heaps of words that have stuck where the wind and the pain could not blow them away.*

A beach with the sea mist coming in across it, a whole tree of driftwood half buried in the sand and bleached white with the salt, a basket of strawberries bought along the road, so that when I kissed her I could taste the sweet tartness of the fruit on her lips.

I remember a tune that we sang together, "The mission bells told me that I mustn't stay, South of the border, down Mexico way." I have forgotten most of the words.

And I remember vaguely how her body was, and the shape of her breasts before the children were born.

But that is all I have left from the good times.

The other memories are clear; stinging, whiplash clear. Each ugly word, and the tone in which it was said. The sound of sobbing in the night, the way our marriage dragged itself on for three long grey years after it was mortally wounded, and both of us using all our strength to keep it moving because of the children.

The children! Oh, God, I mustn't think about them now. It hurts too much. Without the children to complicate it, I must think about her for the last time; I must end this woman Joan. So now finally and for all to end this woman who made me cry. I do not hate her for the man with whom she went away. She deserved another try for happiness. But I hate her for my children and for making shabby the love that I could have given Shermaine as a new thing. Also, I pity her for her inability to find the happiness for which she hunts so fiercely. I pity her for her

*coldness of body and of mind. I pity her for her prettiness that is
now almost gone (it goes round the eyes first, cracking like oil
paint), and I pity her for her consuming selfishness which will
lose her the love of her children.*

My children—not hers! My children!

*That is all, that is an end to Joan, and now I have Shermaine,
who is none of the things that Joan was. I also deserve another
try.*

"Shermaine," he whispered and turned her head slightly to
kiss her. "Shermaine, wake up."

She stirred and murmured against him.

"Wake up." He took the lobe of her ear between his teeth and
bit it gently. Her eyes opened.

"*Bon matin, madame.*" He smiled at her.

"*Bon jour, monsieur,*" she answered and closed her eyes to
press her face once more against his chest.

"Wake up. I have something to tell you."

"I am awake, but tell me first if I am still dreaming. I have a
certainty that this cannot be reality."

"You are not dreaming."

She sighed softly, and held him closer.

"Now tell me the other thing."

"I love you," he said.

"No. Now I am dreaming."

"In truth," he said.

"No, do not wake me. I could not bear to wake now."

"And you?" he asked.

"You know it—" she answered. "I do not have to tell you."

"It is almost morning," he said. "There is only a little time."

"Then I will fill that little time with saying it—" He held her
and listened to her whispering it to him.

No, he thought, now I am certain. I could not be that wrong.
This is my woman.

22

The drum stopped with the dawn. And after it the silence was very heavy, and it was no relief.

They had grown accustomed to that broken rhythm and now in some strange way they missed it.

As Bruce moved around the laager he could sense the uneasiness in his men. There was a feeling of dread anticipation on them all. They moved with restraint, as though they did not want to draw attention to themselves. The laughter with which they acknowledged his jokes was nervous, quickly cut off, as though they had laughed in a cathedral. And their eyes kept darting back towards the ring of jungle.

Bruce found himself wishing for an attack. His own nerves were rubbed sensitive by contact with the fear all around him.

If only they would come, he told himself. If only they would show themselves and we could see men, not phantoms.

But the jungle was silent. It seemed to wait. It watched them. They could feel the gaze of hidden eyes. Its malignant presence pressed closer as the heat built up.

Bruce walked across the laager to the south side, trying to move casually. He smiled at Sergeant Jacque, squatted beside him, and peered from under the truck across open ground at the remains of the bridge.

"Trucks will be back soon," he said. "Won't take long to repair that."

Jacque did not answer. There was a worried frown on his high intelligent forehead, and his face was shiny with perspiration.

"It's the waiting, Captain. It softens the stomach."

"They will be back soon," repeated Bruce. If this one is worried, and he is the best of them, then the others must be almost in a jelly of dread.

Bruce looked at the face of the man on the other side of Jacque. Its expression shrieked with fear.

If they attack now, God knows how it will turn out. An African can think himself to death; they just lie down and die. They are getting to that stage now; if an attack comes they will either go berserk or curl up and wail with fear. You can never tell.

Be honest with yourself—you're not entirely happy either, are you? No, Bruce agreed, it's the waiting does it.

It came from the edge of the clearing on the far side of the laager—a high-pitched inhuman sound, angry, savage.

Bruce felt his heart trip, and he spun round to face it. For a second the whole laager seemed to cringe from it.

It came again, like a whip across aching nerves. Immediately it was lost in the roar of twenty rifles.

Bruce laughed—threw his head back and let it come from the belly.

The gunfire stammered into silence, and others were laughing also. The men who had fired grinned sheepishly and made a show of reloading.

It was not the first time that Bruce had been startled by the cry of a yellow hornbill. But now he recognized his laughter and the laughter of the men around him, a mild form of hysteria.

"Did you want the feathers for your hat?" someone shouted, and the laughter swept round the laager.

The tension relaxed as the banter was tossed back and forth. Bruce stood up and brought his own laughter under control.

No harm done, he decided. For the price of fifty rounds of ammunition, a purchase of an hour's escape from tension. A good bargain.

He walked across to Shermaine. She was smiling also.

"How is the catering section?" He grinned at her. "What miracle of the culinary art is there for lunch?"

"Bully beef."

"And onions?"

"No, just bully beef. The onions are finished."

Bruce stopped smiling. "How much is left?" he asked.

"One case—enough to last till lunch time tomorrow."

It would take at least two days to complete the repairs to the bridge; another day's travel after that.

"Well," he said, "we should all have healthy appetites by the time we get home. You'll have to try and spread it out. Half rations from now on."

He was so engrossed in the study of this new complication that he did not notice the faint hum from outside the laager.

"Captain," called Jacque, "can you hear it?"

Bruce inclined his head and listened.

"The trucks!" His voice was loud with relief, and instantly there was an excited murmur round the laager.

The waiting was over.

They came growling out of the bush into the clearing. Heavily loaded, timber and sheet-iron protruding backwards from under the canopies, sitting low on their suspensions.

Ruffy leaned from the cab of the leading truck and shouted, "Hello, boss. Where shall we dump?"

"Take it up to the bridge. Hang on a second and I'll come with you."

Bruce slipped out of the laager and crossed quickly to Ruffy's truck. He could feel his back tingling while he was in the open, and he slammed the door behind him with relief.

"I don't relish stopping an arrow," he said.

"You have any trouble while we were gone?"

"No," Bruce told him. "But they're here. They were drumming in the jungle all night."

"Calling up their buddies," grunted Ruffy and let out the clutch. "We'll have some fun before we finish this bridge. Most probably take them a day or two to get brave, but in the end they'll have a go at us."

"Pull over to the side of the bridge, Ruffy," Bruce instructed and rolled down his window. "I'll signal Hendry to pull in beside us. We'll off-load into the space between the two trucks and start building the corrugated iron shield there."

While Hendry manœuvred his truck alongside, Bruce forced himself to look down on the carnage on the beach.

"Crocodiles," he exclaimed with relief. The paunching racks

still stood as he had last seen them, but the reeking pile of human remains was gone. The smell and the flies, however, still lingered.

"During the night," agreed Ruffy as he surveyed the long slither marks in the sand of the beach.

"Thank God for that."

"Yeah, it wouldn't have made my boys too joyful having to clean up that lot."

"We'll send someone down to tear out those racks. I don't want to look at them while we work."

"No, they're not very pretty." Ruffy ran his eyes over the two sets of gallows.

Bruce climbed down into the space between the trucks.

"Hendry."

"That's my name." Wally leaned out of the window.

"Sorry to disappoint you, but the crocs have done the chore for you."

"I can see. I'm not blind."

"Very well then. On the assumption that you are neither blind nor paralyzed, how about getting your trucks unloaded?"

"Big deal," muttered Hendry, but he climbed down and began shouting at the men under the canvas canopy.

"Get the lead out there, you lot. Start jumping about!"

"What were the thickest timbers you could find?" Bruce turned to Ruffy.

"Nine by threes, but we got plenty of them."

"They'll do," decided Bruce. "We can lash a dozen of them together for each of the main supports." Frowning with concentration, Bruce began the task of organizing the repairs.

"Hendry, I want the timber stacked by sizes. Put the sheet-iron over there." He brushed the flies from his face. "Ruffy, how many hammers have we got?"

"Ten, boss, and I found a couple of handsaws."

"Good. What about nails and rope?"

"We got plenty. I got a barrel of six inch and—"

Preoccupied, Bruce did not notice one of the coloured civilians leave the shelter of the trucks. The man walked a dozen

paces towards the bridge and stopped. Then unhurriedly he began to unbutton his trousers as Bruce looked up.

"What the hell are you doing?" he shouted, and the man
started guiltily. He did not understand the English words, but
Bruce's tone was sufficiently clear.

"Monsieur," he explained, "I wish to—"

"Get back here!" roared Bruce. The man hesitated in confusion and then he began closing his fly.

"Hurry up—you bloody fool."

Obediently the man hastened the closing of his trousers. Everyone had stopped work, and they were all watching him. His
face was dark with embarrassment and he fumbled clumsily.

"Leave that." Bruce was frantic. "Get back here."

The first arrow rose lazily out of the undergrowth along the
river in a silent parabola. Gathering speed in its descent, hissing
softly, it dropped into the ground at the man's feet and stuck up
jauntily. A thin reed, fletched with green leaves, it looked harmless as a child's plaything.

"Run," screamed Bruce.

The man stood and stared with detached disbelief at the arrow.

Bruce started forward to fetch him, but Ruffy's huge black
hand closed on his arm and he was helpless in its grip. He struck
out at Ruffy, struggling to free himself, but he could not break
that hold.

A swarm of them, like locusts on the move, high arcing, flut-
ing softly, were dropping all around the man as he started to
run.

Bruce stopped struggling and watched. He heard the metal
heads clanking on the bonnet of the truck, saw them falling
wide of the man, some of the frail shafts snapping as they hit the
ground.

Then between the shoulders, like a perfectly placed bander-
illa, one hit him. It flapped against his back as he ran, and he
twisted his arms behind him, vainly trying to reach it, his face
twisted in horror and in pain.

"Hold him down," shouted Bruce as the coloured man ran into the shelter. Two gendarmes jumped forward, took his arms, and forced him face downwards onto the ground.

He was gabbling incoherently with horror as Bruce straddled his back and gripped the shaft. Only half the barbed head had buried itself—a penetration of less than an inch—but when Bruce pulled the shaft it snapped off in his hand, leaving the steel twitching in the flesh.

"Knife," shouted Bruce, and someone thrust a bayonet into his hand.

"Watch those barbs, boss. Don't cut yourself on them."

"Ruffy, get your boys ready to repel them if they rush us," snapped Bruce and ripped away the shirt. For a moment he stared at the crudely hand-beaten iron arrowhead. The poison coated it thickly, packed in behind the barbs, looking like sticky black toffee.

"He's dead," said Ruffy from where he leaned over the bonnet of the truck. "He just ain't stopped breathing yet."

The man screamed and twisted under Bruce as he made the first incision cutting in deep beside the arrowhead with the point of the bayonet.

"Hendry, get those pliers out of the tool kit."

"Here they are."

Bruce gripped the arrowhead with the steel jaws and pulled. The flesh clung to it stubbornly, lifting in a pyramid. Bruce hacked at it with the bayonet, feeling it tear. It was like trying to get the hook out of the rubbery mouth of a catfish.

"You're wasting your time, boss!" grunted Ruffy with all the calm African acceptance of violent death. "This boy's a goner. That's no horse! That's snake juice in him, fresh mixed. He's finished."

"Are you sure, Ruffy?" Bruce looked up, "Are you sure it's snake venom?"

"That's what they use. They mix it with kasava meal."

"Hendry, where's the snake-bite outfit?"

"It's in the medicine box back at the camp."

Bruce tugged once more at the arrowhead, and it came away, leaving a deep black hole between the man's shoulderblades.

"Everybody into the trucks, we've got to get him back. Every second is vital."

"Look at his eyes," grunted Ruffy. "That injection stuff ain't going to help him much."

The pupils had contracted to the size of match heads, and he was shaking uncontrollably as the poison spread through his body.

"Get him into the truck."

They lifted him into the cab and everybody scrambled aboard. Ruffy started the engine, slammed into reverse, and the motor roared as he shot backwards over the intervening thirty yards to the laager.

"Get him out," instructed Bruce. "Bring him into the shelter."

The man was blubbering through slack lips and he had started to sweat. Little rivulets of it coursed down his face and naked upper body. There was hardly any blood from the wound, just a trickle of brownish fluid. The poison must be a coagulant, Bruce decided.

"Bruce, are you all right?" Shermaine ran to meet him.

"Nothing wrong with me." Bruce remembered to check his tongue this time. "But one of them has been hit."

"Can I help you?"

"No, I don't want you to watch." And he turned from her. "Hendry, where's that bloody snake-bite outfit?" he shouted.

They had dragged the man into the laager and laid him on a blanket in the shade. Bruce went to him and knelt beside him. He took the scarlet tin that Hendry handed him and opened it.

"Ruffy, get those two trucks worked into the circle and make sure your boys are on their toes. With this success they may get brave sooner than you expected."

Bruce fitted the hypodermic needle onto the syringe as he spoke. "Hendry, get them to rig some sort of screen around us. You can use blankets."

With his thumb he snapped the top off the ampoule and filled the syringe with the pale yellow serum.

"Hold him," he said to the two gendarmes, lifted a pinch of skin close beside the wound, and ran the needle under it. The man's skin felt like that of a frog, damp and clammy.

As he expelled the serum Bruce was trying to calculate the time that had elapsed since the arrow had hit. Possibly seven or eight minutes; mamba venom kills in fourteen minutes.

"Roll him over," he said

The man's head lolled sideways, his breathing was quick and shallow, and the saliva poured from the corners of his mouth, running down his cheeks.

"Get a load of that!" breathed Wally Hendry, and Bruce glanced up at his face. Hendry's expression was a glow of deep sensual pleasure, and his breathing was as quick and shallow as that of the dying man.

"Go and help Ruffy," snapped Bruce as his stomach heaved with disgust.

"Not on your Nelly. This I'm not going to miss."

Bruce had no time to argue. He lifted the skin of the man's stomach and ran the needle in again. There was an explosive spitting sound as the bowels started to vent involuntarily.

"Jesus," whispered Hendry.

"Get away," snarled Bruce. "Can't you let him die without gloating over it?"

Hopelessly he injected again, under the skin of the chest above the heart. As he emptied the syringe the man's body twisted violently in the first seizure and the needle snapped off under the skin.

"There he goes," whispered Hendry, "there he goes. Just look at him, man. That's really something."

Bruce's hands were trembling, and slowly a curtain descended across his mind.

"You filthy swine," he screamed and hit Hendry across the face with his open hand, knocking him back against the side of the gasoline tanker. Then he went for his throat and found it with both hands. The windpipe was ropy and elastic under his thumbs.

"Is nothing sacred to you, you unclean animal," he yelled into Hendry's face. "Can't you let a man die without—"

Then Ruffy was there, effortlessly plucking Bruce's hands from the throat, interposing the bulk of his body, holding them away from each other.

"Let it stand, boss."

"For that—" Hendry gasped as he massaged his throat. "For that I'm going to make you pay."

Bruce turned away, sick and ashamed, to the man on the blanket.

"Cover him up." His voice was shaky. "Put him in the back of one of the trucks. We'll bury him tomorrow."

23

Before nightfall they had completed the corrugated iron screen. It was a simple four-walled structure with no roof to it. One end of it was detachable, and all four walls were pierced at regular intervals with small loopholes for defense.

Long enough to accommodate a dozen men in comfort, high enough to reach above the heads of the tallest, and exactly the width of the bridge, it was not a thing of beauty.

"How you going to move it, boss?" Ruffy eyed the screen dubiously.

"I'll show you. We'll move it back to the camp now, so that in the morning we can commute to work in it."

Bruce selected twelve men, and they crowded through the open end into the shelter and closed it behind them.

"Okay, Ruffy. Take the trucks away."

Hendry and Ruffy reversed the two trucks back to the laager, leaving the shelter standing at the head of the bridge like a small Nissen hut. Inside it Bruce stationed his men at intervals along the walls.

"Use the bottom timber of the frame to lift on," he shouted. "Are you all ready? All right, lift!"

The shelter swayed and rose six inches above the ground. From the laager they could see only the boots of the men inside.

"All together," ordered Bruce. "Walk!"

Rocking and creaking over the uneven ground, the structure moved ponderously back towards the laager. Below it the feet moved like those of a caterpillar.

The men in the laager started to cheer, and from inside the shelter they answered with whoops of laughter. It was fun. They were enjoying themselves enormously, completely distracted from the horror of poison arrows and the lurking phantoms in the jungle around them.

They reached the camp and lowered the shelter. Then one at a time the gendarmes slipped across the few feet of open into the safety of the laager, to be met with laughter and back-slapping and mutual congratulation.

"Well, it works, boss," Ruffy greeted Bruce in the uproar.

"Yes." Then he lifted his voice. "That's enough. Quiet down all of you. Get back to your posts."

The laughter subsided and the confusion became order again. Bruce walked to the centre of the laager and looked about him. There was complete quiet now. They were all watching him. I have read about this so often—he grinned inwardly—the heroic speech to the men on the eve of battle. Let's pray I don't make a hash of it.

"Are you hungry?" he asked loudly in French and received a chorus of hearty affirmatives.

"There is bully beef for dinner." This time humorous groans.

"And bully beef for breakfast tomorrow." He paused. "And then it's finished."

They were silent now.

"So you are going to be truly hungry by the time we cross this river. The sooner we repair the bridge, the sooner you'll get your bellies filled again."

I might as well rub it in, decided Bruce.

"You all saw what happened to the person who went into the open today, so I don't have to tell you to keep under cover. The sergeant major is making arrangements for sanitation—five-gallon drums. They won't be very comfortable, so you won't be tempted to sit too long."

They laughed a little at that.

"Remember this. As long as you stay in the laager or the shelter they can't touch you. There is absolutely nothing to fear. They can beat their drums and wait as long as they like, but they can't harm us."

A murmur of agreement.

"And the sooner we finish the bridge, the sooner we will be on our way."

Bruce looked around the circle of faces and was satisfied with what he saw. The completion of the shelter had given their morale a boost.

"All right, Sergeant Jacque. You can start sweeping with the searchlights as soon as it's dark."

Bruce finished and went across to join Shermaine beside the Ford. He loosed the straps of his helmet and lifted it off his head. His hair was damp with perspiration, and he ran his fingers through it.

"You are tired," Shermaine said softly, examining the dark hollows under his eyes and the puckered marks of strain at the corners of his mouth.

"No. I'm all right," he denied, but every muscle in his body ached with fatigue and nervous tension.

"Tonight you must sleep all night," she ordered him. "I will make the bed in the back of the car."

Bruce looked at her quickly. "With you?" he asked.

"Yes."

"You do not mind that everyone should know?"

"I am not ashamed of us." There was a fierceness in her tone.

"I know, but—"

"You said once that nothing between you and me could ever be dirty."

"No, of course it couldn't be dirty. I just thought—"

"Well then, I love you, and from now on we have only one bed between us." She spoke with finality.

Yesterday she was a virgin, he thought with amazement, and now—well, now it's no holds barred. Once she is roused a woman is more reckless of consequences than any man. They are such wholesale creatures. But she's right, of course. She's my woman and she belongs in my bed. The hell with the rest of the world and what it thinks!

"Make the bed, wench." He smiled at her tenderly.

Two hours after dark the drum started again. They lay together, holding close, and listened to it. It held no terror now, for they were warm and secure in the afterglow of passion. It was like lying and listening to the impotent fury of a rainstorm on the roof at night.

24

They went out to the bridge at sunrise; the shelter moved across the open ground like the carapace of a multi-legged metallic turtle. The men chattered and joked loudly inside, still elated by the novelty of it.

"All right, everybody. That's enough talking," Bruce shouted them down. "There's work to do now."

And they began.

Within an hour the sun had turned the metal box into an oven. They stripped to the waist, and the sweat dripped from them as they worked. They worked in a frenzy, gripped by a new urgency, oblivious of everything but the rough-sawed timber that drove white splinters into their skin at the touch. They worked in the confined heat, amid the racket of hammers and in the piney smell of sawdust. The labour fell into its own pattern with only an occasional grunted order from Bruce or Ruffy to direct it.

By midday the four main trusses that would span the gap in the bridge had been made up. Bruce tested their rigidity by propping one at both ends and standing all his men on the middle of it. It gave an inch under their combined weight.

"What do you think, boss?" Ruffy asked without conviction.

"Four of them might just do it. We'll put in king-posts underneath," Bruce answered.

"Man, I don't know. That tanker weighs plenty."

"It's no flyweight," Bruce agreed. "But we'll have to take the chance. We'll bring the Ford across first, then the trucks, and the tanker last."

Ruffy nodded and wiped his face on his forearm; the muscles below his armpits knotted as he moved, and there was no flabbiness in the powerful bulge of his belly above his belt.

"Phew!" He blew his lips out. "I got the feeling for a beer now. This thirst is really stalking me."

"You've got some with you?" Bruce asked as he passed his thumbs across his eyebrows and squeezed the moisture from them so it ran down his cheeks.

"Two things I never travel without, my trousers and a stock of the brown and bubbly." Ruffy picked up the small pack from the corner of the shelter and it clinked coyly. "You hear that sound, boss?"

"I hear it, and it sounds like music." Bruce grinned. "All right, everybody." He raised his voice. "Take ten minutes."

Ruffy opened the bottles and passed them out, issuing one to be shared among three gendarmes. "These Arabs don't properly appreciate this stuff," he explained to Bruce. "It'd just be a waste."

The liquor was lukewarm and gassy; it merely aggravated Bruce's thirst. He drained the bottle and tossed it out of the shelter.

"All right." He stood up. "Let's get these trusses into position."

"That's the shortest ten minutes I ever lived," commented Ruffy.

"Your watch is slow," said Bruce.

Carrying the trusses within it, the shelter lumbered out onto the bridge. There was no laughter now, only laboured breathing and curses.

"Fix the ropes!" commanded Bruce. He tested the knots personally, then looked up at Ruffy and nodded. "That'll do."

"Come on, you mad bastards," Ruffy growled. "Lift it."

The first truss rose to the perpendicular and swayed there like a grotesque Maypole with the ropes hanging from its top.

"Two men on each rope," ordered Bruce. "Let it down gently." He glanced round to ensure that they were all ready.

"Drop it over the edge, and I'll throw you bastards in after it," warned Ruffy.

"Lower away!" shouted Bruce.

The truss leaned out over the gap towards the fire-blackened stump of bridge on the far side, slowly at first, then faster as gravity took it.

"Hold it, damn you! Hold it!" roared Ruffy, with the muscles in his shoulders humped out under the strain. They lay back against the ropes, but the weight of the truss dragged them forward as it fell.

It crashed down across the gap, lifted a cloud of dead wood ash as it struck, and lay there quivering.

"Man, I thought we'd lost that one for sure," growled Ruffy, then turned savagely on his men. "You bastards better be sharper with the next one—if you don't want to swim this river."

They repeated the process with the second truss, and again they could not hold its falling length, but this time they were not so lucky. The end of the truss hit the far side, bounced, and slid sideways.

"It's going! Pull, you bastards, pull!" shouted Ruffy.

The truss toppled slowly sideways and over the edge. It hit the river below them with a splash, disappeared under the surface, then bobbed up and floated away downstream until checked by the ropes.

Both Bruce and Ruffy fumed and swore during the lengthy exasperating business of dragging it back against the current and manhandling its awkward bulk back onto the bridge. Half a dozen times it slipped at the crucial moment and splashed back into the river.

Despite his other virtues, Ruffy's vocabulary of curse words was limited, and it added to his frustration that he had to keep repeating himself. Bruce did much better—he remembered things that he had heard and he made up a few.

When finally they had the dripping balk of timber back on the bridge and were resting, Ruffy turned to Bruce with honest admiration.

"You swear pretty good," he said. "Never heard you before, but no doubt about it, you're good! What's that one about the cow again?"

Bruce repeated it for him a little self-consciously.

"You make that up yourself?" asked Ruffy.

"Spur of the moment." Bruce laughed.

"That's 'bout the dirtiest I ever heard." Ruffy could not conceal his envy. "Man, you should write a book."

"Let's get this bridge finished first," said Bruce. "Then I'll think about it."

Now the truss was almost servile in its efforts to please. It dropped neatly across the gap and lay beside its twin.

"You curse something good enough, and it works every time," Ruffy announced sagely. "I think your one about the cow made all the difference, boss."

With two trusses in position they had broken the back of the project. They carried the shelter out and set it on the trusses, straddling the gap. The third and fourth trusses were dragged into position and secured with ropes and nails before nightfall.

When the shelter waddled wearily back to the laager at dusk, the men within it were exhausted. Their hands were bleeding and bristled with wood splinters, but they were also mightily pleased with themselves.

"Sergeant Jacque, keep one of your searchlights trained on the bridge all night. We don't want our friends to come out and set fire to it again."

"There are only a few hours' life left in each of the batteries." Jacque kept his voice low.

"Use them one at a time then." Bruce spoke without hesitation. "We must have that bridge lit up all night."

"You think you could spare a beer for each of the boys that worked on the bridge today?"

"A whole one each!" Ruffy was shocked. "I only got a coupla cases left."

Bruce fixed him with a stern eye, and Ruffy grinned. "Okay, boss. Guess they've earned it."

Bruce transferred his attention to Wally Hendry, who sat on the running board of one of the trucks, cleaning his nails with the point of his bayonet.

"Everything under control here, Hendry?" he asked coolly.

"Sure, what'd you think would happen? We'd have a visit

from the archbishop? The sky'd fall in? Your French thing'd have twins or something?" He looked up from his nails at Bruce. "When are you jokers going to get that bridge finished instead of wandering around asking damn-fool questions?"

Bruce was too tired to feel annoyed. "You've got the night watch, Hendry," he said, "from now until dawn."

"Is that right, hey? And you? What're you going to do all night, or does that question make you blush?"

"I'm going to sleep, that's what I'm going to do. I haven't been lolling around camp all day."

Hendry pegged the bayonet into the earth between his feet and snorted. "Well, give her a little bit of sleep for me too, bucko."

Bruce left him and crossed to the Ford.

"Hello, Bruce. How did it go today? I missed you," Shermaine greeted him, and her face lit up as she looked at him.

It is a good feeling to be loved, and some of Bruce's fatigue lifted. "About half finished, another day's work." Then he smiled back at her. "I won't lie and say I missed you—I've been too damn busy."

"Your hands!" she said with quick concern and lifted them to examine them. "They're in a terrible state."

"Not very pretty, are they?"

"Let me get a needle from my case. I'll get the splinters out."

From across the laager Wally Hendry caught Bruce's eye and with one hand made a suggestive sign below his waist. Then, at Bruce's frown of anger, he threw back his head and laughed with huge delight.

25

Bruce's stomach grumbled with hunger as he stood with Ruffy and Hendry beside the cooking fire. In the early morning light he could just make out the dark shape of the bridge at the end of the clearing. That drum was still beating in the jungle, but they hardly noticed it now. It was taken for granted, like the mosquitoes. "The batteries are finished," grunted Ruffy. The feeble yellow beam of the searchlight reached out tiredly towards the bridge.

"Only just lasted the night," agreed Bruce.

"Christ, I'm hungry," complained Hendry. "What I could do to a couple of fried eggs and a porterhouse steak!"

At the mention of food Bruce's mouth flooded with saliva. He shut his mind against the picture that Wally's words had evoked in his imagination.

"We won't be able to finish the bridge and get the trucks across today," he said, and Ruffy agreed.

"There's a full day's work left on her, boss."

"This is what we'll do then," Bruce went on. "I'll take the work party out to the bridge. Hendry, you will stay here in the laager and cover us the same as yesterday. And Ruffy, you take one of the trucks and a dozen of your boys. Go back ten miles or so to where the forest is open and they won't be able to creep up on you. Then cut us a mountain of firewood—thick logs that will burn all night. We will set a ring of watch fires round the camp tonight."

"That makes sense." Ruffy nodded. "But what about the bridge?"

"We'll have to put a guard on it," said Bruce, and the expressions on their faces changed as they thought about this.

"More pork chops for the boys in the bushes," growled

Hendry. "You won't catch me sitting out on the bridge all night."

"No one's asking you to," snapped Bruce. "All right, Ruffy. Go and fetch the wood, and plenty of it."

Bruce completed the repairs to the bridge in the late afternoon. The most anxious period was in the middle of the day when he and four men had to leave the shelter and clamber down onto the supports a few feet above the surface of the river to set the king-posts in place. Here they were exposed at random range to arrows from the undergrowth along the banks. But no arrows came, and they finished the job and climbed back to safety again with something of a sense of anticlimax.

They nailed the crossties over the trusses and then roped everything into a compact mass.

Bruce stood back and surveyed the fruit of two full days' labour.

"Functional," he decided, speaking aloud. "But we certainly aren't going to win any prizes for aesthetic beauty or engineering design."

He picked up his jacket and thrust his arms into the sleeves; his sweaty upper body was cold now that the sun was almost down.

"Home, gentlemen," he said, and his gendarmes scattered to their positions inside the shelter.

The metal shelter circled the laager, squatting every twenty or thirty paces, like an old woman preparing to relieve herself. When it lifted and moved on, it left a log fire behind it. The ring of fires was completed by dark, and the shelter returned to the laager.

"Are you ready, Ruffy?" From inside the shelter Bruce called across to where Ruffy waited.

"All set, boss."

Followed by six heavily armed gendarmes, Ruffy crossed quickly to join Bruce, and they set off to begin their all-night vigil on the bridge.

Before midnight it was cold in the corrugated iron shelter,

for the wind blew down the river and they were completely exposed to it, and there was no cloud cover to hold the day's warmth against the earth.

The men in the shelter huddled under their gas capes and waited. Bruce and Ruffy leaned together against the corrugated iron wall, their shoulders almost touching, and there was sufficient light from the stars to light the interior of the shelter and allow them to make out the guard rails of the bridge through the loopholes.

"Moon will be up in an hour," murmured Ruffy.

"Only a quarter of it, but it will give us a little more light," Bruce concurred as he peered down into the black hole between his feet where he had prised up one of the newly laid planks.

"How about taking a shine with the torch?" suggested Ruffy.

"No." Bruce shook his head and passed the flashlight into his other hand. "Not until I hear them."

"You might not hear them."

"If they swim downstream and climb up the piles, which is what I expect, then we'll hear them all right. They'll be dripping water all over the place," said Bruce.

"Kanaki and his boys didn't hear them," Ruffy pointed out.

"Kanaki and his boys weren't listening for it," said Bruce.

They were silent then for a while. One of the gendarmes started to snore softly, and Ruffy shot out a huge booted foot that landed in the small of his back. The man cried out and scrambled to his knees, looking wildly about him.

"You have nice dreams?" Ruffy asked pleasantly.

"I wasn't sleeping," the man protested, "I was thinking."

"Well, don't think so loudly," Ruffy advised him. "Sounds as though you were sawing through the bridge with a cross cut."

Another half hour dragged itself by like a cripple.

"Fires are burning well," commented Ruffy, and Bruce turned his head and glanced through the loophole in the corrugated iron behind him at the little garden of orange flame-flowers in the darkness.

"Yes, they should last till morning."

Silence again, with only the singing of the mosquitoes and the rustle of the river as it flowed by the piles of the bridge. Shermaine has my pistol, Bruce remembered with a small trip in his pulse; I should have taken it back from her. He unclipped his bayonet from the muzzle of his rifle, tested the edge of the blade with his thumb, and slid it into the scabbard on his web belt. Could easily lose the rifle if we start mixing it in the dark, he decided.

"Christ, I'm hungry," grunted Ruffy beside him.

"You're too fat," said Bruce. "The diet will do you good."

And they waited.

Bruce stared down into the hole in the floorboards. His eyes began weaving fantasies out of the darkness; he could see vague shapes that moved, like things seen below the surface of the sea. His stomach tightened, and he fought the impulse to shine his flashlight into the hole. He closed his eyes to rest them. I will count slowly to ten, he decided, and then look again.

Ruffy's hand closed on his upper arm; the pressure of his fingers transmitted alarm like a current of electricity. Bruce's eyelids flew open.

"Listen," breathed Ruffy.

Bruce heard it. The stealthy drip of water on water below them. Then something bumped the bridge, but so softly that he felt rather than heard the jar.

"Yes," Bruce whispered back. He reached out and tapped the shoulder of the gendarme beside him, and the man's body stiffened at his touch.

With his breath scratching his dry throat, Bruce waited until he was sure the warning had been passed to all his men. Then he shifted the weight of his rifle from across his knees and aimed down into the hole.

He drew in a deep breath and switched on the flashlight. The beam shot down, and he looked along it over his rifle barrel.

The square aperture in the floorboards formed a frame for the picture that flashed into his eyes. Black bodies, naked, glossy with wetness, weird patterns of tattoo marks, a face staring up at him, broad sloped forehead above startlingly white eyes and flat nose. The long gleaming blade of a panga. Clusters of humanity clinging to the wooden piles like ticks on the legs of a beast. Legs and arms and shiny trunks merged into a single organism, horrible as some slimy sea creature.

Bruce fired into it. His rifle shuddered against his shoulder, and the long orange spurts from its muzzle gave the picture a new flickering horror. The mass of bodies heaved and struggled like a pack of rats trapped in a dry well. They dropped, splashing into the river, swarmed up the timber piles, twisting and writhing as the bullets hit them, screaming, babbling over the sound of the rifle.

Bruce's weapon clicked empty and he groped for a new magazine. Ruffy and his gendarmes were hanging over the guard rails of the bridge, firing downwards, sweeping the piles below them with long bursts, the flashes lighting their faces and outlining their bodies against the sky.

"They're still coming!" roared Ruffy. "Don't let them get over the side."

Out of the hole at Bruce's feet thrust the head and naked upper body of a man. There was a panga in his hand; he slashed at Bruce's legs, his eyes glazed in the beam of the flashlight.

Bruce jumped back—and the knife missed his knees by inches. The man wormed his way out of the hole towards Bruce. He was screaming shrilly, a high meaningless sound of fury.

Bruce lunged with the barrel of his empty rifle at the contorted black face. All his weight was behind that thrust and the muzzle went into the Baluba's eye. The foresight and four inches of the barrel disappeared into the head, stopping only when it hit bone. Colourless fluid from the burst eyeball gushed from around the protruding steel.

Tugging and twisting, Bruce tried to free the rifle, but the foresight had buried itself like the barb of a fish hook. The Baluba had dropped his panga and was clinging to the rifle barrel with both hands. He was wailing and rolling on his back upon the floorboards, his head jerking every time Bruce tried to pull the muzzle out of his head.

Beyond him the head and shoulders of another Baluba appeared through the aperture.

Bruce dropped the rifle and gathered up the fallen panga; he jumped over the writhing body of the first Baluba and lifted the heavy knife above his head with both hands.

The man was jammed in the hole, powerless to protect himself. He looked up at Bruce and his mouth fell open.

Two-handed, as though he were chopping wood, Bruce swung his whole body into the stroke. The shock jarred his shoulders and he felt blood splatter his legs. The untempered blade snapped off at the hilt and stayed imbedded in the Baluba's skull.

Panting heavily, Bruce straightened up and looked wildly about him. Baluba were swarming over the guard rail on one side of the bridge. The starlight glinted on their wet skins. One of his gendarmes was lying in a dark huddle, his head twisted back and his rifle still in his hands. Ruffy and the other gendarmes were still firing down over the far side.

"Ruffy!" shouted Bruce. "Behind you! They're coming over!" He dropped the handle of the panga and ran towards the body of the gendarme. He needed that rifle.

Before he could reach it, the naked body of a Baluba rushed at him. Bruce ducked under the sweep of the panga and grappled with him. They fell locked together, the man's body slippery and sinuous against him, and the smell of him fetid as rancid butter.

Bruce found the pressure point below the elbow of the man's knife arm and dug in with his thumb. The Baluba yelled and his panga clattered on the floorboards. Bruce wrapped his arm around the man's neck while with his free hand he reached for his bayonet.

The Baluba was clawing for Bruce's eyes with his fingers, his nails scored the side of Bruce's nose, but Bruce had his bayonet out now. He placed the point against the man's chest and pressed it in. He felt the steel scrape against a rib, and the man redoubled his struggles at the sting of it. Bruce twisted the blade, working it in with his wrist, forcing the man's head backwards with his other arm.

The point of the bayonet scraped over the bone and found the gap between. As in taking a virgin, suddenly the resistance to its entrance was gone and it slid home full length. The Baluba's body jerked mechanically and the bayonet twitched in Bruce's fist.

Bruce did not even wait for the man to die. He pulled the blade out against the sucking reluctance of tissue that clung to it and scrambled to his feet in time to see Ruffy pick another Baluba from his feet and hurl him bodily over the guard rail.

Bruce snatched the rifle from the gendarme's dead hands and stepped to the guard rail. They were coming over the side, those below shouting and pushing at the ones above.

Like shooting a row of sparrows from a fence with a shotgun, thought Bruce grimly, and with one long burst he cleared the rail. Then he leaned out and sprayed the piles below the bridge. The rifle was empty. He reloaded with a magazine from his pocket. But it was all over. They were dropping back into the river, the piles below the bridge were clear of men, their heads bobbed away downstream.

Bruce lowered his rifle and looked about him. Three of his gendarmes were killing the man that Bruce had wounded, standing over him and grunting as they thrust down with their bayonets. The man was still wailing.

Bruce looked away.

One horn of the crescent moon showed above the trees; it had a gauzy halo about it.

Bruce lit a cigarette, and behind him those gruesome noises ceased.

"Are you okay, boss?"

"Yes, I'm fine. How about you, Ruffy?"

"I got me a terrible thirst now. Hope nobody trod on my pack."

About four minutes from the first shot to the last, Bruce guessed. That's the way of war—seven hours of waiting and boredom, then four minutes of frantic endeavour. Not only of war either, he thought. The whole of life is like that.

Then he felt the trembling in his thighs and the first spasm of nausea as the reaction started.

"What's happening?" A shout floated across from the laager. Bruce recognized Hendry's voice. "Is everything all right?"

"We've beaten them off," Bruce shouted back. "Everything under control. You can go to sleep again."

And now I have got to sit down quickly, he told himself.

Except for the tattoos upon his cheeks and forehead, the dead Baluba's features were little different from those of the Bambala and Bakuba men who made up the bulk of Bruce's command.

Bruce played the flashlight over the corpse. The arms and legs were thin but stringy with muscle, and the belly bulged from years of malnutrition. It was an ugly body, gnarled and crabbed. With distaste Bruce moved the light back to the features. The bone of the skull formed harsh angular planes beneath the skin, the nose was flattened, and the thick lips had about them a repellent brutality. They were drawn back slightly to reveal the teeth, which had been filed to sharp points like those of a shark.

"This is the last one, boss. I'll toss him overboard." Ruffy spoke in the darkness beside Bruce.

"Good."

Ruffy heaved and grunted, the corpse splashed below them, and Ruffy wiped his hands on the guard rail, then came to sit beside Bruce.

"Goddam apes." Ruffy's voice was full of the bitter tribal antagonism of Africa. "When we get shot of these U.N. people there'll be a bit of sorting out to do. They've got a few things to learn, these bloody Baluba."

And so it goes, thought Bruce, Jew and Gentile, Catholic and Protestant, black and white, Bambala and Baluba.

He checked the time, another two hours to dawn. His nervous reaction from physical violence had abated now; the hand that held the cigarette no longer trembled.

"They won't come again," said Ruffy. "You can get some sleep now if you want. I'll keep an eye open, boss."

"No, thanks. I'll wait with you." His nerves had not settled down enough for sleep.

"How's it for a beer?"

"Thanks."

Bruce sipped the beer and stared out at the watch fires around the laager. They had burned down to puddles of red ash, but Bruce knew that Ruffy was right. The Baluba would not attack again that night.

"So how do you like freedom?"

"How's that, boss?" The question puzzled Ruffy, and he turned to Bruce questioningly.

"How do you like it now the Belgians have gone?"

"It's pretty good, I reckon."

"And if Tshombe has to give in to the Central Government?"

"Those mad Arabs!" snarled Ruffy. "All they want is our copper. They're going to have to get up early in the morning to take it. We're in the saddle here."

The great jousting tournament of the African continent: I'm in the saddle, try to unhorse me! As in all matters of survival it was not a question of ethics and political doctrine (except to the spectators in Whitehall, Moscow, Washington, and Peking). There were big days coming, thought Bruce. My own country, when she blows, is going to make Algeria look like an old ladies' sewing circle.

26

The sun was up, throwing long shadows out into the clearing, and Bruce stood beside the Ford and looked across the bridge at the corrugated iron shelter on the far bank.

He relaxed for a second and let his mind run unhurriedly over his preparations for the crossing. Was there something left undone, some disposition which could make it more secure?

Hendry and a dozen men were in the shelter across the bridge, ready to meet any attack on that side.

Shermaine would take the Ford across first. Then the trucks would follow her. They would cross empty to minimize the danger of the bridge collapsing, or being weakened for the passage of the tanker. After each truck had crossed, Hendry would shuttle its load and passengers over in the shelter and deposit them under the safety of the canvas canopy.

The last truck would go over fully loaded. That was regrettable but unavoidable.

Finally Bruce himself would drive the tanker across. Not as an act of heroism, although it was the most dangerous business of the morning, but because he would trust no one else to do it, not even Ruffy. The five hundred gallons of fuel it contained was their safe-conduct home. Bruce had taken the precaution of filling all the gasoline tanks in the convoy in case of accidents, but they would need replenishing before they reached Msapa Junction.

He looked down at Shermaine in the driver's seat of the Ford.

"Keep it in low gear, take her over slowly but steadily. Whatever else you do, don't stop."

She nodded. She was composed and she smiled at him. Bruce felt a stirring of pride as he looked at her, so small and lovely, but today she was doing man's work. He went on. "As soon as you are over, I will send one of the trucks after you. Hendry will put six of his men into it and then come back for the others."

"*Oui, Monsieur Bonaparte.*"

"You'll pay for that tonight," he threatened her. "Off you go."

Shermaine let out the clutch and the Ford bounced over rough ground to the road, accelerated smoothly out onto the bridge.

Bruce held his breath, but there was only a slight check and sway as it crossed the repaired section.

"Thank God for that." Bruce let out his breath and watched while Shermaine drew up alongside the shelter.

"*Allez,*" Bruce shouted at the coloured engine driver who was ready at the wheel of the first truck. The man smiled his cheerful chubby-faced smile, waved, and the truck rolled forward.

Watching anxiously as it went onto the bridge, Bruce saw the new timbers give perceptibly beneath the weight of the truck, and he heard them creak loudly in protest.

"Not so good," he muttered.

"No—" agreed Ruffy. "Boss, why don't you let someone else take the tanker over?"

"We've been over that already," Bruce answered him without turning his head. Across the river Hendry was transferring his men from the shelter to the back of the truck. Then the shelter started its tedious way back towards them.

Bruce fretted impatiently during the four hours that it took to get four trucks across. The long business was the shuttling back and forth of the corrugated iron shelter, at least ten minutes for each trip.

Finally only the fifth truck and the tanker were left on the north bank. Bruce started the engine of the tanker and put her into auxiliary low, then he blew a single blast on the horn. The driver of the truck ahead of him waved an acknowledgement and pulled forward.

The truck reached the bridge and went out into the middle. It was fully loaded, twenty men aboard. It came to the repaired section and slowed down, almost stopping.

"Go on! Keep it going, damn you," Bruce shouted in impotent anger. The fool of a driver was forgetting his orders. He crawled forward and the bridge gave alarmingly under the full weight, the high canopied roof rocked crazily, and even above the rumble of his own engine Bruce could hear the protesting groan of the bridge timbers.

"The fool, oh, the bloody fool," whispered Bruce to himself. Suddenly he felt very much alone and unprotected here on the north bank with the bridge being mutilated by the incompetence of the truck driver. He started the tanker moving.

Ahead of him the other driver had panicked. He was racing his engine, the rear wheels spun viciously, blue smoke of scorched tires, and one of the floorboards tore loose. Then the truck lurched forward and roared up the south bank.

Bruce hesitated, applying the brakes and bringing the tanker to a standstill on the threshold of the bridge.

He thought quickly. The sensible thing would be to repair the damage to the bridge before chancing it with the weight of the tanker. But that would mean another day's delay. None of them had eaten since the previous morning. Was he justified in gambling against even odds, for that's what they were? A fifty-fifty chance, heads you get across, tails you dump the tanker in the middle of the river.

Then unexpectedly the decision was made for him.

From across the river a Bren gun started firing. Bruce jumped in his seat and looked up. Then a dozen other guns joined in and the tracer flew past the tanker. They were firing across towards him, close on each side of him. Bruce struggled to drag from his uncomprehending brain an explanation of this new development. Suddenly everything was moving too swiftly. Everything was confusion and chaos.

Movement in the rear-view mirror of the tanker caught his eye. He stared at it blankly. Then he twisted quickly in his seat and looked back.

"Christ!" he swore with fright.

From the edge of the jungle on both sides of the clearing Baluba were swarming into the open—hundreds of them running towards him, the animal-skin kilts swirling about their legs, feather headdresses fluttering, sun bright on the long blades of their pangas. An arrow rang dully against the metal body of the tanker.

Bruce revved the engine, gripped the wheel hard with both hands, and took the tanker out onto the bridge. Above the sound of the guns he could hear the shrill ululation, the excited squealing of two hundred Baluba. It sounded very close, and he snatched a quick look in the mirror. What he saw nearly made him lose his head and give the tanker full throttle. The nearest Baluba, screened from the guns on the south bank by the tanker's bulk, was only ten paces away—so close that Bruce could see the tattoo marks on his face and chest.

With an effort Bruce restrained his right foot from pressing down too hard, and instead he bore down on the repaired section of the bridge at a sedate twenty miles an hour. He tried to close his mind to the squealing behind him and the thunder of gunfire ahead of him.

The front wheels hit the new timbers, and above the other sounds he heard them groan loudly, and felt them sag under him.

The tanker rolled on and the rear wheels brought their weight to bear. The groan of wood became a cracking, rending sound. The tanker slowed as the bridge subsided, its wheels spun without purchase, it tilted sideways, no longer moving forward.

A sharp report, as one of the main trusses broke, and Bruce felt the tanker drop sharply at the rear; its nose pointed upwards and it started to slide back.

"Get out!" his brain shrieked at him. "Get out, its falling!" He reached for the door handle beside him, but at that moment the bridge collapsed completely. The tanker rolled off the edge.

Bruce was hurled across the cab with a force that stunned him; his legs wedged under the passenger seat and his arms tangled in the strap of his rifle. The tanker fell free, and Bruce felt his stomach swoop up and press against his chest as though he rode a giant roller coaster.

The sickening drop lasted only an instant, and then the tanker hit the river. Immediately the sounds of gunfire and the screaming of Baluba were drowned out as the tanker disappeared below the surface. Through the windscreen Bruce saw now the cool cloudy green of water, as though he looked into the window of an aquarium. With a gentle rocking motion the tanker sank down through the green water.

"Oh, my God, not this!" He spoke aloud as he struggled up from the floor of the cab. His ears were filled with the hiss and belch of escaping air bubbles; they rose in silver clouds past the windows.

The truck was still sinking, and Bruce felt the pain in his eardrums as the pressure built up inside the cab. He opened his mouth and swallowed convulsively, and his eardrums squeaked as the pressure equalized and the pain abated. Water was squirting in through the floor of the cab and jets of it spurted out of the instrument panel of the dashboard. The cab was flooding.

Bruce twisted the handle of the door beside him and hit it with his shoulder. It would not budge an inch. He flung all his weight against it, anchoring his feet on the dashboard and straining until he felt his eyeballs starting out of their sockets. It was jammed solid by the immense pressure of water on the outside.

"The windscreen," he shouted aloud. "Break the windscreen." He groped for his rifle. The cab had flooded to his waist as he sat in the passenger's seat. He found the rifle and brought it dripping to his shoulder. He touched the muzzle to the windscreen and almost fired. But his good sense warned him.

Clearly he saw the danger of firing. The concussion in the confined cab would burst his eardrums, and the avalanche of broken glass that would be thrown into his face by the water pressure outside would certainly blind and maim him.

He lowered the rifle despondently. He felt his panic being slowly replaced by the cold certainty of defeat. He was trapped fifty feet below the surface of the river. There was no way out.

He thought of turning the rifle on himself, ending the inevitable, but he rejected the idea almost as soon as it had formed. Not that way, never that way!

He flogged his mind, driving it out of the cold lethargic clutch of certain death. There must be something. Think! Damn you, think!

The tanker was still rocking; it had not yet settled into the ooze of the river bottom. How long had he been under? About twenty seconds. Surely it should have hit the bottom long ago.

Unless! Bruce felt hope surge into new life within him. The tank! By God, that was it.

The great, almost empty tank behind him! The five-thousand-gallon tank which now contained only four hundred gallons of gasoline—it would have a displacement of nearly eighteen tons! It would float.

As if in confirmation of his hope, he felt his eardrums creak and pop. The pressure was falling! He was rising.

Bruce stared out at green water through the glass. The silver clouds of bubbles no longer streamed upwards; they seemed to hang outside the cab. The tanker had overcome the initial impetus that had driven it far below the surface, and now it was floating upwards at the same rate of ascent as its bubbles.

The dark green of deep water paled slowly to the colour of chartreuse. And Bruce laughed. It was a gasping, hysterical giggle and the sound of it shocked him. He cut it off abruptly.

The tanker bobbed out onto the surface, water streamed from the windscreen, and through it Bruce caught a misty distorted glimpse of the south bank.

He twisted the door handle, and this time the door burst open readily, water poured into the cab and Bruce floundered out against its rush.

With one quick glance he took in his position. The tanker had floated down twenty yards below the bridge, the guns on the south bank had fallen silent, and he could see no Baluba on the north bank. They must have disappeared back into the jungle.

Bruce plunged into the river and struck out for the south bank. Vaguely he heard the thin high shouts of encouragement from his gendarmes.

Within a dozen strokes he knew he was in difficulties. The drag of his boots and his sodden uniform was enormous. Treading water, he tore off his steel helmet and let it sink. Then he tried to struggle out of his battle jacket. It clung to his arms and chest and he disappeared under the surface four times before he finally got rid of it. He had breathed water into his lungs and his legs were tired and heavy.

The south bank was too far away. He would never make it. Coughing painfully, he changed his objective and struck upstream against the current towards the bridge.

He felt himself settling lower in the water; he had to force his arms to lift and fall forward into each stroke.

Something plopped into the water close beside him. He paid no attention to it; suddenly a sense of disinterest had come over him, the first stage of drowning. He mistimed a breath and sucked in more water. The pain of it goaded him into a fresh burst of coughing. He hung in the water, gasping and hacking painfully.

Again something plopped close by, and this time he lifted his head. An arrow floated past him; then they began dropping steadily around him.

Baluba hidden in the thick bush above the beach were shooting at him; a gentle pattering rain of arrows splashed around his head. Bruce started swimming again, clawing his way frantically upstream. He swam until he could no longer lift his arms clear of the surface, and the weight of his boots dragged his feet down.

Again he lifted his head. The bridge was close, not thirty feet away, but he knew that those thirty feet were as good as thirty miles. He could not make it.

The arrows that fell about him were no longer a source of terror. He thought of them only with mild irritation.

Why the hell can't they leave me alone? I don't want to play any more. I just want to relax. I'm so tired, so terribly tired.

He stopped moving and felt the water rise up coolly over his mouth and nose.

"Hold on, boss. I'm coming!"

The shout penetrated through the grey fog of Bruce's drowning brain. He kicked, and his head rose once more above the surface. He looked up at the bridge.

Stark naked, big belly swinging with each pace, thick legs flying, the great dangling bunch of his genitals bouncing merrily, black as a charging hippopotamus, Sergeant Major Ruffararo galloped out along the bridge.

He reached the fallen section and hauled himself up onto the guard rail. The arrows were falling around him, hissing down like angry insects. One glanced off his shoulder without penetrating and Ruffy shrugged at it, then launched himself up and out, falling in an ungainly heap of arms and legs to hit the water with a splash.

"Where the hell are you, boss?"

Bruce croaked a water-strangled reply, and Ruffy came plowing down towards him with clumsy overarm strokes.

He reached Bruce. "Always playing around," he grunted. "Guess some guys never learn!" His fist closed on a handful of Bruce's hair.

Struggling unavailingly, Bruce felt his head tucked firmly under Ruffy's arm and he was dragged through the water. Occasionally his face came out long enough to suck a breath, but mostly he was underwater. Consciousness receded and he felt himself going, going.

His head bumped against something hard but he was too weak to reach out his hand.

"Wake up, boss. You can have a sleep later," Ruffy's voice bellowed in his ear. He opened his eyes and saw beside him the pile of the bridge.

"Come on. I can't carry you up here."

Ruffy had worked round the side of the pile, shielding them from arrows, but the current was strong here, tugging at their bodies. Without the strength to prevent it, Bruce's head rolled sideways and his face flopped forward into the water.

"Come on, wake up." With a stinging slap Ruffy's open hand hit Bruce across the cheek. The shock roused him, he coughed, and a mixture of water and vomit shot up his throat and out of his mouth and nose. Then he belched painfully and retched again.

"How's it feel now?" Ruffy demanded.

Bruce lifted a hand from the water and wiped his mouth. He felt much better.

"Okay? Can you make it?"

Bruce nodded.

"Let's go then."

With Ruffy dragging and pushing him, he worked his way up the pile. Water poured from his clothing as his body emerged, his hair was plastered across his forehead and he could feel each breath gurgle in his lungs.

"Listen, boss. When we get to the top we'll be in the open again. There'll be more arrows—no time to sit around and chat. We're going over the rail fast and then run like hell—okay?"

Bruce nodded again. Above him were the floorboards of the bridge. With one hand he reached up and caught an upright of the guard rail, and he hung there without strength to pull himself the rest of the way.

"Hold it there," grunted Ruffy and wiggled his shiny wet bulk up and over.

The arrows started falling again; one pegged into the wood six inches from Bruce's face and stood there quivering. Slowly Bruce's grip relaxed. I can't hold on, he thought, I'm going.

Then Ruffy's hand closed on his wrist, he felt himself dragged up, his legs dangled. He hung suspended by one arm and the water swirled smoothly past twenty feet below.

Slowly he was drawn upwards, his chest scraped over the guard rail, tearing his shirt, then he tumbled over it into an untidy heap on the bridge.

Vaguely he heard the guns firing on the south bank, the flit and thump of the arrows, and Ruffy's voice.

"Come on, boss. Get up."

He felt himself being lifted and dragged along. With his legs boneless soft under him, he staggered beside Ruffy. Then there were no more arrows; the timbers of the bridge became solid earth under his feet. Voices, and hands on him. He was being lifted, then lowered face down onto the wooden floor of a truck. The rhythmic pressure on his chest as someone started artificial respiration above him, the warm gush of water up his throat, and Shermaine's voice. He could not understand what she was saying, but just the sound of it was enough to make him realize he was safe. Darkly through the fog he became aware that her voice was the most important sound in his life.

He vomited again.

Hesitantly at first, and then swiftly, Bruce came back from the edge of oblivion.

"That's enough," he mumbled and rolled out from under Sergeant Jacque, who was administering the artificial respiration. The movement started a fresh paroxysm of coughing, and he felt Shermaine's hands on his shoulders restraining him.

"Bruce, you must rest."

"No." He struggled into a sitting position. "We've got to get out into the open," he said, gasping.

"No hurry, boss. We've left all the Balubes on the other bank. There's a river between us."

"How do you know?" Bruce challenged him.

"Well—"

"You don't!" Bruce told him flatly. "There could easily be another few hundred on this side." He coughed again painfully and then went on. "We're leaving in five minutes, get them ready."

"Okay." Ruffy turned to leave.

"Ruffy!"

"Boss?" He turned back expectantly.

"Thank you."

Ruffy grinned self-consciously. " 'At's all right. I needed a wash anyway."

"I'll buy you a drink when we get home."

"I won't forget," Ruffy warned him and climbed down out of the truck. Bruce heard him shouting to his boys.

"I thought I'd lost you." Shermaine's arm was still around his shoulders, and Bruce looked at her for the first time.

"My sweet girl, you won't get rid of me that easily," he assured her. He was feeling much better now.

"Bruce, I want to—I can't explain—" Unable to find the

words, she leaned forward instead and kissed him, full on the mouth.

When they drew apart, Sergeant Jacque and the two gendarmes with him were grinning delightedly.

"There is nothing wrong with you now, Captain."

"No, there isn't" Bruce agreed. "Make your preparations for departure."

From the passenger seat of the Ford, Bruce took one last look at the bridge.

The repaired section hung like a broken drawbridge into the water. Beyond it on the far bank were scattered a few dead Baluba, like celluloid dolls in the sunlight. Far downstream the gasoline tanker had been washed by the current against the beach. It lay on its side, half submerged in the shallows, and the Shell insignia showed clearly.

And the river flowed on, green and inscrutable, with the jungle pressing close along its banks.

"Let's get away from here," said Bruce.

Shermaine started the engine, and the convoy of trucks followed them along the track through the belt of thick river bush and into the open forest again.

Bruce looked at his watch. The inside of the glass was dewed with moisture and he lifted it to his ear. "Damn thing has stopped. What's your time?"

"Twenty minutes to one."

"Half the day wasted," Bruce grumbled.

"Will we reach Msapa Junction before dark?"

"No, we won't. For two good reasons. First, it's too far, and second, we haven't enough gas."

"What are you going to do?" Her voice was unruffled; already she had complete faith in him.

I wonder how long it will last, he mused cynically. *At first you're a god. You have not a single human weakness. They set a standard for you, and the standard is perfection. Then the first time you fall short of it, their whole world blows up.*

"We'll think of something," he assured her.

"I'm sure you will," she agreed complacently, and Bruce grinned. The big joke, of course, was that when she said it he also believed it. Damned if being in love didn't make you feel one hell of a man.

He changed to English so as to exclude the two gendarmes in the back seat from the conversation.

"You are the best thing that has happened to me in thirty years."

"Oh, Bruce." She turned her face towards him, and the expression of trusting love in it and the intensity of his own emotion struck Bruce like a physical blow.

I will keep this thing alive, he vowed. *I must nourish it with care and protect it from the dangers of selfishness and familiarity.*

"Oh, Bruce, I do love you so terribly much. This morning when—when I thought I had lost you, when I saw the tanker go over into the river—" She swallowed and now her eyes were full of tears. "It was as though the light had gone—it was so dark, so dark and cold without you."

So absorbed with him that she forgot about the road, Shermaine let the Ford veer and the offside wheels pumped into the rough verge.

"Hey, watch it!" Bruce cautioned her. "Dearly as I love you also, I have to admit you're a lousy driver. Let me take her."

"Do you feel up to it?"

"Yes, pull into the side."

Slowly, held to the speed of the lumbering vehicles behind them, they drove on through the afternoon. Twice they passed deserted Baluba villages beside the road, the grass huts disintegrating and the small cultivated lands about them thickly overgrown.

"My God, I'm hungry. I've got a headache from it, and my belly feels as though it's full of warm water," complained Bruce.

"Don't think you're the only one. This is the strictest diet I've ever been on—must have lost two kilos! But I always lose in the wrong place, never on my bottom."

"Good," Bruce said. "I like it just the way it is—never shed an ounce there." He looked over his shoulder at the two gendarmes. "Are you hungry?" he asked in French.

"*Mon Dieu!*" exclaimed the fat one. "I will not be able to sleep tonight if I must lie on an empty stomach."

"Perhaps it will not be necessary." Bruce let his eyes wander off the road into the surrounding bush. The character of the country had changed in the last hundred miles. "This looks like game country. I've noticed plenty of spoor on the road. Keep your eyes open."

The trees were tall and widely spaced with grass growing beneath them. Their branches did not interlock so that the sky showed through. At intervals there were open glades filled with green swamp grass and thickets of bamboo and ivory palms.

"We've got another half hour of daylight. We might run into something before then."

In the rear-view mirror he watched the lumbering column of transports for a moment. They must be almost out of gasoline by now, hardly enough for another half hour's driving. There were compensations however; at least they were in open country now and only eighty miles from Msapa Junction.

He glanced at the petrol gauge—half the tank. The Ranchero still had sufficient to get through even if the trucks were almost dry.

Of course! That was the answer. Find a good camp, leave the convoy, and go on in the Ford to find help. Without the trucks to slow him down he could get through to Msapa Junction in two hours. There was a telegraph in the station office, even if the junction was still deserted.

"We'll stop on the other side of this stream," said Bruce and slowed the Ford, changed into second gear, and let it idle down the steep bank.

The stream was shallow. The water hardly reached the hubcaps as they bumped across the rocky bottom. Bruce gunned the Ford up the far bank into the forest again.

"There!" shouted one of the gendarmes from the back seat, and Bruce followed the direction of his arm.

Standing with humped shoulders, close beside the road,

bunched together with mournfully drooping horns, heads held low beneath the massive bosses, bodies very big and black, were two old buffalo bulls.

Bruce hit the brakes, skidding the Ranchero to a stop, reaching for his rifle at the same instant. He twisted the door handle, hit the door with his shoulder, and tumbled out onto his feet.

With a snort and a toss of their ungainly heads the buffalo started to run.

Bruce picked the leader and aimed for the neck in front of the plunging black shoulder. Leaning forward against the recoil of the rifle, he fired and heard the bullet strike with a meaty thump. The bull slowed, breaking his run. The stubby forelegs settled and he slid forward on his nose, rolling as he fell, dust and legs kicking.

Turning smoothly without taking the butt from his shoulder, swinging with the run of the second bull, Bruce fired again, and again the thump of bullet striking.

The buffalo stumbled, giving in the legs, then he steadied and galloped on like a grotesque rocking horse, patches of baldness grey on his flanks, big-bellied, running heavily.

Bruce shifted the bead of the foresight onto his shoulder and fired twice in quick succession, aiming low for the heart, hitting each time, the bull so close he could see the bullet wounds appear on the dark skin. The gallop broke into a trot; head swinging low, mouth open, legs beginning to fold. Aiming carefully for the head, Bruce fired again. The bull bellowed, a sad lonely sound, and collapsed onto the grass.

The trucks had stopped in a line behind the Ford, and now from each of them swarmed black men. Jabbering happily, racing each other, they streamed past Bruce to where the buffalo had fallen in the grass beside the road.

"Nice shooting, boss," applauded Ruffy. "I'm going to have me a piece of tripe the size of a blanket."

"Let's make camp first." Bruce's ears were still singing with gunfire. "Get the trucks into a ring."

"I'll see to it."

Bruce walked up to the nearest buffalo and watched for a

while as a dozen men strained to roll it onto its back and begin butchering it. There were clusters of grape-blue ticks in the folds of skin between the legs and body.

A good head, he noted mechanically, forty inches at least.

"Plenty of meat, Captain. Tonight we eat thick!" said one of his gendarmes, grinning as he bent over the huge body to begin flensing.

"Plenty," agreed Bruce and turned back to the Ranchero. In the heat of the kill it is a good feeling: the rifle's kick and your stomach screwed up with excitement. But afterwards you feel a little bit dirtied; sad and guilty, as you do after lying with a woman you do not love.

He climbed into the car, and Shermaine sat away from him, withdrawn.

"They were so big and ugly—beautiful," she said softly.

"We needed the meat. I didn't kill them for fun." But he thought with a little shame, I have killed many others for fun.

"Yes," she agreed. "We needed the meat."

He turned the car off the road and signalled to the truck drivers to pull in behind him.

27

Later it was all right again: the meat-rich smoke from a dozen cooking fires drifting across the camp, the dark treetops silhouetted against a sky full of stars, the friendly glow of the fires, and laughter, men's voices raised, someone singing, the night noises of the bush—insects and frogs in the nearby stream —a plate piled high with grilled fillets and slabs of liver, a bottle of beer from Ruffy's hoard, the air at last cooler, a small breeze to keep the mosquitoes away, and Shermaine sitting beside him on the blankets.

Ruffy drifted across to them, in one hand a stick loaded with meat from which the juice dripped, and in the other hand a bottle held by the throat.

"How's it for another beer, boss?"

"Enough." Bruce held up his hand. "I'm full to the back teeth."

"You're getting old, that's for sure. Me and the boys going to finish them buffalo or burst trying." He squatted on his great haunches and his tone changed. "The trucks are flat, boss. Reckon there's not a bucketful of gas in the lot of them."

"I want you to drain all the tanks, Ruffy, and pour it into the Ford."

Ruffy nodded and bit a hunk of meat off the end of the stick.

"Then first thing tomorrow morning you and I will go on to Msapa in the Ranchero and leave everyone else here. Lieutenant Hendry will be in charge."

"You talking about me?" Wally came from one of the fires.

"Yes. I'm going to leave you in charge here while Ruffy and I go on to Msapa Junction to fetch help." Bruce did not look at Hendry, and he had difficulty keeping the loathing out of his voice. "Ruffy, fetch the map will you?"

They spread it on the earth and huddled around it. Ruffy held the flashlight.

"I'd say we are about here." Bruce touched the tiny black vein of the road. "About seventy, eighty miles to Msapa." He ran his finger along it. "It will take us about five hours there and back. However, if the telegraph isn't working we might have to go on until we meet a patrol or find some other way of getting a message back to Elisabethville."

Almost parallel to the road and only two inches from it on the large-scale map ran the thick red line that marked the Northern Rhodesian border. Wally Hendry's slitty eyes narrowed even further as he looked at it.

"Why not leave Ruffy here, and I'll go with you." Hendry looked up at Bruce.

"I want Ruffy with me to translate if we meet any Africans along the way." Also, thought Bruce, I don't want to be left on the side of the road with a bullet in my head while you drive on to Elisabethville.

"Suits me," grunted Hendry. He dropped his eyes to the map. About forty miles to the border. A hard day's walk.

Bruce changed to French and spoke swiftly. "Ruffy, hide the diamonds behind the dashboard of your truck. That way we are certain they will send a rescue party even if we have to go to Elisabethville."

"Talk English, bucko," growled Hendry, but Ruffy nodded and answered, also in French, "I will leave Sergeant Jacque to guard them."

"*No!*" said Bruce. "Tell no one."

"Cut it out!" rasped Hendry. "Anything you say I want to hear."

"We'll leave at dawn tomorrow." Bruce reverted to English.

"May I go with you?" Shermaine spoke for the first time.

"I don't see why not." Bruce smiled quickly at her, but Ruffy coughed awkwardly.

"Reckon that's not such a good idea, boss."

"Why?" Bruce turned on him, his temper starting to rise.

"Well, boss"—Ruffy hesitated, then went on—"you, me, and

the lady all shoving off towards Elisabethville might not look so good to the boys. They might get ideas, think we're not coming back or something."

Bruce was silent, considering it.

"That's right," Hendry cut in. "You might just take it into your head to keep going. Let her stay, sort of guarantee for the rest of us."

"I don't mind, Bruce. I didn't think about it that way. I'll stay."

"She'll have our boys to look after her, she'll be all right," Ruffy assured Bruce.

"All right then, that's settled. It won't be for long, Shermaine."

"I'll go and see about draining the trucks." Ruffy stood up. "See you in the morning, boss."

"I'm going to get some more of that meat." Wally picked up the map carelessly. "Try and get some sleep tonight, Curry. Not too much grumble and grunt."

In his exasperation Bruce did not notice that Hendry had taken the map.

28

It rained in the early hours before the dawn, and Bruce lay in the back of the Ranchero and listened to it drum on the metal roof. It was a lulling sound, and a good feeling to lie warmly listening to the rain with the woman you love in your arms.

He felt her waking against him, the change in her breathing and the first slow movements of her body.

There were buffalo steaks for breakfast but no coffee. They ate swiftly, and then Bruce called across to Ruffy. "Okay, Ruffy?"

"Let's go, boss."

They climbed into the Ford, and Ruffy filled most of the seat beside Bruce. His helmet perched on the back of his head, rifle sticking out through the space where the windscreen should have been, and two large feet planted securely on top of the case of beer on the floor.

Bruce twisted the key and the engine fired. He warmed it at a fast idle and turned to Hendry, who was leaning against the roof of the Ford and peering through the window. "We'll be back this afternoon. Don't let anybody wander away from camp."

"Okay." Hendry breathed his morning breath full into Bruce's face.

"Keep them busy, otherwise they'll get bored and start fighting."

Before he answered Hendry let his eyes search the interior of the Ford carefully and then he stood back. "Okay," he said again. "On your way!"

Bruce looked beyond him to where Shermaine sat on the tailboard of a truck and smiled at her.

"Bon voyage!" she called, and Bruce let out the clutch.

They bumped out onto the road amid a chorus of cheerful

farewells from the gendarmes around the cooking fires, and Bruce settled down to drive. In the rear-view mirror he watched the camp disappear around the curve in the road. There were puddles of rain water in the road, but above them the clouds had broken up and scattered across the sky.

"How's it for a beer, boss?"

"Instead of coffee?" asked Bruce.

"Nothing like it for the bowels," grunted Ruffy and reached down to open the case.

Wally Hendry lifted his helmet and scratched his scalp. His short red hair felt stiff and wiry with dried sweat, and there was a spot above his right ear that itched. He fingered it tenderly.

The Ranchero disappeared around a bend in the road, the trees screening it abruptly, and the hum of its motor faded.

Okay, so they haven't taken the diamonds with them. I had a bloody good look around. I guessed they'd leave them. The girl knows where they are like as not. Perhaps—no, she'd squeal like a stuck pig if I asked.

Hendry looked sideways at Shermaine; she was staring after the Ranchero.

Silly bitch! Getting all broody now that Curry's giving her the rod. Funny how these educated johnnies like their women to have small tits—nice piece of arse though. Wouldn't mind a bit of that myself. Jesus, that would really get to Mr. High-Class Bloody Curry, me giving his pretty the business. Not a chance though. These niggers think he's a God or something. They'd tear me to pieces if I touched her. Forget about it! Let's get the diamonds and take off for the border.

Hendry settled his helmet back on his head and strolled casually across to the truck that Ruffy had been driving the day before.

Got a map, compass, coupla spare clips of ammo—now all we need is the glass.

He climbed into the cab and opened the cubbyhole.

Bet a pound to a pinch of dung that they've hidden them somewhere in this truck. They're not worried—think they've got me tied up here. Never occurred to them that old Uncle Wally might up and walk away. Thought I'd just sit here and wait for them to come back and fetch me—take me in and hand me over to a bunch of nigger police aching to get their hands on a white man.

Well, I got news for you, Mr. Fancy-talking Curry!

He rummaged in the cubbyhole and then slammed it shut.

Okay, they're not there. Let's try under the seats. The border is not guarded, might take me three or four days to get through to Fort Rosebery, but when I do I'll have me a pocketful of diamonds, and there's a direct air service out to Ndola and the rest of the world. Then we start living!

There was nothing under the seats except a greasy dust-coated jack and wheel spanner. Hendry turned his attention to the floorboards.

Pity I'll have to leave that bastard Curry. I had plans for him. There's a guy who really gets to me. So goddam cocksure of himself. One of them. Makes you feel you're shit—fancy talk, pretty face, soft hands. Christ, I hate him.

Viciously he tore the rubber mats off the floor, and the dust made him cough.

Been to university, makes him think he's something special. The bastard. I should have fixed him long ago—that night at the road bridge I nearly gave it to him in the dark. Nobody would have known, just a mistake. I shoulda done it then. I shoulda done it at Port Reprieve when he ran out across the road to the office block. Big bloody hero. Big lover. Bet he had everything he ever wanted, bet his Daddy gave him all the money he could use. And he looks at you like that, like you crawled out of rotting meat.

Hendry straightened up and gripped the steering wheel, his jaws chewing with the strength of his hatred. He stared out of the windscreen.

Shermaine Cartier walked past the front of the truck. She had a towel and a pink plastic toilet bag in her hand; the pistol swung against her leg as she moved.

Sergeant Jacque stood up from the cooking fire and moved

to intercept her. They talked, arguing, then Shermaine touched the pistol at her side and laughed. A worried frown creased Jacque's black face, and he shook his head dubiously. Shermaine laughed again, turned from him, and set off down the road towards the stream. Her hair, caught carelessly at her neck with a ribbon, hung down her back onto the rose-coloured shirt she wore, and the heavy canvas holster emphasized the unconsciously provocative swing of her hips. She went out of sight down the steep bank of the stream.

Wally Hendry chuckled and then licked his lips with the quick-darting tip of his tongue. "This is going to make it perfect," he whispered. "They couldn't have done things to suit me better if they'd spent a week working it out."

Eagerly he turned back to his search for the diamonds. Leaning forward, he thrust his hand up behind the dashboard of the truck, and it brushed against the bunch of canvas bags that hung from the mass of concealed wires.

"Come to Uncle Wally." He jerked them loose and, holding them in his lap, began checking their contents. The third bag he opened contained the gem stones.

"Lovely, lovely grub," he whispered at the dull glint and sparkle in the depths of the bag. Then he closed the drawstring, stuffed the bag into the pocket of his battle jacket and buttoned the flap. He dropped the bags of industrial diamonds onto the floor and kicked them under the seat, picked up his rifle, and stepped down out of the truck.

Three or four gendarmes looked up curiously at him as he passed the cooking fires. Hendry rubbed his stomach and pulled a face.

"Too much meat last night!"

The gendarme who understood English laughed and translated into French. They all laughed, and one of them called something in a dialect that Hendry did not understand. They watched him walk away among the trees.

As soon as he was out of sight of the camp Hendry started to run, circling back towards the stream.

"This is going to be a pleasure!" He laughed aloud.

29

Fifty yards below the drift where the road crossed the stream Shermaine found a shallow pool. There were reeds with fluffy heads around it and a small beach of white river sand, black boulders, polished round and glossy smooth, the water almost blood warm and so clear that she could see a shoal of fingerlings nibbling at the green algae that coated the boulders beneath the surface.

She stood barefooted in the sand and looked around carefully, but the reeds screened her, and she had asked Jacque not to let any of his men come down to the river while she was there.

She undressed, dropped her clothes across one of the black boulders, and with a cake of soap in her hand waded out into the pool and lowered herself until she sat with the water up to her neck and the sand pleasantly rough under her naked behind.

She washed her hair first and then lay stretched out with the water moving gently over her, soft as the caress of silk. Growing bold, the tiny fish darted in and nibbled at her skin, tickling, so that she gasped and splashed at them.

At last she ducked her head under the surface, and then, with the water streaming out of her hair into her eyes, she groped her way back to the bank.

As she stooped, still half blinded, for her towel, Wally Hendry's hand closed over her mouth and his other arm circled her waist from behind.

"One squeak out of you and I'll wring your bloody neck." He spoke hoarsely into her ear. She could smell his breath, warm and sour in her face. "Just pretend I'm old Bruce—then both of us will enjoy it." And he chuckled.

Sliding quickly over her hip, his hand moved downwards,

and the shock of it galvanized her into frantic struggles. Holding her easily, Hendry kept on chuckling.

She opened her mouth suddenly and one of his fingers went in between her teeth. She bit with all her strength and felt the skin break and tasted blood in her mouth.

"You bitch!" Hendry jerked his hand away and she opened her mouth to scream, but the hand swung back, clenched, into the side of her face, knocking her head across. The scream never reached her lips for he hit her again and she felt herself falling.

Stunned by the blows, lying in the sand, she could not believe it was happening until she felt his weight upon her and his knee forced cruelly between hers.

Then she started to struggle again, trying to twist away from his mouth and the smell of his breath. "No, no, no." She repeated it over and over, her eyes shut tightly so she did not have to see that face above her, and her head rolling from side to side in the sand. He was so strong, so immensely powerful.

"No," she said, and then, "Ooah!" at the pain, the tearing, stinging pain within and the thrusting heaviness above. And through the pounding, grunting, thrusting nightmare she could smell him and feel the sweat drip from him and splash into her upturned unprotected face.

It lasted forever, and then suddenly the weight was gone and she opened her eyes.

He stood over her, fumbling with his clothing, and there was a dullness in his expression. He wiped his mouth with the back of his hand and she saw the fingers were trembling. His voice when he spoke was tired and disinterested. "I've had better."

Swiftly Shermaine rolled over and reached for the pistol that lay on top of her clothes. Hendry stepped forward with all his weight on her wrist, and she felt the bones bend under his boot and she moaned. But through pain she whispered, "You pig, you filthy pig," and he hit her again, flat-handed across the face, knocking her onto her back once more.

He picked up the pistol and opened it, spilling the cartridges into the sand, then he unclipped the lanyard and threw the pistol far out into the reed bed.

"Tell Curry I say he can have my share of you," he said and walked quickly away among the reeds.

The white sand coated her damp body like sugar icing. She sat up slowly holding her wrist, the side of her face inflamed and starting to swell where he had hit her.

She started to cry, shaking silently, and the tears squeezed out between her eyelids and matted her long dark lashes.

30

Ruffy held up the brown bottle and inspected it ruefully. "Seems like one mouthful and it's empty." He threw the bottle out of the side window. It hit a tree and burst with a small pop.

"We can always find our way back by following the empties." Bruce smiled, once more marveling at the man's capacity. But there was plenty of storage space. He watched Ruffy's stomach spread onto his lap as he reached down to the beer crate.

"How we doing, boss?"

Bruce glanced at the milometer. "We've come eighty-seven miles."

Ruffy nodded. "Not bad going. Be there pretty soon now."

They were silent. The wind blew in on them through the open front. The grass that grew between the tracks brushed the bottom of the chassis with a continuous rushing sound.

"Boss—" Ruffy spoke at last.

"Yes?"

"Lieutenant Hendry—those diamonds. You reckon we did a good thing leaving him there?"

"He's stranded in the middle of the bush. Even if he did find them they wouldn't do him much good."

"Suppose that's right." Ruffy lifted the beer bottle to his lips and when he lowered it he went on. "Mind you, that's one guy you can never be sure of." He tapped his head with a finger as thick and as black as a blood sausage. "Something wrong with him—he's one of the maddest Arabs I've found in a long time of looking."

Bruce grunted grimly.

"You want to be careful there, boss," observed Ruffy. "Any time now he's going to try for you. I've seen it coming. He's working himself up to it. He's a mad Arab."

"I'll watch him," said Bruce.

"Yeah, you do that."

Again they were silent in the steady swish of the wind and the drone of the motor.

"There's the railway." Ruffy pointed to the blue-gravelled embankment through the trees.

"Nearly there," said Bruce.

They came out into another open glade, and beyond it the water tank at Msapa Junction stuck up above the forest.

"Here we are," said Ruffy and drained the bottle in his hand.

"Just say a prayer that the telegraph lines are still up and that there's an operator on the Elisabethville end."

Bruce slowed the Ford past the row of cottages. They were exactly as he remembered them, deserted and forlorn. The corners of his mouth were compressed into a hard angle as he looked at the two small mounds of earth beneath the cassia flora trees. Ruffy looked at them also but neither of them spoke.

Bruce stopped the Ford outside the station building and they climbed out stiffly and walked together onto the veranda. The wooden flooring echoed dully under their boots as they made for the door of the office.

Bruce pushed the door open and looked in. The walls were painted a depressing utility green, loose paper was scattered on the floor, the drawers of the single desk hung open, and a thin grey skin of dust coated everything.

"There she is," said Ruffy and pointed to the brass and varnished wood complexity of the telegraph on a table against the far wall.

"Looks all right," said Bruce. "As long as the lines haven't been cut."

As if to reassure him, the telegraph began to clatter like a typewriter.

"Thank God for that," Bruce sighed.

They walked across to the table.

"You know how to work this thing?" asked Ruffy.

"Sort of," Bruce answered and set his rifle against the wall. He was relieved to see a Morse table stuck with adhesive tape to the wall above the apparatus. It was a long time since he had memorized it as a Boy Scout.

He laid his hand on the transmission key and studied the table. The call sign for Elisabethville was "EE."

He tapped it out clumsily. Almost immediately the set clattered back at him, much too fast to be intelligible, and the roll of paper in the repeater was exhausted. Bruce took off his helmet and laboriously spelled out, "Transmit slower."

It was a long business, with requests for repetition. "Not understood" was made nearly every second signal, but finally Bruce got the operator to understand that he had an urgent message for Colonel Franklyn of President Tshombe's staff.

"Wait," came back the laconic signal.

And they waited. They waited an hour, then two.

"That mad bastard's forgotten about us," grumbled Ruffy and went to the Ford to fetch the beer crate. Bruce fidgeted restlessly on the unpadded chair beside the telegraph table. He reconsidered anxiously all his previous arguments for leaving Wally Hendry in charge of the camp, but once again decided that it was safe. He couldn't do much harm. Unless, unless Shermaine! No, it was impossible. Not with loyal gendarmes to protect her.

He started to think about Shermaine and the future. There was a year's mercenary captain's pay accumulated in the Crédit Banque Suisse at Zurich. He made the conversion from francs to pounds—about two and a half thousand. Two years' operating capital, so they could have a holiday before he started working again. They could take a chalet up in the mountains— there should be good snow this time of the year.

Bruce grinned—snow that crunched like sugar and a twelve-inch-thick eiderdown on the bed at night.

Life had purpose and direction again.

"What you laughing at, boss?" asked Ruffy.

"I was thinking about a bed."

"Yeah? That's a good thing to think about. You start there, you're born there, you spend most of your life in it, you have plenty of fun in it, and if you're lucky you die there. How's it for a beer?"

The telegraph came to life at Bruce's elbow. He turned to it.

"Curry . . . Franklyn," it clattered. Bruce could imagine the wiry, red-faced little man at the other end: ex-major in the third brigade of the Legion; a prime mover in the O.A.S., with a sizeable price still on his head from the de Gaulle assassination attempt.

"Franklyn . . . Curry," Bruce tapped back. "Train unserviceable. Motorized transport stranded without fuel. Port Reprieve road. Map reference approx . . ." He read the numbers off the sheet on which he had noted them.

There was a long pause, then, "Is U.M.C. property in your hands?" The question was delicately phrased.

"Affirmative," Bruce assured him.

"Await air-drop at your position soonest. Out."

"Message understood. Out." Bruce straightened from the telegraph and sighed with relief. "That's that, Ruffy. They'll drop gas to us from one of the Dakotas. Probably tomorrow morning." He looked at his wrist watch. "Twenty to twelve. Let's get back."

Bruce hummed softly, watching the double tracks ahead of him, guiding the Ford with a light touch on the wheel.

He was contented. It was all over. Tomorrow the fuel would drop from the Dakota under those yellow parachutes. He must lay out the smudge signals this evening. And ten hours later they would be back in Elisabethville.

A few words with Carl Engelbrecht would fix seats for Shermaine and himself on one of the outward-bound Daks. Then Switzerland, and the chalet with icicles hanging from the eaves. A long rest while he decided where to start again. Louisiana was under Roman–Dutch Law, or was it Code Napoléon? He might even have to take another bar examination, but the prospect pleased rather than dismayed him. It was fun again.

"Never seen you so happy," grunted Ruffy.

"Never had so much cause," Bruce agreed.

"She's a swell lady. Young still—you can teach her."

Bruce felt his hackles rise, and then he thought better of it and laughed.

"You going to sign her up, boss?"

"I might."

Ruffy nodded wisely. "Man should have plenty wives—I got three. Need a couple more."

"One I could only just handle."

"One's difficult. Two's easier. Three, you can relax. Four, they're so busy with each other they don't give you no trouble at all."

"I might try it."

"Yeah, you do that."

And ahead of them through the trees they saw the ring of trucks.

"We're home," grunted Ruffy, then he stirred uncomfortably in his seat. "Something going on."

Men stood in small groups. There was something in their attitude: strain, apprehension. Two men ran up the road to meet them. Bruce could see their mouths working but could not hear the words.

Dread, heavy and cold, pushed down on the pit of Bruce's gut.

Gabbling, incoherent, Sergeant Jacque was trying to tell him something as he ran beside the Ford.

"Tenente Hendry—the river—the madame—gone." French words like driftwood in the torrent of dialect.

"Your girl," translated Ruffy. "Hendry's done her."

"Dead?" The question dropped from Bruce's mouth.

"No. He's hurt her. He's—you know!"

"Where is she?"

"They've got her in the back of the truck."

Bruce climbed heavily out of the car. Now they were silent, grouped together, not looking at him, faces impassive, waiting.

Bruce walked slowly to the truck. He felt cold and numb. His legs moved automatically beneath him. He drew back the canvas and pulled himself up into the interior. It was an effort to move forward, to focus his eyes in the gloom.

Wrapped in a blanket, she lay small and still.

"Shermaine . . ." It stuck in his throat.

"Shermaine," he said again and knelt beside her. A great livid swelling distorted the side of her face. She did not turn her head to him but lay staring up at the canvas roof.

He touched her face and the skin was cold, cold as the dread that gripped his stomach. The coldness of it shocked him so he jerked his hand away.

"Shermaine . . ." This time it was a sob. The eyes, her big haunted eyes, turned unseeing towards him, and he felt the lift of escape from the certainty of her death.

"Oh, God," he cried and took her to him, holding the unresisting frailty of her to his chest. He could feel the slow even thump of her heart beneath his hand. He drew back the blanket and there was no blood.

"Darling, are you hurt? Tell me, are you hurt?" She did not answer. She lay quietly in his arms, not seeing him.

"Shock," he whispered. "It's only shock," and he opened her clothing. With tenderness he examined the smoothly pale body; the skin was clammy and damp, but there was no damage.

He wrapped her again and laid her gently back down on the floor.

He stood, and the thing within him changed shape. Cold still, but now burning cold as dry ice.

Ruffy and Jacque were waiting for him beside the tailboard.

"Where is he?" asked Bruce softly.

"He is gone."

"Where?"

"That way." Jacque pointed towards the southeast. "I followed the spoor a short distance."

Bruce walked to the Ford and picked up his rifle from the floor. He opened the cubbyhole and took two spare clips of ammunition from it.

Ruffy followed him. "He's got the gem diamonds, boss."

"Yes," said Bruce and checked the load of his rifle. The diamonds were of no importance.

"Are you going after him, boss?"

Bruce did not answer. Instead he looked up at the sky. The sun was halfway towards the horizon and there were clouds thickly massed around it.

"Ruffy, stay with her," he said softly. "Keep her warm."

Ruffy nodded.

"Who is the best tracker we've got?"

"Jacque. Worked for a safari outfit before the war as a tracker boy."

Bruce turned to Jacque. The thing was still icy cold inside him, with tentacles that spread out to every extremity of his body and his mind.

"When did this happen?"

"About an hour after you left," answered Jacque.

Eight hours start. It was a long lead.

"Take the spoor," said Bruce softly.

31

The earth was soft from the night's rain and the spoor deep trodden; the heels had bit in under Hendry's weight, so they followed fast.

Watching Sergeant Jacque work, Bruce felt his anxiety abating, for although the footprints were so easy to follow in these early stages that it was no test of his ability, yet from the way he moved swiftly along—half crouched and wholly absorbed, occasionally glancing ahead to pick up the run of the spoor, stooping now and then to touch the earth and determine its texture —Bruce could tell that this man knew his business.

Through the open forest with tufted grass below, holding steadily south by east, Hendry led them straight towards the Rhodesian border. And after the first two hours Bruce knew they had not gained upon him. Hendry was still eight hours ahead, and at the pace he was setting eight hours' start was something like thirty miles in distance.

Bruce looked over his shoulder at the sun where it lay wedged between two vast piles of cumulus nimbus. There in the sky were the two elements which could defeat him.

Time. There were perhaps two more hours of daylight. With the onset of night they would be forced to halt.

Rain. The clouds were swollen and dark blue around the edges. As Bruce watched, the lightning lit them internally, and at a count of ten the thunder grumbled suddenly. If it rained again before morning there would be no spoor to follow.

"We must move faster," said Bruce.

Sergeant Jacque straightened up and looked at Bruce as though he were a stranger. He had forgotten his existence.

"The earth hardens." Jacque pointed at the spoor, and Bruce saw that in the last half hour the soil had become gritty and compacted. Hendry's heels no longer broke the crust. "It is unwise to run on such a lean trail."

Again Bruce looked back at the menace of gathering clouds. "We must take the chance," he decided.

"As you wish," said Jacque and transferred his rifle to his other shoulder, hitched up his belt, and settled the steel helmet more firmly on his head.

"*Allez!*"

They trotted on through the forest towards the southeast. Within a mile Bruce's body had settled into the automatic rhythm of his run, leaving his mind free.

He thought about Wally Hendry, saw again the little eyes and around them the puffy folded skin, and the mouth below, thin and merciless, the ginger stubble of beard. He could almost smell him. His nostrils flared at the memory of the rank red-head's body odour. Unclean, he thought, unclean mind and unclean body.

His hatred of Wally Hendry was a tangible thing. He could feel it sitting heavily at the base of his throat, tingling in his fingertips and giving strength to his legs.

And yet there was something else. Suddenly Bruce grinned, a wicked baring of his teeth. That tingling in his fingertips was not all hatred—a little of it was excitement.

What a complex thing is a man, he thought. *He can never hold one emotion—always there are others to confuse it. Here I am hunting the thing that I most loathe and hate, and I am enjoying it. Completely unrelated to the hatred is the thrill of hunting the most dangerous and cunning game of all, man.*

I have always enjoyed the chase, he thought. *It has been bred into me, for my blood is that of the men who hunted and fought with Africa as the prize.*

The hunting of this man will give me pleasure. If ever a man deserved to die, it is Wally Hendry. I am the plaintiff, the judge, and the executioner.

Sergeant Jacque stopped so suddenly that Bruce ran into him and they nearly fell.

"What is it?" said Bruce, panting, coming back to reality.

"Look!"

The earth ahead of them was churned and broken.

"Zebra," Bruce groaned, recognizing the round uncloven hoofprints. "Goddammit to hell—of all the filthy luck!"

"A big herd," Jacque agreed. "Spread out. Feeding."

As far ahead as they could see through the forest the herd had wiped out Hendry's tracks.

"We'll have to cast forward." Bruce's voice was agonized by his impatience. He turned to the nearest tree and hacked at it with his bayonet, blazing it to mark the end of the trail, swearing softly, venting his disappointment on the trunk.

"Only another hour to sunset," he whispered. "Please let us pick him up again before dark."

Sergeant Jacque was already moving forward, following the approximate line of Hendry's travel, trying vainly to recognize a single footprint through the havoc created by the passage of thousands of hoofs. Bruce hurried to join him and then moved out on his flank. They zigzagged slowly ahead, almost meeting on the inward leg of each tack and then separating again to a distance of a hundred yards.

There it was! Bruce dropped to his knees to make sure. Just the outline of the toecap showing from under the spoor of an old zebra stallion. Bruce whistled, a windy sound through his dry lips, and Jacque came quickly.

One quick look, then, "Yes, he is holding more to the right now." He raised his eyes and squinted ahead, marking a tree that was directly in line with the run of the spoor.

They went forward.

"There's the herd." Bruce pointed at the flicker of a grey body through the trees.

"They've got our wind."

A zebra snorted and then there was a rumbling, a low blurred drumming of hoofs, as the herd ran. Through the trees Bruce caught glimpses of the animals on the near side of the herd: too far off to show the stripes, looking like fat grey ponies as they galloped, ears up, black-maned heads nodding. Then they were gone, and the sound of their flight dwindled.

"At least they haven't run along the spoor," muttered Bruce, and then bitterly; "Damn them, the stupid little donkeys! They've cost us an hour. A whole priceless hour."

Desperately searching, wild with haste, they worked back and forth. The sun was below the trees; already the air was cooling in the short African dusk. Another fifteen minutes and it would be dark.

Then abruptly the forest ended and they came out on the edge of a vlei. Open as wheatland, pastured with green waist-high grass, hemmed in by the forest, it stretched ahead of them for nearly two miles. Dotted along it were clumps of ivory palms with each graceful stem ending in an untidy cluster of leaves. Troops of guinea fowls were scratching and chirruping along the edge of the clearing, and near the far end a herd of buffalo formed a dark mass as they grazed beneath a canopy of white egrets.

In the forest beyond the clearing, rising perhaps three hundred feet out of it, stood a kopje of tumbled granite. The great slabs of rock with their sheer sides and square tops looked like a ruined castle. The low sun struck it and gave the rock an orange warmth.

But Bruce had no time to admire the scene; his eyes were on the earth, searching for the prints of Hendry's jungle boots.

Out on his left Sergeant Jacque whistled sharply, and Bruce felt the leap of excitement in his chest. He ran across to the crouching gendarme.

"It has come away." Jacque pointed at the spoor that was strung ahead of them like beads on a string, skirting the edge of the vlei, each depression filled with shadow and standing out clearly on the sandy grey earth.

"Too late!" Bruce groaned. "Damn those bloody zebra!" The light was fading so swiftly it seemed as though it were a stage effect.

"Follow it." Bruce's voice was sharp with helpless frustration. "Follow it as long as you can."

It was not a quarter of a mile farther on that Jacque rose out of his crouch. Only the white of his teeth showed in the darkness as he spoke. "We will lose it again if we go on."

"All right." Bruce unslung his rifle with weary resignation. He knew that Wally Hendry was at least forty miles ahead of them—more, if he kept travelling after dark. The spoor was cold. If this had been an ordinary hunt he would long ago have broken off the chase.

He looked up at the sky. In the north the stars were fat and yellow, but above them and to the south it was black with cloud.

"Don't let it rain," he whispered. "Please, God, don't let it rain."

The night was long. Bruce slept once for perhaps two hours and then the strength of his hatred woke him. He lay flat upon his back and stared up at the sky. It was all dark with clouds; only occasionally did they open and let the stars shine briefly through.

"It must not rain. It must not rain," he repeated like a prayer, staring up at the dark sky, concentrating upon it, as though by the force of his mind he could control the elements.

There were lions hunting in the forest. He heard the male roaring, moving up from the south, and once his two lionesses answered him. They killed a little before dawn, and Bruce lay on the hard earth and listened to their jubilation over the kill. Then there was silence as they began to feed.

That I might have success as well, he thought. I do not often ask for favours, Lord, but grant me this one. I ask it not only for myself but for Shermaine and the others.

In his mind he saw again the two children lying where Hendry had shot them, the smear of mingled blood and chocolate across the boy's cheek.

He deserves to die, prayed Bruce, so please don't let it rain.

As long as the night had been, that quickly came the dawn— a grey dawn gloomy with low cloud.

"Will it go?" Bruce asked for the twentieth time, and this time Jacque looked up from where he knelt beside the spoor.

"We can try now."

They moved off slowly with Jacque leading, doubled over to peer shortsightedly at the earth, and Bruce close behind him, be-devilled by his impatience and anxiety, lifting his head every dozen paces to the dirty grey roof of cloud.

The light strengthened and the circle of their vision opened from six feet to as many yards, to a hundred, so they could make out the tops of the ivory palms, shaggy against the grey cloud.

Jacque broke into a trot, and ahead of them was the end of the clearing and the beginning of the forest. Two hundred yards beyond rose the massive pile of the kopje, in the early light look-ing more than ever like a castle, turreted and sheer. There was something formidable in its outline. It seemed to brood above them, and Bruce looked away from it uneasily.

Cold and with enough weight behind it to sting, the first rain-drop splashed against Bruce's cheek.

"Oh no!" he protested and stopped.

Jacque straightened up from the spoor and he too looked at the sky. "It is finished. In five minutes there will be nothing to follow."

Another drop hit Bruce's upturned face and he blinked back the tears of anger and frustration that pricked the rims of his eyelids.

Faster now, tapping on his helmet, plopping onto his shoul-ders and face, the rain fell.

"Quickly," cried Bruce. "Follow as long as you can."

Jacque opened his mouth to speak, but before a word came out he was flung backwards, punched over as though by an in-visible fist, his helmet flying from his head as he fell and his rifle clattering on the earth.

Simultaneously Bruce felt the bullet pass him, disrupting the air, so the wind of it flattened his shirt against his chest, crack-ing viciously in his ears, leaving him dazedly looking down at Sergeant Jacque's body.

It lay with arms thrown wide, the jaw and the side of the head below the ear torn away, white bone and blood bubbling over it. The trunk twitched convulsively and the hands fluttered like trapped birds. Then, flat-sounding through the rain, he heard the report of the rifle.

The kopje, screamed Bruce's brain, *he's lying in the kopje!* And Bruce moved, twisting sideways, starting to run.

32

Wally Hendry lay on his stomach on the flat top of the turret. His body was stiff and chilled from the cold of the night and the rock was harsh under him, but the discomfort hardly penetrated the fringe of his mind. He had built a low parapet with loose flakes of granite, and he had screened the front of it with the thick bushy stems of broom bush.

His rifle was propped on the parapet in front of him and at his elbow were the spare ammunition clips.

He had lain in this ambush for a long time now—since the preceding afternoon. Now it was dawn and the darkness was drawing back; in a few minutes he would be able to see the whole of the clearing below him.

I coulda been across the river already, he thought, coulda been fifty miles away. He did not attempt to analyze the impulse that had made him lie here unmoving for so many hours.

Man, I knew old Curry would have to come. I knew he would only bring one nigger tracker with him. These educated johnnies got their own rules—man-to-man stuff, and he chuckled as he remembered the two minute figures that he had seen come out of the forest in the fading light of the previous evening.

The bastard spent the night down there in the clearing. Saw him light a match and have himself a smoke in the night—well, I hope he enjoyed it, his last.

Wally peered anxiously out into the gradually gathering dawn.

They'll be moving now, coming up the clearing. Must get them before they reach the trees again.

Below him the clearing showed as a paleness, a leprous blotch, on the dark forest.

The bastard! Without preliminaries Hendry's hatred returned to him. This time he don't get to make no fancy speeches. This time he don't get no chance to be hoity-toity.

The light was stronger now. He could see the clumps of ivory palms against the pale brown grass of the clearing.

"Ha!" Hendry exclaimed.

There they were, like two little ants, dark specks moving up the middle of the clearing.

The tip of Hendry's tongue slipped out between his lips and he flattened down behind his rifle.

Man, I've waited for this. Six months now I've thought about this. And when it's finished I'll go down and take his ears.

He slipped the safety catch; it made a satisfying mechanical click.

Nigger's leading. That's Curry behind him. Have to wait till they turn, don't want the nigger to get it first. Curry first, then the nigger.

He picked them up in his sights, breathing quicker now, the thrill of it so intense that he had to swallow, and it caught in his throat like dry bread.

A raindrop hit the back of his neck. It startled him. He looked up quickly at the sky and saw the rain coming.

"Goddammit!" He looked back at the clearing. Curry and the nigger were standing together, a single dark blob in the half light. There was no chance of separating them. The rain fell faster, and suddenly Hendry was overwhelmed by the old familiar feeling of inferiority, of knowing that everything, even the elements, conspired against him; the knowledge that he could never win, not even this once.

They, God and the rest of the world.

The ones who had given him a drunk for a father.

A squalid cottage for a home and a mother with cancer of the throat.

The ones who had sent him to reform school, had fired him from two dozen jobs, had pushed him, laughed at him, jailed him twice. They, all of them (and Bruce Curry who was their figurehead), they were going to win again. Not even this once, not even ever.

"Goddammit," he cursed in hopeless, wordless anger against them all.

"Goddammit, goddammit to hell," and he fired at the dark blob in his sights.

33

As he ran Bruce looked across a hundred yards of open ground to the edge of the forest.

He felt the wind of the next bullet as it cracked past him.

If he uses rapid fire he'll get me even at three hundred yards.

And Bruce jinked his run like a jack rabbit. The blood roared in his ears, fear drove his feet.

Then all around him the air burst asunder, buffeting him so he staggered. The vicious whip-whip-whip of bullets filled his head.

I can't make it.

Seventy yards to the shelter of the trees, seventy yards of open meadow land, and above him the commanding mass of the kopje.

The next burst is for me—it must come, now!

And he flung himself to one side so violently that he nearly fell. Again the air was ripping to tatters close beside him.

I can't last! He must get me!

In his path was an antheap, a low pile of clay, a pimple on the open expanse of earth. Bruce dived for it, hitting the ground so hard that the wind was forced from his lungs out through his open mouth.

The next burst of gunfire kicked lumps of clay from the top of the ant heap, showering Bruce's back.

He lay with his face pressed into the earth, wheezing with the agony of empty lungs, flattening his body behind the tiny heap of clay.

Will it cover me? Is there enough of it?

And the next hail of bullets thumped into the ant heap, throwing fountains of earth but leaving Bruce untouched.

I'm safe. The realization came with a surge that washed away his fear.

But I'm helpless, answered his hatred. Pinned to the earth for as long as Hendry wants to keep me here.

The rain fell on his back, soaking through his jacket, coldly caressing the nape of his neck, and dribbling down over his jaws.

He rolled his head sideways, not daring to lift it an inch, and the rain beat down on the side of his face.

The rain! Falling faster, thickening, hanging from the clouds like the skirts of a woman's dress. Curtains of rain. Greying out the edge of the forest, leaving no solid shapes in the mist of falling, liquid mother-of-pearl.

Still gasping but with the pain slowly receding, Bruce lifted his head.

The kopje was a vague blue-green shape ahead of him, then it was gone, swallowed by the eddying columns of rain.

Bruce pushed himself up onto his knees and the pain in his chest made him dizzy. Now! he thought. Now, before it thins, and he lumbered clumsily to his feet.

For a moment he stood clutching his chest, sucking for breath in the haze of water-filled air, and then he staggered towards the edge of the forest.

His feet steadied under him, his breathing eased, and he was into the trees.

They closed around him protectively. He leaned against the rough bark of one of them and wiped the rain from his face with the palm of his hand. The strength came back to him and with it his hatred and his excitement.

He unslung the rifle from his shoulder and stood away from the tree with his feet planted wide apart.

"Now, my friend," he whispered, "we fight on equal terms." He pumped a round into the chamber of the FN and moved towards the kopje, stepping daintily, the weight of the rifle in his hands, his mind suddenly sharp and clear, vision enhanced, feeling his strength and the absence of fear like a song within him, a battle hymn.

He made out the loom of the kopje through the dripping rain-heavy trees and he circled out to the right. There is plenty of time, he thought. I can afford to case the joint thoroughly. He completed his circuit of the rock pile.

The kopje, he found, was the shape of a galleon sinking at the head. At one end were the high double castles of the poop, from which the main deck canted steeply forward as though the prow were already under water. This slope was scattered with boulders and densely covered with dwarf scrub, an interwoven mass of shoulder-high branches and leaves.

Bruce squatted on his haunches with the rifle in his lap and looked up the ramp at the twin turrets of the kopje. The rain had slackened to a drizzle.

Hendry was on top. Bruce knew he would be at the highest point. Strange how height makes a man feel invulnerable, makes him think he is a god.

And since Hendry had fired upon them he must be in the turret nearest the vlei, which was slightly the higher of the two, its summit crowned by a patch of stunted broom bush.

So now I know exactly where he is and I will wait half an hour. He may become impatient and move; if he does I will get a shot at him from here.

Bruce narrowed his eyes, judging the distance. About two hundred yards.

He adjusted the rear-sight of the FN and then checked the load, felt in the side pocket of his jacket to make sure the two extra clips of ammunition were handy, and settled back to wait.

"Curry, you son-of-a-bitch, where are you?" Hendry's shout floated down through the drizzling rain.

Bruce stiffened. I was right—he's on top of the left-hand turret.

"Come on, bucko, I've been waiting for you since yesterday afternoon."

Bruce lifted the rifle and sighted experimentally at a dark patch on the wall of the rock. It would be difficult shooting in the rain, the rifle slippery, the fine drizzle clinging to his eyebrows and dewing the sights of the rifle with little beads of moisture.

"Hey, Curry, how's your little French piece of pussy? Man, she's hot, that thing, isn't she?"

Bruce's hands tightened on the rifle.

"Did she tell you how I gave her the old business? Did she tell you how she loved it? You should have heard her panting like a steam engine. I'm telling you, Curry, she just couldn't get enough!"

Bruce felt himself start to tremble. He clenched his jaws, biting down until his teeth ached.

Steady, Bruce my boy, that's what he wants you to do.

The trees dripped steadily in the silence and a gust of wind stirred the scrub on the slope of the kopje. Bruce waited, straining his eyes for the first hint of movement on the left-hand turret.

"You yellow or something, Curry? You scared to come on up here? Is that what it is?"

Bruce shifted his position slightly, ready for a snap shot.

"Okay, bucko, I can wait. I've got all day. I'll just sit here thinking about how I mucked your little bit of French. I'm telling you it was something to remember. Up and down, in and out, man it was something!"

Bruce came carefully up onto his feet behind the trunk of the tree and once more studied the layout of the kopje.

If I can move up the slope, keeping well over to the side, until I reach the right-hand turret, there's a ledge there that will take me to the top. I'll be twenty or thirty feet from him, and at that range it will all be over in a few seconds.

He drew a deep breath and left the shelter of the tree.

Wally Hendry spotted the movement in the forest below him; it was a flash of brown quickly gone, too fast to get a bead on it.

He wiped the rain off his face and wriggled a foot closer to the edge. "Come on, Curry. Let's stop buggering about," he shouted and cuddled the butt of his rifle into his shoulder. The tip of his tongue kept darting out and touching his lips.

At the foot of the slope he saw a branch move slightly, stirring when there was no wind. He grinned and snuggled his hips down onto the rock. Here he comes, he gloated, he's crawling up under the scrub.

"I know you're sitting down there. Okay, Curry, I can wait too."

Halfway up the slope the top leaves of another bush swayed gently, parting and closing.

"Yes!" whispered Wally, "Yes!" He clicked off the safety catch of the rifle. His tongue came out and moved slowly from one corner of his mouth to the other.

I've got him, for sure! There—he'll have to cross that piece of open ground. A coupla yards, that's all. But it'll be enough.

He moved again, wriggling a few inches to one side, settling his aim into the gap between two large grey boulders; he pushed the rate-of-fire selector onto rapid, and his forefinger rested lightly on the trigger.

"Hey, Curry, I'm getting bored. If you're not going to come up, how about singing to me or cracking a few jokes?"

Bruce Curry crouched behind a large grey boulder. In front of him were three yards of open ground and then the shelter of another rock. He was almost at the top of the slope, and Hendry had not spotted him. Across the patch of open ground was good cover to the foot of the right-hand turret. It would take him two seconds to cross, and the chances were that Hendry would be watching the forest at the foot of the slope.

He gathered himself like a sprinter on the starting blocks.

"Go!" he whispered and dived into the opening—and into a hell storm of bullets. One struck his rifle, tearing it out of his hand with such force that his arm was paralyzed to the shoulder; another stung his chest, and then he was across. He lay behind the far boulder, gasping with the shock, and listened to Hendry's voice roaring triumphantly.

"Fooled you, you stupid bastard! Been watching you all the way up from the bottom."

Bruce held his left arm against his stomach; the use of it was returning as the numbness subsided, but with it came the ache. The top joint of his thumb had caught in the trigger guard and been torn off; now the blood welled out of the stump thickly and slowly, dark blood, the colour of apple butter. With his right hand he groped for his handkerchief.

"Hey, Curry, your rifle's lying there in the open. You might need it in a few minutes. Why don't you go out and get it?"

Bruce bound the handkerchief tightly around the stump of his thumb and the bleeding slowed. Then he looked at the rifle where it lay ten feet away. The foresight had been knocked off, and the same bullet that had amputated his thumb had smashed into the breech, buckled the loading handle and the slide. He knew that it was damaged beyond repair.

"Think I'll have me a little target practice," shouted Hendry from above, and again there was a burst of automatic fire. Bruce's rifle disappeared in a cloud of dust and flying rock fragments, and when it cleared the woodwork of the rifle was splintered and torn and there was further damage to the action.

Well, that's that, thought Bruce. Rifle's wrecked, Shermaine has the pistol, and I have only one good hand. This is going to be interesting.

He unbuttoned the front of his jacket and examined the welt that the bullet had raised across his chest. It looked like a rope burn, painful and red, but not serious. He rebuttoned the jacket.

"Okay, Bruce baby, the time for games is over. I'm coming down to get you." Hendry's voice was harsh and loud, filled with confidence.

Bruce rallied under the goading of it. He looked around quickly. Which way to go? Climb high so he must come up to get at you. Take the right-hand turret, work around the side of it and wait for him on the top.

In haste now, spurred by the dread of being the hunted, he scrambled to his feet and dodged away up the slope, keeping his head down, using the thick screen of rock and vegetation.

He reached the wall of the right-hand turret and followed it around, found the spiral ledge that he had seen from below and went onto it, up along it like a fly on a wall, completely exposed, keeping his back to the cliff of granite, shuffling sideways up the eighteen-inch ledge, with the drop below him growing deeper with each step.

Now he was three hundred feet above the forest and could look out across the dark green land to another row of kopjes on the horizon. The rain had ceased but the cloud was unbroken, covering the sky.

The ledge widened, became a platform, and Bruce hurried across it around the far shoulder and came to a dead end. The ledge had petered out and there was only the drop below. He had trapped himself on the side of the turret—the summit was unattainable. If Hendry descended to the forest floor and circled the kopje he would find Bruce completely at his mercy, for there was no cover on the narrow ledge. Hendry could have a little more target practice.

Bruce leaned against the rock and struggled to control his breathing. His throat was clogged with the thick saliva of exhaustion and fear. He felt tired and helpless; his thumb throbbed painfully, and he lifted it to examine it once more. Despite the tourniquet it was bleeding slowly, a wine-red drop at a time.

Bleeding! Bruce swallowed the thick gluey stuff in his throat and looked back along the way he had come. On the grey rock the bright red splashes stood out clearly. He had laid a blood spoor for Hendry to follow.

All right then, perhaps it is best this way. At least I may be able to come to grips with him. If I wait behind this shoulder until he starts to cross the platform, there's a three-hundred-foot drop on one side, I may be able to rush him and throw him off.

Bruce leaned against the shoulder of granite, hidden from the platform, and tuned his ears to catch the first sound of Hendry's approach.

The clouds parted in the eastern sector of the sky and the sun shone through, slanting across the side of the kopje.

It will be better to die in the sun, thought Bruce, a sacrifice to the sun god thrown from the roof of the temple, and he grinned without mirth, waiting with patience and with pain.

The minutes fell like drops into the pool of time, slowly measuring out the ration of life that had been allotted to him. The pulse in his ears counted also, and this breath that he drew and held and gently exhaled—how many more would there be?

I should pray, he thought, but after this morning when I prayed that it should not rain, and the rains came and saved me, I will not presume again to tell the Old Man how to run things. Perhaps he knows best after all.

Thy will be done, he thought instead, and suddenly his nerves jerked tight as a line hit by a marlin. The sound he had heard was that of cloth brushing against rough rock.

He held his breath and listened, but all he could discern was the pulse in his ears and the wind in the trees of the forest below. The wind was a lonely sound.

Thy will be done, he repeated without breathing and heard Hendry breathe close behind the shoulder of rock.

He stood away from the wall and waited. Then he saw Hendry's shadow thrown by the early morning sun along the ledge, a great distorted shadow on the grey rock.

Thy will be done. And he went round the shoulder fast, his good hand held like a blade and the weight of his body behind it.

Hendry was three feet away, the rifle at high port across his chest, standing close in against the cliff, the cup-shaped steel helmet pulled low over the slitty eyes and little beads of sweat clinging to the red-gold stubble of his beard. He tried to drop the muzzle of the rifle, but Bruce was too close.

Bruce lunged with stiff fingers at Hendry's throat and he felt the crackle and give of cartilage. Then his weight carried him on, and Hendry sprawled backwards onto the stone platform with Bruce on top of him.

The rifle slithered across the rock and dropped over the edge, and they lay chest to chest with legs locked together in a horrible parody of the love act. But in *this* act we do not procreate, we destroy.

Hendry's face was purple and swollen above his damaged

throat, his mouth open as he struggled for air, and his breath smelled old and sour in Bruce's face.

With a twist towards the thumb Bruce freed his right wrist from Hendry's grip and, lifting it like an axe, brought it down across the bridge of Hendry's nose. Twin jets of blood spouted from the nostrils and gushed into his open mouth.

With a wet, strangling sound in his throat Hendry's body arched violently upwards, and Bruce was thrown back against the side of the cliff with such force that for a second he lay there.

Wally was on his knees, facing Bruce, his eyes glazed and sightless, the strangling, rattling sound spraying from his throat in a pink cloud of blood. With both hands he was fumbling his pistol out of its canvas holster.

Bruce drew his knees up to his chest, then straightened his legs in a mule kick. His feet landed together in the centre of Hendry's stomach, throwing him backwards off the platform. Hendry made that strangled bellow all the way to the bottom, but at the end it was cut off abruptly, and afterwards there was only the sound of the wind in the forest below.

For a long time, drained of strength and the power to think, Bruce sat on the ledge with his back against the rock.

Above him the clouds had rolled aside and half the sky was blue. He looked out across the land and the forest was lush and clean from the rain. *And I am still alive.* The realization warmed Bruce's mind as comfortably as the early sun was warming his body. He wanted to shout it out across the forest. *I am still alive!*

At last he stood up, crossed to the edge of the cliff, and looked down at the tiny crumpled figure on the rocks below. Then he turned away and dragged his beaten body down the side of the turret.

It took him twenty minutes to find Wally Hendry in the chaos of broken rock and scrub below the turret. He lay on his side with his legs drawn up as though he slept. Bruce knelt beside him and drew his pistol from the olive-green canvas holster;

then he unbuttoned the flap of Hendry's bulging breast pocket and took out the white canvas bag.

He stood up, opened the mouth of the bag, and stirred the diamonds with his forefinger. Satisfied, he jerked the drawstring closed and dropped them into his own pocket.

In death he is even more repulsive than he was alive, thought Bruce without regret as he looked down at the corpse.

The flies were crawling into the bloody nostrils and clustering around the eyes.

Then he spoke aloud.

"So Mike Haigh was right and I was wrong—you can destroy it."

Without looking back he walked away. The tiredness left him.

34

Carl Engelbrecht came through the doorway from the cockpit into the main cabin of the Dakota.

"Are you two happy?" he asked above the deep drone of the engines, and then, a grin on his big brown face, "I can see you are!"

Bruce grinned back at him and tightened his arm around Shermaine's shoulders. "Go away! Can't you see we're busy?"

"You've got lots of cheek for a hitchhiker—bloody good mind to make you get out and walk," Carl grumbled as he sat down beside them on the bench that ran the full length of the fuselage. "I've brought you some coffee and sandwiches."

"Good. Good. I'm starving." Shermaine sat up and reached for the thermos flask and the greaseproof paper packet. The bruise on her cheek had faded to a shadow with yellow edges—it was almost ten days old. With his mouth full of chicken sandwich Bruce kicked one of the wooden cases that were roped securely to the floor of the aircraft.

"What have you got in these, Carl?"

"Dunno," said Carl and poured coffee into the three plastic mugs. "In this game you don't ask questions. You fly out, take your money, and let it go." He drained his mug and stood up. "Well, I'll leave you two alone now. We'll be in Nairobi in a couple of hours, so you can sleep or something!" He winked. "You'll have to stay aboard while we refuel. But we'll be airborne again in an hour or so, and the day after tomorrow, God and the weather permitting, we'll set you down in Zurich."

"Thanks, old cock."

"Think nothing of it—all in the day's work."

He went forward and disappeared into the cockpit, closing the door behind him.

Shermaine turned back to Bruce, studied him for a moment,

and then laughed. "You look so different—now you look like a lawyer!"

Self-consciously Bruce tightened the knot of his Old Michael-house tie. "I must admit it feels strange to wear a suit and tie again." He looked down at the well-cut blue suit—the only one he had left—and then up again at Shermaine. "And in a dress I hardly recognize you either."

She was wearing a lime-green cotton frock, cool and crisp looking, white high-heeled shoes, and just a little make-up to cover the bruise. A damn fine woman, Bruce decided with pleasure.

"How does your thumb feel?" she asked, and Bruce held up the stump with its neat little turban of adhesive tape.

"I had almost forgotten about it."

Suddenly Shermaine's expression changed and she pointed excitedly out of the perspex window behind Bruce's shoulder. "Look, there's the sea!"

It lay far below them, shaded from blue to pale green in the shallows, with a rind of white beach and the wave formation moving across it like ripples on a pond.

"That's Lake Tanganyika." Bruce laughed. "We've left the Congo behind."

"Forever?" she asked.

"Forever!" he assured her.

The aircraft banked slightly, throwing them closer together, as Carl picked out his landmarks and altered course towards the northeast.

Four thousand feet below them the dark insect that was their shadow flitted and hopped across the surface of the water.

☞ The Gang That Couldn't Shoot Straight

☞ ALSO BY JIMMY BRESLIN

CAN'T ANYBODY HERE PLAY THIS GAME?

THE WORLD OF JIMMY BRESLIN

The Gang That Couldn't Shoot Straight

Jimmy Breslin

NEW YORK ☞ THE VIKING PRESS

☞ The Gang That Couldn't Shoot Straight

Chapter 1

The idea for the six-day bike race came out of a meeting held in November, in Brooklyn, in the offices of Anthony Pastrumo, Sr. He is a sixty-eight-year-old man who is called "Papa" when he is at home and "Baccala" by his friends and business associates, all of whom share a common feeling toward Baccala. They are scared to death of him.

Baccala is one of the five big bosses of the Mafia gangsters in New York. He is also a very great dog-lover. Last year he bought a Russian wolfhound for his four-year-old niece so she could grow up in an atmosphere of teeth. The dog was stolen. Baccala had somebody write a form letter that was mimeographed and sent to every veterinarian and animal hospital in the New York area. It offered a reward of $250 to anybody who reported if a Russian wolfhound with specific markings was brought around for shots.

"I look to make a stool pigeon out of a dog doctor," Baccala explained. "All he tells me is who the guy is with-a my dog. I pay the $250. I go to the guy who stole my-a dog. I speak to him nice. Then I cut out his heart and feed it to the dog."

The bike race was Baccala's idea. He nominated a chubby real-estate man named Joseph DeLauria to be the actual promoter of the race. DeLauria has made large sums of money fronting for Baccala in business deals. DeLauria also has received many slaps in the face when he has irritated Baccala during these deals.

Baccala's office in Brooklyn is in a building which is listed as the home of the Lancer Trucking Company. There is no trucking company. If Baccala wants a trucking company, he will steal one from a Jew. Baccala held the meeting to deal with a dissident group in his gang: Reform Italians. The gang was headed by Salvatore Palumbo. He is known, among all illegitimate people and cops in Brooklyn, as Kid Sally Palumbo. In Brooklyn waterfront dialect, this often comes out as "Sally Kid." He is twenty-nine and he has a power base of five cousins and sixty others who live on the South Brooklyn waterfront and work, under Kid Sally's direction, at mayhem for the Baccala gang. For some time Kid Sally Palumbo and his group have wanted to get their hands on a major revenue-producing enterprise. Violence still pays less than any other job in crime. Baccala was of the opinion that Kid Sally Palumbo couldn't run a gas station at a profit even if he stole the customers' cars. But the level of annoyance from Kid Sally Palumbo and his people was becoming inordinately high. You could see that at a big meeting held to discuss the rift.

"You sit-a here, okay? you sit-a here, okay? you sit-a here, okay?" Baccala was saying, assuming his role of *don cheeche*. One of the major rewards for being a big shot in the Mafia is that you are in charge of seating arrangements at all restaurants or meetings. You tell everybody where to sit and keep the best seat for yourself.

Everybody in the meeting sat down except Kid Sally Palumbo.

"You sit-a," Baccala said, pointing at a chair in the corner.

"I don't feel like sittin'."

"You sit-a."

"I think I'm going to stand."

The two glared at each other. Baccala shrugged and sat down. He is known as the Sicilian Dean Rusk. Be a little smooth and give a little on the surface now. After the conference ends amicably, send in the B-52s.

"So what you want?" Baccala said.

"Do the right thing," Kid Sally said.

"What's?" Baccala said.

"We got to go around with a gun with loaded bullets. What do we get for it? You get everything, we get ungotz."

"You shut up you face," Baccala said.

"You old guys, we got to do deuces and treys in the can and you leave the money for your kids. What's this? You send your kids to West Point. We go to West Point, all right. Sing Sing West Point."

"You show no respect," Baccala said.

"I'm good people," Kid Sally said.

"You no act like good people."

"I'm good people!"

Kid Sally's grandmother, Mrs. Big Mama Ferrara, had rehearsed him carefully. "You just say you good people and you take-a no bullasheet," she told him.

The meeting broke up on that note. Baccala, watching Kid Sally and his cousins leave the office, realized they constituted political pressure. As Baccala is sensitive to this sort of thing, he decided to do something about it.

What Baccala wanted to do at first was not good. *"Ciciri,"* he muttered one night. The three people with him at dinner became nervous. The word *ciciri* means bean, but to Baccala the meaning is much deeper. The only history he knows of is the rebellion of Sicilians in Palermo in 1282 against the French. A French soldier tried to rape a housewife in front of her husband in Palermo. The husband killed the soldier and all Palermo took to the streets. They surrounded French soldiers and told them to say the word *ciciri*. It is supposed to be an impossible set of syllables for the French tongue to handle. So the people of Palermo, with a great shout, slit the throats of the soldiers. Baccala, who knows the story by heart, loves to talk about the part where the hero of the uprising, Nicola Pancia, boarded a French ship in the harbor and had seventy French sergeants and their wives and children thrown overboard. Nicola Pancia and his men hung over the side and cheered each time a baby drowned.

"The baby makes-a bubbles in the water," Baccala always says, crying from laughter.

In more recent history, each time Baccala mutters this particular word, somebody in Brooklyn gets invited on a deep-sea fishing trip from Sheepshead Bay. Out in the ocean, a rope is put around the man's neck. The other end of the rope is attached to an old jukebox. The jukebox is thrown overboard. The man invariably follows.

On this particular occasion, however, Baccala spent a week glaring and muttering and then he called in Kid Sally Palumbo again and told him he was getting a chance to make money. A bike race.

Bike-racing is a thing out of the 1930s. It used to be called "the Ride to Nowhere." The only thing Baccala really knows about bike-racing is that Italians ride bikes. But it was indicative of Baccala's age that, when pressed, he went for an idea out of the 1930s instead of something modern, such as selling cocaine to grammar-school kids. During the Depression, when even fine gangsters were broke, Baccala went to a bike race at Madison Square Garden and quickly noticed that when everybody stood up to cheer they left their coats draped over the seats. On the second sprint of the night Baccala grabbed a great camel-hair from Row B, Section 205. A while later he took a black Chesterfield out of the last row of the end arena. He got into the side arena and came off with a terrific storm coat. He happened to look around, and he saw so many guys running around the arena and stealing coats that he thought he was having a vision of heaven.

Over the loudspeaker, later on that night, the announcer for the bike race said, "The score at this point . . ."

"Forty-nine coats!" somebody screamed from the mezzanine.

Despite the different era, Baccala was certain his new bike race would make immense amounts of money. He intended to have open gambling on it. The event would be held in a field-artillery armory in the 91st Precinct in Brooklyn. The only thing not for sale in the 91st Precinct is the captain's bowling trophy. As Baccala saw it, the bike race would be a roulette wheel for six days and nights. He would let Kid Sally Palumbo handle the whole thing and keep nearly all the money. This would keep the fresh bum quiet.

This bike race is another example of how Mafia bosses weave their way into the fabric of society. The Mafia of New York is split into five groups known as "families." The Baccala Family runs all organized crime in Brooklyn. The gang has been in Brooklyn longer than the Ferris wheel at Coney Island. It was formed in 1890 under the leadership of Raymond the Wolf. He ate babies. Raymond the Wolf passed away in his sleep one night from natural causes; his heart stopped beating when the three men who slipped into his bedroom stuck knives in it. Joe the Wop, who had sent the three men, took over the mob. Joe the Wop shot nuns. A year later he dropped dead while being strangled. At this point Baccala heard that three people he had known and loved for twenty years were discussing ways to take over the gang. So was Baccala. This, of course, made his three great friends become treacherous enemies. One night Baccala stepped into the Roma Gardens Lounge to visit the three people. Baccala also brought a machine gun with him. The three old friends were eating dinner.

Baccala caught them with the machine gun between the veal. A waiter was so close to Baccala's gun that he got powder burns all over the front of his waiter's jacket.

When the police arrived, they found the waiter nervously twisting a napkin between his hands. An inspector looked at the powder burns on the waiter's jacket.

"What shooting?" Louis the Waiter said.

For several months thereafter, whenever some hero would come into the Roma Gardens Lounge and order a meal, a hand would come up from under the table and set down a dish of veal Parmigiana.

After the machine-gunning was out of the headlines, Baccala took command of the gang. He has lasted as head of the family since 1944, which is a new record for gangsters, Brooklyn, single individual.

Kid Sally Palumbo came toward the top of the Baccala Family through personal service, great greed, and also great luck. His objectives were the power to say, "You sit here," and money. They go together. The financial structure of the Mafia is the same as in the film industry. Ten stars walk around earning millions, and thousands of unknowns get little pieces of work here and there and mainly earn nothing. They wait for the key role to pop up.

One day, in Kid Sally Palumbo's presence, Baccala announced he was very mad at one Georgie Paradise.

"Georgie Paradise, he's-a no do the right thing," Baccala said. "Georgie Paradise, he's a rat *basset*."

Kid Sally immediately got very mad at Georgie Paradise too.

"That dirty rat bastard Georgie Paradise," Kid Sally Palumbo said. He had never met Georgie Paradise.

Kid Sally called a saloon where he was told Georgie Paradise hung out.

"Hey! Is Georgie Paradise there?" Kid Sally said.

The phone on the other end dropped and then it was picked up again. "Hey! This is Georgie Paradise."

"You be on the corner in ten minutes. We got a important message from Baccala that you got to handle," Kid Sally said.

Georgie Paradise was on the corner in front of the saloon in ten minutes. Kid Sally and three of his people, Big Lollipop and his cousin Little Lollipop and Mike the Driver, who was driving, came to pick up Georgie Paradise.

"Hey!" Kid Sally Palumbo called out from the car.

"Hey!" Georgie Paradise said. He walked up to the car.

Big Lollipop jumped on Georgie Paradise's head as Georgie Paradise came into the car. Little Lollipop put both hands on Georgie Paradise's throat. Sensing something unusual, Georgie Paradise began twisting. Kid Sally Palumbo took a gun out. He tried to hold the gun against Georgie Paradise's head. Georgie moved his head around. Kid Sally's gun slipped off Georgie Paradise's head. Kid Sally fired three shots which went out the window. Georgie Paradise got a hand on the door and opened it and threw himself out onto the street. He began to run. Mike the Driver, who was driving, was afraid Georgie Paradise would start screaming and bring the cops. Mike the Driver put his foot to the floor so he could drive the car away. The car shot forward just as Georgie Paradise was trying to run around it. The car did some job of squashing Georgie Paradise.

The newspapers the next day wrote that Georgie Paradise had been the victim of a hit-run driver.

Baccala was elated. "You know that Kid Sally, he's a nice-a boy," he told everybody. "He does-a things with style. They no even investigate Georgie Paradise."

This great doing away with Georgie Paradise made Kid Sally a comer in the Baccala Family.

This Mafia of Baccala and Kid Sally Palumbo got into American life the same way the Greeks got into Buckingham

Palace. They came by boat and worked their way up. The Mafia is known as the "Cosa Nostra" in publications and on witness stands. In America today it is a federation of gangsters, ninety-seven per cent of whom are Italian or of Italian origin. The other three per cent is comprised of Irish, who run the docks; Jews, who handle the money; and Greeks, who are the most underrated thieves in the world. The members of the federation work together as well, and have the same trust in each other, as members of Congress. At a wake of a Mafia leader who has been shot six times in the head, one huge floral piece always arrives with the ribbon saying, "I'm Sorry It Had to Come to This."

The foundation of the Mafia is its Sicilian blood. Calabrese and Napolitano bloodlines mean very much. But Sicilian stands over all. The older founders of the American Mafia refer to their group as the *onorata società,* or honored society. It was formed centuries ago in Sicily to protect the people from being robbed and tortured by foreigners who constantly invaded and controlled the island. Like any such organization, including the police in America, it was most responsive to the needs of the rich Sicilian landowners. Their property was most protected. The poor were robbed. Soon the rich were robbed too.

The basis of the Mafia was that it ignored all local laws, as they were laws set down by foreigners. The Mafia ruled by its own code. The Mafia liked this way of life so much that it has not given it up through the centuries. A true Sicilian in America today must smoke in the subway. Baccala himself goes three blocks out of his way for the privilege of going the wrong way on a one-way street. At the same time, the Mafia is very strict in upholding its own laws. Once a member of Baccala's gang cheated Baccala just a little bit on profits from a bookmaking operation. Baccala took the man to a dentist's office that night and put the drill just a little bit through the man's tongue.

In Sicily, in one thousand years of existence, the Mafia has never been able to spread from Palermo and Agrigento on the southwestern side of the island. There is no Mafia in Siracusa or any other place on the island's eastern coast. And today, when a Mafia member is arrested in Italy, he is treated with extraordinary disdain by authorities. In Palermo the shifting of the wholesale fruit market to a new location produced a wave of murders. Authorities indicted 118 hoodlums. A high-school gymnasium was used for the mass trial. Bleachers for the defendants were set up along one wall, and plumbers constructed a cage of thick steam pipes around the bleachers. Whenever one of the defendants would jump up from the bleachers and grip the steam pipes and shout out his innocence, policemen would reach up and smash his fingers with clubs. Late one afternoon one of the defendants, charged with cutting off a man's head among the tomato stalls, had to attend the men's room. Guards manacled his hands and ankles, looped a chain around his middle, and walked him like a dog. One of the magistrates, a magnificent gray-haired woman from Verona, watched the Mafioso shuffle helplessly at the end of his chain. In precise, cultured tones, the woman magistrate inquired from the bench as to why the police did not have another chain wrapped around the prisoner's neck so he could be yanked around more easily.

But in America, where violence is loved and respected in all sectors, the Mafia leaped and spread to every major city and its suburbs as the nation grew. When the protection-minded Mafia people came to America, they found the land-owners had so many guards it was ludicrous. The National Guard shot down women and children during a strike against a Rockefeller mine in Ludlow, Colorado. The fiercest dons of them all threw up their hands in defeat and admiration. "No can match," Giuseppe (Extreme Unction) Magaddino of the Kansas City outfit said. The Mafia was left with only the poor to protect. As only so much can be taken from the poor by terror, subtler methods must be used. Sell women or narcotics or the chance to gamble or whisky to the poor. So the Mafia originally became a national success during Prohibition, as evil everywhere flourishes under repression. Then there is the matter of Americans relying on a dedicated lawman and lifetime bachelor named J. Edgar Hoover. He is the head of the FBI. The original job of the FBI was to prevent interstate crime, the foremost practitioners of which are the Mafia. But in the years of Hoover the Mafia grew into a crime cartel and an FBI arrest of a Mafia member was rare except on the FBI radio programs and, later, television shows. Hoover himself kept announcing that he did not believe there was any such thing as the Mafia. The answer can only be either that Hoover was a member of the Mafia or that he regarded Communist literature on 14th Street in New York as far more dangerous than narcotics on 108th Street. So many FBI agents penetrated the Communist Party that meeting halls became referred to as "the squad room." The agents, graduates of Catholic colleges in the North or dedicated Southerners, both varieties of which can be counted upon to hate Communism and suspect its presence everywhere, always have been helpless around the Mafia.

"Don't we have anybody who infiltrated this organization these people have?" the new United States Attorney General asked at his first FBI crime briefing.

"We've tried, but we've had no success," the assistant director handling the briefing said.

"Why is that?" the Attorney General said.

"Well, we do have several agents who could *pass* for Italian, but each time one of them gets close he is asked for the names of all his cousins," the assistant director said.

Hoover knows better than anybody that stool pigeons, not electronic eavesdropping, are the backbone of law-enforcement. Hoover himself would be merely another retired cop at the racetrack if a girl hadn't once called him up and told him what movie John Dillinger was at. Yet for decades Hoover had no contacts around or within the Mafia, and the Mafia grew into a part of American life. Of course, even with a clear field, the Italians in the Mafia never have come close to the magnitude of larceny committed here by English Protestants, but they have been formidable, given the limits of education and intelligence.

And now, here, in Brooklyn, the Mafia was starting to stretch out and wrap its tentacles, as the newspapers write it, around another part of American life. The Six-Day Bike Race. And Joseph DeLauria was presenting himself around town as a bike-race promoter. He rented an armory, put his name on letterheads, contacted a booking agent in Rome, and awaited other ceremonial duties. The real job of putting on the show, getting the track built, and organizing the gambling was left to Kid Sally Palumbo and his people.

Chapter 2

The cold wind from the mountains ran through the stone streets that have no trees. When Mario Trantino came out of the house into the early-morning emptiness, the air forced his eyes to widen. The street was an alley built on a sharp hill, which started in the center of town and ended in the rocks and mud where the hill became the start of a mountain. The alley ran between attached two-story stone houses which were pastel-colored but tiny and dirty inside and with running water only in the daylight hours. The narrow sidewalks were lined with cars parked half on the sidewalk. A new gray Fiat was in front of Mario's door. The auto-rental agency where he worked had given him its best car, at an employee's rate, for his trip. It was a fine car, but all Mario cared was that the machine knew enough to move. He despised cars. His job was apprentice mechanic and handyman at the auto-rental agency, but he really considered himself a young artist.

Mario always went around town with his shoelaces untied. He did not care for this, because he always tripped on the laces. And then his arches ached constantly because he had to walk in a way that would both get him where he was going and keep the loose shoes from falling off his feet. Mario told everybody that he did not like shoelaces because this is the first way that society ties up the human personality. When people in town said he was crazy, Mario beamed. He did not need glasses, but he would take his uncle's, thick, silver-rimmed things, and walk with the glasses perched on the bridge of his nose. When Mario had to see, at a streetcorner, he looked over the tops of the glasses. Otherwise, he kept his eyes looking down. The thick glasses hurt his eyes, so he would close them and pretend he was a blind man and concentrate on visualizing things. Mario said this kept the world from distracting him. It also kept the people in town shaking their heads and clucking. This made Mario feel it was the only way he could make people regard him as artistic.

In his town, the town of Catanzia, in Calabria, in southern Italy, there was no way for an artist to subsist or to be recognized, and his chances of developing his talent were limited. So Mario Trantino had to walk around town with his arches aching and his shoes flopping and his eyes closed, tripping over his shoelaces quite often, but his real suffering began when he had to go to work on his job. Every wipe of a cloth and every turn of a wrench at the auto-rental garage went against Mario. Near the end of a day a pain would shoot through the palm of Mario's right hand. The pain was caused by the nail being driven through his hand and into the cross.

A woman came through the doorway curtain of the next house and smiled good morning to Mario in the cold morning air. A nannygoat with straggly hair, black-tipped with dirt, followed her. The woman put a brazier, black from fire, on the sidewalk. The brazier was filled with tree branches broken into small sticks. She stuffed a fistful of balled-up paper into the sticks and put a match to the paper. The nannygoat sniffed at the brazier and then backed up from the flames and went through the curtain and into the house. The woman was starting the morning fire to warm the house. When the paper burns and the sticks first catch, the flames are too high and wavery to bring into the house. The woman stepped away from the brazier to wait for the flames to become low. Using her skirt as a potholder, she brought the brazier upstairs in the house and put a little pocket of warmth into the morning dampness. The goats and chickens lived downstairs in the house. Mario's house had a striped curtain, more like a bathtowel, on the door. Behind the curtain a cow stood in straw that was wet with urine. The woman stood and watched the flames. She smiled at Mario again and walked over to the gray Fiat and began polishing the fender with her wool skirt. Southern Italy is the same as the rest of the world. People stroke and polish machines while goats urinate in their houses.

In a few minutes Mario would be using this car to leave Catanzia forever. He was driving to Reggio Calabria and the 9:35 a.m. plane to Rome. At Rome he would transfer to the International Terminal and get on the 1:45 p.m. Alitalia flight to America; to Kennedy Airport in New York, to Manhattan, and to Brooklyn, and to all the great things that everybody said that he, Mario Trantino, surprise third-place finisher in the Milan-San Remo amateur bike race, was sure to receive for placing very high in, or winning, the World Championship Six-Day Bike Race in New York. If Mario failed and had to come home, he would sit down backward on the railroad tracks at Reggio Calabria and eat his sandwich and let the Naples express come from behind and do the rest.

When the letter inviting Mario to the bike race had come six weeks ago, it put a flash of brightness in his chest. The letter was from a booking agent in Rome named Rinaldi, who said he was representing an organization of American-Italian men who were anxious to bring back bike-racing to its rightful place in American sports.

In Europe only a few athletes make more than a champion bike-racer. With bike-racing in America unknown in the last twenty-five years, Rinaldi had to produce contestants at a price American promoters could afford. Rather than contact professionals chasing big fees and endorsements on the European circuit, Rinaldi went for reasonably good amateurs and pointed out to them that nobody would notice they were being paid in America. Besides, there was the free trip to America. Any dreams Mario had of becoming a great rich bike-rider were minute compared to his desire to get to America. Rinaldi wanted Mario to team with another fairly good Italian amateur, Carlo Rafetto of Milano. In his letter he said Mario had a fine chance to win. As the sponsors in America had made it plain that they were not about to turn over much money to some oily Turk, Rinaldi was booking only people learning how to ride a two-wheeler, or advanced tuberculars, from countries other than Italy. He was an expert at doing this. Once, for Rossi, the popular but slightly weak Italian lightweight, Rinaldi brought in a German with a broken hand. Rinaldi told the German that if he punched very fast with the broken hand, he would not notice the pain.

For his trip, Mario was guaranteed all expenses plus $1000 American. If his team won the race, the letter said, prizes could run to as much as $2500. There was even a chance the bike race would go on tour throughout America. When Mario took the letter to the bank to look up the money-exchange tables, the teller hung over his shoulder. The teller began shaking when he saw the amounts Mario was inspecting. The teller blessed himself and kissed his fingers. He leaned over the top of the counter and kissed Mario.

Mario took a deep breath of the cold morning air and started walking down the hill. He took long strides. At twenty-three, Mario Trantino was probably the most striking male in Catanzia. If he had grown up in a freer atmosphere than the vacantness of Catanzia, he would have been on the preferred invitation list of every party that had the chance of becoming an orgy. Mario had a proud body that was a little bit over six feet and was contained in 165 pounds. Black hair clung to his head in waves. Sideburns dropped to a point that was a full inch lower than they were on the picture of Garibaldi in Mario's house. His face was clear and had a tone and life to it that comes from the constant breaking of sweat during some form of athletics. His dark brown eyes gleamed with excitement. His nose, just prominent enough to get into trouble with a fast-closing door, put a measure of Roman history onto his face. He wore his only suit, a tight-fitting pepper-and-salt with double vents.

On his job at the auto-rental agency, Mario took interest only at lunchtime when Savona, the fat manager, would sit at his desk and sip *chocolata* and play cards with Mario. Savona wore eyeglasses that were as thick as windshields. The eyeglasses would steam up in the noon heat; Catanzia was very cold at night and on both edges of night and very hot at midday, and at noon Savona would take the glasses off and wipe them. With his glasses off, Savona was technically blind. It is extremely helpful to play cards for money with somebody who is not too good at seeing.

Mario's other small pleasure on the job was to stretch out underneath a car he was working on and pretend he was a gynecologist tinkering with Sophia Loren. When he would get tuckered out from this, he would fall asleep. His head would be on the cement that was covered with oil and grease, but this wouldn't matter to him.

Mario had been putting things on paper since he was eight. Each morning that summer he had bicycled two miles down a twisting road to the small resort hotel on the cliff over the sea. The hotel allowed kids to put out deck chairs and run other small errands for tips. The hotel was out of the way, and the only foreign tourists ever to stay there were a childless couple from Manchester, England. The man was a schoolteacher who liked to paint. He liked vacationing on the Calabrian coast because nobody came up to him and insisted he needed a drink when all he really wanted to do was paint. At first, the kids from Catanzia formed a circle behind the man and watched him paint. They would lose interest and leave. All except Mario. When the schoolteacher came for the second summer, he had a paintbox for Mario. The little boy spent some of his afternoons sitting on the cliffs and putting colors on paper while the man painted. Once in a while he looked at what Mario was doing and made suggestions. The schoolteacher spoke fair Italian and was able to make himself understood. And by the middle of the third summer Mario was starting to pick up enough English for the beginnings of conversation. In the summer of Mario's twelfth year the schoolteacher and his wife did not come, and the hotel never heard from them again. But the man had left his impression on Mario. The boy loved to draw and paint. In school, Mario leaped ahead of the class in English and because it was so easy he worked even harder on the subject. When somebody's relatives from America came to Catanzia for a visit, Mario would show off and talk to them in English that was a couple of shades better than that used by the relatives.

Mario also showed off his art work. He brought a pencil sketch of Christ on the cross to the rectory, and it still hangs in the front room of the rectory. Another of Mario's sketches was far more famous in Catanzia. Mario made the sketch when he was sixteen, and he did it carefully and slowly over several weeks of peeking at his uncle and aunt on Sunday afternoons in order to obtain an immensely detailed sketch of the two of them steaming through knockout sex. When Mario showed it around the street for the first time, so many kids collected around him and made so much noise that a fight started. A stumpy old man named Doto got up from a cane chair in front of his house and waved a stick at the boys and chased them.

When Doto saw Mario's sketch, he pretended to go into a rage. He grabbed it from Mario and told him to go to confession. Doto took the sketch and tottered down to the *pasticceria* and passed it around to the old men having coffee, and the old men choked and doubled up and coffee ran down their chins. Doto brought the sketch home, and he keeps it in the top drawer of his bureau. He looks at it every Sunday afternoon in hopes of being stimulated.

There was no impetus at home for Mario to do anything but work at a job. His mother had died when he was six. His father was a name on a birth certificate, put there for form. He was raised, with four cousins, by his uncle and aunt. The seven people lived on one large bed, and on three cots, in three rooms in the tiny house. Whenever Mario drew anything around the house and showed them his work, the uncle would say, "That's nice, but come with me today and do something good. Pick up almonds with me today." Then Mario had to go out with a burlap sack and long sweepers made of sticks and scratch almonds from the ground and into the burlap, while his uncle walked around hunting chipmunks with a .22 rifle. The family ate the animals and sold the almonds.

There was a girl in town named Carmela and she worked at the dry-goods store, and Mario asked her to go to the movies one night and Carmela's aunt, who was called Zia Nicolina, showed up as chaperon. Zia Nicolina did not look like a chaperon. She looked, from neck to midsection, like a cow. Her stomach looked like a steam boiler wrapped in black cloth. Zia Nicolina was unmarried. During the war, when there had been Italian and then German and then American troops in the town, Zia Nicolina had been able to take care of entire regiments. The Germans used to send a command car to pick her up. As a chaperon, Zia Nicolina was a large bulldog. At the movies she sat directly behind Carmela, with her fat hands draped over the seats between Carmela and Mario. Every time Mario shifted his weight, Zia Nicolina's hands dug into his shoulder. "Stay on your side," Zia Nicolina rasped. The walk home was excruciating because Zia Nicolina got between them, one hand tightly gripping Mario's arm, and she complained of arthritis until they reached the door; then she shooed Carmela inside and told Mario to go away.

Mario endured it because Carmela was the only girl in town who seemed to find any amusement in his untied shoelaces and his eyeglass habits. One night, when he had a date to take Carmela to see a picture billed as *Gangster Story,* Mario arrived to find Zia Nicolina standing outside the house.

"Carmela's sick," Zia Nicolina said.

"Oh," Mario said.

"You can't see her, she sleeps," Zia Nicolina said.

"Well, tell her I was here and that I hope she is better," he said.

He turned to go.

"Hey!" Zia Nicolina said.

"Yes?"

"You take Zia Nicolina to the movie instead?"

A vise closed around Mario's throat and he nodded yes, and Zia Nicolina grabbed his arm and he walked her down to the movie house. She sat next to him all night, her fat legs brushing up against his, her hand grabbing his arm when anything happened. Her face, which needed a shave, was shiny with sweat. Carmela and her family lived in a house at the top of the hill, on the edge of town. On the way home Zia Nicolina made Mario go a block out of the way because she wanted to find a hoe she said she had left in the field her family tilled. Zia Nicolina stepped into the field, and Mario, one hand on her elbow, followed her. Zia Nicolina went a couple of steps and then backed into Mario like a truck. Mario was off balance when Zia Nicolina twisted around and put her hands on the back of his neck. She fell backward, and Mario came down on top of her.

Mario despised the night with Zia Nicolina. He had a great love for the earth and the colors and shadings of ground in the sunlight, and he loved the symmetry of a girl, not just her body, but her hair and her eyes and her mouth and the depth that her face could show, and he loved his mornings up on the hills, with the sounds of his work, the tinkling of water running through the brushes when he rinsed them, the tiny sound of a pencil biting into good paper. Every morning he rode up the road winding along the mountain, pushing his legs until they were on fire and then became numb. When he could go up no more, he stopped and drew. When it was time to leave, he turned and came flying down the mountain and onto the hill at the foot of the mountain and down through the town, and he always headed for the start of the road which led out of town and while he was racing on his bike through the town he imagined he was leaving it forever. At the last corner he would turn and slow down and pedal sullenly to his job at the auto-rental agency.

Riding through the hills made him the best bike-rider in Catanzia by the time he was sixteen, and he entered and won several small races sponsored by the church societies. He entered a townwide race and won that too. Savona, from the auto-rental agency, was a bike-racing fan. The day before Mario stumbled out of high school, Savona offered him a job. Mario took the job and continued bike-racing on weekends. He began entering amateur races all over Italy. He received expenses and also placed in the first twenty finishers often enough to earn silent bonuses. He earned $200 for his first major victory, the 25-kilometer race.

He spent most of this money on expensive art paper. Mario's drawing was put to uses of sorts around Catanzia. At a charity carnival for one of the churches he sketched faces and took in more money for the church than the weight-guesser did. Once Mario did a poster for a local bike race and a man from the race committee in Naples liked it so much he gave it to a sporting newspaper in Naples. The sketch ran in the paper, and when Mario got the clipping in the mail he walked around looking at it so much that the newsprint began to disintegrate.

For one big championship race Mario went to Rome, and he took a guided tour of the Cinecittà film studios. In one building dozens of people were sitting in an air-conditioned room and working at drawing boards. They were animating comic strips that ran on television. One of the artists, about twenty-five, had long straggly hair and wore a flowered shirt, tight chino pants, and cowboy boots. He was whistling while he cut out little strips of gray-speckled cellophane and carefully glued them over parts of the comic strip. The tour conductor was talking about the hard, precise work going on in the room. Mario jumped when he heard the word "work." When he got back to Catanzia and was polishing his cars, he kept hearing the tour conductor say the artists were working.

When he was in Rome, Mario took a walk on the Via Veneto and dawdled in the light from the kiosks on a big corner newsstand across the street from the Hotel Excelsior. Mario's eyes jumped when he saw an entire rack of magazines with titles: *Il Giornale di Artista, The Artist,* and *Studio International of Modern Art.* Mario liked the American magazines best. In one of them the first article was titled, "A Basic Approach to Composition." It was written by Grant Monroe. A picture of Grant Monroe, with great bushy hair and in a T-shirt, ran with the article. The caption read: "Grant Monroe at his studio on 10th Street in New York's East Village." Mario read the article, which was difficult because it referred to a thing called the "Golden Section," which is a triangular way of arranging scenes so that people look into them, rather than see a flat, straight-up-and-down arrangement. He read the magazines for months, always returning to the picture of Grant Monroe and his bushy hair, and he dreamed of meeting him one day. Then the letter from Rinaldi came, and Mario walked around with the magazine under his arm. He would go to America and see Grant Monroe and become an artist and never leave America and never see Catanzia again.

Now, in the cold air of his last morning in Catanzia, Mario walked down the hill from his house as quickly as he could and he came around a corner and went down the block toward the church, which stood facing a square.

Father Marsalano was pacing up and down with the chickens in the cobblestone piazza in front of the church. He carried a prayer book and a Polaroid camera. When Father Marsalano saw Mario turn the corner and come into the square, he brought his hand to his mouth and let out a yell. The chickens flapped up and hung around Father Marsalano's ankles. If he could ever get them to go higher and begin flying in circles around him, he would claim he was Saint Francis of Assisi.

Eleven heads poked from doorways. Father Marsalano pointed to a boy of about seven, who was standing in his bare feet. The boy had short pants and a thin white shirt ripped at the elbows. Black uncombed hair fell onto his face. The boy came running across the square and followed the priest and Mario to the back of the church. A muddy lot covered with rocks and tin cans ran up the hill behind the church.

Father Marsalano held the camera out to Mario. The priest stepped into the lot, and the boy came through the cold mud after him. Father Marsalano grabbed Giovanni's thin shirt and ripped the front of it. Giovanni made a face. Father Marsalano ran a hand through the mud. He wiped his hand on the front of Giovanni's shirt and smeared the mud across Giovanni's face. The kid's mouth almost formed a word.

"All right," Father Marsalano said to Mario, "take the picture."

Father Marsalano stood with the prayer book in his left hand and his right hand on top of Giovanni's head. Father Marsalano's face became somber. Giovanni stuck his tongue out at the camera. Father Marsalano's hand lifted from the top of Giovanni's head. Then it came down hard enough to cause a concussion. Giovanni winced. Mario took the picture.

While Mario was flipping and pulling and peeling to get at the picture, Father Marsalano was on him like a blanket. The priest started saying, "Good! Good!" when he saw the picture. It was nearly as good as a Dr. Tom Dooley poster. Father Marsalano's face was pleading. Giovanni looked only like early death.

Father Marsalano took Mario by the arm and started walking him to the back door of the church. Giovanni stood in the cold mud and made a fist with his right hand and brought his arm up and bent it at the elbow. Giovanni's left hand slapped the inside of his right elbow. This is the classic expression of true Italian regard for the clergy, which first began to appear when Innocent IV was Pope.

Inside, Father Marsalano began writing in pen on the back of the picture:

> Dear Friends Who Left Catanzia to Go to America and Become Rich, the Mother of God is watching always. So is Saint Angelo, who is the patron of Catanzia and everybody who ever lived in our town. This picture on the opposite side shows the place where your beloved church is going to erect a new orphanage. This poor little boy standing with me has no place to sleep or eat. He is very

hungry now. Also very cold. Someday when we have the new orphanage which we will build this little boy will be warm and fed.

It is good to hear from you. Send me some good news in the mail. Then I will have good news for the homeless little children of Catanzia.

Yours in the Lord,
Father Giuseppe Marsalano

The priest put the picture into a manila envelope. The envelope was already stuffed with addresses of people who had gone to America directly from Catanzia, or who were members of families started by people who had gone to America from Catanzia and were now dead.

"All right, you go now?" the priest asked Mario.

"Yes, Father."

"You know what to do in New York?"

"Go to the mailbox with them to make sure they send the money."

"Good." The priest cleared his throat. "Now, I tell you something. You be a good boy."

"Yes, Father."

"Don't steal."

"No, Father."

"Respect womanhood. Remember. Every woman you meet will be the mother of somebody some day. You respect that. Just remember, the Virgin Mary watches when you're near a woman who will become a mother."

At the airport Mario checked his baggage through to New York. He sat in the little waiting room with his ticket in his hand and looked out the window. The whitecapped, very blue waters of the Strait of Messina ran against the edge of the airport. Across the water the dark mountains of Sicily climbed straight up. Mount Etna, dark at the bottom, misty and snow-covered at the top, had gray smoke billowing from its crater.

Mario looked at Sicily. He had been there once, for a bike race at Palermo. The night before the race he had gone into a *pasticceria* on a little street near the hotel and he stood at a table and played brischola with a priest. The priest was cheating, but when Mario complained a man said he would cut off Mario's ears if he complained again. Mario turned white, but he stayed and kept playing with the priest until there was a power failure. Palermo has three or four of them a night. While the owner was getting out his hurricane lamps, Mario's hands swept the table. He scooped up all the money and ran out of the place. The next day, when the bike race started through the streets of Palermo, Mario put his head down in case the man who had threatened him was in the crowd. He did not lift it up until he was out in the hills of the countryside. Sicilians were strange people.

As Mario looked at the water he heard the noise of the plane. A twin-engined Convair was coming out of the sky. It was the plane which goes from Messina to Reggio Calabria to Rome. The date was January 23. In airports all over Europe, in Belgrade and Turin and Warsaw and Copenhagen, there were bike-riders waiting for planes to America and the many thousands of dollars which the six-day bike race would bring.

Chapter 3

Baccala, the executive producer of the six-day bike race, was at home asleep in his $175,000 brick house in Beachhaven, Long Island. Baccala is 5-foot-5. He was in bed on his back with his arms flung out and his mouth open. He looked like a rolled stuffed pork. His wife, Mrs. Baccala, was asleep on her side next to him. Baccala had his toes stuck between the calves of Mrs. Baccala's legs so he would be warm all night. Mr. and Mrs. Baccala were the only people in the nineteen-room house. They had raised three children: Anthony Jr., who attended Georgetown and became a lawyer in Maryland; Vera, who attended Mt. Carmel College in New Hampshire, and now teaches in San Leandro, California: and Joseph, also known as Zu Zu, who dropped out of high school at the behest of a judge who sentenced him to six months in the reformatory. Zu Zu, twenty-six, is a very promising young shylock in Miami.

Of his three children, Baccala is proudest of Zu Zu. "He's a good nice boy," Baccala always says. All Mafia people succumb to an insidious urge to make their children respectable. But they are never comfortable with it. When the dons sit down for coffee and discuss their children, there are many baffled gestures made with the palms up.

"What do I know what he do?" Baccala said to Louis the Chink one day when asked about his decent son. "All the time he read a book. What do I know? He goes to the school."

But when Zu Zu was fifteen and he had just stood his first pinch, felonious assault with a tire iron on his continuation-school teacher, Baccala came bounding into a restaurant and ordered everybody to drink up.

"What do you think-a my kid does today?" he said. "That little rat-a basset. What do you think-a he does? He breaks his teacher's head!"

"A *salut!*" somebody called out.

"Aha!" Baccala said. He threw down a straight scotch.

With the children gone, Baccala's house, with its bowling alleys in the basement, stereophonic-fitted bar and study, and square foot after square foot of Italian marble floors, was silent and empty. Outside, floodlights glared on the fenced-in grounds. Two tawny German shepherds loped around the grounds, ready to chew on anybody coming over the fence. Baccala does not rely on the dogs to wake him up if trespassers arrive. He has every inch of his windows and doors wired. The central alarm system is on the floor under Baccala's bed. Its major component is an air-raid alarm. Next to it are two loaded shotguns.

At eight a.m. Baccala was out of bed and ready to leave for the day. He was standing just inside the kitchen door while his wife, Mrs. Baccala, went out into the driveway in her housecoat. Mrs. Baccala slid behind the wheel of a black Cadillac. Baccala sat down on the kitchen floor and closed his eyes and folded his arms over his face. Mrs. Baccala started the car. When the car did not blow up from a bomb, Baccala got up from the kitchen floor and walked out into the driveway, patted Mrs. Baccala on the head as she came out of the car, got in, and backed down the driveway and went off to start another day.

Baccala was beautiful in his big black car. Covered with pressed black Italian silk, he looked stumpy, rather than dumpy. His head was stuck inside a tiny black fedora. The next size after Baccala's hat is a college beanie. He sat on two overstuffed pillows. Without the pillows, Baccala would be so low in the seat that he would have to peer through the steering wheel. Even with the pillows, Baccala has a big wooden block strapped to the gas pedal.

Baccala pressed a $125 black alligator tasseled loafer onto the gas pedal. The shoes were, after Baccala's heart, the most important part of his make-up. New shoes are the badge of the Mafia. Gangsters come from families who went barefoot in southern Italy and Sicily. The children were raised in America in worn sneakers, summer and winter. The first dollar they steal, on growing up, goes to a shoe store. Even old Mafiosos, the ones who have lived to pile up fortunes from narcotics and shylocking, cannot pass a shoe store without going in and buying a new pair. The danger in this is considerable, and many good law-enforcement people feel the way to break up the Mafia is to hit them in the shoes. This was borne out when a joint venture of Baccala's and the Philadelphia mob's turned into real trouble. Representatives from the two mobs shot four major welshers. Three men from each mob were assigned to a burial detail. The graveyard was a field in Rockland County. The six gravediggers who showed up with the bodies all wore $110 pebble-grained Bronzini customs. They walked on their toes through the mud. When they began digging, they tried to push the shovels down only with their toes. They kept stopping to rub their shoes on the backs of their trousers.

"Dig deep down," one of them said.

"I got a fresh shoeshine," somebody muttered.

"Mud gets in the lines around the dots," one of them said, referring to the pebble grain.

The body never did get down very far. A good rainstorm a week later uncovered the bodies, and the FBI moved two mobile laboratories into the field.

As Baccala drove to work, the hopes of three personal families and of his whole Mafia family rested on him. He has the three personal families because he has two other wives, aside from Mrs. Baccala. One of the other wives is a twenty-nine-year-old cocktail waitress who is in a split-level house which Baccala bought for her in Teaneck, New Jersey. The other is twenty-four and redheaded and she wears fur coats and lives in an apartment on East 56th Street. He also has a sixteen-year-old high-school senior as a friend. The wives are absolutely legal wives as far as the government is concerned. Baccala files joint income-tax returns for all three families. Local authorities might require a divorce in here some place, but nobody has ever complained.

Baccala got married three times to solve a great problem which came to a head one night in 1955. The cocktail waitress he was to marry was sixteen. Baccala had her at the bar of a Chinese restaurant. They were sitting on stools and facing each other. The girl rubbed her young knees against Baccala's. His body started to glow. He swallowed his vodka. It created a stirring in his loins. He waited until the Chinaman behind the bar was busy, and he slipped out of the place with the girl. Baccala would stiff a bishop. They walked up to Seventh Avenue, to the Park West Hotel. Baccala went into the cigar store on the corner. He stuffed a handful of twenty-five-cent cigars in his pocket. He took one from the fifteen-cent box and held it out to the clerk. He gave the clerk a dollar for the cigar. While the clerk made change, Baccala hit the candy stand and came off with six rolls of butterscotch Life Savers. He got the change and grabbed a *Daily News* on the way out.

He took the girl into the hotel lobby. The clerk pushed the registry pad at him. Baccala picked up the pen. He shot his cuffs and held the pen way out. He arranged his feet so his weight would be evenly distributed. Then he bent over the registry pad and brought the pen to it.

Make-a two sticks and put a little v between them, and that's a big M.

He began drawing a capital M, the first letter of "Mr. and Mrs. John Smith."

Baccala's knuckles whitened as he pushed the pen. After he had the capital S in Smith he broke into freehand.

Make a couple of mountains.

He made two mountains for the small m in Smith. It didn't seem right. He went back to make another mountain, and his hand was tired and it slipped and made a mess of the card. Baccala could feel the reservation clerk's eyes boring into him. Baccala dropped the pen and shook his hand. He was angry and too embarrassed to look at the clerk. He put his hand into his pocket and pulled out a roll three inches thick, with hundreds on the top, and snapped a five dollar bill off the roll.

"I got arthrite. You write in for me."

The clerk looked at him haughtily. Baccala was crushed. For his pride, he wanted to bite the clerk on the nose. When he got upstairs with the girl he didn't want to take his clothes off.

After that, Baccala wanted permanent lodgings for his romancing. So he married his two girl friends. Baccala stays home with Mrs. Baccala three nights. The other four are divided among his two other wives and the sixteen-year-old coed.

Baccala is in complete command of his business life. He never touches anything that is illegal. Every year, on Christmas Day, his chief shylock, Moe Fein, arrives with an envelope containing $50,000 in cash. The $50,000 is Baccala's interest for the year on the $250,000 he gave the shylocks a year ago to put on the street for him. The shylocks loan it out for whatever interest they can get. But the first $50,000 must go to Baccala. And the $250,000 can be recalled at any time. Baccala passes on narcotics importing, but is never in the same room with narcotics. It takes large amounts of cash in small bills to pay for a shipment of heroin or cocaine which could earn hundreds of thousands of dollars. If Baccala feels a shipment is worth it, he sends Moe Fein on a plane to Lucerne, Switzerland, to withdraw the money from Baccala's numbered accounts. The accounts total over eleven million dollars. In Switzerland, Fein meets somebody from the Corsican drug-factory organization. Fein and the Corsican are bonded with their lives. Fein flies home, the Corsican disappears, and the narcotics shipment comes into New York from Montreal by car. The narcotics seep down to the street, where Negroes do the selling and much of the using. "We don't hurt-a nobody, we only sell to-a niggers," Baccala reasons. The money rises to Baccala. He is silent about it. But as nobody sees anything wrong with gambling, Baccala openly admits he runs all bookmaking and policy numbers in Brooklyn.

Baccala is one of the many Mafia bosses who generally are depicted as controlling sprawling businesses. He has been involved in a number of legitimate enterprises. At one time he was one of the city's largest dress-manufacturers. He used threats, acid, and non-union help. People in the garment industry referred to a Baccala dress as "the buy or die line." The chief assistant in the dress factory, Seymour Lipman, had a brother-in-law named Dave, who also was in the garment business. Dave sold Seymour material. It took four sets of books to do it, but Seymour Lipman and his brother-in-law Dave wound up with houses in Miami. Baccala was losing eighty cents each time he sold a dress. At the first-anniversary party for his dress business, Baccala arrived at the factory with a can of gasoline in each hand.

In another business venture, Baccala and the chief of the East Harlem mob, Gigi off of 116th Street, entered into what they felt would be a gigantic stock-swindling operation. They were doing business with, they were assured, complete suckers. "High-class Protestant people, what could they know?" Gigi off of 116th Street said. Then the high-class Protestants went to Nassau for a week. Baccala and Gigi suddenly lost $140,000 each in the market and were indicted for illegal trading in potato futures.

After being arraigned, Baccala growled, "I shoot-a somebody, but first I gotta find out-a who I shoot-a and what for I shoot-a him."

It cost him another $35,000 in legal fees before the indictment was dismissed.

But as money makes geniuses of all men, Baccala is known as an immensely successful real-estate holder in Brooklyn. The first thing a Sicilian in America seeks is property. This is a reaction to centuries of peasantry. Baccala's first money went for a small house with a back yard in Canarsie. He planted fig trees in the back yard and when it got cold he covered them with tar paper and put paint cans on the tops of the trees. This, along with religious statues and flamingos on the front lawns, is the most familiar sight in an Italian neighborhood. Baccala bought all his property through Joseph DeLauria. In New York State it costs $100 to form a corporation. Shareholders in the corporation do not have to reveal themselves. They can nominate a person to represent them in a realty corporation. In buying realty, DeLauria forms a new corporation specifically to purchase one parcel. He then nominates his secretary to be the name of record for the new corporation. Anybody attempting to check a realty deal runs into a secretary. She traces back to another corporation. Baccala's name is nowhere, and he owns land worth millions. Many business people understand the connection but don't mind doing business. Money is money.

In the course of the years, many lawyers handling real

estate in these deals went on into politics. Joseph DeLauria always came around with a good campaign contribution. It usually was accepted with deep thanks. Italian politicians had less reason to debate accepting Mafia money than anyone else. Privately, many Italians regard the Mafia as a sort of Knights of Columbus that gets mad. Besides, if it weren't for the Mafia, the closest many Italians would come to holding office in this country would be supervisory jobs in the Department of Sanitation. The discrimination against anybody with an Italian name starts in high school and never really ends. To fight it, some Mafia dons forget greed. When Frank Costello handled the Mafia's political fixing in the East, he did most of his mob business through Jewish bagmen and Irish judges. Costello's pushing of Italians onto court benches mainly was done out of pride in his people. If one of his Italian judges could handle a contract, that was fine. But it was more important that they were Italians and they were judges and that their children would be the children of Italian judges.

Baccala, however, given the choice between a fine, highly promising, dead-honest Italian candidate and a disliked, shifty Irish thief, would at all times go for the Irishman. Baccala's political theories were simple. He had Joseph DeLauria try to bribe every public official in Brooklyn, but he did not expect an inordinate number of breaks to come his way as a result of the bribery. He learned over the years that when it is important, a politician performs for the Mafia about as well as he performs for the public. The popular story is that every big Mafia boss owns one or two appeals-court judges, a few Congressmen, a raft of prosecutors, and, for important contracts, one Supreme Court justice. Now maneuvers with quite a bit of sophistication always do occur. An assistant United States attorney in New York deliberately made reversible errors during a trial so that the Mafia defendant would be certain to win an appeal on a case which was hopeless to win with a jury trial. But endless tales of the Mafia reaching everybody in the world are the result of rumors and fantasies and false promises as much as anything else. Baccala was a political realist. Sure, he'd love to get to a judge. Even higher than that, if possible. But he settled for full ownership of one freshman New York State Assemblyman. The moment the Assemblyman took office, he introduced a private bill which would allow Joseph DeLauria to purchase most of the land under the Hudson River.

In personally vetoing the bill, the Governor remarked to people in his office, "The last person who tried a thing like this was my grandfather."

The drive to the office on this morning took Baccala forty-five minutes. He used the parkway to get to Brooklyn. He came off it onto narrow, puddle-filled streets of warehouses. On one dull street he pulled the car into the empty loading space in front of the dingy two-story Lancer Trucking Company building.

When Baccala came into the building, chairs scraped on the floor of the first-floor office. Four guys jumped to their feet.

"Hey!" Baccala said to them.

The faces of the four screwed into deep thought. Finally one of them said something.

"Hey!" he said to Baccala.

"Hey!" Baccala answered.

"Hey!" another one said.

"Hey!"

"Hey!"

"Hey!"

"Hey!"

The four black suits stood at attention while Baccala started up a flight of narrow wooden stairs. Baccala stamped his Cuban heels on each step as he came up. The noise sounded through the stairwell. A water buffalo in a light blue suit with silver threads appeared at the top of the stairs.

"Hey!" Baccala called out.

"Hey!" the Water Buffalo said.

Baccala walked into the morning silence of his office, which is a sea of snake plants, lamps with ancient frilled shades, and a large wooden desk. Religious statues were everywhere. When Baccala flicked on the light, the room was alive with multicolored lights arranged around the statues. A bank of red imitation candles glowed in front of Saint Anthony. In cream face, brown robes, yellowing Easter palm tied around the waist in big loop knots, Saint Anthony stood directly behind Baccala's desk.

Baccala whipped his hat off for Saint Anthony. *"Buon' giorno,"* he said.

He held his hat against his chest. He bowed his head and started praying out loud.

"Saint Anthony, let me make the good-a living today. And Saint Anthony, let me tell-a you something. I know they a lot of people, they tell you that Baccala is no good. Tell you that I'm bad. Well, you listen to me, please? You remember one thing. Baccala he's on your side. You need, Baccala he goes out and gets it for you. Don't worry about Baccala. He's with Saint Anthony. So Saint Anthony, you be sure you on Baccala's side. Don't listen to these-a creeps. You understand? All right. Amen."

Chapter **4**

At midnight that night, twenty miles away from Baccala's big house, on Marshall Street in Brooklyn, smoke from the first cigarette of the day came against the film of toothpaste on Kid Sally Palumbo's capped teeth. He had just gotten up. Kid Sally straightened his collar. His shirt collar came halfway up the back of his neck. It grazed his ears and came around to a powerful silver tie. He smoothed his hair back. His hair was black and gleamed with brilliantine. It was cut in Madison Avenue button-down. The day Kid Sally saw Artie the Chink, one of the big guys in the East Harlem outfit, walking around with a button-down, he went into Manhattan and got his hair cut at the same barbershop Frank Sinatra uses. The button-down seemed a bit off-center for Kid Sally's face. He has a scar running through his right cheekbone. High cheekbones give his deep brown eyes a hard look. His square chin toughens the look of his mouth. He took another drag on the cigarette. It was an English Oval. Frank Costello smokes English Ovals.

He blew the cigarette smoke at his face in the mirror. His top lip came up in a careful sneer. He giggled. It was a terrific interpretation of Tommy Udo. Tommy Udo is a gangster in an old movie called *Kiss of Death*. Richard Widmark played the part. The big scene in the movie is when Tommy Udo, sneering and giggling, pushes an old lady in a wheelchair to her death down a tenement staircase. Kid Sally Palumbo loved the movie the first time he saw it. He loved it so much that he came back to the movie house that night and saw it again. The next day he was first in line when the movie opened. Kid Sally was fifteen at the time. For the next fourteen years, less twenty-two months in various prisons, Kid Sally Palumbo saw reruns of the movie wherever it played, so he could learn to imitate Tommy Udo. It was not a waste. As Kid Sally looked at himself in the mirror now, he thought he was seeing Tommy Udo, he was giving such a terrific imitation.

One of Kid Sally Palumbo's main men, Tony the Indian, was standing in the bedroom doorway. Tony the Indian is called the Indian because he looks like an Indian. He has olive skin and black hair that combs straight back on either side of his part. Tony the Indian also acts like an Indian. When he is out collecting gambling debts, he comes into a place with a knife between his teeth.

"So what's doin'?" he said to Kid Sally.

"What's doin', I'm gettin' dressed," Kid Sally said. He fingered the tie. He craned his neck to make sure the tie knot and shirt collar sat just right.

"You got a real good *eagle*," Tony the Indian said.

"What should I do, go around thinkin' like I'm a ragpicker?" Kid Sally said.

"That's what I mean," Tony the Indian said. "You got a real terrific *eagle*. You let yourself know you're somethin'."

"You got to get respect off of people. You can't get no respect if you come around actin' like you're just a guy in off of the street. You got to have some class."

"Well, you could *axt* anybody, Sally Kid, they all tell you, that Sally, he got a real *eagle*."

Kid Sally tilted his head to look at himself from another angle.

He and Tony the Indian are always talking to each other. They have stirring conversations, particularly on any telephone they suspect is tapped. Three weeks ago the two spoke over Kid Sally Palumbo's line, which is jointly tapped by the New York City police, the Treasury Department, the FBI, and the Immigration and Naturalization Service.

The phone rang, and a voice the lawmen could identify as Kid Sally Palumbo's answered.

"Yeah," Kid Sally said.

"Hey! What's doin'?" the other voice said. The wiretappers did not know who it was. Kid Sally knew it was Tony the Indian.

"I know you," Kid Sally Palumbo said.

"You do?"

"Yeah, I know you," Kid Sally said.

"All right," the other voice said.

"How we doin'?" Kid Sally said.

"What's goin' on?" the other voice said.

"Did you see that other fella?" Kid Sally said.

"Yeah, I seen him."

"Do you want to see me for somethin'?" Kid Sally said.

"Yeah."

"Meet you right where we was the last time," Kid Sally said.

"You mean the place where that guy—"

"No, not that place. The other place," Kid Sally said.

"What place?"

"The place where we went after the place you're talkin' about."

"Oh, I know that place. Yeah, I was in that place with you."

"What time you be there?" Kid Sally said.

"The same time we was in it last time," the other voice said.

"All right, that's a meet," Kid Sally said.

"We got a meet," the other voice said.

"Take care," Kid Sally said.

"Take care," the other voice said.

When Kid Sally hung up, he stuck his chin out proudly. "Now let them rat mothers, they think they all so smart, let them figger out what that was about."

"Who was it?" one of his men, a dwarf named Beppo who is called Beppo the Dwarf, said.

"Tony the Indian. He seen the guy Levy from Thirty-eighth Street what owed the twenty-five hundred. I got to meet Tony at Ciro's at ten-thirty tonight."

The bug the New York police had put into Kid Sally's desk picked this up. That night two detectives were at the bar when Kid Sally and Tony the Indian came in. The next day a marginal dress manufacturer, David Levy, was brought in for questioning by the District Attorney. Levy said just enough to provoke a new investigation into shylocking.

Kid Sally always seemed to have troubles of this sort. Baccala gave him a clear field in the jukebox business in a few busy sections. Kid Sally established the Ace Vending Machine Company. One of his main men, Joe the Sheik, was in charge of supplying records. Joe the Sheik detested any loud, fast music that reminded him of niggers. "There ain't enough of niggers in the world, people havin' to go around soundin' like them," Joe the Sheik said. Ace Vending jukeboxes carried only Italian numbers. Many people say this is what led to the resurgence of weekend piano-players in Irish bars. Ace Vending went broke, and Baccala laughed openly about it.

Baccala did not laugh so much when Kid Sally Palumbo, without official sanction, tried to take over businesses by using only muscle. This style went out with Al Capone. The Mafia today tries to emulate Protestant bankers. First, loan money. Then collect souls as interest. Kid Sally Palumbo tried to do it with beatings and acid and terror.

He became particularly attracted to Weight Watchers clubs, which were springing up throughout Brooklyn. The clubs were run at great profit by reedy Jewish women who warned clients, mainly fat Italian women, that "your husband is going to get himself a little girl friend so he can feel her ribs." Weight Watchers profits soared and pasta sales slumped. Soon Kid Sally Palumbo began making visits to the Jewish women running the clubs. He dropped veiled hints: "You could be dead in a bomb accident."

The most faithful member of the Weight Watchers club on Saypole Street was Carmela Russo. At thirty-five, she was 5-foot-2 and weighed 217 pounds. When Carmela Russo bent over to touch her toes, her breasts hit the floor before her fingertips. She regarded Weight Watchers as the last chance for her marriage; two months ago her husband, Tony, had started buying dirty books. One afternoon Carmela Russo was in the Weight Watchers club, exercising very hard. She glanced up and saw Kid Sally Palumbo and two of his group swagger in and begin shouting at Mrs. Millie Lewin, who ran the club. Carmela Russo picked her chest off the floor and let out the first of many loud hollers, the last several of which were heard by the District Attorney's office.

However, as a gangster, Kid Sally is very good at some of the basics. The big thing was his knowledge of Good People. In his circles, you say, "He's good people" when you speak of anybody who has at least one legitimate extortion murder under his belt. Kid Sally is the Walter Winchell of the Good People. When he goes to the jukebox he always plays a record by Phyllis McCarthy because she goes out with Sam Giardine, who is the big guy in *Chick*-ago. He knows that Gigi from the Bronx takes out a barmaid from the Silhouette Lounge. If Kid Sally is in the area he stops in at the Silhouette and leaves the barmaid a $10 tip and says, "My regards to your friend." He knows the barmaid will describe him to Gigi and Gigi will say,

"That's-a that nice-a kid, Sally. He's a real nice-a boy." And Kid Sally knows other important things, such as that Georgie Brown from Mott Street lives in Seaview, Long Island; Johnny Brown from Bath Beach lives in Greendale, Long Island; Jackie Brown from East Harlem lives in Pelham Park, Westchester; and Tommy Brown, Eddie Brown, Tony Brown, and Jimmy Brown all go to New Jersey to play golf. Kid Sally never met, but knows all about, Rocky from Detroit, Rocky from Buffalo, Rocky from Cleveland, and Rocky from Topeka.

While Kid Sally stood and looked at himself in the mirror, he began his crap-game singsong. Until he handled the Georgie Paradise contract, he was best known in Brooklyn for the way he could remember all the sayings and keep saying them, over and over, at the crap games he worked at for Baccala. Kid Sally's job was to stand and watch and keep his right hand ready. At the first squawk from a player, Kid Sally would make a V for victory with the two fingers of his right hand and then jab them into the player's eyes. And while he stood and waited to poke eyes, Kid Sally would singsong to the players. When Kid Sally began doing it here in the bedroom, Tony the Indian smiled. He liked Kid Sally to do this.

"Hey! The game's not hard and nobody's barred. . . . Pick a hunch and grab a bunch. . . . Hey! The more you bet, the more you get. . . . Let it go and watch it grow. . . . Hey! Slow it down. Bet fast and you can't last, bet slow and you got to go. . . . We go every night at ten, come along and bring a fren. . . . Hey! The game's not hard and nobody's barred. . . ."

"Who's got the moneys?" Tony the Indian said.

"Yeah, who got the moneys?" Kid Sally said. "I know it ain't us."

Kid Sally took the English Oval and put it in his mouth. He clenched the cigarette between his teeth. He wanted to see how he looked with the cigarette like this. It was all right, but the cigarette was too short. You can put your teeth on a filter cigarette. But who can smoke filters? You got to smoke English Ovals. Frank Costello smokes English Ovals. Kid Sally let the cigarette hang from his lower lip. He looked through the smoke. That's pretty good. Kid Sally thought he looked pretty good. He felt real good.

Then, as it always happens to him, he became uneasy. Somewhere in his mind, just beneath where he is thinking of all these big things and how he looks, there is this jumbled scene that always lies there waiting for him to come on it, and he always seems to come on it and it makes him feel uneasy.

It is a rainy day in Samuel J. Morse High School. The grade adviser for the first-term boy students has gone over the charts, trying to find a class in which Salvatore Palumbo can sit for the 1:45 to 2:40 period. Salvatore Palumbo has already been placed in all the shop courses and gym periods available. The grammar-school record and Youth Court probation notice attached make it plain that Salvatore Palumbo belongs in chains, not classrooms. The grade adviser notes that Salvatore is only two months away from being sixteen, when he can be ejected from school. "You like Spanish?" the grade adviser says finally. Kid Sally shrugs. "He says he likes Spanish," the grade adviser says.

Kid Sally comes into the Spanish class in his sneakers and brown corduroy pants and blue windbreaker with RED WINGS s.c. printed across the back. The s.c. stands for Screwing Club. The class is made up of Jewish girls in neat blouses and plaid skirts and they peer through Chinese-slanted eyeglasses when Kid Sally comes into the room. The boys are thin Jewish kids who sit erect and with their eyes riveted on the teacher, a tall, balding man named Goldstein. Goldstein grimaces when he sees Kid Sally. Then Goldstein walks slowly back and forth in front of the classroom and starts the lesson. Kid Sally

Palumbo sits down and hunches his neck inside the top of his windbreaker and goes into a trance.

"Wouldn't you say so, Mr. Palumbo?"

There is a roar from the class. Kid Sally Palumbo looks up, and all these black-haired girls are looking at him through their Chinese-slanted eyeglasses and the boys with the bumpy noses are looking at him and everybody is laughing at him. Laughing loudly, and laughing down their noses at him. In the front of the room, Goldstein is smiling.

"Well, give us your answer to the question, Mr. Palumbo," Goldstein says.

Kid Sally Palumbo, flustered, his face red while everybody laughs at him, pulls himself together and does the only thing he knows how to do.

"You could go and fuck yourself!" he shouts at Goldstein.

Every time Kid Sally comes onto this scene in his mind, his stomach begins turning over and he has trouble thinking, and he snarls at Goldstein and the snarl comes up out of Kid Sally's insides and right into the present. And Kid Sally, standing in front of his mirror, moves his mouth around the cigarette. He snarls.

"You could go and fuck yourself!"

"Hey! What you say this for?"

Big Mama had come into the bedroom with her hands on her hips.

"Nothin'," Kid Sally said.

"You watch-a you mouth in the house," Big Mama said.

Big Mama is a short, wrinkled woman with a parrot's bill for a nose. Her gray hair is pulled back in a bun. Her dark brown eyes move quickly. She was dressed in traditional Italian mourning black: black dress, black stockings, black tie-lace shoes. Big Mama's husband, a game but inept extortionist, died twenty-three years ago.

Kid Sally calls her Big Mama because he grew up in an apartment with both his mother, whom he called Little Mama, and his grandmother, who became Big Mama. His mother died of pneumonia when he was nine. The father, Papa Albert Palumbo, did nine years in jail for being an accessory after the fact of a murder. Albert got to the scene too late to do the thing himself, as contracted, but he did arrive just in time to be seen stuffing the body into a cement-mixer. He died a year after he got out of prison. Big Mama raised Kid Sally Palumbo and watched with pride while he headed for stardom, with her urging him on.

"Now you know what to do?" she said to Kid Sally.

"Yeah."

"Make sure you know what to do."

"Yop."

She whispered, "Just remember, all these others, they *bassets*. Rat *bassets*."

Kid Sally's face brightened. Big Mama always made him feel strong. Like the day he was sitting in the back of the courtroom with Big Mama while they waited for an assault case to be called. It was one of Kid Sally's first contracts for Baccala, and he had beaten up the wrong guy. The victim let out a sucker's holler. Kid Sally and Big Mama sat in the brown-paneled courtroom and there was a case on before Kid Sally's and the lawyer in the front of the courtroom was questioning a Negro kid who was on the stand.

"Now the racial tensions in your neighborhood are the result of it being a Negro neighborhood, isn't that correct?" the lawyer said.

"*Ahont* know," the black kid said.

"Well, are there many Negro families living in your neighborhood?"

"Guess so."

"Tell me about the block you live on. What kind of people live on your block?"

"Le's see. There's eight houses that got all Negro people livin' in them, then there's one white family, and then we got one eyetalian family."

"*Mulagnon!*" Big Mama screamed from the back of the courtroom.

"Rat *mulagnon basset!*" Big Mama was on her feet now, shaking a finger at the black kid on the witness stand.

"You, you, you—you get you ass whipped."

The judge was directing a court attendant to grab her, and the lawyer, a little man with a mustache, whirled around and shouted, "Please!"

"Jew mocky lawyer!" Big Mama yelled.

The judge, Irish, took no real offense at this. He only had Big Mama and Kid Sally thrown out of the room.

Out in the hallway, Big Mama got up on her tiptoes and looked through the small pane in the door and put the Evil Eye on everybody inside. Kid Sally stood next to her and felt great.

Kid Sally ran manicured fingernails, the polish glistening in the light, over the scar on his right cheek. The scar was one of the prices he has paid for this uncertainty that runs through him sometimes. Once, very early in his career, he was assigned to a good arson job by the Baccala family. His job was to do whatever the arsonist, Benny the Bug, wanted. A row of five attached shops, all losing business in a changing neighborhood, had formed a sort of association and paid Benny to turn their businesses into a large empty lot. Benny spent hours splashing gasoline in the cellars of the stores. He had Kid Sally flatten out the empty gas cans and take them to Erie Basin and throw them in the water. If a fire marshal finds an old gas can in the ruins, he will report this to the police, which is very bad, and to the insurance company, which is far worse. After careful checking, Benny the Bug left the scene and repaired to an el station overlooking the stores. One of the merchants, who had the dry-goods store on the end of the row, was with him. The merchant was worried about a good fire wall in his store.

"You're dealing with professionals," Benny told the merchant.

Presently flames began showing in the windows of the first four stores. Nothing showed from the dry-goods store. "I tol' you," the dry-goods-store man wailed. Benny took out a dollar cigar, licked it with his tongue, then put it in his mouth. All the stores erupted in smoke. The dry-goods shop remained solid. "Ohhhhh!" the shopkeeper moaned. The front of the dry-goods store then blew out into the middle of the street. The roof turned into a geyser of timbers, bricks, and tar paper. A side wall exploded and disintegrated. The flames licked at the fire wall like it was candy.

Benny the Bug took the cigar out of his mouth and sneered at the merchant next to him.

"Nuclear," Benny the Bug said.

Kid Sally Palumbo thought he knew the whole game after that day. He pestered Baccala for arson jobs he could handle himself. Baccala gave him a special, a nightclub in Greenwood Lake which was owned by a cousin of Baccala's and which was losing money. This made the nightclub a candidate for the usual restaurant fire, a grease fire in the kitchen, helped along by fifteen gallons of gasoline. Kid Sally sloshed gasoline all over the place late one night. He kept remembering all the things Benny the Bug had done. He was satisfied that he had done everything. He started a small fire in a corner and stepped outside. He strode out like Mussolini. "Beautiful," he said to Tony the Indian, who was waiting in the car. Kid Sally's foot hit something. He looked down to see a gas can.

He had forgotten to pick up the gas cans. Kid Sally ran back to the nightclub just as the place exploded. Flying glass cut Kid Sally's face. The next day fire marshals found four gas cans in the embers.

"If Eisenhower owned the place we wouldn't pay," an insurance adjuster said.

Kid Sally looked carefully at the scar on his cheek, then stepped back and put the English Ovals in his inside jacket pocket. Sinatra keeps his cigarettes there.

"Take care," Kid Sally said to Big Mama.

He walked out of his bedroom and into a hallway. The staircase going down to the street is in the middle of a dark hallway. Tony the Indian went down the stairs first. As Kid Sally started down, a door at the far end of the hallway opened and a girl with a pink quilted robe pulled around her stood with the light from her room flooding around her. She had long black hair and off-olive skin. Oriental eyebrows slashed away at an angle from long narrow eyes.

"You going out this late?" she said.

"He got business," Big Mama called out. "You in college. You keep studying. That's-a you business. He got-a his business."

"Take care," Kid Sally said.

"You take care," the girl said.

She shut the door. Kid Sally started down the stairs. Big Mama leaned over the banisters. "You forget," she whispered. She was holding out a black pistol.

"I don't need it," Kid Sally said.

"All right. But you watch you ass."

Chapter 5

Kid Sally bounced down the stairs and through the scarred vestibule and came out onto the street. The building Kid Sally lives in is two stories of old brick with a storefront office taking up the first floor. Gold lettering on the streaked window says ACE VENDING MACHINE. This is a business he ran. His people stole pistachio nuts from the big Washington Market and filled machines with them and put the machines into bars. It was a fair business, but then the Washington Market moved up to the Bronx and security was tighter at the new place and nobody could steal pistachio nuts, so Ace Vending went out of business.

Beppo the Dwarf, with hair hanging in his face, sat in the office. The office was a good place to sit because it wasn't cold like the street. The dwarf had on a plaid short-sleeved sportshirt. He sat at a scarred desk. The wall behind the dwarf was covered with a poster of the front of a nude girl lying on a fat right hip. When the dwarf saw Kid Sally standing outside the office, he twisted around in the straight-backed chair. He got onto his knees, stood up straight, and then got way up on his toes and leaned out and kissed the girl on the poster somewhere around the top of the legs.

"That Beppo, he's crazy," Kid Sally said.

"You bet he's crazy," Tony the Indian said.

In the office, Beppo the Dwarf stood clapping his hands. He had just touched on one of the major sore points of all gangsters, and he knew he was small enough to get away with it. From the day a man is inducted into the Mafia he feels he is God or, at the very least, Saint Michael the Archangel. This ego, coupled with the normal lack of imagination and caring which goes with his IQ, makes the average hoodlum the worst sex partner imaginable. "I'd rather have a cold German than a hot wise guy," Sandra the Hooker announced one night. To overcome this, the wise guys will do anything to leave a girl feeling thrilled, up to, including, and mainly the little scene Beppo had just acted out with the poster. If there is one thing a Mafia guy fears, outside of a narcotics conviction, it is having the girl tell anybody what he does to her.

"If you ever tell," Tony the Indian warned his girl friend one night, "I'll choke you on the throat and make your eyes fall out."

The building Kid Sally lives in is in the middle of the block. The block is made up of single-story tan stucco laundry-truck garages set between four- and five-story tenements that have fire escapes creeping down their fronts. The block seeps to an end against dreary wharves which are part of the South Brooklyn waterfront. A lone tanker, with only a couple of small lights showing on the bridge, sat in the oil-covered water.

For most people who live on Marshall Street there are two directions that can be taken in life. One is to get up early in the morning and walk down to the end of the street, to the docks and hatches and baling hooks and shape-ups which are the life of the longshoreman. The other way is to get up at night and go out and steal. Marshall Street, of course, is most crowded in the late afternoons when the people come out to compare cut hands received while breaking through warehouse skylights the night before.

This situation once led Nathan Glaser, director of the Brooklyn Regional Social Security Office, to observe, "These people don't take out Social Security cards even once in their lives. If we had a few more places like Marshall Street we'd be mailing tambourines to retired people."

Kid Sally Palumbo and Tony the Indian started up the cracked sidewalk toward the corner. Kid Sally's shoulders swung, and his legs were close together. His steps began with the toes and the balls of his feet pushing against his big black thick new shoes. Kid Sally had spent a long time learning how to walk this way. An alert, quick walk is rare in a poor neighborhood. People usually react to environment right down to their feet. In crumbling surroundings people walk with a wide, aimless gait. On Marshall Street a woman going to buy tripe for dinner slumps into three or four people each way. On Madison Avenue, women coming for fittings swing their legs out of taxicabs and flick across the sidewalk through a wall of businessmen without bumping. On Marshall Street, only Kid Sally Palumbo, who is trying to be a general in the Mafia, has direction to his stride.

Tony the Indian went to one of a row of brown-doored garages near the corner. He opened the doors and went in and backed out a black Cadillac. Kid Sally shut the doors and got into the car. Ten minutes later Tony the Indian slowed the car as it came to the corner of a dark street. He inched the car past the building line of a red brick supermarket. Kid Sally looked down the neon-lit sidewalk of Flatbush Avenue. It was empty. Tony the Indian hit the gas and the car swerved around the corner and came to a stop, tires squealing, in a flood of neon formed by a long sign:

THE ENCHANTED HOUR

A poster in one window said:

INDOOR CLAM BAKE, SUNDAY AFTERNOONS.
CHICKEN CACCIATORE, LINGUINE AND GO GO GIRLS!

The noise of the tires squealing made the people near the windows in the Enchanted Hour look out. They saw Kid Sally Palumbo step out onto the sidewalk and march like Mussolini to the door. Tony the Indian swung around the car after him. Kid Sally waited at the door for Tony to open it. Kid Sally arranged his lips in a Tommy Udo sneer. Then he walked into the Enchanted Hour and he could feel everybody in the place looking at him.

"Hey!" somebody said to Kid Sally. He nodded and kept walking.

"Hey!" somebody else said. Kid Sally nodded again.

Kid Sally went down the bar to an empty black leather stool. He stood alongside the stool. Never sit. You sit and you look all bent over. Kid Sally stood at the bar with the English Oval hanging from his bottom lip and his chin out and his chest out and his shirt cuffs showing nice, feeling real soft and good on his wrists. The mirror behind the bar made everything look blue because the place was so dark. Kid Sally tilted his chin higher, and the smoke came out of his nose and mouth at the same time. One stream of blue smoke running up and one stream of blue smoke coming down. In the mirror, Kid Sally saw a guy who really knows what he's doing. *Good People,* Kid Sally said to himself.

He put a hundred-dollar bill on the bar. His index finger waved. "Take care of us, here," he said.

The bartender flung himself in front of Kid Sally. "Scotch?"

"For me and my friend." The finger waved. "And buy the bar a drink."

The bartender nodded. He threw straight scotches and water in front of Kid Sally and Tony the Indian. Then he ran up and down the rest of the bar, filling the order. Kid Sally would borrow at shylock interest rates before he would put anything less than a hundred-dollar bill on the bar at the Enchanted Hour.

A short guy in a black suit came down the bar and stood with him.

"You got somethin' for me, pal?" Kid Sally said.

"The guy give me long stories," the little guy said.

"What stories?" Kid Sally said.

"I think he's a broken-down suitcase," the little guy said. "I don't know if he got."

Kid Sally was leaning against the bar. He pushed away from it and stood up straight, his shoulders squaring.

"Who does this guy think he is? I'm going to break both his legs and throw in a arm for good measure," Kid Sally said. "Who is this guy, not payin'? Does he know who he's doin' business with?"

"I told him it was good people," the little guy said.

"I'm gonna do what I have to do," Kid Sally said.

"I tol' him," the little guy said.

Kid Sally looked at the little guy. "All right," he said. The little guy left. Kid Sally turned back and looked at himself in the mirror. Huh. The whole place was looking at him. They all got respect for Kid Sally Palumbo, he told himself. He began to think of the day when he could walk into the big places in Manhattan, the Copa and Jilly's, and get the respect the big guys over there get.

At his left elbow was a small railing that separates the regular bar from the service bar. The service bar has an aluminum top for draining. The red and blue neon from the jukebox was reflected in watery light on the aluminum. The waitress, her long black hair swinging across her shoulderblades, brushed behind Kid Sally and came up to the service bar, just on the other side of the little railing. She put a tray down on the aluminum.

"One C.C. and water, a vodka gimlet, and two Dewar's on the rocks," she said.

Kid Sally took his shot glass of scotch and flicked it down in a gulp.

The waitress stood at the aluminum with her lips pursed. She clucked in rhythm to the music from the jukebox.

The bartender was reaching for a bottle on the back bar to start filling her order. Kid Sally put his shot glass down. He waited until the bartender was right in the middle of reaching for the bottle.

"Take care of me and my friend," Kid Sally said. His finger waved.

The bartender stopped in the middle of his motion. He grimaced. Then he turned around with a big smile. "Sure, Sally Kid," he said.

The waitress looked at Kid Sally. "Really!"

Kid Sally made his Tommy Udo sneer.

"You!" the waitress said.

Kid Sally felt great. He loved being a big shot like this.

Tony the Indian tapped him on the arm. "That guy is in the booth waitin' for you."

Kid Sally threw down his drink and lit a fresh cigarette. He squared his shoulders. This was a very important match for him. He walked to a booth in the back of the place. He slid in on the empty side. The man sitting opposite him grinned. The man was wearing a hand-stitched light brown glen-plaid suit. His reddish hair was closely cut. He wore hornrimmed glasses. His name was Izzy Cohen and he was Baccala's chief Jew. The Mafia relies heavily on Jews. Boss gangsters are usually able to count only when they take off their shoes and use their toes. Every big outfit has a Jew who can count money and mastermind gambling and swindling operations. As the hood-lums do not understand exactly what the Jew is doing, but suspect the worst, they threaten the Jew periodically. Baccala always tells Izzy Cohen, "You steal and I make you put you tongue on the third rail." Izzy Cohen throws up his arms in horror. The next morning he takes out his Jewish revolver, a ballpoint pen, and goes to work and steals some more. Izzy comes out of a family of pushcart peddlers on the East Side of Manhattan. The north end of his brain has clear, almost impressive university tendencies. The south end is cluttered with worms which become active only when the word larceny is programed into them. This situation makes Izzy Cohen a literate thief. As the master figure man for the Brooklyn mob, he is thought to be as brilliant as the late Abba Dabba Bernstein. Abba Dabba worked for Dutch Schultz and became famous for his ability to fix the Cincinnati Clearing House total, used for policy numbers payoffs.

"Where do we stand?" Kid Sally Palumbo said. He wanted to let Izzy know who was in charge. Kid Sally was. Kid Sally had a button in the Mafia. Izzy was only a Jew. They can't join.

"My work was finished before it started," Izzy said.

"What do you mean?" Kid Sally said.

"I know my business. Let me ask you something. Where do you stand?"

"Stand where?"

"Stand with everything."

Kid Sally reached inside his jacket for his cigarettes. He carefully took one from the pack. He picked up his lighter and flicked it open. He wanted to show this Jew who he was.

"You want a Monte Carlo made up around a bike race, right?" Izzy Cohen said.

"Right," Kid Sally said.

"I got that already," Izzy said. "Now let me ask you one thing. Suppose a chain breaks? What do you do then?"

"A chain? What chain?"

"The chain on the bike breaks. What do you do then? You can't have a price on a bike-rider if his chain breaks. What do you have for that?"

Kid Sally felt all this uncertainty running through him. He put the cigarette in his mouth and gave Izzy the Tommy Udo sneer.

"I got the fat man takin' care of all the details. What do you think, I'm some little kid runnin' around fixing bikes?"

"What do you mean by everything?" Izzy Cohen said.

"Just what I said. The fat man does all my work for me. He's terrific at takin' care of things like this."

The fat man was Big Jelly Catalano, and he is 425 pounds slabbed onto a 6-foot-3 frame and topped by a huge owl's face with a mane of black hair. He looks at the world through milk-bottle eyeglasses. What he thinks the world should be has made him, at thirty-two, a legend in South Brooklyn. In grammar school, with 280 pounds of him lopping over both sides of his seat and blocking the aisles, he spent his years with his hands covering his mouth while he whispered to the girls:

"Sodomy!"

"Period!"

"Come!"

Since that time he has done so many bad things that Judge Bernard Dubin, Part 2B, Brooklyn Criminal Court, one day was moved to observe, "If this man ever could have fit on a horse, he would have been a tremendous help to Jesse James."

While Kid Sally guaranteed on this night that all things were being handled by Big Jelly, while the bike-riders were due in the country in a matter of hours and the race was only a week off, Big Jelly was doing what he always does at night.

"I'm telling you it's all right," Big Jelly was saying to the maitre d'. The maitre d' was nervously fingering three menus while he stood in the foyer and tried to block Big Jelly's entrance into the Messina, a restaurant on East 55th Street in Manhattan.

"Meester Jelly, please, we got a nice-a place here. You a circus."

"Carlo, will you stop it," Big Jelly said. "This is my wife. Say hello to Carlo, honey."

A thin ebony-wood carving with a tremendous chest bursting against a white blouse held out her hand to Carlo.

"*Howyou,* my good man," she said.

"And this here is my mother-in-law," Big Jelly said.

A cocoa-colored girl built like a middleweight and dressed in a blond wig and yellow miniskirt began to giggle. "If Jelly my son-in-law, then that make him a mother-in-law fucker!"

Carlo turned his head to see if anybody inside had heard her, and the two girls began to shriek and Big Jelly reached out and mussed Carlo's patent-leather hair, and he pushed past Carlo and the two girls came with him and Carlo had to trot to get ahead of them and he was scowling while he led Big Jelly and his two girls to a table in a corner in the back of the room.

Big Jelly sat down and untied his pearl-gray tie. He took off the jacket of his size-64 black mohair suit. He unbuttoned his white shirt and took it off and arranged it over the back of the chair. Big Jelly now sat in a T-shirt that had broad pink stains on it from some previous powerhouse linguine sauce which would not come out in the wash. Big Jelly always takes his clothes off when he eats because his stomach and chest stick out so far that the fork always brushes against them and food drops down his front. So Big Jelly strips down and lets the linguine sauce fall where it may.

All around the carpeted dining room people were looking at

Big Jelly in shock, then smirks and a chuckle or two. Big Jelly's mother-in-law leaned across the table and began rubbing the two cow udders that Big Jelly has for a chest.

"You make a girl for somebody," the mother-in-law said.

Big Jelly laughed loudly. He cupped his hands under his cow udders and he swung back and forth in his seat.

"That's it, that's it," the mother-in-law said.

The wife began to clap her hands and sing a smoker song.

Carlo came plunging between tables, running his hands over his hair and then waving them.

"Please, please."

"Please what?" Big Jelly said.

"This is no pigsty," Carlo said.

"A pig!" Big Jelly shouted. "You call me a pig? Who's a pig!"

He picked up a butter plate and bounced it off Carlo's head. Carlo grabbed a glass of water and threw it in Big Jelly's face. Big Jelly got his size-13 shoe out from under the table and he kicked Carlo in the ankle. Carlo let out a scream and clutched his ankle. Big Jelly bounced another plate off Carlo's head. A waiter in a red jacket came over and grabbed Big Jelly. The girl with the big breasts got her nails into the waiter's face. He screamed. Another waiter grabbed the girl. Big Jelly missed a right-hand punch but he got a fork in his hand and brought it down hard into the waiter's hand. The two girls got up from the table. Big Jelly grabbed his shirt, tie, and jacket and fought with one hand while he and the girls made their way to the door. Big Jelly came out into the cold air in his T-shirt, and his hair was all over his face.

"I'll burn that joint down," he screamed.

The two girls waved a cab. The three of them got in, and Big Jelly said he wanted a drink. They went to Clarke's on Third Avenue for straight vodka. The cab waited outside. Then Big Jelly took his girl friends to a place on Madison Avenue, where he drank scotch with a wine chaser. They told the cab-driver to take them to Jilly's on 52nd, but they made a stop at the Wagon Wheel on the way, and now Big Jelly was clapping his hands and rolling his eyes and saying, "Sodomy!" and the two girls slapped their thighs and the wife fished into her purse and Big Jelly yelled, "Find it for paper." When the cab-driver saw the girl come out with three marijuana ciga-rettes and pass them around, he stopped the cab and got out and leaned against the hood.

"If I'm goin' to take a pinch, it's goin' to be for my own habit, not yours," he announced.

"It's all right, I'm with my mother and she lets me," Big Jelly said.

At 6:30 a.m. the two girls were standing naked in Room 625 of the Hotel West Virginia. The bathroom door opened and Big Jelly came out naked with a black beret tilted over his right eye.

"Ooooooo la la," he said.

Chapter 6

At 7:05 p.m. Alitalia flight 101 came in on its approach to Kennedy Airport. The plane whined across the last of the Atlantic with its landing floodlights striking the black water and then running onto the gray sand of Rockaway Beach. In the tourist section of the plane Mario Trantino and seven other bike-riders tumbled around the windows like monkeys, trying to see America for the first time. The plane came down on the winter-wet runways and Mario Trantino came down the steps with his eyebrows up, mouth open, eyes afire.

Joseph DeLauria was waiting in the lobby in his function as president of the bike-race association. A crowd of men stood with him. When the passenger agent brought Mario and the other riders out, DeLauria pushed through people and hugged Mario. He stepped aside, and a thin old man wearing the red, green, and white sash of the Society of San Gennaro kissed Mario on both cheeks. Two fat doctors wearing reception-committee rosettes waited in line. Another man in a sash stood behind them.

Joseph DeLauria was next to Mario, rattling off names, "Mr. Riccobona . . . Mr. Scola . . . Mr. Cirillo . . . Dr. Palermo . . . Mr. DiLorenzo . . ."

Mario jumped. "Mr. DiLorenzo!"

The fat man hugging Mario nodded eagerly. Mario reached into his jacket pocket for the list from the priest. "DiLorenzo, DiLorenzo," he said. His finger shook while it went over the list and stopped at the name.

"Are your people from Catanzia?"

The fat man nodded yes. His eyes became filled. He hugged Mario tightly. Mario put the list back in his pocket and wrapped his arms around the doctor.

"You know Father Marsalano? He put your name down on the list here."

The fat man pushed backward against Mario's arms.

"He said you'd help," Mario said.

The man broke out of his arms and went backward through the crowd.

"Hey!" Mario called out to him.

"*Bafongool*," the fat man said. He fled into a crowd.

Mario tried to follow him in the crowd, but his eyes fell on two Air France stewardesses. The committee led Mario out of the airport while he kept twisting to see the stewardesses, and when Mario got into Manhattan the lights in the theater district, and the crowds walking in them, made him dizzy.

Mario passed out when he got to the room. He woke up in the morning with his head under a pillow. He rolled over on his back and began to run his legs back and forth against the white sheets. His body tingled with its first brush of luxury. He swung out of bed and went over to the window. Manhattan in the morning in the silence drifts across the eyes, and the buildings seem to be moving into each other. Beyond the buildings was the river. The river water was winter-gray and the January wind blew onto the water from an angle and made a windowscreen pattern on the surface. Mario went into the bathroom and unwrapped the soap. It was the biggest bar of soap he had ever seen. He held the soap to his nose. There was a clean smell with an undertone of cologne. It did not have the cleaning-fluid smell of Italian soap. He twisted the shined silver handle in the stall shower. Warm water, becoming hot, came down on him. He turned and let the water fall on his neck. He stood there with the hot water hitting his neck, and he was using more water with this one shower than entire families use during a day in Catanzia. Mario began thinking while the hot water fell on his neck. He began thinking of the same things anybody who lands in America thinks of. Mario was thinking about staying in America forever.

He came out of the shower and sat on the edge of the bed and flipped through the telephone directory. He was surprised to find Grant Monroe listed. He dialed the hotel operator and gave her the number.

"You can dial that yourself," she said.

"I'm blind," Mario said.

"Oh, I'm sorry, I'll get it for you," she said.

Mario spoke away from the phone. "Do your own work, I don't do it for you."

Grant Monroe's number rang several times. Finally a foggy voice answered. Mario stood up in excitement.

"Mr. Grant Monroe?" Mario said.

"Of course, he's always up answering phones this time of day."

"Oh, good," Mario said. "Could I please to speak to him?"

"Oh, I see. You're not putting me on. You *are* sick."

The phone clicked.

Mario got dressed and went downstairs, where he waited for Joseph DeLauria. Since Mario could speak English, DeLauria was taking him around town for publicity interviews. When DeLauria arrived he was grumpy because he didn't like being an errand boy, and he was also afraid the bike race would be a flop and he would be blamed for it. "My guys don't even know what a bike race is," Bobby Scola of Hodcarriers Local 43 told DeLauria. DeLauria gave the desk clerk envelopes addressed to the bike-riders. He handed Mario one. It contained a hundred-dollar bill for expenses. Mario put the bill in the watch pocket of his suit. He went to the newsstand and took two Hershey bars for breakfast. He stepped aside so DeLauria could pay. DeLauria remained immobile. Mario made a face like a beggar in pain. DeLauria muttered and fished in his pocket for change.

DeLauria took Mario to the offices of a scratch sheet which ran little sports-news items, to two small radio stations, and then to the big chain afternoon newspaper. By custom, it was the easiest to crack for publicity. The custom called for DeLauria to step into a small office with the sports editor and pay money. The sports editor then called out to a young guy who was sitting at a desk and writing a headline for a basketball story. The headline said, "St. John's Splinters Holy Cross." The young guy put down his work and interviewed Mario.

Back at the hotel, Mario called Grant Monroe again. There was no answer. He watched television all afternoon. At night three fat men on the race committee took the riders to dinner at a restaurant across the street from the hotel. The riders, mixed up by the time changes, began to fall asleep at the table.

In the morning Mario called Grant Monroe again. After many rings, the foggy voice answered.

"The wake is tomorrow," the voice said. "He died yesterday. He cut his throat." The voice trailed off. "Hey, it's seven-thirty in the freaking morning. Are you crazy? What do you do, sleep in the streets?" The phone clicked.

The bikes had arrived by air freight. They were being kept in a park building at Central Park. Mario and the other riders went for a workout at ten. Many of them were asking when the indoor track would be ready for practice. Joseph DeLauria laughed and clapped a few of them on the back. After the workout DeLauria walked out of the park to hail a cab. Mario, who was wearing a black sweatsuit and had sweat dripping from his chin, ran after DeLauria. He got in the cab with him. Mario showed DeLauria Grant Monroe's address on 10th Street.

DeLauria shook his head. "Puerto Rican neighborhood."

Mario did not answer.

DeLauria held his hands out. "So go get killed." DeLauria told the cabbie to go down the East Side to 10th Street.

Tenth Street was narrow, and tin cans and spilled garbage bags were on the curb and in the gutter. The blacktop was covered with swatches of broken glass, which glistened in the pale winter-morning sunlight. The sidewalks were empty in the cold. The houses were five- and six-story adjoining walkups, some dirty red, some dirty brown, some dirty tan, with chalk-marked stoops and high, bare soot-covered windows. Number 288 was dirty red. The brass mailboxes in the vestibule were scarred and bent from being pried open by junkies. The names on some of them were printed by hand on cardboard and were so smudged Mario had to look closely to see Ruiz and Torres and Maldonado. The other slots had no names on them. Mario couldn't find Monroe. He tried the vestibule door. It was unlocked and he came into a lightless hallway with a staircase in front of him and an apartment, the door half open, on his left.

Mario knocked on the half-open door. There was no answer. He stepped inside. He was in a bare-floored front room. The walls were covered with floor-to-ceiling posters of pop art. One showed a caveman chiseling "Nobel Peace Prize" onto a stone tablet. An old bathtub was against one wall. It had a curved lip at the top and it stood on ornate legs. The bathtub was painted in psychedelic swirls. In the middle of the room were easels and tables with brushes and paints and palettes. A high stool was placed in front of the three windows looking onto the street.

"Hello," Mario called out.

There was a muffled sound from the back of the apartment. A door opened and a little man pushed himself into the room in a wheelchair. He was bald and wore glasses and he had a brown bottle of whisky in his lap and a cup in his left hand. He pushed the chair with his free hand. He brought the chair to a stop at a long table.

"In that case," he said. He put the cup and the whisky bottle on the table. He opened the whisky bottle and poured into a glass. He swallowed the whisky in a gulp. He picked up the cup and spilled something on a large sheet of art paper on the table. He began rubbing his fingers on the wet paper.

"He knows I only want tea and the son-of-a-bitch doesn't buy me any and he tells me use coffee. Use coffee, and he'll see what he gets."

"What's that?" Mario said.

The little man kept rubbing the paper. "Tea, I said tea, can't you even hear? He wants something to look ten years old. I use tea on the new paper to make it look old. Tea does it good. This son-of-a-bitch, what does he care? He says use coffee if I don't have tea. Oh, he's a lazy bastard."

"Who?" Mario said.

"Who? Who do you think? What's the difference anyway? I'm so freaking stewed now I don't care."

He poured himself another drink. After he swallowed it, he ran his hands over his face.

"All night I work, and twice in a row now some dirty bastard calls here early in the morning and wakes me up. Two days in a row. So this morning I said to hell with it. I just took myself into the kitchen and had a pick-me-up. And I'm still picking myself up. Freaking telephones."

The little man's head was flopping toward his left shoulder, and he had to raise his eyebrows to focus on Mario.

"Where are you from, dressed like that?"

"I'm Mario Trantino. I am from Catanzia in Italy."

"How's the Pope?"

"His Holiness?"

"Yeah. I think he wants to make sex a contest. See whose wife gets caught tonight."

He spun around in the wheelchair and whirred over to the bathtub. He fumbled with his fly and went in the bathtub. He ran the water, shut it off, and whirred back to the table.

He held the bottle out to Mario. "Treat it like it's your own."

Mario looked at him. "Come on," the man said. Mario walked over to him, took the bottle, and put it inside his mouth as if it were a tongue-depressor. He was not going to do anything to have this man in the wheelchair get mad and make him go away. With his lips outside the bottle, there was no way for Mario's mouth to close by reflex and block the flow of whisky. When he tilted the bottle, the whisky poured free and a string of small bubbles beaded through the bottle, and then more of them came, and finally an air pocket gurgled through the whisky.

"Hey," the man said. "When I was young I was taught that whisky is better for you than jerking off, but you're ridiculous." Mario's stomach was turning. He breathed out of his mouth so he wouldn't gag.

"Now what do you want?" the guy said. He took a drink for himself. "You want Grant?" Mario said yes. "Then what the hell are you doing here? Don't you know him?"

"Oh, yes, I know him very well," Mario said.

"Well, then, you know that he's never here. What the hell would he do here? There's work here. He can't do any of this. He doesn't even know to pour tea. Use coffee if you don't have tea, he says." The little man looked up. "Say, what the hell is that outfit you got on?"

"It's a—well, the clothes I wear, in the—ah—they are my clothes—ah—"

"It's your game, not mine," the little man said. "Jeez, I'm stewed. And I got to have this work done by tomorrow morning. An early work. Huh. Where is the thing now?" He leaned over and went through a pile of paper on a small table and pulled out a street scene that was obviously New York. "Here we are," he said.

"It's very nice work," Mario said.

"Nice work? It's great work. The guy broke his back doing things like this. But people are pigs. You know he never sold this? He never knew how to push himself, so he never sold this? That's one thing you can say about Grant. For somebody who never drew a stroke in his life, he has taste. He knows where to get some obscure thing and sell it around. Hell, we'll push ten of these things out. I can do one of these in a day. Just as long as we don't get jammed. Jeez, I *am* stewed." He picked up the bottle.

"He leaves me here with nobody. Christ, he wants nobody around to see. All right. But get me somebody to bring me tea. He forgets about me being in the chair here. You know what he said to me once? He said, 'Meet me uptown right away.' Me. How'm I going to get down the stairs here? I told him, if I could just leave here like that, I would be playing football and screwing young cheerleaders. When do I get out of here? He's supposed to come around and he never does. He sends a cabbie to take me out. I go up to Harlem. The Glamour Inn. You get stewed and they let a broad wheel me into the back room. Beautiful. So what does the cabbie do? He takes a fare and he leaves me there. I'm trying to get a cab from the curb and all these bastards are pullin' the money out of my pockets and I can't stop them. Son-of-a-bitch. Then I ask him for an answering service and he won't even get me that. So freak him. I got woken up two mornings in a row, freak him. I'm drunk."

He stopped talking and looked at Mario. "If you go to the Plaza and see him, don't start telling him Sidney is sitting here drunk. Sidney is good and drunk. Only don't tell him."

He frowned for a moment and looked cockeyed at Mario. "Say, how did you get in here? Did Grant give you a key?"

Mario smiled and decided not to tell him the door was just open. He said good-by and walked backward out of the room. He waved good-by at the door. "Don't say I'm drinking," Sidney called after him. Mario shut the door.

Mario went outside and walked the streets in his black sweatsuit, asking directions for his hotel every few blocks. In the lobby he asked where the Plaza was and what it was and the bellhop told him it was a very good hotel. Mario went upstairs, showered, and changed into his suit. At two, he went to the Plaza, with its horse-carriages and Rolls-Royces and hot-dog venders parked around a fountain, and the scrubbed steps, under an ornate heated marquee, leading to the lobby. Mario asked at the desk for Grant Monroe. He was not registered. Mario began to walk around the lobby.

Grant Monroe was sitting at a small table in the corner of the Palm Court. His long fingers, which had a couple of dusty orange paint streaks on them, were wrapped around a small china coffee cup. Grant Monroe was dressed in a shapeless tweed topcoat that was splattered with red and blue and gray paint. His hair was uncombed and it came down the back of his neck and stood out where the coat collar brushed up into the back of his neck. Underneath the coat he had on a gray turtleneck and an array of multicolored love beads. He sipped the coffee, put it down, and peered through his glasses. His left hand went into his topcoat pocket. It twisted around inside. It came out slowly, while Grant looked around to see who was watching him. The hand came up holding a tugged-off piece of salami sandwich on rye bread. He pushed the whole piece into his mouth, and his jaws worked violently to compress the salami and rye bread before they choked him.

The minute Mario saw Grant, he brushed through a row of potted palms and came up to the table. Mario was starting to introduce himself when the violins struck up and his words were lost.

Grant was up on his feet, pushing Mario away with one hand and waving with the other. "Oh, Mrs. Tyler! Here, Mrs. Tyler. Essie, right here!"

A tall slim woman in a white wool coat with black leather trim waved a gloved hand at Grant and walked toward his table. Grant began pushing Mario hard. "I'm quite busy at the moment; oh, you look stunning, Essie. Come sit." Grant Monroe put his hand onto Mario's chest and gave a shove.

The woman slipped into a seat at the table and opened her coat, and Grant helped her put it on the back of her chair. Grant then reached under the table and brought up a huge black leather folder and pulled a chair up next to the woman, and he sat down and held open the folder and spoke excitedly to her while he showed her the painting. It was the same street scene Sidney had just shown Mario. He could hear snatches of Grant talking.

". . . You see, I am accepting a Guggenheim to work abroad and I just felt I could not simply leave and have this hanging nowhere. It was always my favorite and now that I have my Guggenheim I feel I must dispose of it . . ."

Mario stepped through the potted palms and onto the carpeted walkway which goes around the Palm Court. The walkway was empty. Mario bent over and snatched at his shoelaces. He pulled them open and out of the holes so they flopped loose. He reached into the breast pocket of the suit and took out his uncle's eyeglasses. He pulled his tie half open and out of his jacket. Feet flopping, his eyes shut, Mario pushed back into the Palm Court.

He opened his eyes and looked over the top of the glasses once so he could aim himself at Grant Monroe's table.

"Grant Monroe?" he said.

"Yes, I'm quite busy now if you'll excuse me," Monroe said. "Now, Essie, this is the perfect thing for your sitting room."

"It *is* charming."

"I saw Sidney and he told me where you were," Mario said.

Grant Monroe's eyes became large behind his glasses. His mouth became set.

"Grant," the woman said, "now you must talk to me sensibly about price. I can see that it's . . ."

Mario stumbled away from the table and went out into the lobby.

"Say there!" Grant Monroe rushed into the lobby behind him. Grant was breathing quickly. He took Mario by the arm and walked him to a row of telephone booths.

"Now where did you see Sidney?" he said.

"This morning."

"This morning where?"

"At your place where he works. On Tenth Street."

Grant Monroe's lip was trembling. His eyes flashed. He ran a hand through his hair. He plunged into a phone booth. His paint-streaked, bony fingers fumbled a dime into the phone and stuttered through the dialing process.

"Come on, answer the phone, come on, come on, oh, hello, Sidney? . . .

"Sidney? Who do you think it is? Of course. Sidney? What's the matter with you? Sidney, are you drinking?" Grant put a hand over the phone and looked at Mario. "Was he drinking?" Mario nodded yes. Grant went back to the phone. "Sidney, listen to me. Did a person come in this morning, a person from

Italy? He did? Well, Sidney, how many times have you been told . . . Hey! Don't you say that to me. Sidney! Sidney, don't you ever talk like that to me. WHAT! What did you just say? Sidney, that goes for your mother too. Sidney?" He looked at the phone and hung it up.

Grant Monroe slumped in the phone booth. His legs stuck out. He was wearing chino pants and white socks and loafers. His hand dug into the coat pocket and came up with the torn salami on rye. He took a bite of it.

"The first thing you do," Monroe said, talking with his mouth full, "is to bring your own lunch. You order a sandwich in there, they charge you two-fifty for a piece of Kraft's cheese on bread. The coffee is bad enough. A dollar."

He looked at Mario. "Now I have to go back in and talk to that woman. What is it you have on your mind?"

"Nothing, I just wanted to meet you," Mario said.

He who catches a thief at work and who wants to take part in the work must show patience or risk disturbing the entire operation. Mario did not have to be taught the basics of larceny. He nodded good-by and left. Back at the hotel, a note in his box said there would be a cocktail party at 5:30 the next night and all riders were asked to attend. Practice as usual in Central Park in the morning. Mario thought for a while. It was just as well. He'd need a couple of days to get an idea together and then he could take it to Grant Monroe for help. He went to a movie and to bed early and he woke up in the morning feeling very happy.

Chapter 7

The police dog had the garbage bucket overturned on the sidewalk and he had his head flattened and his nose was rooting at the garbage when Big Mama came out on the stoop with a broom to start the morning. Big Mama pulled the black shawl around her and came clumping down the steps with the broom held out. "Shooooo!" she was saying. The dog's head stopped twisting inside the bucket. He watched Big Mama out of the sides of his eyes. "Shoooo!" she said again. The dog's lips parted and long yellow teeth showed. A growl came through the teeth. Big Mama stamped her foot on the pavement. "Shooo!" The dog's head came up and he growled loudly and his teeth reached for Big Mama. Big Mama let out one yelp in outrage. She swung the broomstick with her right arm. She swung it so hard the broomstick whirred in the air, and when it caught the dog in the mouth the dog's head turned and the growl became a whine. Big Mama swung the broomstick backhanded and caught the dog in the face again. The dog was trying to get away when Big Mama got both hands on the broom and hit the dog across the back with a full-armed shot. The police dog howled and scrambled away. "Shoooo, sonomabeetch!" Big Mama said.

Big Mama, muttering to herself, swept the garbage back into the can. She righted the can, covered it, put the broom up against the building, and began carrying the can out to the curb. She had to arch her back against the heaviness of the can. Other women were out in the street, dressed in the black uniform of old Italian women. They came up cellar stairs or down stoops or out of doorways, and they all carried garbage cans in hands that had deep wrinkles over the knuckles. After this they walked slowly up to the corner and turned onto Columbia Avenue to buy bread for breakfast.

The avenue runs parallel to the river for the entire length of the South Brooklyn waterfront. It is made up of stores set into the bottom floors of five-story brownstone walkup buildings which have flat tar roofs, and jutting out from the roofs are cornices of cement swirled into faces of kings and lions, or scrolls and tablets. The buildings were put up at a time when design was as important to a workingman as wash-up time is today. In the summer Columbia Avenue has pushcarts set up on the curbs and crates set up under the awnings in front of the stores. People walk on the narrow aisle in the sidewalks between the pushcarts and the crates. They walk with bright fruit piled up to form a wall on each side of them, with cheap dresses at their fingertips and cheeses and bright pink pork hanging from the awnings and the merchants talking in Italian into their ears. In the winter the sidewalks are empty and newspapers blow in the wind which always comes off the river. The shop doors are closed and the windows are steamy. When you reach the corner of Marshall Street you turn right and walk halfway down the block to the bakery, Cafiero's bakery. The neighborhood stops at the building line which ends at Cafiero's.

The next store after Cafiero's was empty, and beaverboard covered the broken windows. Once it was Bisceglia's jewelry store. The big clock which had been put into the curb in front of the store, a clock that goes high into the air and can be seen for blocks, was plastered with ripped political campaign posters. The store next to Bisceglia's had a green bread-delivery box on the sidewalk, and a sign in the window read: BODEGA. Across the avenue, directly across from Cafiero's, was Pagano's shoe store. Next to Pagano's was a store with a shabbily painted sign which said, TV REPAIR, and a poster in the window advertised Chu Chu Perez singing on WHOM, a foreign-language radio station.

In the reghettoization of New York, a knife comes down the middle of a block and leaves the last of the old minorities on one side of the blade and the new minorities on the other side of the blade. And both sides live together and apart and they hate each other in a way which only people who are the same and will not admit it always hate each other. On one side of the knife cutting through the building lines, and stretching for blocks, are Italians: Italians in stores and in the linoleum-floored apartments over the stores, Italians in the tenements on the blocks running off the avenue. On the other side of the knife, and running for many blocks, are Puerto Ricans: Puerto Ricans in stores and over the stores in the broken, community-bathroom apartments. Puerto Ricans living in the tenements on the blocks running off the avenue. Puerto Ricans with dented, ripped, used convertibles parked at the curbs, the willowy radio antennas they like so much sticking out of the rear fenders. Puerto Ricans standing in garbage in the doorways and on the sidewalks and in the gutters. Drinking from beer cans in brown paper bags and throwing the cans in the bags out into the middle of the street. In San Juan you get a ticket if you do not throw garbage into the middle of the street, because the trucks pick up garbage by moving down the middle of a street with a cowcatcher and a brush. In Brooklyn you are called a pig if you do this. And the Puerto Ricans do not understand, and the sanitation workers, mainly Italians, do not understand and they will collect garbage on Columbia Avenue past Cafiero's building line only when inspectors come around and force them.

Big Mama bought three loaves of bread and some rolls in Cafiero's. When she came back to the apartment, Angela had the refrigerator open and she was looking into it. She yawned and clasped her hands and stretched them high over her head. The skirt of her short blue woolen dress came up to her thighs and left a bit of white girdle gartered to white net stockings showing.

"Hiya," Angela said.

"You go to school like that?" Big Mama said.

"Uhuh." She brought her arms down. "It's only when I stretch."

"What do you do, tempt?"

"Mama, nobody even cares any more. The whole world is short skirts."

"I fan you behind."

Angela laughed and sat down to a cup of coffee. "Did brother bring home a paper?"

"No," Big Mama said.

Kid Sally Palumbo always falls asleep with the *Daily News* over his face or on the covers next to him. The paper always carries its share of headlines saying such things as: RAID "KID SALLY" HANGOUT. And particularly now, with Sally doing exactly what Big Mama wanted him to do, pushing to get into the real money, she didn't want Angela seeing any newspapers until she had checked them, and there was no time for checking them this morning. And over the years Angela knew enough never to buy a paper unless it had been read through. It was one of the silent understandings by which she lived.

Angela drank her coffee quickly. She went into her room and came out in a dark blue coat and with a brown briefcase, thick with books, crooked in her arm.

"I go to the corner with you," Mama said.

Angela came onto the sidewalk waving at two kids looking out the windows from across the street and a fat woman who opened her window and waved a bare arm out into the cold air. A college student on the block is still an adventure on Marshall Street. Toregressa stood guard duty halfway up the block. Toregressa leaned on a cane. He had a cap pulled down over his ears and a plaid scarf covering his chin. It was his third day out of bed after the flu. Yesterday he had spent an hour telling people on the block how he had resisted death. When he saw Angela he let his mouth sag and he began blinking his eyes to show pain. He shuffled his feet and inched the cane along the sidewalk.

"Oh, you look good today," Angela said to him. "By tomorrow you'll be as good as new." She was smiling and walking quickly and she and Big Mama moved past Toregressa while he was trying to make himself cry so Angela would stop and pet him.

Up at the corner, Beppo, eyes roughed up from sleeping on his face on a couch in the back of the office, was standing in his shirtsleeves.

"Learn the lessons," he said.

Big Mama waved a hand. "Shut up-a you, I teach you."

"I'd tell you to be a good boy," Angela said.

"Tell me then," Beppo said.

"I don't think you'd know how."

Beppo giggled. Angela laughed. She came onto the avenue laughing and waved a hand at Mama and began walking toward the subway four blocks down. Big Mama stood on the corner and watched her granddaughter and shook her head at the amount of legs a girl shows today.

"Saint Anthony protect," she mumbled.

New York University is in reclaimed office buildings that face the grimy frost-yellowed grass of Washington Square. It is an impersonal place to go to school. Thousands of students come out of the subways, cram the hallways from morning until late at night, and then go back into the subways. The campus hero is the job they get when they graduate. For Angela, the impersonalness was important.

In grammar school, in the fourth grade, when she was ten, there was an afternoon when one of the boys in the class walked around filling the inkwells with a large smeared bottle of ink and the ether smell of ink was all over the room, and the nun looked around when the front door to the classroom opened. Big Mama looked into the room. When Angela saw her, she became afraid, the way all kids do when their world is suddenly disturbed. The nun went over to the door and Big Mama whispered to her and the nun turned around and told Angela to get her coat and go with her grandmother. Big Mama kept Angela home, in the house, until the next Monday, when the stories about Kid Sally Palumbo being sentenced to thirteen months were gone from the newspapers. When Angela got to school at twenty of nine on Monday, the girls clustered around two eighth-graders who were twisting a rope all turned and looked at Angela as if she had polio. The ether smell of ink came into Angela's nose, as it was to come into her nose for years when she was frightened.

Angela always went home from school wordlessly, head down, books held up to her face. When she came across the avenue and turned onto Marshall Street, the books would come down and the chin would go up and life would flood back into her eyes and mouth. At home she was kept away from everything, and she knew everything.

In poor neighborhoods everywhere, there were signs hanging out to welcome kids back from the Korean war. On Marshall Street one night, everybody hung out signs saying, WELCOME HOME SALLY and flags hung from windows and there was a big block party for Kid Sally Palumbo, who was home from the battle of Sing Sing. The kids Angela played with ran around getting sips of red wine from the adults drinking on the stoops. Then they all went up to the corner and told strangers passing by, "Her brother come home today." And the strangers would say, "Oh, isn't that wonderful." And Angela and all the kids would shriek, "He was a prisoner!" Laughing, they'd run down the block again. If Big Mama had heard this, she would have erupted into hand-swinging anger.

As Sally and the five cousins on the block grew older and were involved in continuous trouble, Angela thickened the screen around herself, and her life became the books on the table in her room. In school she became the moody little girl who made the honor roll. In high school, at the Dominican Girls' Academy, she outgrew her head-hanging walk. She began to notice that girls either were overfriendly to her, which she knew was an expression of superiority, or went out of their way to ignore her. Boys, who understand power, always treated her with deference. In her third year of high school her class of thirty-eight girls sat and talked before class started, and it was February 15 and they were talking about Valentine cards they had gotten. A redheaded girl in the front of the room called out, "How come Angela got Valentine Day cards with a picture of a garage?"

Laughter fell around Angela. For a small instant she was nervous and confused. Then the embarrassment ran out of her face and her eyes narrowed. When the laughter stopped, she called out, saying each word by itself, "You . . . rat . . . stool . . . pigeon . . . son . . . of . . . a . . . bitch."

Nobody was overfriendly and nobody made a show of trying to ignore her after that. Everything became correct, and Angela spoke to girls only when she felt like it.

In her neighborhood most of the girls went to vocational or commercial high schools and spent their afternoons smoking cigarettes in DiLorenzo's candy store with boys who had dropped out of school and were waiting to get into jobs or trouble. The girls went to filing-clerk jobs in insurance offices in Manhattan, or, mainly, into knitting mills. They rode in cars with boys, and sex and marriage came quickly. Angela found she had nothing in common with the girls. And the boys were overly careful of her because Kid Sally Palumbo had promised to cut the fingers off anybody touching his sister. For a few years Angela was close to Carmine Pollino, who lived at Number 25 Marshall Street and attended Brooklyn Automotive High. Then one afternoon she was coming home from school and she stopped to talk to Carmine, who was sitting on the stoop doing homework.

"A composition, I don't know why I got to do a composition," he said. "You don't have to write no compositions to fix up cars."

She came up and sat next to him on the stoop and looked at his composition.

> My friend Jonny Lombardo isn't nervouse of anything. The other day he sent away for a brochure on a fuel injector. Then the mailman came in the morning and what did Jonny receive but the brochure. It was outasight and he come right over to the house to show it to me so I could see what a outasight thing he had received in the mail.

Carmine's budding masculinity crumbled away in Angela's eyes as she read the painful scrawl.

"Is that how you spell Johnny?" she said.

"Yeah, Johnny," he said. "J-o-n-n-y. That's right, isn't it?"

"An H," she said.

"H?"

"Oh, you know that," she said.

Carmine shrugged and crossed out the name the first time and wrote it out correctly and then he skipped over the second misspelling and resumed his scrawling. After this, Angela found she had very little to say to him.

At school she went to basketball games on Friday nights at Bishop McCarthy Boys' High School. After the games she danced with Irish boys who were breathing heavily even before the music started. She did not see the boys at any other time. When one of them asked for her phone number, she told him she had no phone. One of the things Angela knew without being told was never to use a telephone. At home, Angela was always given a running lecture by Big Mama on the evils of Irish boys. Big Mama kept saying that Irishers take the bread out of their children's mouths to buy whisky. Big Mama said this in a high-pitched voice, with her hands waving. Among the most overlooked racial problems in the country is the division between Irish and Italians. "Go with nice Italian boys," Big Mama said.

The trouble was, Big Mama's idea of a nice Italian boy was a strangler's son. For the big event of Angela's four years in high school, Big Mama went to the South Brooklyn version of the *Social Register*. Just as any decent Protestant would enter the hospital if his daughter tried to make her debut on the arm of somebody with an unknown family name, so do the old-breed Mafia try to match their offspring with children of other Mafia families. Royal blood can be preserved only with the strictest of breeding. Big Mama insisted Angela invite to her prom a nice Italian boy named Henry Gallante. He was the nineteen-year-old son of Sammy (the Timber Wolf) Gallante, the Canarsie section of Brooklyn's answer to John Dillinger. On the night of the dance, Henry Gallante arrived with three huge orchids. He gave them to Angela reluctantly because he really wanted to wear the orchids himself. One strangulation too many in the yard behind his house had turned Henry Gallante very far from violence.

Outside of trying to steer her toward Italian boys of shaky antecedents, Big Mama went to great lengths to shield Angela from what was going on around her. Kid Sally Palumbo never spoke of what he did for a living, in front of his sister. And by her own instincts Angela never went into the vending-machine office. She developed the habit of never walking past it, either. She did not want to see or know what was going on in the office. At the same time, she knew everything. There was an organization of Good People and it was an old Italian thing and her brother and his cousins were in it some place, and Big Mama knew all about it, and so did Angela. But the Kid Sally Palumbo in the newspapers was not her brother. Her brother was the person in the house with her who could make her laugh.

One day, in the spring of her last year in high school, she came into the vestibule to go upstairs and the sound of loud voices came through the wall from the vending-machine office.

"Do the right thing," her brother's voice shouted.

"I'm trying to do the right thing," another voice said.

"Then where's the freakin' money?" Big Jelly's voice said.

A chair scraped and there was the sound of flesh being slapped. Then another sound. And then a loud shriek. "You Jew mocky son-of-a-bitch!" her brother shouted. "Oh, you dirty bastard."

"Are you all right, Sally Kid?" Big Jelly's voice yelled.

"My hand, the dirty bastard. Kick his head in."

There was a commotion, and through the door Angela saw a man in a neat gray suit running onto the sidewalk. Big Jelly ran after him and threw a kick at him that missed. The man got into a car at the curb and pulled away.

Angela went up to her room and dropped her schoolbooks on the bed and sat there for an hour. When it was out of her, she left the room as if nothing had happened. Her brother came home that night with his hand in a cast. Kid Sally Palumbo had a willing, but inaccurate right hand. In the afternoon melee he had bounced a punch against the edge of the desk and broken two knuckles.

When she graduated from high school, Angela had the marks and units to enter several colleges. But the Palumbos were not yet in the stratum of gangsters who sent their daughters in fur coats to exclusive schools. Angela entered NYU. She liked the idea of being swallowed in its size. Only people directly familiar with her from months of sitting in the same class knew that she was the sister of New York's reputedly roughest young racketeer. She kept an uninterested attitude about everything but the classwork. One boy, Robert Dineen, who was in her late-afternoon classes, always spoke to her. One day at the end of class he asked her if she felt like a cup of coffee. He took her to a bar that was three steps down from the sidewalk of Sheridan Square. Angela drank Coke. Dineen drank beer with a motion that caused the rim of the glass to strike the bridge of his nose so hard Angela was afraid he would wound himself. After that she met him one time at the Brooklyn Public Library on a Saturday night. They walked to a place on Flatbush Avenue called Flynn's. Dineen drank beer and talked sports with the young guys in the neighborhood who hung out in the place. He had his back turned to Angela much of the time. She noticed the bar was filled with young girls whose companions treated them the same way. But when she walked to the jukebox Angela could feel Dineen watching her very carefully. She went home alone by cab that night. She met Dineen there a couple more times. She liked his openness and the way everybody else in the bar was open and spoke out. Nobody was withdrawn and there was no whispering.

One day after school, when they were going out that night,

Angela said she had to go and change and Dineen insisted on coming with her. Angela said yes. She was empty while she rode the subway with Dineen and then walked him down the street to the house.

Big Mama got Dineen in the front room. She sat directly across from him.

"You want a pear?"

"No, thank you," he said.

"Where you go tonight?"

"To a movie, I guess."

"Then you be home by eleven o'clock?"

"Well—uh—I guess around then."

"You name Dineen. What's-a you mother's name?"

"Collins."

"Uh. You go to mass?"

"Yes, ma'am."

"Our family goes to church." Big Mama turned and looked at a picture of the Sacred Heart. "You want a sandwich?"

"No, thank you."

"What's-a you father do?"

"Oh, he's dead."

"Oh, that's-a bad. I'm sorry."

"That's all right."

"What did this-a father do?"

"Policeman."

Big Mama said it very slowly. "You . . . father . . . cop?"

"He was a sergeant. I have two uncles on the job in Long Island."

Big Mama blessed herself and looked up at the ceiling. "*Gesù Cristo,*" she muttered.

When Angela came out, dressed, and started to leave with Dineen, Big Mama snarled at them, "You be home eleven-fifteen the latest."

Angela looked at her, puzzled. "All right," she said.

They were halfway down the stairs when Big Mama leaned over the banisters.

"*No fagia mal!*"

"Pardon me?" Dineen said.

"Never mind. She know."

Later, when Dineen brought her home, they stood inside the vestibule talking to each other quietly. Through the wall came the well-enunciated words of her cousin, Larry (Kid Blast) Palumbo.

"I still think we should go and shoot his whole freakin' head off. Then set the son-of-a-bitch on fire. That's what I say we should do."

Dineen grabbed the doorknob for support. He stuttered through a good-by. As Angela started up the staircase, a light flicked on and Big Mama looked down the stairs at them.

"You kiss-a her?"

"I'm afraid to close my eyes here," Dineen said.

Dineen kept going to school in the summer so he could finish quickly and go on to law school. Angela stayed in school for the summer too. On Friday nights Dineen drove her to Sheepshead Bay for clams and beer. Afterward they sat in the car, looking at the lights on the dark water which ran up to the fishing-boat piers. On the first night there Dineen leaned over and kissed Angela and she brought up her face to his and he ran a hand over her body for the first time.

On the July Fourth weekend Dineen took her to a beach party at Breezy Point. His cousin had a house three doors from the beach. There was a big crowd of people Angela knew from Flynn's. Dineen started the night off by drinking beer from a keg and talking to the other boys. He came and sat on a blanket with Angela for a while. Then at 11:30 he said he wanted to go up to his cousin's house for cigarettes. He took Angela by the hand and they walked away from the wood fire and across the dark sand to the street. Dineen said nothing.

He was breathing too hard to talk. The house was a one-story white wooden bungalow with a screened-in porch. A lamp on the porch was the only light in the house.

"I'll wait outside," Angela said. She said it automatically. Dineen held her hand and took her up the walk and held the screen door for her. On the porch he took her hand again and started into the darkened living room. Inside, he headed for a door. "Where are we going?" Angela said automatically. And he opened the door and led her in by the hand and he was kissing her and she went down onto the bed on her back with him still kissing her, and she wriggled her legs onto the bed. He was surprised when she did not stop him. His hands were at the top of her blouse and he was pulling at it so hard it was lifting her shoulderblades off the bed. The button went in his hands.

"Stop it," she said. He was tugging at the next button. "Stop it!" she said sharply. Her tone brought Kid Blast's voice back into his ears. *She'll have my head cut off.* Dineen tumbled from her and stood next to the bed.

"Don't get mad," he said.

"I'm not mad, I just want to have clothes to wear," she said. She unbuttoned the blouse and reached down and unzipped the side of her Capri pants.

"Don't tell your brother," he said.

The day Angela was supposed to have her period, the phone rang at eight a.m. Big Mama looked at the phone suspiciously. Kid Sally was inside, asleep. The few people who called never called before noon. Big Mama picked it up. It was Robert Dineen, calling the house for the first time.

"Well, how do you feel?" he asked Angela.

"Fine," she said.

"Everything's all right?"

"Oh, that? Oh, I don't know. No, not yet. Don't worry about it."

"I do worry."

"Oh, stop."

"Stop? I don't want to get strangled."

For three days Robert Dineen called in the morning and saw Angela during the afternoon at school, and each time the answer was no. He began to look like a defendant. On the fourth day Angela told him everything was all right. Dineen went to the bar on Sheridan Square and drank whisky. By seven p.m. he was looking at himself in the mirror behind the bar. "I play with death!" he said.

Chapter **8**

A few months after this, a man named Theodore Kaplowitz, who owned four bars in Brooklyn, walked into the office of the District Attorney. He said that Kid Sally Palumbo and three others had come into his best place, the Esquire, and walked behind the bar and opened the cash register and taken half the money. Kid Sally Palumbo announced he was a partner in the place from now on. Kaplowitz began to argue. Kid Sally Palumbo took Kaplowitz's arm and tried to break it over the edge of the bar.

The assistant district attorney handling the complaint had bodyguards placed on Kaplowitz. He also had him wired for recording in case Kid Sally Palumbo returned. Kid Sally had intended to return and get some more money and give Kaplowitz another beating, but he never got around to it. The police thought Kid Sally was smelling the trap. The assistant district attorney, Frank Rogin, twenty-nine, decided to bring in Kid Sally for questioning. Assistant Chief Inspector Cornelius J. Gallagher, fifty-nine, commanding officer, Brooklyn South detectives, had Kid Sally picked up. Kid Sally came into Rogin's office at eight p.m. Gallagher and two detectives stood in the doorway. Kid Sally was chewing gum. The 100-watt bulbs in the cracked plaster ceiling made Kid Sally's black hair glisten.

"What could I tell you, Mr. Rogin?" Kid Sally said. "What could I tell you?" He held his hands out and sat in silence while Rogin kept asking questions.

Gallagher lit a cigarette. His pouchy eyes became slits as the smoke ran over his face.

"You're just a guinea," he said to Kid Sally.

"All right on that stuff," Rogin said.

"Why not?" Gallagher said. "Why be nice to a guinea like this?"

"I said forget it," Rogin said sharply.

Gallagher glared through the slits of his pouchy eyes. Gallagher went into another office and sat with his two detectives. Gallagher leafed through the file on Kid Sally Palumbo. "What's this with his sister?" he said.

"She goes to school," one of the detectives said.

"She must do the bookkeeping for them," Gallagher said. "You know these other guinea bastards can't read or write."

"I just know she goes to school," the detective said.

"Uhuh," Gallagher said. He went back to the doorway of Rogin's office.

"Sally?"

Kid Sally Palumbo didn't turn his head. "Yeah?"

"Does the sister handle the money for you, or does she just keep the records?"

Kid Sally Palumbo swung around in his chair with his eyes flashing wildly. "Your mother!"

Gallagher smiled. "No, your sister, Sally."

Rogin's hand slammed the desk. "I'll do the talking here," he said to Gallagher.

When Kid Sally Palumbo left, Rogin told Gallagher, "I'm

very interested in this guy we had here. I'm not interested in anything else. The sister doesn't interest me. Am I understood? Leave the girl alone. I don't do business this way."

Gallagher looked at Rogin the way every man who is fifty-nine looks at a twenty-nine-year-old who is above him in life. Driving back to the precinct, Gallagher said to the two detectives, "Bring the sister in tomorrow."

"Where do we get the warrant?" one of them said.

"You don't need a warrant for a guinea. Pick her up after school and bring her to the Charles Street house. I'll use the office there."

Angela Palumbo was coming out the back door of the English 101 classroom at 3:40 the next afternoon. The ones in front of her were having some kind of trouble getting out the door. Angela stood in line and shuffled forward. When she saw the two faces in the hallway, her breath caught in her throat.

Two Irish faces, tilted back to look past the crowd, and also tilted back with the sense of authority all policemen like to use. Angela stopped just outside the door. The other students were walking past, but going only a few steps and turning to watch. One of the detectives, the one in a black topcoat with the collar turned up, held out his right hand with a gold shield in it. Angela was shaking. She felt a hand on her shoulder. Robert Dineen stood with her.

"Could you come with us, please?" the detective said.

"It'll just be for a little while," the other one said.

The hallway was crowded now. Faces were looking at Angela from everywhere. Her hands began to shake. She couldn't speak.

"Do you have a warrant?" Dineen said.

"It's okay, don't worry," the detective said. He was ignoring Dineen and looking at Angela. The other detective put a hand on Dineen's arm. "You can go," he said.

"Let me see the warrant," Dineen said.

"Why don't you come with her, then?" the detective in the black coat said. "Then you can see that it's nothing."

With the crowded hallway watching her, Angela went with the detectives and Dineen. Outside on the sidewalk, all the heads turned to watch her get into a black unmarked Plymouth. She sat in the back seat with Dineen. They were driven to the Charles Street precinct house, which covers the NYU area. The precinct house is at the end of a block of warehouses. The flag hanging from the second-floor window whipped in the wind coming from the Hudson River, a half-block away. Angela Palumbo walked into the station with her schoolbooks huddled in her arms and her head down, and the detectives guided her toward the metal staircase in the lobby. One of them turned around and put a hand on Dineen's chest. "You wait here," he said.

Cornelius Gallagher sat in a bare upstairs office. He wore a brown suit, a drinker's stomach pressing against the middle button.

"Sit down," he said. He pointed to a chair next to him. You always sit next to a girl when you question her. It gives that little intimacy women need. If you sit across a desk from her, it puts everything on a cold business basis. Women cannot react to it.

"Here, let me take your books," Gallagher said.

Angela shook her head.

"All right. Would you like a cigarette?" He held out a pack of filter cigarettes. Angela's hand shook and her fingers fumbled with the top of the pack while she took one. Gallagher lit it for her. He put a tin ashtray in front of her. He reached over and put the match into the ashtray. Always use the same ashtray with a girl.

"Angela, I just wanted to ask you a few things," he said. "You can answer if you want, and if you don't want, you don't have to answer. But you don't have to worry about what you say. We're just having a conversation here."

The cigarette shook in her fingers and she had trouble getting it into her mouth.

"You know, Angela, I've been around a long time and seen a lot of things. There's nothing you could tell me that I don't know already. Oh, I tell you, the things I've seen in my life. I couldn't be surprised by anything you tell me. I've heard it all. Why, you could sit there right now and tell me that your brother killed Georgie Paradise and I wouldn't get excited at all. Sally killed Georgie Paradise? What's it mean to me? I've been all through it."

The voice was rasping and unreal, and Angela Palumbo's breath kept falling to the bottom of her stomach.

"What's he waiting for?" the desk sergeant asked a patrolman downstairs. The sergeant nodded at Robert Dineen.

"I don't know," the patrolman said. "Hey, buddy, something you want?"

Dineen had been standing against a rusted radiator. "I'm waiting for somebody," he said.

"Waiting for who?"

"Somebody upstairs."

"Well, you better wait outside, then. This isn't a waiting room."

The patrolman's voice went through Dineen. It carried the sharpness a cop puts into his voice when he is carrying out an order for somebody he wants to impress.

Dineen waited on the sidewalk. Newspapers blew down the street in swirls of dust. The flat late-afternoon sun came through a garbage-strewn alley between two warehouses. Late-afternoon sun in the winter depresses anybody watching it. After a short while it makes the person feel sick to his stomach. Dineen felt like he had been riding in a closed car filled with exhaust fumes. Fear and disgust mixed with the sickness.

The detectives' and desk patrolman's voices kept running through him, and the fear grew stronger. What the hell was he doing in a thing like this? He could get in trouble in law school.

The street was empty and the shadows were becoming longer when Robert Dineen began walking toward the subway five blocks away.

It was 5:30 when Angela Palumbo came down the stairs alone. She had her face buried in the books. She had not spoken a word since she came into the precinct house. She had sat in a trance while this red pouchy face cooed at her and smiled and showed her reports she looked at but did not see. Now she walked through the lobby and stepped outside and she needed Robert Dineen badly, just to hold her arm and talk to her, and she came out into the evening on the sidewalk of the empty street.

Angela Palumbo did not mention the precinct questioning to anybody when she got home. She went to her room. In the morning she did not go to school. She did not go to school for the rest of the term. When Big Mama and Sally tried to talk to her, she said she didn't feel well. When they told her to see a doctor, she shrugged.

"Girls," Big Mama said to Kid Sally one night. "Girls can be strange sometimes. She get over it."

One day in late December, Angela was coming back from the store and as she came into the vestibule she heard shouts coming through the wall and the sound of somebody being slapped, and one of the voices started pleading. When she heard another slap, she spat a word out of her mouth.

"Good."

In January she went back to school. Robert Dineen was not in any of her classes, and she did not see him in the hallway because she never looked up when she walked from room to room.

On a Thursday night, at the midnight show at the Copacabana, she sat at ringside with Buster Capanegro, a bookmaker and shylock with the East Harlem mob. The comedian told a joke. "Kids from mixed marriages are very confused. I tell you. I know a kid who had an Italian father and a Jewish mother. Every time he passes a department store he doesn't know whether to buy it or rob it."

"Hey! What's so funny about that?" Buster Capanegro snapped.

The comedian looked at him. Buster looked at the comedian. The comedian nearly fainted.

"I didn't like that at all, that fresh punk," Angela said.

When Big Mama told her one night that there would be some nice Italian boys around for a big bike race soon, Angela shrugged. When Big Mama told her it was important for her to go to a cocktail party and be Mama's eyes, Angela was more interested.

"It be good if you go," Big Mama said. "You watch and come back and tell me what everybody does."

Angela nodded. Now she wanted to go to the party.

Chapter 9

The press cocktail party for the six-day bike race was held upstairs at Keefe's Steak House. The crowd featured some newspaper and television reporters, many copy boys from the *Daily News* who passed themselves off as sports reporters and drank whisky with a beer motion, the president of the Queens chapter of a Greek society, and several stumpy members of the Polish Eagles of Greenpoint.

Several young girls were interspersed through the crowd as hostesses. Name cards were pinned to their dresses. When Angela Palumbo came up the stairs to the room, she automatically looked away from the table that had the name cards. She knew there would not be a card for her. If one happened to be there by mistake, she knew enough not to wear it. She was dressed in a short canary-yellow coat. Her black hair fell onto her shoulders. Joseph DeLauria saw her and left the bar and came up to her.

"I'm Joseph DeLauria," he said. "Here, let me take your coat." She turned and began to come out of the coat. She was wearing a matching dress. "God bless, you're pretty," DeLauria said. She saw his eyes go to her shoulder to make sure she wasn't wearing a name card. Then to her hands, to make sure she wasn't holding one of the cards and about to put it on.

She went to the bar and ordered ginger ale. She was not going to start drinking around this DeLauria. He began introducing Angela to people: a gray-haired man who was the New York correspondent for *Il Giornale* of Milan, one of the Polacks from Greenpoint, and a chubby kid with a crewcut whose face was beet-red from the unfamiliar brandy hitting a system used only to tap beer. He said his name was Tommy something and that he worked for the *Daily News*. Angela looked away. Another Irisher drunk.

She stiffened when DeLauria took her arm. "I want you to meet some of the great riders from Italy," he said. He began showing her around the room. "Here, Carlo Rafetto, I'd like you to meet Angela." DeLauria was careful to give only the first name. "And, hey, this is Mario Ciariello. Mario, meet Angela. And now where's the other Mario? Mario Trantino. Oh, there he is in the back. Look at this."

Mario was sitting alone at a table in the back of the room. He was bent over and had the tablecloth pulled up, and he was working with a pencil. Under his left hand there was a small picture, torn from a sightseeing book, of a $35,000 Modigliani which had hung in a Madison Avenue gallery. With his right hand Mario was just doodling a little, trying to see if he could copy even a bit of the Modigliani. *Who knows, Sidney says they all have the taste of a pig. Maybe you just make a little change here and there and they don't even know.*

When Mario saw DeLauria leading a girl in a yellow dress toward him, he quickly pulled the red-checked tablecloth back into place over his work.

DeLauria made introductions and patted Angela on the back. "Why don't you sit down and visit with Mario? He's all alone here. We can't have that, can we?"

"Am I supposed to make him buy me champagne?" Angela said.

Joseph DeLauria laughed with his mouth and called her a son-of-a-bitch with his eyes. He walked away.

As Angela started to sit down, she looked directly at Mario. The casualness went out of her body and she slipped into the chair with her hands smoothing her skirt and coming up gracefully and her eyes staying on Mario's face. Mario caught an impression of her as she started to sit down, and his eyes ran from her hips to her chest and onto her face. A picture of his hotel room came into his mind.

"Hello," she said.

"Hello."

She thought for a moment. "Uh, *si recreon'?*" She said it stiffly and with the key syllables slurred. Her Italian was terrible.

"Nice," he said.

"Oh, you know English?"

"From the school and this man teaches me home."

"That's good. Do most of the young people speak English where you come from?"

"Young people go away."

"Oh, I'll bet they do. But they have to go to Germany or Australia, don't they? Nobody can get in this country any more."

"You must do a special thing to stay here," Mario said.

"Well, if you win the race that will make you special maybe," she said.

Mario pulled the tablecloth back and looked down at his drawing. He took a pencil from his breast pocket and copied a little curve from the Modigliani. This was the something special that was going to keep him in the country.

"What's that?" she said.

"Nothing, nothing." He pulled the tablecloth back quickly.

He's sitting there probably drawing dirty pictures for the whole time, Angela thought. *I'll bet you he's got me in them.* She picked up the glass to finish it. It's always easier to leave when the glass is empty. *Moron,* she said to herself.

"Well, have fun," she said. She got up.

He looked up, flustered. "No, I just was . . ." his hand made a pinwheel motion.

"What is it?" she said.

"Oh . . ." His hand said it was nothing.

"Oh, what is it?" she said. She decided she'd embarrass him. She came around the table. He put both hands on top of the cloth. Angela grabbed an edge of the tablecloth and pulled the whole thing out from under Mario's hands.

When she saw what he had been doing, she was surprised. "Oh, I couldn't imagine," she said. "You're an artist?"

"I am going to be one," Mario said. "I am going to stay here and work to be an artist. This is—uh—just—uh—trying to—uh—"

"Practice," she said.

"Yes, practice." He stuffed the two sheets of paper in his jacket pocket.

"It's wonderful," she said. "Where did you study? What university did you attend?"

"In Catanzia nobody goes to the university," he said.

"Mario," Joseph DeLauria called. "Mario, come over here for a minute. I want you to meet somebody."

"Don't get up," Angela said.

"He wants me."

"Don't get up."

Mario shrugged. Angela glanced at DeLauria and turned her head from him. She sat and thought about what she could do to upset DeLauria. She had met him today for the first time. He was a bastard, and he also worked for Baccala. She didn't know Baccala, either. But she knew he was the "people" her brother and grandmother were arguing about.

"Why don't you go somewhere where you can do what you want?" she said to Mario.

"I stay?" he said.

"No, let's go some place else," she said.

She got up and began walking through the tables. Mario bent over quickly. He pulled his shoelaces open. He got up and followed Angela. Joseph DeLauria caught a glimpse of them while they were leaving. "Smart," he said to himself. "That's nice and smart."

Out in the street, Mario put on his uncle's glasses. He took a step and tripped on a lace and bumped into Angela.

"Excuse," he said.

They began walking down the street. She glanced down. "Your laces are untied," she said.

"That is the way I have them," he said.

"Oh," she said. She saw he was walking with his eyes closed. "Do you have something the matter?" she said.

"I save my eyes for looking at colors," he said.

"Oh," she said.

He had no coat.

"You'll freeze," she said.

"I think of hot colors and they make me warm," he said. "I sweat."

"Oh," she said.

He felt good. He was impressing her very much that he was an artist.

They rode the subway downtown and came onto the narrow tenement streets of Little Italy. On Mulberry Street, Italian music came from a record shop. Cheeses hung in the store windows. A meat-delivery truck was parked in front of an Italian butcher's. The white-coated deliveryman was carrying sheep's heads, *capozzelle,* into the store. The red vein lines ran in a spiderweb over the white bone and fat of the sheep's heads. Water was dripping from the back of the truck and turning to ice on the curb. The butcher from the store was shaking a bag of rock salt onto the freezing water. Mario put his hands deeper into his pockets.

"Oh, you'll freeze," she said.

He closed his eyes. "I think of hot colors," he said.

She took him into a place called Raymond's, which is on a corner. Raymond's has a bar on one side and a clam bar on the other. Tables are in the rear. Three men work behind the clam bar, putting breaded shrimp and *calamare* and blowfish tails into wire baskets. They drop the wire baskets into boiling grease and the grease turns to brown foam over the cold breaded fish, and in a minute or so one of the men pulls the wire basket out and dumps the fish on a plate. He covers it with red sauce and slaps it on the counter. The sauce is made of red peppers and cayenne primarily, with a little tomato in passing. The signs behind the counter say: SAUCES: 1. HOT. 2. MEDIUM. 3. LIGHT.

Raymond's is one of the places in New York tourists and out-of-town businessmen hear about. One of the hobbies of the people in the neighborhood is to sit in Raymond's and watch one of these visitors go against the sauce. Angela slid onto a stool at the clam bar. Mario sat next to her. Angela nudged Mario when a man in a plaid hat called out in a flat Midwestern accent for number-one sauce on his shrimp. They put the plate in front of the man. The plaid hat forked a shrimp dripping with number-one sauce into his mouth. His mouth clamped down on the shrimp. He started his first chew. He then made a face as if he had just been shot. He opened his mouth and made a sound like a trombone. The counter-man automatically gave him a glass of Coke. The man swallowed it. The plaid hat now bellowed as the sauce bit into his tongue. The counterman gave him another Coke. The man drank it, paid for the shrimp, and walked out of the door. He stood on the sidewalk. Everybody inside could see the man's shoulders heaving while he gulped in the cold air.

"Another score for the house," the counterman said. Everybody laughed.

Angela and Mario ate *calamare* with number-one sauce and a side order of linguine. The linguine was slick with olive oil, and the bottom of the bowl was covered with clams and parsley. Italians being immune to sauce, they happily swallowed the *calamare*. The counterman wrote out the check and put it on the counter and Mario reached for the watch pocket. Her hand stopped him.

"Now, don't be silly," she said.

"Oh, no," he said.

"I said."

She picked up the check and went through her purse and paid. They left and she guided him by the elbow around the corner to Ferrara's, which has show windows that take up half the block. The windows are filled with speckled cookies and pastries that have cream coming out of both ends. Inside, brilliant lights glare from the ceiling and come off the mirrored walls and spill onto the white tile floor and polished tabletops. The place smells of whipped cream and coffee. They ordered *cappuccino*, heavily creamed coffee that froths at the top of the glass, and *cannoli*, which are filled with thick rum cream.

"Now tell me," she said.

"With the painting?"

"Yes."

"It must come from here." He held his hands to his stomach. "It must come from me. There is nothing to put down if it does not come from me. There is no way for this to happen at home. We eat chipmunks in Catanzia. You must spend too much time hunting them to be an artist."

"Chipmunks! Still?" she said.

"Oh, and dandelions. Or the good grass," he said.

"Oh, really now," she said.

"No, it is true," he said. When he saw how she was reacting, he thought of saying he had a brother who died because he had no food.

"When are you going to do any painting here?" she said.

"Tomorrow maybe," he said.

"I'd like to see what you do, but I have school all day. Then I have to go right home."

"You could come another day," he said. The picture of his hotel room came into his mind again. There were, his instinct told him, great resources in anybody who seemed to like him and was this beautiful. But Mario's mind operated one step at a time, and his vision of a future with Angela consisted of her in his hotel room.

"What other day?" she said. "You have the race."

He shrugged.

"I'll see you at the race, and when it's all over I'll come and watch you paint," she said.

"You'll be at the race?" he said.

"Every night," she said.

She paid the check on the way out and walked to the subway with him. She pointed to the entrance for the uptown trains. She started to walk across the street to the Brooklyn train entrance and then she turned around and came back. "Do you have change for the subway?" she said.

Mario said yes.

She said, "Let me see to be sure you've got the right change."

He showed her his silver. She nodded and went to the subway. When her head disappeared down the stairs, Mario put his hand into the watchpocket and began looking for a taxi. The hundred-dollar bill was still intact. He decided to keep it that way. When the taxi got him to the hotel, the doorman held the door and Mario took out his change. There wasn't enough. He looked at the doorman. "You put it on my room bill?"

"We don't do that here," the doorman said.

"In Italy, yes," Mario said.

Mario showed the doorman his key. The doorman and the cab-driver looked at each other. Mario got out of the cab and walked into the lobby and went to the elevators. When the doorman came in and asked the desk clerk for the cab money and told him what room to charge, the clerk shook his head.

"One of those bike-riders they booked in here. The bastards sure come with nerve."

"They know," the doorman said.

When Angela got home, Big Mama called out from the kitchen. "You have a nice time?"

"It was all right."

"Who you meet there?"

"Some boys."

"Italian boys?"

"I met one. A nice young Italian boy."

"Young?"

"A kid," Angela said.

Chapter **10**

When the job of producing a sports event had started, several weeks before, Kid Sally Palumbo and Big Jelly arrived at the 987th Field Artillery Armory with two carpenters named Mulqueen and Keefe. The carpenters had a superior reputation, particularly for their work on the chapel of Attica State Prison, where they each spent thirty months for poor usage of a gun. Big Jelly and the carpenters stood with an armory worker who unrolled the floor plan and went over it with them.

Kid Sally Palumbo walked away. The click of his heels sounded throughout the gloomy armory. Kid Sally lifted his feet up and brought the heels down harder. The sound went high up, to the olive steel beams that crisscross in the pale light coming through the windows. Now Kid Sally started taking big tramping strides and he walked the length of the armory listening to his footsteps making the only sound in the place. Trucks and jeeps, with 105-mm. howitzers coupled to them, were parked along the armory walls. At the far end of the floor a green corrugated-metal sliding door was halfway down from the ceiling. When the green corrugated door came all the way down to the floor it chopped off the armory floor. The area behind the door was the motor pool for the field-artillery outfit housed in the armory. The equipment now happened to be parked out around the floor. But it was always kept in the motor-pool area.

Kid Sally Palumbo didn't bother with any of this. He just kept walking and listening to his footsteps echo around the building. Big Jelly and the carpenters stood and went over the plans. The carpenters were taking notes and Big Jelly was waving his arm around the empty building like a foreman. The armory worker had gone back to his office. He left Big Jelly and the carpenters to work out the floor plan for the track and bleachers. When they told Kid Sally they were through, Kid Sally said he was tired from all this detail work and he needed a nap. The carpenters, holding paper with floor measurements, said they were going to get the lumber and the workers needed to put together a fine track for bike-racing. Big Jelly looked at his watch. It was 2:30. He was just in time to meet his new girl friend. "She gets off in half an hour," Big Jelly said. His new girl friend was in her third year in high school.

With three days to go before the race, a final meeting was held in Baccala's office.

"I don't know where we stand," Joseph DeLauria said. He held his palms up. "I do the right thing every day, that's all I can say."

"I go to a joint yesterday," Big Jelly said, "and I tell the guy, 'Hey, take some tickets,' and he says, 'Who tickets?' I tell him for the bike race, make the waiters go, and he says to me, 'Hey, believe me, they'd rather get shot than have to go to a bike race.'"

"That's what everybody says," Kid Sally Palumbo said. "*Axt* anybody, they tell you, get lost."

"So you get two *tousan*, three *tousan* people," Baccala said.

"They all bring money. Be plenty for everybody."

"Who wins the race?" Kid Sally said.

"Whoever wins," Izzy Cohen said.

"Why?" Kid Sally asked.

"Because we have six sprints a night. The riders bunch up so's they're all even and then we announce odds on each rider over the loudspeaker and then you guys make book in the stands and we run the sprint off. What do we care who wins? We got them bettin' into our odds. We take off the top. You got to give a man some kind of a shot for his money. If we try to screw them completely, they walk out on us and then where are we?"

"All right," Kid Sally said.

"One-a thing," Baccala said.

"What?"

Baccala leaned forward with his chubby hands clasped together. "What about the bike-riders looking to rob us?"

"How could they rob us?" Izzy said.

"Never mind, trust in-a only Christ and Saint Anthony." Baccala's eyes narrowed. "We make sure. We lock-a them in the cage."

"What cages?" Kid Sally said.

"We get cages, regular cages with-a bars on them. When the rider is not riding the bike, he goes into the cage. He can no talk to the other riders. When it is time for him to come and ride, boop! Out of the cage. He rides."

"Where do we get a cage from?" Kid Sally said.

"That's your job," Baccala said.

"I got all the jobs," Kid Sally said. "I don't like the jobs and I don't like the whole idea. This race is gonna get us nothin' but grief. A breadline, we could do better on a breadline than with this thing."

"Shut up-a you face," Baccala said.

"I say what I freakin' please," Kid Sally said.

"Shut up-a you face."

"Go screw," Kid Sally said.

Baccala's face did not change expression. The Water Buffalo, standing by the door, took his cue from Baccala. He kept his face straight too. Izzy shrugged and looked at the newspaper. Big Jelly looked through his glasses, unblinking.

Kid Sally took out a cigarette. He opened the lighter with a loud snap. His thumb hit the wheel and the flame shot up. He put the lighter away. He took the cigarette in the thumb and forefinger of his left hand and held it to his mouth. Smoke hung in front of his face. He stared at Baccala.

He stood up. "Well, the thing better be right, what else could I tell you?" he said. He and Big Jelly left the room, slamming the door after them.

"*Ciciri,*" Baccala snarled.

Kid Sally and Big Jelly spent the afternoon in the vending office, looking through the Yellow Pages for cages. Big Jelly finally found two theatrical renting places. Between them they had eleven circus cages which they could rent for two weeks. They needed them back for the Ed Sullivan show. This left the bike race one cage short. There were twenty-four riders, divided into two-man teams. While one rider was on the track, the teammate would be in the cage, sleeping on the cot. A woman at one of the agencies suggested they call Thompson's, a large pet-supply house in Manhattan which services zoos around the country. The man at Thompson's said he had one cage he could lease for a week. Sally and Big Jelly drove over to Thompson's. It was in a warehouse. A man in the office took Sally and Jelly through a triple-locked steel door and into a hot cement room that was smelly and filled with the squeal of birds. In a tall cage at the front of the warehouse, a zebra shouldered against thick bars. Next to him, in another cage, an antelope stood quietly. Cages filled with multicolored birds, were stacked on top of each other. Up against the back wall there was a small cage on wooden blocks. Next to it was a big circus cage. A tan form was rolled up in one corner of the cage.

"Here's the cage," the man said, stopping at the small one.

"Not big enough," Big Jelly said.

"We need it big enough for a guy," Kid Sally Palumbo said.

"We're startin' slavery," Big Jelly said.

"Well, that's all I got," the man said. "If I move the lion next week, you could have the cage then."

"Who lion?" Kid Sally said.

The man pointed to the larger cage. "That's a lion in there." The tan form in the corner stirred and came up on four legs. Wisps of mane, darker than the coat, straggled from its head. It stood on four puppy legs that were too long. The lion had feet too big for the body.

"That's a real baby, only five months old," the man said.

Kid Sally slapped his hand on the bars. The lion jumped up and pushed into the corner of the cage.

"What's a matter with him?"

"He's scary. He's only a baby."

"He looks like he could eat my freakin' leg," Big Jelly said.

"You have to put meat in front of him," the man said. "He'll be afraid of people for a few months yet."

Kid Sally yelled at the lion. "Yaaaaaahhhh!" The lion shook. The left side of Kid Sally's mouth came up in a sneer. His eyes squinted. He began to giggle.

"Yaaaaahhhhh!" Tommy Udo snarled.

"You sell him?" Kid Sally said.

"Sure, he's for sale. Two hundred and fifty dollars."

Kid Sally kept giggling and looking at the lion. "Give him the money, Jelly."

At six p.m. there was a roar and then a scream which ran through Marshall Street. People rushed to the windows. They looked out to see Kid Sally Palumbo, giggling, dragging a lion across the sidewalk from a panel truck. Women, screaming, ran away. The lion had a rope attached to a makeshift leather collar around his neck. Kid Sally pulled on the rope. The lion, head down, fear sounding from his throat, tried to dig into the sidewalk. Kid Sally Palumbo began yelling at the lion and pulling hard on the rope. The lion roared in fear. Big Jelly got behind the lion and pushed. They got the lion into the vending-machine office, opened the door to the cellar, and pushed the lion down the stairs. Kid Sally slammed the door and giggled. Big Jelly went out and waddled back with a paper bag, meat in waxed paper showing at the top.

"Eight pounds of chopped meat, that should fill his belly," Big Jelly said. He opened the cellar door and ripped the top of the waxed paper. He threw the bag down the stairs. The meat scent hit the lion while the bag was still in the air. Two floppy paws slapped down on the bag the moment it touched the floor.

"Look at that," Big Jelly said.

"Wait'll we feed him *people*," Kid Sally Palumbo said. He began to giggle.

Kid Sally and Big Jelly locked the office and went out for their night's business. They drove to a lumber mill. The lights were on. Mulqueen and Keefe were hammering bolts into a section of boards planked together to form a curved section of track. All over the lumber mill pieces like this were stacked or sat on sawhorses. A table in the middle of the floor was covered with a layout of the armory.

"We're right up to here," Mulqueen said. He put his finger on a spot in the plans. The spot was even with the doorway for the motor pool. The white lines on the blueprint paper, with long arrows and short arrows and numbers with apostrophes after them, irritated Kid Sally. He didn't know what they meant. He wanted to go back and play with the lion. "We just have to get the turn done, it goes in here," Mulqueen said, tapping his finger on the motor-pool area.

"It looks good," Kid Sally said. "Just don't let us down."

He and Big Jelly went out and sat in the car.

"We got things to do yet," Kid Sally said.

"What?" Big Jelly said.

"Well, we got to do things."

"I know what we got to do," Big Jelly said. "We got to go and do things to a couple of girls. Do them certain things to girls, that's what we got to do." He started the car.

Izzy sat in the Enchanted Hour from midnight until 1:30 a.m. He had an important appointment with Kid Sally Palumbo. At 1:30 he told the waiter to give him the check. *This kid is going to make a good memory of himself,* Izzy thought.

At seven p.m. on Friday, January 23, the World Championship Six-Day Bike Race, sponsored by the Americans of Italian Descent Amity Committee of New York, was one hour away from its official start. Only a few people were coming up the brightly lit armory steps. Ticket clerks began to shift uneasily and talk about a small crowd. When Izzy walked into the armory, he asked the head clerk what the advance sale was. The clerk said 1100. Actual attendance usually works out to be double the size of the advance. This would mean a crowd of about 2200 for the night's racing. Opening night. It all goes downhill after that. The ticket clerk laughed at the ridiculous situation. "Don't laugh," Izzy said. "Right now they don't have enough to pay you."

Inside, banners from Italian, Greek, French, and Polish societies hung from the balcony. Smoke from the first few black DeNobili cigars came up from the seats and hung in the floodlights. The old men smoking the cigars obviously were bike-race veterans. They kept their overcoats on.

In the middle of the floor, directly in front of the center of the grandstands, were twelve red, yellow, and blue circus cages with black bars. Each cage had a cot in it, and a folding tray for eating. The cages were in a General Custer circle. One side of each cage, the side facing the stands, was open. The other side, the side facing the inside of the wagon-train circle, was boarded up. In this way the riders in the cages would be unable to talk to each other through the backs of their cages.

Around the cages ran a beautiful wooden track. Neat, varnished pine wood gleamed in the light. The track had straightaways gently bending into a fine saucer curve. The lip of the saucer was banked high up from the bottom of the track. This was to create thrilling scenes of bike-riders seemingly on their sides, but protected by simple speed while they raced around the curve and came zooming into the straightaway. The straightaway ran the full length of the armory. The other turn of the track was not yet down. The beautiful curved boards that would form the turn were piled atop each other in front of the green corrugated-metal door, which was pulled down to the floor.

Mulqueen and Keefe stood with ten workers. "Get the door up now so we can finish this thing," Mulqueen was telling an armory worker dressed in fatigues.

The armory worker pressed a large button. Black, heavily greased chains began to make a zzzzzzzzzng sound. The green corrugated-metal shed door grumbled up from the armory floor. It rose steadily to reveal, foot by foot, first, five 105-mm. howitzers, neatly spaced, canvas tied to the muzzles. The howitzers were attached to five half-ton trucks. As the door rose more, the rest of the scene came into view. Packed together in neat rows, shining dully in the dim light, were the jeeps, half-tracks, ambulances, and trucks of the 987th Field Artillery Regiment, New York National Guard.

Mulqueen spat out curses. "Look at this. It'll take a half-hour to move this mess the hell out of there."

"Move them?" the armory worker said. "You don't move anything in there. That's the motor pool. Everything in there stays where it is."

"No, you don't understand," Mulqueen said. "We need that space for the track."

"That's the motor pool," the armory worker said. "It don't move."

It was now 7:15 p.m. Mulqueen walked the length of the armory floor quickly. He went out into the lobby. He saw Joseph DeLauria, dressed in a tuxedo, greeting old men who had sashes draped over their shoulders. Mulqueen tried to talk to DeLauria. DeLauria shook his head and wouldn't listen. Mulqueen saw Izzy leaning against a wall. "I don't do woodwork," Izzy said. Mulqueen finally saw Kid Sally Palumbo standing in the middle of a circle of his people.

"That's nothin', just have them move the trucks," Kid Sally Palumbo said. He turned back to his people.

"They won't move the trucks," Mulqueen said.

"Hey, that's nothin'," Big Jelly said. "Sally Kid, go over to the office there and tell the guy and he'll do it for you."

"It's always me," Kid Sally said. "I got to do everything." He stepped through the people and went into the armory office.

"You got to move the cannons for us," Kid Sally said. A man in civilian clothes sat at the desk.

"Where to?" the man said.

"Out in the street, anywhere, I don't care. Just move them."

"Move our motor pool? That's the property of the United States government. We can't move one jeep."

Kid Sally closed his eyes and ran a hand over them. "Who's in charge of this place?"

"The colonel."

"Where is he?"

"Home."

"Get him on the phone and straighten this thing out."

The man dialed a number. "Hello, is Colonel Rudershan there? Oh, I see. Yes, I forgot all about that. Well, thanks, I'll try him tomorrow then."

He hung up. "The colonel went to a movie with his wife and his brother and sister-in-law. It's the sister-in-law's birthday."

"Move the cannons," Kid Sally said.

"That's government property," the man said.

"MOVE THE CANNONS!" Kid Sally screamed.

"Hey!"

Baccala stood in the doorway, shoes gleaming, black hat tilted on his head, a DeNobili fuming in his mouth.

"How you no measure the track right?"

"This guy won't move the cannons," Kid Sally said.

"So he no move the cannons, then you move the track," Baccala said. "Make the track little."

Mulqueen, the carpenter, closed his eyes. "You can't do it. The thing is measured to fit like it is."

"Fix," Baccala said. His eyes were narrow. He walked out of the office.

A haze formed inside Kid Sally Palumbo's head. The haze solidified and turned into a throbbing knot in the middle of his forehead. He began to punch himself on the forehead. He didn't see Baccala walk away.

Down at the end of the armory floor, Mulqueen and Keefe stood and looked at the track.

"Eight hours," Keefe said. "Eight hours at least."

It was 8:17 p.m. now. Nearly 2500 people sat in the stands. In the age of numbers, 2500 at a sports event is painfully few on paper. But when you have 2500 people sitting and waiting for an event to start that you can't get started and you stand in the middle of the floor and look up at these 2500 people, they look like a million people.

A voice from an empty part of the balcony started it. *"Hey, what you do?"*

A growl ran through the rest of the people. A Polack jumped up in the end balcony. *"Come on."*

The Greeks in the seats behind their society banner began to clap their hands. The clapping spread and now the whole place was clapping, and then the people started stamping their feet and the noise sounded like a building coming down. Kid Sally Palumbo stood in the infield with his eyes shut. His cousin Albert Palumbo said he had an idea. Albert went downstairs to the locker room and called the riders, who were sitting on wooden benches between the green lockers and looking up at the ceiling. The stamping coming through the ceiling had them frightened. Albert led them up the stairs and onto the armory floor. The rhythmic clapping turned to cheers for the riders. Albert led them across the track and into the infield.

"All right, inside," Albert yelled. He began motioning to the riders. The riders looked at the cages and did not move. Big Jelly and Carmine and Albert had to come and start pushing them into their assigned cages. Grumbling in several languages began. The riders got into the cages, and the doors were slammed.

Bike-riders race in T-shirts and black knit swimming trunks. Because they sit on hard bike seats for hours at a time, they stuff things down the front of their trunks to cushion themselves against the steady chafing, biting motion of the bike seat. In a normal six-day bike race, the riders, by the last day, have so much stuffed down their fronts that they appear to have elephantiasis. Towels are used for stuffing. Many oldtime bike-riders used to stuff steaks into their trunks. They found the grease was very good for the insides of their thighs. Also the steaks could be eaten after the race was over.

The riders were in the cages and the crowd stirred and again began to clap. At 9:30 p.m., a Greek in a cage started it. Contestant Constantine Caras turned his back on the audience and stuffed three large bathtowels down the front of his trunks. Proudly, Caras turned and faced the crowd with this great bulge between his legs.

"Yip, yip," the Greek yelled. He gripped the bars and began jumping up and down in the cage. He stopped jumping and started scratching behind his neck. He scratched under his arms. He had his hands down and he was scratching his waist when the crowd saw what was coming. A roar went out when the Greek stuck his tongue out of one side of his mouth and his hands began tearing at the bulge between his legs.

Caras' Greek partner had been sitting on the edge of the cot. Now he came off the cot onto all fours. He padded up to the bars and began barking like a dog. He raised one leg into the air.

The crowd was in tears. People were standing, bent over, and slapping their thighs.

Mario Trantino and Carlo Rafetto, who were in the cage next to the Greeks, saw the crowd becoming helpless with laughter. Mario took the folding tray and began banging it against the bars, the way he had seen them do it in American prison movies. The sound of the tin tray carried. One of the Polacks on the other side of the circle of cages picked up his tray and began banging it. Soon the steady rhythm of trays banging against the bars sounded everywhere and the people in the seats clapped along with the banging trays. Up at the end of the armory Mulqueen was ripping out sections of track and scratching his ear while he tried to figure out what to do, and then the clapping from the crowd started to die down and the first people got up and began to file to the exits. More people started to file out. There was a tangle at the exits because people were turning back from the exits, growling, and trying to push their way back into the arena. Everybody was pushing and getting nowhere, and then one old Italian, face shaking with anger, threw his cigar into the air and held out his hands like the Pope and screamed in Italian that the ticket clerk wouldn't give him his money back.

An old woman in a black cloth coat was out of the grandstands first. She came with a stumpy walk. She came with a shopping bag filled with food for the entire night in her right hand. She came across the track with this stumpy walk and with the shopping bag full of food in her right hand and she saw Joseph DeLauria standing in his tuxedo and she went right for the tuxedo and swung the bag of food and the bag broke on Joseph DeLauria's head. Sausage sandwiches with rich red sauce flew all over the place.

A fat man in a truck-driver's cap came running across the track. He began skipping around with his right leg drawn back. He was trying to figure out who to go after when Albert Palumbo came around the side of the cage, and the guy looked at Albert and then let go and kicked Albert in the ankles. A fat, bald Greek came pounding over the track with a folding chair held over his head. He swung the chair at Big Jelly. The Greek missed, but he kept the chair in motion and the chair caught Tony the Indian on the head and he went down like an air-raid victim. Now people were coming from everywhere, throwing punches and chairs, and the bike-riders held their bulges and jumped up and down like monkeys.

An old man in a cap and overcoat grabbed a bike from the front of the Polish riders' cage. The old man walked the bike onto the track and got on it. He started pumping the bike up to the turn. He hit the saucer and pumped wildly around it and then shot down onto the straightaway and flew along it. There was a rumble from the far end of the armory. The big green corrugated door was coming down and the carpenters and workers ducked under it and into the safety of the motor pool. The door came all the way down the floor. The old man riding the bike was in ecstasy while he shot down the straight-away. Three-quarters of the way down he felt the handlebars for brakes. Then he pushed the pedal backward. This made only a zizzzziiiing sound. The bike did not slacken.

The old man got excited and his foot fumbled and pushed the pedal violently forward by mistake. When he and the bike hit the green door, he went halfway up the door like a human fly. He fell like a sack of cement.

The first call was made to the 91st Precinct by the man in the armory office. When the squad car responded, the patrol-man took a look at the crowd milling around the track and went back to the car and put in a Signal 16, which is the riot call.

The next morning, the court attendant looked up and saw the judge was ready. With an unhurried municipal walk, the attendant went over to open the door to the detention pens and bring the morning's defendants into the courtroom. A wave of snarling people slapped into the attendant. Kid Sally Palumbo was leading them. He was in his T-shirt. His suit jacket was folded over his arm. Both knees of his pants were ripped. Behind him came a crush of bandaged, splattered, ripped people from the bike-race riot.

"And what's this?" the judge said.

"A company returning," the docket clerk said.

When everybody was released on bail, Kid Sally began to whisper and glance around to let his people know they were to show up at the street later in the day.

They came through the double doors of the courtroom and out into a shabby high-ceilinged lobby. Cigarette butts and candy wrappers littered the floor. Revolving doors opened onto the cold street. Through the door, Kid Sally could see photographers jamming together to get pictures of him coming out of court. Pictures ordinarily were all right, in fact Kid Sally once tried to pay a *Daily News* cameraman $25 to take a color picture for the Sunday roto section. But Kid Sally didn't want New York to see a picture of him in a T-shirt and with ripped pants. He stopped and looked around. The two old men working the shoeshine stand looked at him.

"Shine?" one of them said.

"No," Kid Sally said. "No, not a shine." He came over to the stand and took a tin of black polish. Using a courtroom-door window as a mirror, Kid Sally put his fingers into the polish and printed FUCK YOU across his forehead. Kid Sally came through the revolving doors waving his arm at the pack of crouching, jostling, swearing cameramen, who laughed and then froze when they saw his forehead.

Chapter 11

Mario had gotten back to the hotel at three a.m. At nine a.m. the hotel cashier woke him up. The room bill had been paid, the cashier said, and Mario had until one p.m. to check out. After that, all bills run up by the bike-riders would be their own responsibility. If Mario intended to remain, the hotel suggested a deposit. Mario came down to the lobby, where the bike-riders were waving airline tickets and arguing over what had happened. The girl at the airlines counter in the lobby was busy booking the bike-riders on the afternoon and evening flights back to Europe. Mario handed the girl his ticket and said he wanted to cash it in. The girl gave him $311.35.

Mario took a cab down to 10th Street. He leaned forward on the seat and went through his inside pocket for the picture Father Marsalano had given him the morning he left for America. A small warmth ran through Mario when he felt the envelope. He looked at the words on the back of the picture: "Dear Friends Who Left Catanzia to Go to America and Become Rich . . ." Mario patted the picture. No matter how tough it could get in America, he always had the envelope from home.

When the cab stopped on 10th Street, Mario saw the meter

was $1.45. He became immobile. Slowly he handed the driver a dollar bill, two dimes, and a lire piece he hoped would pass for a quarter. The cabbie's hand felt $1.45. The cabbie's thumb ran over the palm trying to find a tip. The thumb found no tip. The cabbie wanted to shout, but his tongue already had gone into shock. Mario was halfway across the sidewalk when the cabbie finally broke the numbness.

"I could understand it if you was a Puerto Rican," he yelled at Mario.

The veins on the sides of the cabbie's head popped out in anger. Two blocks later, he was still muttering when he began to put the coins in his change-maker. When he saw the lire piece, he suffered a heart spasm.

Sidney had a more positive reaction when he opened the door and Mario pushed into the apartment.

"Kill yourself," Sidney said.

Sidney was edgy because he did not like Mario, and also because he had been living without whisky. After Mario had shown up at the Plaza Hotel, Grant Monroe, in a rage, had come down to the apartment and frisked the place for whisky. Now Mario, who had caused all the trouble for Sidney, was sitting across from him. And Mario, as payment for having discovered Grant Monroe's particular brand of larceny, was expecting help.

"Grant says we got no room for you," Sidney said. "We'll give you all the help we can, but we got no room."

"Just show me how you do this thing," Mario said. He thought that if he could just learn the game, the next step would take care of itself.

"Well, where are you staying?" Sidney said.

"The *chiti*," Mario said. Sometimes English words beginning with C came out "Ch."

"Cheatey is the right name," Sidney said. "I don't know what I can tell you. I think you're a natural thief myself."

He described his operation, which was very simple. Five years back, when Grant Monroe and Sidney met each other and started off, the usual route in art forging was to copy a Chagall or Modigliani. But apartments on Fifth and Park Avenues were becoming as crowded as subway trains with all the thieves selling phony Chagalls and Modiglianis to rich idiots. Grant came up with the idea of finding work done by artists who had lived in unrecognized ability and who died virtually unknown. Sidney would copy their works and sign Grant Monroe's name to them. Grant's great sales personality would carry it from there. He was great at selecting customers who lived far away from each other. They could be sold the same paintings. All Sidney had to do was sit in the apartment and work like a Xerox machine. It was a fine arrangement. Rather than pushing fake Chagalls for big, risky money, Grant Monroe sold phony Grant Monroes on a solid volume basis. The hundred-dollar bills added up. Of course, everything depended on Sidney's remaining hidden. This was all right with Sidney. He couldn't sell his own work. His personality was so bad the Chinese would not take free missiles from him. Besides, Sidney appreciated Grant. He felt Grant was removing the ultimate hazard of an art thief's life: a guard who won't allow you to mix paint in your cell.

"Just remember, only use dead artists," Sidney told Mario. "If they can breathe, they can sign warrants."

Sidney tugged open the doors of an old cabinet. Inside was a pile of reproductions and scarred originals of work done by people dead and unremembered. "Take your pick," he said to Mario. "Whichever you think is best for you. Don't worry what people like. They all got the taste of pigs. You can sell anything. The biggest art-collector in this city got a bum Picasso right in his living room."

Mario went through the pile. "Which one do you think I should use?" he asked.

Sidney said, "Hey, I don't even know if you can put a straight line on paper. Grant said help you out. That's what I'm doing. But you got to be able to do this yourself. If you're not a half an artist, then go find another way to steal."

Mario's chin came out in pride. "I can do it myself," he said. He pulled out an original of a nude girl in her apartment. There was a rip through the girl's face. The rest of her was intact. Sidney said the picture was particularly safe to use. The artist, Peppis, was caught by the Depression and he wound up painting station signs in the subway for the WPA. He became drunk and tumbled off the platform and was killed by the Broadway local. "Even the motorman who killed him is dead," Sidney said.

Mario nodded and stepped around Sidney and Sidney tried to roll the wheelchair after Mario, but Mario was already whisking sheets from a stack of art paper. "The hell you will, they cost a dollar-fifty apiece," Sidney said. Mario was grabbing at charcoal nubs, paint tubes, brushes, anything that could be picked up.

"Thief bastard!" Sidney yelled as Mario walked out the door.

When Mario got back to the hotel there was a message from Angela. She would be at the hotel at 12:30. Mario was in front of the hotel at 12:15. He had his suitcase between his feet and the art paper tucked under his arm. The winter wind swirled out of a lifeless gray sky. The wind lifted newspaper pages and carried them along the sidewalk. Angela came around the corner from the subway. She had her chin buried into the collar of a navy-blue coat. She did not smile when she saw him. Her eyes teared in the wind and her face seemed drained. People who have been up all night always show it in cold weather.

She looked at the suitcase. "You're going home?" she said. Her voice had a hopeful rise.

"No, I'm staying here."

"Oh," she said. "Then what's the suitcase for?"

"The hotel costs too much. I have to find another place."

"You have to move *already?*" she said to him.

"They want money in deposit if I stay."

Angela's eyes narrowed. "*Quecottsadiablo!*"

Mario thought he heard her say this, but he decided he had not. A woman hasn't talked like this since Mary Magdalene reformed.

"DeLauria," Angela said. "Chew!" She spat at the air.

The scowl on her face surprised Mario. He didn't think the girl was this tough. He immediately made his eyes wide and he let the rest of his face hang. He was pretty sure he looked like an orphan with sad eyes.

Angela looked at him and sighed. "Come on in and we'll have coffee and figure out something," she said.

She bought a copy of the *Village Voice* at the hotel newsstand, and they sat in the coffee shop while she read the ads. She went to the phone booth and made several calls. She came out smiling. "There's one down on Eleventh Street that's cheap."

The apartment was at 293 East 11th. The superintendent, a red-faced man in a dirty woolen shirt, led them up scarred staircases to the top floor. Pale afternoon light came through a skylight. The superintendent opened the door to number 20. It was three rooms in railroad-car alignment. There also was a small dusty kitchen and a crumbling bathroom. The wooden floor squeaked. White plaster showed through the dirt-streaked blue wall paint. The apartment was $36 a month. The superintendent wanted one month in advance and a month's security. Mario grimaced and took money out of his pocket.

"What can you do?" Angela said. "The least DeLauria could've done."

She spat at the air again. Mario paid the superintendent and was handed a key and a scrawled receipt. "It's yours as of now," the man said. "What do you want on the mailbox, Mr. and Mrs.?"

"What business is it of yours?" Angela said.

"I couldn't care less," the superintendent said.

"Well, then, don't ask," Angela said.

Downstairs, Angela looked at her watch. She had to get going.

"Good luck," she said. "I have a lot to do now."

She started down the stoop and turned to say good-by to Mario. He was standing on the top step with his face saying "War Orphan."

Angela stopped. "What are you going to sleep on?"

He shrugged and looked even sadder.

"Well, come on with me, you can't sleep on the floor," she said. He bounded down the steps. They walked up to First Avenue and went past coffee shops and bars filled with young boys and girls wearing bell-bottom pants and Saint-John-the-Baptist hair styles. Two blocks up there was a store called Cheap John's. Angela left Mario on the sidewalk. She went inside and came out with a pillow.

"At least for your head," she said, holding the pillow out to Mario.

Two boys stopped on the sidewalk and watched. "We hope you'll be very happy together," one of them said.

Angela buried her face in the pillow. She was flushed with embarrassment. Mario was surprised to see her react this way. But when her face came out of the pillow it was straight and cold again. She handed Mario the pillow.

"All right," she said, "take care of yourself."

"When do you come again?" he asked her.

"In a couple of days," she said.

She was frowning as she went down the subway steps.

"No miss!" Big Mama said to Tony the Indian. He nodded.

"No miss!" Big Mama said to Big Jelly.

"Nobody miss!" she hissed at everybody.

They were crowded into the kitchen and the living room, thirty of them, standing around with plates in their hands, and when they came up to the stove Big Mama would plunge a serving spoon into this big aluminum restaurant pot of lobster fra diavolo and heap it on the plates, all the time muttering, "No miss!"

They were going to shoot everything they could. The trouble had started predictably and easily. Kid Sally Palumbo, chewing a toothpick, leaned against the wall in Baccala's office. Kid Sally had been summoned because of the bike-race failure. The Water Buffalo and two black suits stood by the door. Baccala sat at his desk and looked at his hands in his lap.

"I like-a lunch," Baccala said.

Kid Sally said, "You wanna eat and talk? Good."

Baccala kept looking at his hands. "I said, *I* like-a lunch. I no say *you* like-a lunch. So *you* shut up-a you face!"

"Hey you!" Kid Sally said.

"Shut up-a you face," the Water Buffalo said. The two black suits stirred. Kid Sally bit his bottom lip.

Baccala looked up. His eyes were so narrow he could barely see through the slits. "What you do," he said to Kid Sally softly, "you drive-a me to lunch. You wait-a outside. When I finish-a lunch, I come out and you drive-a me back here." Baccala's voice rose. "Every day you come here and you drive-a Baccala."

Coldly, almost offhandedly, Baccala was perpetrating the

worst of all crimes against a gangster. He was trying to kill Kid Sally's ego. He was telling Kid Sally face to face—worse, in front of others—that from now on he was not the leader of a faction of a gang. He was to be a chauffeur for Baccala. Chauffeur, errand boy, footman, and lackey. And Kid Sally Palumbo, his face stinging, had to stand against the wall and take it without a sound. The Water Buffalo and the pair of black suits were only a few feet from him. The Water Buffalo had his eyes on the ceiling and he was praying to a saint whose name he knew, in hopes Kid Sally would say something fresh so Baccala would let the Water Buffalo kill Kid Sally right in the office.

The toothpick in Kid Sally Palumbo's mouth moved up and down. He said nothing. When he walked out of the place he took a deep breath because he was glad to be alive. Then he took a second deep breath. He would be back in that office someday with all of his people and they would make headlines because of the way they would kill Baccala and the Water Buffalo.

Kid Sally Palumbo stood alone, looking out the kitchen window. He trembled a little. Over the centuries, revolts in the Mafia have always been heavily sanctioned affairs. Just as no smart political legislator brings his bill to a vote unless he knows beforehand that he has the votes to win, so does an ambitious Mafioso operate. A revolt normally consists of the ambitious one becoming restless with an old boss, then subtly asking around the organization to determine if he has any support. If enough people in command tell him, "Old men, sometimes they better off they die," he knows he has assent. He then invites his boss out to dinner, and on the way home he drops the boss off in the nearest sewer.

But in this revolt Kid Sally Palumbo was starting, he had no official sanction at all. Instead, he was shaking the structure of the entire organization. This, he knew, normally was as sure a way to get killed as sky-diving from the Empire State Building. He had a group of, in all, 125 hoodlums from Marshall Street and the adjoining blocks. They were going against an organized Mafia family of perhaps 1000 members, full- and part-time. But Kid Sally Palumbo's group had youth and hunger for the money which Baccala had been denying them. And the Baccala Family, like any other institution in the country, was old and essentially sick with success. A small, determined group could topple it. The victory would require close teamwork and extensive brainwork. But the rewards could be incredible. If Kid Sally won control of the Baccala gang, all the other Mafia families in the country would automatically recognize him. He could get at millions. And there would be something so much more important than money. Revenge. As Kid Sally stared out the window, the wind gusted off the docks and the telephone lines began waving in the streetlights. Kid Sally could see Baccala hanging from the wires, his head flopping over on his broken neck, the wind blowing the body like wash.

"No miss!" Big Mama was saying. She was calling it out now.

Kid Sally knew she was right. It is not too good when you shoot at a guy and miss him. Sometimes the guy comes back and finds you asleep in your bed. Kid Sally also knew that it does not matter what you do in life, as long as you do it effectively. The people who shoot and miss are the ones who get in trouble. In a city like New York, failure is the real crime. But for those who shoot straight and get the job done, the rewards are immense. Society not only approves but gives adulation. They still write of Lucky Luciano as if he had been a fine Mayor of New York. Willie Moretti, who could have been as big as Luciano but happened to mess up a couple of key murders, was classified as a cheap hoodlum when he died.

"When you're broke, you're a joke," Kid Sally said. He took out a pack of cigarettes. He flicked the lighter deliberately. He took a drag on the cigarette. Everybody in the room watched him: young guys with dark hair and mean faces and cigarettes hanging from their lips. Kid Sally blew the smoke out in a stream. His lip curled. He began to giggle. Everybody in the room began to giggle with him.

"Old fuckin' greaseballs," Kid Sally said.

"I put out his mother's eyes," Big Jelly said.

"He don't give me nothin', I take it. I take it over his fuckin' dead body," another one of them called out.

Big Mama stood in the kitchen doorway, drying her hands on her apron. Angela leaned in the doorway with her. Big Mama put out a hand to push her away. "Shoo. Go to your room."

Angela pushed Big Mama's hand back. "I spit on their graves," Angela said.

Big Mama clasped her hands and looked up at the ceiling. *Madre di Cristo.*

"Nothin' means nothin' until we give them a present," Kid Sally said. "We give them a present of somebody's head in a box."

"Maybe they don't like it and they quit," Big Jelly said.

"We'll see what kind of chops they got," Kid Sally said.

Chapter 12

Joey Miranda, a good car thief, and his best friend, Julie DiBiasi, who does all sorts of evil things from his base as a gas-station attendant, were standing together and remembering certain things. This was a herculean thing for them to be doing. Joey Miranda had an IQ of 67 in grammar school and since has retrogressed to the point where he forgets his home phone number. And Julie DiBiasi always sneers at people and says, "At least I know I'm a dope."

With their heads together, the brain worms pulsed with great information. The much-hated Water Buffalo, Baccala's chief aide, always parks his car at night in the same spot on Bushwick Avenue. The spot is always open for Water Buffalo's car because there is a fire hydrant there. The cops put a $25 ticket on the car each night. The Water Buffalo uses the tickets to pick his teeth. When he parks the car at night, the Water Buffalo is well covered by another car, which pulls alongside him, the people in the back seat holding machine guns at the ready. The Water Buffalo lives in a two-family house around the corner from the fire hydrant. When he gets to his house, the cover car leaves him, and his wife, Mrs. Water Buffalo, takes up the coverage. She peers out the door with a shotgun.

In the morning the Water Buffalo has no coverage. However, he walks on the street very close to people. He usually picks out a lady wheeling a baby carriage and he walks alongside her. If he sees any suspicious car, he bends down and kisses the baby. "Who could shoot if they thought they might hit a baby?" the Water Buffalo says. "The only person I know of who would do a thing like that is me."

"What happens," Julie DiBiasi wondered, "if he starts driving away in his car some morning and then the car stops on him and he has to get out and see what's wrong?"

Joey Miranda thought about this. "So many things could happen to you when the car stops and you have to get out and look at what made the car stop," he said.

"He could get his throat strangled," Julie DiBiasi said.

"No strangle!" Big Mama said. "It takes too long. Everybody walks by and see what you do. Just shoot-a him."

"The Water Buffalo gets hit right in the head," Kid Sally Palumbo announced.

Early the next morning Julie DiBiasi, working very carefully with a knife, started a slow leak around the valve of the Water Buffalo's left rear tire. At 11:30 the Water Buffalo came out from behind a lady who had twins in a stroller and got into his car and drove it off and turned a corner and went down three blocks and turned another corner. He felt the car pulling on the turn and he slowed down and stopped at the curb of a street that had garages and a factory on it. The car following him was driven by the best driver on Marshall Street, Ezmo the Driver. He was terrific at trailing people and not being noticed. Julie DiBiasi and Joey Miranda were in the back seat. They got out and strolled up to strike a blow for freedom.

The Water Buffalo was crouched over and feeling the flat tire. Joey Miranda and Julie DiBiasi swaggered up to him. The Water Buffalo saw them and he dove under the car and came up on the other side like a guy coming out of the pool. Joey

Miranda and Julie DiBiasi bent over so they could shoot the Water Buffalo while he was under the car. But all they could see was the Water Buffalo's $110 Bostonians on the sidewalk on the other side of the car. They fired twice at the Bostonians, but the Bostonians were clomping up and down so fast that the bullets pinged off the cement sidewalk, and the Water Buffalo raced down an alley. Joey Miranda and Julie DiBiasi came rushing around the car and started into the alley. There was this big puddle in the way. The Water Buffalo, who had his adrenalin pumping because it was life and death, had taken the puddle in a big leap and hadn't gotten his $110 Bostonians wet. He was beating down the alleyway. But Joey Miranda pulled up short at the puddle in his $120 Footjoys, and Julie DiBiasi stopped dead in his $115 Johnson Murphys. They tiptoed around the puddle. Then they started down the alley in a fury. Running, running, running with guns in their hands and the fury of centuries racing through their blood. The alley was quite short, and the Water Buffalo had gone beating to the end of it. He skidded on his leather heels around the turn. Joey Miranda and Julie DiBiasi came around the turn flying, guns straight out. They ran into a ramshackle fence made of rotting wood. The fence closed off an area between two buildings. Joey bounced up and looked on the other side of the fence. Nobody was there.

"What do we do?" Julie said.

"We're in some trouble," Joey said.

"Yeah," Julie said.

"We could go back and say we got him and then we could go out tonight and get him for real," Joey said.

"What about Ezmo out in the car? He knows we didn't get him," Julie said.

"I know what to do," Joey said. He pointed his pistol at the fence and closed his eyes and pulled the trigger twice.

"Now run like we just done somethin'," Joey said.

The two of them came racing back out of the alley. Ezmo the Driver had the car rolling just slow enough for them to dive into the back seat. He hit the pedal, and the car was doing 60 by the time Julie pulled the door shut after him.

"Right in the head," Joey said loudly.

"Boy," Ezmo said.

"Right between the ears," Julie said.

"Boy," Ezmo said.

"What blood," Joey said.

"Boy," Ezmo said.

There was a large but quiet celebration at Big Mama's that night. There were fifteen guys sitting there like pirates but saying nothing about anything and Big Mama cooked zuppa di clams and spaghetti alla Carbonara and veal scaloppine alla Romana. There was Soave Bolla on the table, and after it was finished, everybody went to the Bardolino. They toasted Joey Miranda and Julie DiBiasi without saying what they were toasting them about because it was one of those things you don't talk about, and Joey and Julie looked at each other with nervous glances and then Julie decided the only way out was to go to the Bardolino heavy, and pretty soon his head was hanging in the spaghetti alla Carbonara and he was saying to himself, "I'm Al Capone."

The story of the Water Buffalo's murder was not in the *Daily News* when Beppo the Dwarf brought the early edition up at 9:30 p.m. And the story was not on the eleven-o'clock news on television. Big Mama stood in the doorway, drying a pot, and her eyes narrowed.

"Hey, Joey, what you do?"

Kid Sally Palumbo got up and walked over to Julie DiBiasi and slapped his face, and then he walked over to Joey Miranda and slapped his face.

"What is this?" he said.

"The body was in a alley, maybe nobody looked yet," Julie mumbled.

"Yeah," Joey said.

Kid Sally looked at them. "Maybe they're all keeping it quiet to see if we do anything stupid."

"That could-a be," Big Mama said. She glared at Joey and Julie. "It better."

"We seen the blood," Joey mumbled.

The party broke up and Joey Miranda was so drunk he got into the car and fell asleep at the wheel. Julie couldn't feel a thing and he stumbled along the street and tried to take in deep breaths to clear his head, but the wine was still coming up from his stomach and exploding in his head. He walked over to the gas station and passed out in a chair at the desk. You could have stuck pins in Julie, and he would not have felt anything. Which was a good thing because at 4:30 in the morning the Water Buffalo and three other guys walked into the gas station, and the Water Buffalo dragged Julie into the grease pit and it was a good thing Julie couldn't feel much of anything. The police-emergency-squad guy observed, "Dracula never did anything as bad as this."

At 9:30 p.m. the *Daily News* did carry news of the gang war. It read:

DI BIASI—Julie. Very suddenly. Beloved son of Carmela and Ralphie DiBiasi. Dear brother of Frankie, Anthony, and Salvatore DiBiasi. Dear brother of Mrs. Laura Ruocco. May he live forever in a thousand hearts. Reposing CAMPION'S Funeral Home, Inc., 56 Lockman Street, Brooklyn. Interment Thursday 9 a.m. private.

All over South Brooklyn, in every railroad flat, there could be heard the sound of hangers clicking while people took good black funeral clothes out of the closets. They began to get ready for as good a gangland funeral as Kid Sally Palumbo could put together under the circumstances of not having the big money to blow on the kind of funerals all gangsters dream of for themselves.

All major funerals in New York, including the funerals of some people who may have led legitimate lives, such as a Cardinal, basically are copies of Frankie Yale's funeral. Frankie Yale was a very good guy who lived in Brooklyn until 1932, and then he became a very bad guy and somebody put a bomb in his car motor. The bomb worked.

They ran a funeral for Frankie Yale that was bigger than the Democratic National Convention. The great moment in the wake came when Dominic Monzalulu, the man who had coupled the bomb to Frankie Yale's car, stood in front of the casket and began crying and held out his hands and wailed to the flowers over the casket, "You got no idea of the respect I had for this here man." On the day of the funeral there were 21 flower cars and 103 limousines and 225 private cars following Frankie Yale's body. It was terrific, and all good undertakers have a mimeographed copy of the order of Frankie Yale's funeral just in case they get lucky with a bombing victim who was rich.

The funeral of Julie DiBiasi was different. Usually a gangland murder occurs as part of a drive by the established organization. A man drifting away from the fold is the target. The action is both approved and carried out by organization members. All attend the funeral. But for Julie DiBiasi's funeral, there was no way for the Baccala people to attend. Nobody likes to kneel in front of a casket if he knows somebody from the bereaved family is likely to open fire from his folding chair.

Campion, the undertaker, had an easy time with the funeral. Usually he has to spend a lot of time making up the deceased's face so everybody can say how good he looks. But after what the Water Buffalo did to Julie DiBiasi, Campion needed Rembrandt to straighten it out. It would be a closed coffin. Campion also had no argument about the clothes. Usually Campion pushed for the family to buy a new suit for the body and then Campion would pull the suit off the body just before the burial and go out and sell the suit or wear it himself. But with the closed coffin, Julie DiBiasi could be buried in his underwear. The problem of flowers was easily solved too. At an event like this, the prospect of a bomb in the middle of a cluster of roses is disturbing. But Campion had not had the body for an hour when a florist's delivery truck pulled up across the street and a deliveryman came in with a twenty-dollar piece. Campion didn't have to look up from the desk to know that it was a rat cop delivering the flowers. Only the Irish would send such a cheap piece of flowers to a funeral. The deliveryman went back to the truck. The truck did not move. This meant there was a camera in the back of the truck, taking movies through a peephole. This also meant that many strangers, more cops, would be attending the wake. Everybody in the Kid Sally Palumbo gang could now come to the wake. The Baccala mob would know the cops were on the scene, and Baccala's people would not do anything that might get a cop hurt.

The wake for Julie DiBiasi started officially at four o'clock in the afternoon, when Ezmo the Driver picked up old man Toregressa's wife in front of her house on Marshall Street and took her to Campion's. Toregressa's wife is called Mrs. Toregressa. She is the finest mourner in all of South Brooklyn. People from all over get in fights over Mrs. Toregressa so they can have her at their wakes.

Now Mrs. Toregressa sat quietly in the car while Ezmo the Driver drove the car to the funeral home. Mrs. Toregressa had a black shawl over her head and rosary beads twisted in her wrinkled hands. She had stayed up all night so she could have some good coffee circles under her eyes. She started warming up.

"*Gesù*," she said softly.

"*Gesù.*"

"Gesù!" She was quite loud this time. Her hands shook. She was ready.

She came into Campion's walking just behind Julie DiBiasi's brother-in-law and two of his sisters-in-law. There were eleven of Julie's cousins in the place already. The mourners walked in the pale sunlight coming through the windows of Campion's lobby and then into the dim hallway choking-sweet with the smell of roses. When Toregressa's wife came into the chapel with the flickering candles showing on the wallpaper, Toregressa's wife let out a wail which started low in her throat and then came higher and louder. It became a wonderful pitched scream.

"GESÙ! GESÙ!"

"A BONOM' JULIE!"

Julie DiBiasi's sister slumped against her cousin. The sister's legs buckled. Both women fell on the casket in screams. Mrs. Toregressa was directly behind them, screaming.

The immediate family, which includes to the fifth cousins, sat on the right-hand side of the front of the room. The father and mother sat on cushioned chairs facing the doorway so they could wail at each person coming in. The rest of the family sat on wooden folding funeral-parlor chairs with the stenciled CAMPION FUNERAL HOME on the backs. Toregressa's wife sat on the left side of the casket, in the third row, so she could generate mourning that would run through the entire room. All people came in black. The only person who would wear a gray suit to a wake would be a rat cop. The conversation in the funeral chapel was standard. Between the wailing, a mourner observes that God took the deceased. He has six machine-gun bullets in him, or, in this case, was strangled by the Water Buffalo, but God took him. The only alluding to the manner of death is done with a gentle, "At least he didn't suffer." And in recounting the life he led, one sentence suffices: "He had a good life." Nothing else is said. If you begin to search for nice things to say about Julie DiBiasi you stumble onto the ten guys he helped to kill.

The big moment in the wake at Campion's came when Kid Sally Palumbo arrived. Entrances signify rank at gang funerals. A big shot does not walk in from the hallway and stand in front of the casket like any other mourner. A big shot forms up in the hallway with his bodyguards and he waits until the front of the room is clear and the seats are filled. Then he sweeps in. The level of murmur in the room attests to his rank. A buttonman gets a little gasp. A lieutenant gets a louder gasp. A captain gets tears. A *don beppe* or generalissimo creates screams. If you come in front of a casket and create only silence, it usually means that you too could be on the road to the cemetery.

Kid Sally Palumbo came into the lobby of Campion's at 9:15 p.m. to make his entrance. In the absence of the Baccala organization, Kid Sally Palumbo now was the highest-ranking person at the funeral. When Kid Sally came through the door, he was with Big Jelly. He waited in the lobby while Big Jelly ambled down the hall to check the room. Campion asked Kid Sally if he wanted to sit down. Kid Sally shook his head no. He didn't want to crease the thighs of his black Italian-silk suit. Big Jelly stuck out his head and waved. Kid Sally came down the hallway, brushing against floral pieces. Big Jelly held him up for a moment in the hallway. Kid Sally stood clenching and unclenching his hands, waiting to go onstage. Big Jelly tapped him on the shoulder. Kid Sally Palumbo walked into the room like Maurice Evans.

His head was high and his chin was out and his shoulders

weaved as he walked. He stood in front of the casket with his hands clasped in front of him. His feet were apart. He kept shifting from one foot to the other.

"*Che peccat'*," Toregressa's wife screamed.

"*O Dio.*"

Kid Sally Palumbo looked down fondly at the body.

"*È con Dio!*"

A woman in the back of the room picked it up. "*Gesù!*"

An old man in the center mumbled, "*A bonom' Julie.*"

"*Gesù!*" Toregressa's wife screamed.

The father and mother came up and threw themselves, wailing, onto the casket, and Kid Sally Palumbo put his arms around them and rosaries were twisting in almost every hand and crying men kissed each other on the cheeks and bit their knuckles and women flung up their arms in despair. The wake of the beloved Julie DiBiasi, New York City Police Department identification number B-765379, FBI file number 129368742, United States Immigration and Naturalization Case 112-20-7143, was a great success.

Chapter **13**

After the funeral mass, Angela did not go to the cemetery. She took the subway to school. She came up the subway stairs reluctantly and dawdled over a cup of coffee in a place on the corner. She started toward the school building and stopped. She felt like walking instead of sitting in a classroom. There was no use in going to school. Her nerves wouldn't let her concentrate. Nor was there much sense in going on any other day, as long as this business was going on. She began walking down truck-clogged streets toward the East Side. She knew vaguely where she was going, but she didn't think about it until she was on 11th Street and walking toward Mario's. It was all right to look in on him, she told herself. She didn't know anybody else she could stop to see at this time of day.

She was almost to Mario's building when he came out the door and stood on the top of the stoop. Mario had been up since seven o'clock, working on his painting. Since he had no easel or table in his apartment, he worked on his hands and knees, the art paper spread on the floor under him. Mario worked with his head hanging down like a collie's. After many hours of doing this, he became accustomed to having the inside of his head filled to the brim with downrushing blood.

When Mario couldn't work any more, he stood up straight and the blood went rushing down from the inside of his head so quickly that his eyes rolled and he had to put his hands against the wall to keep from falling down. Now, outside on the stoop, he was still swaying. He held out his arms to make airplane wings for balance.

"What are you doing, exercising?" Angela called to him.

Mario felt himself falling. He rotated his arms violently to stay up.

"My knees hurt," he said.

"Oh," Angela said.

He came down the steps, keeping his legs stiff. He resembled Frankenstein.

They went up to a place on the corner and talked, over coffee. Mario was vague about the type of work he was doing, and Angela listened vacantly. She was still unnerved from Julie DiBiasi's funeral. He mentioned that he wanted to see some of the museums in New York. "Modern Art is only a few minutes from here," she said. "You ought to learn the way. Why don't we ride up there and I'll show it to you."

Mario pushed out of the booth and walked eagerly out of the coffee shop. Angela had to stop at the counter and pay the check. When they came out of the subway onto 53rd Street, Mario stooped down and pulled his shoelaces apart. He took his uncle's eyeglasses out of his jacket pocket. He immediately plowed into a woman. Angela had to take his arm and guide him across the street.

The museum had a weekday afternoon crowd of women in their sixties, their sagging chalk necks spilling onto the soft bristles of mink coat collars. There were a few college students, and also many men in the uniform of Wall Street retirement: black Chesterfield coat, rimless glasses, and the *Times* folded to the obituary page.

Two women were standing in front of a work by Andrew Wyeth. Angela and Mario stood alongside them.

"Simply fascinating," one of them said.

"God, such talent," the other said.

Sidney's voice was in Mario's ears. *Pigs.*

Mario stepped up and put his face inches away from the painting. He stared intently at it. *"Fromage,"* he said.

"Fromage," he said again.

The women stopped talking.

Mario stepped back. His arm waved. *"Fromage!"* he shouted.

The women looked at the eyeglasses sitting on his nose, and his open shoelaces.

"Maybe this really isn't one of his best works," one of the women whispered.

"Well, to tell you the truth, I really don't see much in it myself," the other one said.

Mario took Angela's arm and they walked away. Sidney was right; they all knew nothing. Now Mario was sure he would be able to sell somebody some of his work. He stuck his chin out like he was Mussolini. *"Fromage!"* he shouted at a group watching a Picasso.

In one hallway there was a spot from which a painting had been recently removed. Plain wooden brackets for holding the picture frame remained. The painting which had been removed had obviously been there for some time. The wall plaster inside the brackets was covered with a thick layer of dust. Mario stopped. He poked Angela.

A man in a Chesterfield coat and his mink-coated wife were walking along slowly.

Mario stared at the rectangle of dust. "Magnificent," he said.

The man and woman stopped and began inspecting the dust.

"Magnificent!" Mario roared.

The woman sighed. "I wish the frame were nicer," she said.

"The frame doesn't bother me," the man said.

"There's just something," the woman said.

"Could it be hanging upside down?" the man said.

Angela was still laughing when the subway came into the Second Avenue stop, where Mario was to get off. She pointed to the door. He got up. He looked at her sadly. She started to get up with him. Then she sank back in her seat.

"G'by, I'll see you again," she said.

He went out the doors and the train started up again, and when it left the station the day's fun went out of Angela and Brooklyn came on her. She pulled the coat around her.

Between visits from Angela, Mario put together a narrow standard of living. It was unsatisfying, but he felt every day brought him closer to the afternoon when he could sell his first work to one of those ignorant women at the Plaza. He worked in three-hour shifts, resting for two hours, through an entire day, and brought the results to Sidney for help. Most evenings he sat in the coffee shop on the corner and went to the cheapest price on the sign, a 40-cent egg-salad sandwich. The place was frequented by wanderers who lived in the East Village. Mario got to know Simon Krass, a writer who specialized in articles on eroticism. Simon Krass usually came into the coffee shop carrying his cat, High Yellow, under his arm. He sat and commented on the world's latest sex habits. "Airedales are just magnificent," Simon Krass said. He thought Mario, with his eyeglasses and untied shoelaces, would be interested.

One morning the superintendent put Mario into shock by announcing the $36 rent was due. All day Mario was edgy. He kept walking downstairs to stand on the stoop and look for Angela. She did not come. He went to bed heartsick over being stuck with the rent. In the morning he paid the superintendent the $36, went up to the coffee shop, and sat in the telephone booth. He looked at the names he had gotten from Father Marsalano. The third man on the list, Dominic Laviano, had two big checks after his name. The address was the Andrea Doria Club, 724 Knickerbocker Avenue, Brooklyn. Mario looked up the number and called the place. The old man who answered said Dominic Laviano was always there at seven p.m. Mario went through the classified directory and looked for religious listings. Nearly all the Catholic stores were on Barclay Street. He asked the waitress for directions.

After a month in the apartment, Mario had $159 left, and a little fear went through him when he began ordering things in McGowan's Religious Outfitters, 78 Barclay Street. Mario paid $85 for a priest's black suit. He told the salesman the suit was for his twin brother, who was a priest in Italy. The tailor at home would fix the cuffs, Mario said. He also bought a Roman collar and a black shirtfront to wear with it. The salesman wanted to mail the things to Italy. "We just don't like to give our clothes to anyone but a priest," the salesman said. "All these impostors." Mario sent the man to the back of the store for a cape and then ducked out of the door with the box. At 6:30 p.m., dressed as a priest, the pants cuffs dragging, Mario arrived on Knickerbocker Avenue.

The Andrea Doria Club was next to Dominic's Fruit and Vegetables, D. Laviano, prop. The store had crates of greens around the entrance. The greens had been washed and the outer leaves were glazed with ice. The club next door was an old storefront. The bottom halves of the windows were painted over with green and trimmed with red and black. The place had been an ice-cream parlor when Germans lived in the neighborhood. The Italians, who followed the Germans, sought out ice-cream parlors. They made fine social clubs, which are as important to an Italian neighborhood as dairy restaurants are to a Jewish neighborhood. The old marble fountain counter is perfect for holding a $1500 espresso machine imported from Milano. The wire-backed chairs and round tables are fine for card games. Even the big Coca-Cola syrup jugs have a purpose. They get filled with homemade wine.

There were a dozen old men playing cards at the tables when Mario walked in. Dominic Laviano sat at the counter by the wine jugs. He was a bald man with heavy-lidded eyes. Mario handed him the picture. Dominic Laviano's eyes glistened. Mario showed him the message on the back. Dominic Laviano's eyes narrowed. He had a basic conflict about matters religious.

Some years ago the pastor at his church in Brooklyn, Our Lady of Mount Carmel Church, had begun pointing out that the statue of the patron saint had no crown. The old women donated their rings to be melted down for a crown. Their diamonds studded the crown. It was worth $250,000 when finished. The crown was put on display in a glass case set in front of the church. Only the pastor and the sexton had keys. An electric eye would set off a burglar alarm louder than an air-raid siren if anybody tried breaking into the case. One night, with no breaking glass or siren, the crown disappeared. The pastor knelt in church and conducted a prayer vigil for its return. The old women knelt and prayed with him. The men of the church, led by Dominic Laviano, took the matter to another authority. They went to Baccala's office. That night Baccala appeared at the church. He walked up the center aisle and looked at the priest praying. He looked at the sexton, who was trying to hide behind a bank of candles.

Hey!" Baccala called out. The sexton came out from behind the candles. Baccala whispered something in the sexton's ear. The sexton wet his pants. When the women came to the church to start praying the next morning, the crown was back in the case. It had slipped in and out without the alarm's sounding. The women began to thump their breasts. *Mirac'*.

Dominic knew otherwise. But there was a time when Dominic Laviano's sister from Poughkeepsie, Mrs. Regina Barbella, went home to Catanzia, and it still made Dominic wonder. During his sister's visit, Father Marsalano showed her the church doors, which were rotted. She said she would pay for new doors. The doors took so long to arrive and be hung that she missed her return trip on the *Andrea Doria* from Genoa to New York. The *Andrea Doria* sank off Nantucket. Mrs. Regina Barbella still thumps her breast and tells everybody, *"Mirac'."*

Dominic Laviano was not too sure it wasn't a miracle. He named his club after the ship. As he looked at the picture and the note on the back from Father Marsalano, Dominic was holding a little argument with himself. He really didn't trust priests. But he had also had a few whips of pain across the left side of his chest in recent months. Who knows?

"I had my own horse when I was a boy in Catanzia," Dominic Laviano said finally.

Mario could feel the money now. "The church doors of your sister are very beautiful," he said.

"They saved her life," Dominic said.

The two sat at the counter and talked about home for an hour. Across the street, Big Jelly twisted uncomfortably in the cold in his parked car. He and Tony the Indian had been there for two hours on the odd chance that Baccala might drop in to the club and see his friend Dominic. Every ten days or so, Baccala showed up at the Andrea Doria Club for coffee and messages.

"What's the priest doin' in there for so long?" Tony the Indian said.

"He's robbing that old man Dominic, what do you think he's doin'?" Big Jelly said. "Look at him. You could see he got more con in him than a legitimate thief."

At nine o'clock the fencing ended. Dominic took one more look at the picture of the ragamuffin in the lot. Eyes misting,

Dominic told Don Mario, as he called him now, that he would have a contribution for him at four o'clock the next afternoon. Mario blessed him and left.

He walked across the street and he was almost up to the car when he remembered the subway was the other way and he turned around.

Big Jelly looked at Mario closely. "Young priest. I didn't think they hung out with old greaseballs like Dominic," he said.

"He could have them," Tony the Indian said.

"Let's go home," Big Jelly said.

Mario barely slept. He was back at 3:30 the next afternoon. Dominic came into the club with a stack of envelopes that were stamped and addressed to Father Marsalano. He showed the insides of the envelopes to Mario. In each, wrapped in paper, was a ten-dollar bill. "I mail them all," Dominic said. "If a letter gets lost, then we don't lose all the moneys." He asked Mario for the picture. During the night Dominic had woken up with a sharp chest pain. He was afraid it was the Lord, not marinara sauce. On the back of the picture Dominic wrote Baccala's name and the address of the trucking company. "I tell him you come to see him," Dominic said. Dominic felt better about the chest pain now. He was sure he had just saved his soul.

"Grazie," Mario said. He held out his hand. Dominic handed him the picture. Mario held out his hand for the envelopes. Dominic sniffed. He led Mario out of the club and up to a mailbox on the next corner. "You watch, I mail," Dominic said. He stuffed the envelopes into the box. Mario smiled and shook hands good-by. Dominic went back to the fruit-and-vegetable store. Mario pretended to head for the subway. Dominic went into the store. Mario ducked into a doorway.

An hour and a half later the mail truck pulled up, and the driver was starting to shovel the letters into his bag when a hand came past his nose and started digging into the box.

"Scoose, please."

"Hey!" the mailman said. He grabbed the hand. He let go when he saw it was a priest. "Oh, I'm sorry, Father. Can I help you?"

"I mail all the letters and I forget to put something in them," Mario said. "I need back."

"Father, I'm not supposed to . . ."

Mario's hand kept digging. "Ah, here they are," he said. He grabbed a stack of Dominic Laviano's envelopes. "See, they addressed to my pastor, Don Giuseppe Marsalano," Mario said. "I send, but I forget to put inside."

"All right, Father," the mailman said. "Just don't say I let you do this. It's a big violation."

Mario counted the envelopes on the way home in the subway. There were fifty envelopes. He took forty of them, pulled out the ten-dollar bills, and ripped up the envelopes. At the Second Avenue stop he dropped the remaining ten into the mailbox. He walked with his hand over the $400 in his pocket. In the coffee shop he looked over Father Marsalano's list. There were a number of women on it. Women are less suspicious than men, he knew. He wouldn't even need his priest's suit with the women. They would trust him to mail the envelopes himself. He ordered a meat-loaf dinner. The sign said it was $1.65, the most money Mario had spent for food. Soon he would spend much more, he told himself.

Kid Sally Palumbo was in the office. A cigarette was hanging from his mouth. The smoke ran up in front of his eyes.

Angela opened the door. "Well?" she said.

"Getoutahere, I thinkin'," Kid Sally said.

"Just think of one person," she said. She held up a finger. "One is all that it takes. Get Baccala, and the rest will fall in line." She shut the door.

"She's right," Kid Sally said. "This is one-hit proposition. We can't go after everybody. We just concentrate on the boss."

"Whatever you say," Big Jelly said. He picked up a paper bag of chopped meat from the butcher's. He opened the door to the cellar. There was a low roar from the lion, which was at the foot of the stairs. Big Jelly threw the bag of chopped meat. At the bottom of the stairs two lion paws snatched it. Big Jelly started to close the door. The lion's smell rolled up the stairs and hit him in the face. Big Jelly turned blue. Everybody in the office put a hand to his mouth and started to choke. Big Jelly just did get the door closed before the odor smothered them.

"Somebody got to train the lion," Big Jelly said.

"I never dreamt of the lion goin' to the bat'room," Kid Sally said.

"He could kill you quicker than anything they got in the drugstore," Big Jelly said.

"Look," Kid Sally said, "somebody figure out about the bat'-room. I got to try and think like Baccala." He began hitting himself on the forehead to make his head think.

On the other side of Brooklyn, Baccala's manicured fingernails tapped his desk. He looked down at the desk as if it were a sand table. He saw all the great maneuvers of war spread in front of him.

"We just go slow," he said. "So far, it's nice. The other punks, they run around. They think they cowboys. We just go slow and we get every one of them." He leaned forward. "And I strangle Kid Sally personal!"

He got up to leave. Then he looked at the group of black suits standing around the office. "Somebody take a ride down-a their street. Be careful. Just look. You never know. They all craz'. Maybe one of them be standin' right there for you. Go see."

On Marshall Street the next afternoon, nobody was around. Who could get shot if he's not around to get shot at? Kid Sally's cousin Carmine Palumbo and Beppo the Dwarf were on guard in the office. Beppo had performed his duty. He had stolen two license plates in Staten Island. Carmine Palumbo was waiting around to kill somebody. They sat for an hour. Then Beppo the Dwarf's nose crinkled like a rabbit's. Carmine Palumbo's nose looked like a saxophone. He took a deep breath. When the air finally got up to the top of Carmine's nose, his eyes watered. The lion's smell had come all the way up the cellar stairs and was all over the office now. Five hundred cats on a rainy day could not match the lion in Kid Sally Palumbo's cellar.

"I can't take this," Carmine Palumbo said. He took a beach chair and set it up on the sidewalk in front of the office. Beppo the Dwarf came out and sat on the stoop.

"We better keep a eye open," Beppo the Dwarf said. "Who could tell?"

"I keep a eye open," Carmine Palumbo said. "I also want to keep my nose open. Jeez, that lion could put you on the critical list. Maybe the son-of-a-bitch don't bite good, but he sure as hell knows how to go to the bat'room."

Carmine Palumbo sat there with his eyes open, watching everything on the block, for about fifteen minutes. Because he could not concentrate on anything, even nothing, for any longer than this, Carmine Palumbo leaned back in the chair and closed his eyes.

Beppo the Dwarf was sitting on the stoop, looking at his fingernails, he was just looking at his fingernails, when the corner of his eye saw these two cars rushing down the street,

☞ 149

rushing along close to the curb. The windshields showed both cars were filled with heads. Beppo let out a yell and threw himself back over a railing. Carmine Palumbo opened his eyes and he was pulling himself upright in the beach chair when the cars slowed and the lead car came up even with Carmine Palumbo in the beach chair. Carmine Palumbo saw machine guns coming out the front and back windows. The scene was just about to register in his mind when the machine guns blew Carmine through the back of the beach chair.

> PALUMBO—Carmine. Unexpectedly. Greatly loved son of the late Joseph Palumbo and Teresa Palumbo. Dearly beloved brother of Alphonse, Anthony, Nicholas, Michael, and Pasquale Palumbo and Mrs. Loretta DeSalvio. Mourned uncle of Danny DeSalvio. May St. Michael the Archangel recognize his great strength. Reposing CAMPION'S Funeral Home, Inc., 56 Lockman Street, Brooklyn. Interment Tuesday 10 a.m. Private.

On the second night of the wake, late in the going, when Toregressa's wife had shrieked herself into laryngitis, Beppo the Dwarf stood in front of Carmine Palumbo in the casket.

"It's all on account of the rat bastard lion," Beppo the Dwarf wailed.

In the afternoon, after Carmine Palumbo's funeral, Joe Mangoni was driving along Flatbush Avenue, humming and slapping his right hand against the steering wheel in time to the music on the car radio. Joe felt very bad about losing his good friend Carmine, but the music coming into the car was making him feel better. A great scream came out of the radio: James Brown singing. Joe Mangoni began slamming his hand hard against the steering wheel. He glanced at the clock. He was right on time. At four o'clock every day Joe Mangoni came into the College Diner, right down the block from Saint

Joseph's College, and he had coffee and a Danish and he collected money. Customers who owed shylock payments shuffled in, handed him the money, and walked out. Joe Mangoni always liked to collect money, even though it was just money he turned over to somebody else. But today Joe Mangoni had come up with a very terrific idea. Normally he collected the money and gave it to one of Baccala's messengers. But now, being that he was with Kid Sally Palumbo and being that there was all this trouble, Joe Mangoni would not see any of Baccala's messengers. This means, Joe Mangoni reasoned, that if there is no messenger to give the money to, and if you still collect the money, then the money is yours.

"Smart guys do good when there's trouble," Joe Mangoni said out loud in the car. He looked at himself in the mirror. "You look real smart, baby," he said.

Joe parked his car on a side street and walked around to the diner, which was on the avenue. Only a couple of people were in the diner. "Hi, guys," Joe said to the countermen when he walked in. The countermen stared at him. When Joe ordered coffee, the counterman was so nervous he nearly scalded himself.

"What's the matter, you get nervous in the service?" Joe said. He laughed. This was one of Joe's best jokes.

Two priests came walking across the avenue from the block the college was on. The priests wore black fedoras and sunglasses and carried prayer books. The priests came into the diner and came up to take seats at the counter next to Joe Mangoni. Then the priests both stopped and came out from under the coats with guns. Each held the prayer book in one hand and the gun in the other. It was blasphemous, but highly effective.

MANGONI—Joseph. Very suddenly. Beloved, dear son of the late, beloved Luigi and Rose Mangoni. Mourned

☞ 151

brother of Dominic Mangoni. "An eye for an eye. A tooth for a tooth." Reposing CAMPION'S Funeral Home, 56 Lockman Street, Brooklyn. Interment Saturday 11 a.m., private.

"We gotta do somethin'," Kid Sally said when he got back from the funeral. "We got to get one back."

"I said just get Baccala," Angela said.

"We got no time for that today, we got to get one right away," Kid Sally said.

"She's-a right, just think of Baccala," Big Mama said.

"No, somebody right now. Today. They got three of our guys and we got nothin'." Trailing 3-0, Kid Sally was ready to bunt in order to get onto the scoreboard.

"You know who's a good friend of mine?" Big Jelly said.

"Who?" Kid Sally said.

"Albie."

"How good a friend?" Kid Sally said.

"He'd come and meet me," Big Jelly said.

The two of them got in a car with Tony the Indian and Ezmo the Driver and went to Patrissy's Lounge. The place was empty except for the porter. It was two in the afternoon, and Patrissy's doesn't open until nine p.m. The porter was told to get lost. The moment the porter left, Big Jelly reached inside his shirt and pulled out a coil of nylon rope. Sally began snapping the rope between his hands to make sure it wouldn't split while they were garroting Albie.

Albie was home. He never gets out of bed before the six-o'clock news at night. Albie is an air inspector. He stands all night on a streetcorner next to the newsstand on Coney Island Avenue and he breathes the air in and out. Once in a while Baccala sends somebody around to get Albie for something at which Albie is good. What Albie does best is to swing a baseball bat in a crowded bar. Albie has one personal weakness, which accounts for his friendship with Big Jelly. Albie is helpless in the matter of girls. "I like you," he told Big Jelly one night. "You are a real degenerate. Just like me."

All night while he stands on the streetcorner and breathes the air in and out, Albie reads the magazines from the newsstand. Albie reads *Sexology* and *Pervert* and *The American Orgasm*. His favorite is *Orgy Manual,* but this publication appears only when its publisher is between Supreme Court appearances.

So Big Jelly knew exactly how to activate Albie when he called Albie up at his house on the telephone.

"I'm at Patrissy's, where are you?" Big Jelly said.

"I'm home," Albie said.

"Oh, you're home," Big Jelly said.

"You're in some trouble," Albie said.

"What of?" Big Jelly said.

"You know," Albie said.

While Big Jelly talked, Kid Sally stood in front of the phone booth, pretending he was hanging himself with the rope. Big Jelly giggled while he talked.

"What's goin' on?" Albie said.

"I got a girl in the phone booth with me and she is doing all these things to me," Big Jelly said. He giggled at the rope some more.

"She in the phone booth with you?" Albie said.

"Sure, the joint's closed and I'm in here with her. What do I care about what's goin' on? That's Sally's business. My business is bein' a degenerate with broads. You know that. Here, honey, stop it. You're drivin' me crazy here." Big Jelly giggled.

"Stay there," Albie said. "I'll be right down."

While they waited, Ezmo the Driver plugged in the jukebox and put the sound up very high so when it played it would drown out the noise of what they were going to do to Albie. Ezmo was proud of this move. "Sometimes I'm very shrewd," he said.

Albie came a half-hour later. He came into the place with a sex sweat on his forehead. He was so busy looking for a girl in the bar that he never knew what hit him. Kid Sally Palumbo jumped on his head and Tony the Indian got a thumb in Albie's eyes and Ezmo and Big Jelly fell on him and out came the rope and they looped it around Albie. They were going to garrote him, which is the best way in the world to murder somebody, particularly if the perpetrators are demented. Ezmo the Driver ran over to the jukebox with two quarters to play some loud music to drown out Albie's screams. Ezmo's eyes ran down the selections and he saw the Beatles. *Rock-'n'-roll. The Beatles. Good and loud kid stuff.* Ezmo dropped in the money and punched the Beatles' record, number B-6. He punched it for six plays. He ran back to help them garrote Albie.

Albie was in the middle of the floor and the rope was all around his throat and body and he opened his mouth for his first scream when the record on the jukebox came on. The record was "Penny Lane" by the Beatles. It is a soft, lovely tune, the new kind of thing the Beatles do, and even with the jukebox turned up full force, you have to cup your ear to hear the words. Albie's first scream drowned out the soft music.

"Change the music," Kid Sally Palumbo yelled.

Albie let out another shriek.

Here was Ezmo the Driver at the jukebox, kicking it with his foot to try and make the record reject so he could play something loud, and the Beatles kept singing "Penny Lane," and here was Albie on the floor, yelping with the rope around him, yelping way louder than the music, and old ladies began looking out the window across the street.

Kid Sally Palumbo, thinking under intense pressure, thought of an idea so terrific he didn't know why everybody hadn't tried it before. He had Big Jelly take one end of the rope in his hands and face the rear door of the saloon. He and Tony the Indian took the other end and faced the front door. This left Albie in the middle with the rope looped around his neck.

"When I say go, run as fast as you can to the door with the rope," Kid Sally said.

"Go!"

Big Jelly gripped the rope and started. Kid Sally Palumbo and Tony the Indian headed in the opposite direction. Each side in the tug of war had its back to the other. They did not see what was happening in the middle, where Albie, almost out of it, wobbled to his feet and hooked one leg over the rope, the end running to Kid Sally and Tony the Indian. Big Jelly barged ahead to the back door. Kid Sally and Tony started running to the front door. Albie's leg hooked down on the rope, and the rope snapped out of Kid Sally and Tony's hands. When the line slackened suddenly on Big Jelly's end, the fat man went into the door head first. Albie fell to the floor like a sack. Big Jelly stumbled out to the street knocked half dizzy. Kid Sally and Tony kept flying and they hit the car while Ezmo the Driver had it in motion. Big Jelly dove at the moving car, and they barely hauled him in.

"Boy, that was terrific," Big Jelly said to Kid Sally in the car. "His whole head must of come off."

"Wow! We got to do that again," Tony the Indian said.

Kid Sally Palumbo had his eyes half closed while he blew out smoke. "I know what I'm doin'," he said.

When the police arrived at Patrissy's and took Albie to the hospital, there was no way of telling what had happened. Certainly Albie couldn't tell them. The rope had done so much damage to his neck that when the people in the hospital finally revived him with ammonia capsules he couldn't talk. His throat was closed. It would be days before he would be able to make a sound. When a detective gave him a pad and pen, Albie wrote down: "I got a bad stiff neck."

Chapter **14**

After a week of working on copying the painting of the naked girl, Mario got off his knees and carried it over to Sidney's apartment. Right away, it was obvious to Sidney that the ripped face on the picture Mario was copying had caused him to shy away from that part of the body and invest great time and energy on other parts.

"Here and there it looks like a caveman worked on this thing," Sidney said. "But over-all, I want to tell you something, you got a lot of long, hard work ahead of you, but you know how to express yourself all right. Oh, I don't think you can try with this thing yet. You still got a long way to go. For one thing, you're concentrating on this too much."

"What?" Mario said.

"The top of the thing."

"Top?" Mario said.

Sidney shouted. "The top of the tit!"

"Oh," Mario said.

"It gives you away that you're just beginning. Too much detail, it's no good. It's what you suggest and leave out that gives a thing its strength. You paint every eyelash on somebody's eye? So why do you put down every bump on the top of her thing?"

When he got back, Angela was standing in front of the house. He started upstairs to put his work away. When she asked to see it, he covered it and ran. Then they walked up to the corner. In the early darkness the brightly lit coffee shop on the corner looked inviting to Mario. He hadn't eaten since morning.

"Let's go some place nicer," Angela said. "Have you ever had Chinese food?"

He shook his head no.

"There's a place right up there," she said, pointing up First Avenue.

They sat in a booth and she ordered. Mario did not inquire what he was eating. He put his head down and swallowed egg rolls, shrimp and lobster sauce, and sweet-and-sour pork without noticing what it was. Angela was comfortable in the place. It was empty and warm and dim and the booths and the white tablecloths and the curtained door closed around her and kept the cold wind of Brooklyn out of her mind. She held a cup of tea up and looked at Mario. She liked his thick hair. She liked his eyes too. He always looked directly at her, as if she were important. When she went to the ladies' room, she combed her hair carefully. She wondered what it would be like if Mario ever became even a slight success as an artist. She looked at herself in the mirror and shrugged. When she came back to the table, she was eager to take the check from the waiter. After all, Mario had nothing.

Outside the restaurant, Mario half waited for her to go to the subway, but instead she started walking with him. *Well,* she said to herself. *Well, who knows?*

The flights of stairs to Mario's apartment left the two of them panting when they reached his door. He opened it and stepped into the darkness with her. Mario shut the door with one hand and pulled her to him with the other. He kissed her with all the great romance of the Italian mountain country. She twisted her head. She couldn't breathe from the stairs, and now, with his pressing on her, she thought she'd faint.

Angela pushed him back. "Stop for a minute," she said. "Give me a second." She took a deep breath. "Where's the light?"

He flicked the switch. One bare bulb in the ceiling came on. Angela's mouth fell open. On the floor in the center of the room was the pillow. It was covered with a towel Mario had taken from the hotel. Over by the windows were the art supplies and a few smears of paint on the floor. Otherwise, there was nothing in the room.

"You didn't even buy a bed?" she said.

Mario, his eyes glistening, tugged on her arm. Angela went one step toward the pillow and then pulled back. Mario put both hands on her and tried to drag her as if she were a donkey.

"Are you crazy?" she said.

He tried to tug her again, but she wouldn't move. She kept looking at the bare floor. One word kept running through her mind.

Splinters!

She twisted away from him and got out into the hallway.

"What you want?" Big Mama said when she saw Angela in the kitchen the next morning.

"I'm just looking," Angela said. She was fishing in the papers on top of the refrigerator. When she felt her bankbook, she waited until her grandmother wasn't looking, and then she walked out of the kitchen with it. *The hell with it,* she said to herself. *Nobody can live like he is.*

An hour later, Angela banged on Mario's door. She stood in the hallway until he got his coat on. They spent the rest of the morning having a cheap kitchen set sent to his place, buying a second-hand easel and carting it back to the apartment, and going uptown to buy a studio couch at a furniture warehouse that was listed in the *Village Voice*. Mario spent the day staring out windows whenever the price was mentioned. In the furniture warehouse, the price tag on the studio couch read $219. Mario asked the manager if the men's room was available. When Mario came out, Angela said, "They can't deliver it for three days."

Mario put a hand under one end of the couch and lifted. It was light enough. Angela reached down. Her end of it came up easily. They walked out of the warehouse and through the people on the sidewalk and down the subway stairs. Mario stopped at the bottom of the stairs. He timed his move with the subway change clerk. As the clerk's head went down to make change for someone, Mario rushed ahead, kicking open the gate with the NO ENTRANCE sign. When the downtown train came in, Mario backed into it, swinging the couch around until it was lengthwise in the middle of the aisle. He sat down on the couch, and Angela sat next to him. At 42nd Street, the first swirl of the rush hour came into the car. People fell into each other trying to go around the couch.

"Are you comfortable?" a man snarled down at Mario.

"Yes," Mario said.

An old lady with a shopping bag turned around and started sitting down. Mario tried to block her with his elbow. The old lady swung her shopping bag into Mario's face and wedged her way between Mario and Angela. The old lady spread her arms, the elbows coming out like gates. She was ready to hold her position.

The old lady made a sound like a whippoorwill and flew up from the couch. Angela put a hand over her face.

Mario was proud of himself.

Mario and Angela got the studio couch to his building. The

superintendent looked out into the hallway to see what the noise was. Angela looked at him. The superintendent swore to himself. He took Angela's end of the couch. She reached over and grabbed the thick hair on the back of Mario's neck. She held it for a moment. It was just as well the superintendent had come out.

"I'll see you, get a night's sleep for once," she said.

Joe Quarequio is a cousin of Tony the Indian, and he is a very confident guy. His last name means "happy death" and Joe Quarequio always tells himself, "Nothing bad could happen to me because I'm going to have a happy death." So Joe Quarequio is not afraid of doing many things. To satisfy a curious parole officer, Joe works at construction. When he is not at work, he is open to any proposition. One day Joe was on a job in Long Island where they were excavating for an office building. The engineer planted dynamite and the workers spread huge steel mesh mats on the ground over the area to be blasted. An engineer blew his whistle and everybody scurried out onto the sidewalk. Joe saw the engineer take what seemed to be a television channel-selector out of his breast pocket. The engineer pressed a button. The dynamite went off. The sound was muffled by the woven mats. The exploding dirt and rock were held down by the mats. The whole thing worked beautifully. Joe strolled over to the engineer and asked him about the channel-selector. The engineer said it was an electronic detonator. Instead of the old-fashioned, time-consuming stringing of wires from the dynamite to a plunger-type detonator, the electronic detonator merely has to be pressed and a signal explodes the dynamite.

"It's *sim-u-lar* to changin' television programs, ain't it?" Joe Quarequio said to the engineer.

"With slightly heavier results," the engineer said.

"Oh, boy, I seen that," Joe Quarequio said.

Joe Quarequio also saw the toolshed where the engineer kept the dynamite sets. And when Joe Quarequio went home from work that night, he sat against the window in the train and whistled little tunes to himself. In Joe's shirt pocket was the electronic thing. In Joe's lap, inside a paper bag, was enough dynamite to end the rush hour. Joe Quarequio couldn't wait to show it to Kid Sally Palumbo.

"Infuckincredible," Kid Sally Palumbo said. He looked at the neat stapled pink and blue wires, batteries, brass conductors, and sticks of dynamite inside the paper bag. He fondled the electronic detonator.

"We change programs for Baccala," he said. "From livin' to dead."

Kid Sally giggled. Big Jelly slapped the desk. Joe Quarequio was very proud. He had done a very good thing. The bomb would give them a great chance at Baccala. There would be none of this work under the car hood, wiring dynamite to the ignition system. It was slow and therefore quite dangerous. Anybody caught toying with Baccala's car would be immeasurably better off convicted of a major crime in the Orient. The new bomb merely required somebody to slip it onto the floor in the back of Baccala's car, where it would not be noticed, and then stand a block away with the electronic detonator and wait for Baccala to get into the car. A mere press of the thumb would handle the rest of it.

Big Jelly patted the dynamite sticks. "Beautiful," he said. He looked at a small dial. His fat fingers touched it. "What's this for?" he said. Big Jelly twisted the dial. "It goes around in a circle," he said.

"Geez, don't freak with nothin'," Kid Sally said.

"Yeah, I better not," Big Jelly said. He twisted the dial back to where he remembered it had been.

Kid Sally and Joe Quarequio left the office and got into a car with Ezmo the Driver at the wheel. For three days and nights they tried to find Baccala's car. They caught a glimpse of it one night, and Ezmo was about to step on the gas and catch up when he saw a second car slip in behind Baccala's. Ezmo knew the second car was a gun ship. He slowed down. On the fourth day, tired of looking, Kid Sally said he felt like something to eat at a place called the Lercarafriddi on Sackman Street. When Ezmo the Driver came onto Sackman Street he hit the brakes and put the car in reverse. Baccala's Cadillac, with the Water Buffalo riding shotgun, was pulling up in front of the Lercarafriddi. Baccala and the Water Buffalo got out. They went inside the restaurant. A black suit got out of the back seat and took up guard duty in front of the entrance.

Kid Sally peered around the corner. Any experienced thief, he figured, should be able to sneak up to the car on the street side, slip the paper bag with the bomb under the car, and then sneak away without being noticed. After that, all that remained to be done was to wait for Baccala to get into the car. A press on the electronic detonator would make the dynamite blow through the bottom of the car. The bottom of a car made in Detroit is not quite as sturdy as the woven mats used on construction jobs. The bottom of Baccala's car not only would not muffle the sound of the dynamite going off, but it also would not do much to prevent Baccala from riding in the lead funeral car.

"I tell you what," Kid Sally said. "There's been so freakin' much gone wrong, this one I wanna do personal."

"Hey," Joe Quarequio said, "what about me? Who brung you the bomb?"

Kid Sally fingered the detonator. "All right, Joe, you go put the bomb under the car."

Joe Quarequio held the paper bag in front of him as if it were being presented to the queen. Walking in a crouch, so he would be hidden by parked cars, Joe Quarequio slipped down the opposite side of the street from the restaurant. He took a deep breath and began to duck-waddle across the street to Baccala's car.

Inside the restaurant, Baccala had his head inside a big menu. The Water Buffalo watched the sidewalk to make sure the black suit was patrolling properly. The black suit looked up and down the street. He nodded to the Water Buffalo. Everything was all right. By now, Joe Quarequio was in the middle of the street, duck-waddling with his head so low it was impossible to see him as he came at Baccala's car.

Kid Sally leaned against the wall of the building up at the corner. He shook with excitement. It was unbelievable that he was getting this clear a shot at Baccala. He had imagined the death of Baccala would come after a pitched battle which would claim half of Brooklyn. He saw it with guns and ropes and curses and screams. But here in his hand was just a simple, innocuous plastic thing with a button on it. Just press it. "Inventions is unbelievable," he said to Ezmo. Kid Sally fondled the detonator. All the James Bond movies and the television spy shows, things Kid Sally had maintained were jerkoff shows, seemed like the Bible to him now.

A mile away, at the Bergen Street police station house, the desk lieutenant wanted to speak to Patrolman George Cusack, who was on traffic duty. In order to speak to Cusack, the desk lieutenant, under a system installed that day, was to push a button on a monitor board. This would activate a pocket beeper in Patrolman Cusack's pocket, and he would go to a telephone and call in. Patrolman Cusack's beeper was on wavelength 151.190.

When the desk lieutenant pressed the beeper, two things happened. A high-pitched but soft noise began in the beeper in Patrolman Cusack's breast pocket. And on Sackman Street, Joe Quarequio disappeared in the middle of a waddle.

> QUAREQUIO—Joseph. Very, very suddenly. Son of Thomas and Donnette Quarequio. Beloved brother of

George, Frank, Peter, Louise, and the honored Todo (Tommy Scratch) Quarequio. "Fire and brimstone shall descend on our enemies!" Family receiving mourners at CAMPION'S Funeral Home, Inc., 56 Lockman Street, Brooklyn. No interment.

Kid Sally Palumbo was rubbing his fist across his forehead so hard that the skin was peeling. Upstairs, his grandmother was sitting with her hands out while the water boiled in two big pots for the day's number-10 macaroni. There would be a little oil and garlic with it, and that would do it. The lobster fra diavolo and chicken cacciatore and veal rollatini were of the past. The organization not only was having trouble keeping its members alive, but also was having supply trouble.

There were two reasons for this. First were the supply routes. One morning Ezmo the Driver and Tony the Indian decided that at ten a.m. nothing could happen to them. They walked down to Columbia Avenue to buy some meat and a few cans of paint. They thought that fresh paint on the office walls would overcome the lion's smell coming up from the basement. They were two doors down from the paint store, hugging the building line so the people on the crowded sidewalk would be between them and the street. This gave them great natural protection, they felt. The trouble with this was that the Water Buffalo uses the same type of defense every morning and he understands its basic weakness. The basic weakness is that the people standing between you and the danger have a marked tendency to flee, leaving you alone with the danger. This is not good.

The Water Buffalo was driving slowly along Columbia Avenue just to see if he could get lucky. The Water Buffalo saw Ezmo and Tony and he rushed his car to the curb. He came bounding out with a gun in his hand. All the people on the sidewalk ran. This left Tony the Indian, Ezmo the Driver, and the Water Buffalo alone with each other. When the Water

Buffalo got back in his car and began speeding away, he was swearing to himself. He had hit Tony the Indian only two out of three times. And all he had done to Ezmo the Driver was shoot him in the ankle. But after this everybody on Marshall Street was afraid to go off the block except in an armed caravan.

The other reason for the lack of food was the lack of money in the Palumbo organization. The subsistence payments—they amounted to little more than welfare—which Baccala paid to the Palumbo organization had been shut off. The few gambling and shylocking accounts which Kid Sally had kept for himself had displayed coolness to Kid Sally since the start of the revolt.

"What's doin', pal?" Kid Sally said to Norton the Gambler on the phone.

"Gee, I'm glad to hear from you," Norton the Gambler said.

"Don't you want to see me with somethin'?" Kid Sally said.

"Gee, I wouldn't like to get killed just now," Norton the Gambler said.

"Never mind that, what about what you're supposed to see me with?" Kid Sally said. Norton owed Kid Sally $500 interest on a shylock loan.

"Oh, that? Oh, I give that to Jamesy," Norton said. Jamesy was one of Baccala's finest black suits.

"You give it to who?"

"You see Jamesy," Norton the Gambler said. "And if he's not there, just ask for Baccala. I'm sure he'd be glad to talk to you and tell you."

Norton the Gambler hung up. Kid Sally began banging his head against the side of the outdoor phone booth he was using.

He walked back down the block to the office and sat down. The fist started rubbing across the forehead. He took a deep breath. The ammonia smell from the lion caused his eyes to tear. "Geez." He took another deep breath. "Murder."

He put his hand over his mouth and opened the door. The lion slipped past Kid Sally's legs and came into the office. The guys in the office threw themselves at the front door. Big Jelly jumped up on the desk. After six weeks in Kid Sally's cellar, the lion had grown a full foot longer and gained about a hundred pounds, much of it in his head, which made him look frightening.

"He'll fuckin' eat me!" Big Jelly yelled.

Inspiration flooded through Kid Sally's head. He grabbed a rope and reached for the lion. "C'mere, you!" The lion ducked his head. He was still just a trifle young. But strangers to the lion would not know this. "He'll give out heart attacks," Kid Sally said, roughing the lion's mane. Kid Sally sniffed. "He needs a bath," he said.

There was, a little while later, a tangle of bumping cars and people threading their way through the cars and sprinting for their lives away from the Clean-Brite Car Wash on Carroll Street. An immense, prolonged roar came from inside the car wash. The lion was tied to a stanchion. The water came on and hit the lion from all sides. The lion came up on his hind legs, fighting against the rope and shaking his head in the water spray. After five minutes, Kid Sally pushed the lion into the rear of the panel truck. Ezmo the Driver was driving, Big Jelly sat in the middle with a shotgun, and Kid Sally was crushed against the outside door. The truck pulled away from the deserted car wash with the lion in the back growling and shaking himself dry.

Chapter **15**

Nearly all the people in South Brooklyn play the policy numbers. And within close range of Kid Sally's headquarters there were a considerable number of places used as drops for the numbers gambling. The numbers play from these places belonged technically to the Baccala gang. But loyalty dips as chances of death rise. Kid Sally knew there was a chance, if proper strength was displayed, to grab the numbers play from these places. It amounted, each week, to a figure large enough to support a gang in a war. Once a week people handed a numbers runner anywhere from $1.50, to cover a quarter bet each day, to $12 and $18, to cover $2 and $3 play per day. Kid Sally knew his presence, or the threat of it, would not hold these places in line permanently. People figured, correctly, that Kid Sally was so busy defending himself against Baccala's mob that he couldn't concentrate on them. Kid Sally knew he needed something that would produce lasting fear.

The biggest numbers drop was Herman's Luncheonette on Fourth Avenue. It was around the corner from two big taxicab garages. The place was always filled with drivers who left their numbers business with Herman, the owner. Herman stood ready to turn over his numbers each week to the collector who frightened him most. "Yell, shout, scream, but don't get physical," Herman kept saying. Herman was at one end of the counter, smoking a cigarette, when Kid Sally came into the place with the lion. Herman did not move. He stood with his cigarette held out and his eyes bulging. He then wet his pants. Ida, the waitress, had her back to the counter. She was looking in the refrigerator for sandwich meat. The lion's nose twitched. He jumped up on the counter. The customers at the counter, all male, wet their pants. The lion teetered on the counter, reached out with a paw and brushed it against Ida's shoulder, and pulled an eye round out of the refrigerator. Ida glanced at the lion and fainted. Herman was too frozen to look. He could hear the lion chewing on the eye round. He retched. He thought the lion was chewing on Ida the waitress.

"Are we friends?" Kid Sally said to him.

Herman, between trembles, was able to nod yes.

Kid Sally spent the next couple of days building a numbers route. At Jack Goldfarb's candy store, Mrs. Jack Goldfarb was bent down behind the counter looking for a box of El Productos. When Mrs. Jack Goldfarb looked up, she saw a lion eating her Hershey bars. Mrs. Jack Goldfarb went home later that day and was not to come out again for six weeks. In Ackerman's Bar, the lion gauged his distance and leaped onto the bar and began eating peanuts. Mickey, the bartender, broke a quart soda bottle off at the neck and stood with it in his hand, ready to fight for his life. His legs buckled and he passed out.

At the end of a week Kid Sally had things lined up. The numbers route was just large enough to support his outfit, and it was just small enough to be safe for a few weeks. By the time the Baccala people were ready to react to the loss by throwing in a large number of gunmen, Kid Sally expected to have Baccala dead and be in charge himself. Kid Sally was going to take over everything on Monday, the big day in the numbers business. On Monday people leave their bets for the week.

Early Monday morning, Kid Sally felt better. He stood in front of the mirror, flipping his tie and making faces.

"I'm starting to put things together now," he said.

"I hope so, I'm tired of goin' to funerals," Big Jelly said.

Kid Sally put the lion in the back of the truck and started out with Ezmo, Big Jelly, and Beppo the Dwarf. Beppo held a sawed-off shotgun and sat on Kid Sally's lap. They stopped at Herman's Luncheonette first. Kid Sally held the back door of the truck open so the lion could stick his head out. Which was all Herman had to see. He reached behind the counter and came up with a big shopping bag holding slips and money. The shopping bag is the carrying case of the numbers business. Numbers is the racetrack of the poor, and many women serve as runners. A shopping bag is their best disguise. Kid Sally took the bag and had a cup of coffee and left Herman's. At ZuZu's Bar and Grill, Kid Sally took the play, stuffed it into the shopping bag, and had a beer. At Ackerman's they all went inside and had a shot of whisky and a beer. Big Jelly went next door to the butcher and bought chopped meat. When he came back they had another drink and left. At Zanetti's Saloon they all had another round of shots and beer. By the time they hit the Cameo Lounge, three hours and five joints later, they all were shaky from drinking.

The Cameo is not much of an afternoon place. It has a barmaid whose name is Del.

"Hello, Del," Beppo the Dwarf said.

"Don't even talk to me, you're too small for me," Del said.

"I got a five-and-a-half-inch tongue," Beppo the Dwarf said.

Ezmo the Driver gripped the bar and began jumping up and down. Kid Sally sat Beppo the Dwarf on the bar. Del spilled water down the front of his pants. Beppo kissed her in the ear with his tongue. Big Jelly reached for a bottle of scotch. They all kept laughing and drinking and they were still laughing an hour later, when Ezmo was driving them back to Marshall Street. In the back of the truck, the lion was growling. Kid Sally remembered the lion hadn't been fed. "I put the meat on the floor," Big Jelly said. Kid Sally, still giggling, reached down and felt the paper bag. He threw it back over his shoulder. The lion fell on it.

Back on Marshall Street, everybody fell out of the truck, laughing, and Kid Sally reached down for the shopping bag. He felt the paper bag and fumbled for the handles. He didn't feel any. Instead, his fingers touched waxed paper from the butcher store. In the back of the truck, the lion was coughing to clear his throat of a ten-dollar bill.

Kid Sally did not remember coming out of the truck. He was unable to breathe, hear, or see. He went upstairs, like Stalin, locked himself in his room for two days.

Big Jelly sat downstairs with his eyes closed. *"Calamare,"* he said to himself. "Zuppa di mussels."

"You're makin' me hungry," Tony the Indian said.

"Shut up, I'm imaginin' I'm out eatin'," Big Jelly said.

That night Georgie, who was Tony the Indian's cousin, became uncomfortable staying on the block. He was uncomfortable because, as he complained, "My thing don't know we got troubles, all my thing knows is that it's good and ready." At 10:30 Georgie wandered from Marshall Street and got in a cab to go to his girl friend's house in Bensonhurst. Bensonhurst was a bad place for Georgie. It was Baccala's home grounds. Georgie didn't care. "I follow my thing," he always says. "I trust it."

A guy got into the apartment elevator with him. Georgie stood facing the guy, just in case. In a one-on-one situation,

Georgie was not afraid. Georgie's girl was on the fifth floor. The guy pushed the button for the second floor. Georgie relaxed. The guy was all right. When the elevator door slid open at the second floor, Georgie just did catch a glimpse of the four black suits before they came in on him.

At this point there were six dead and the situation was beginning to reach people beyond the Brooklyn South Homicide Squad. The matter by now had come to the attention of M. E. Landsman, a reporter on the *Times*. Mr. Landsman is in charge of the "Crime, Organized" department of the *Times* city desk. Mr. Landsman's first name is Morris, but the *Times*, German-Jewish oriented, apparently seems not to like the Eastern European "Morris" or "Abraham" to be used in its bylines. Landsman and all Abrahams on the paper either use initials or go on home relief. He has been writing stories about organized crime for three years. Landsman was born in White Plains and lives in Larchmont. The only real Italians he ever saw were atop a garbage truck.

As a reporter, however, he is considered an expert in what is known as Italian Geography. This is a practice of such as the FBI, various police intelligence units, and newspaper and magazine writers. Italian Geography is the keeping of huge amounts of information on gangsters: the prices they pay for clothes, the restaurants in which they eat, the names of all relatives out to the fifth cousins, their home addresses, and their visible daily movements. All this information is neatly filed and continually added to. It is never used for anything, and the gangster goes on until death. But Italian Geography keeps many people busy and collecting salaries, and thus is a commendable occupation. M. E. Landsman, just by digging into the cabinet behind his desk, could tell you the home address of Baccala (55 Royal Street), the number of guests at

Anthony (Tony Boy) Boirado's wedding (732), the birthplace of Lucky Luciano (Lercara Friddi, Sicily), and the favorite dining spot and meal of dock boss Mike Rizzuto (Della Palma; veal marsala). All these little facts always add up to nothing in the geographer's mind. And every evening, sitting over a martini in the Oyster Bar at Grand Central Station, M. E. Landsman waits for his train to Larchmont and he says to himself, "I wonder what these people really *do*."

In the security of his office, however, he was without doubt. He submerged himself in his geography and wrote authoritative stories about the Mafia. Now, with the bare police details of the six recent murders in front of him, M. E. Landsman went to work. He went into his cabinet for the M's and brought out Joe Mangoni's file. It showed that Joe Mangoni had a cousin who married Carlo Gambino's niece in Saint Fortunata's Church in Bensonhurst. M. E. Landsman studied this information. He reached for the phone and called Sergeant Paul DiNardo at police headquarters.

Sergeant DiNardo was on the streets as a precinct patrolman for the first month of his first year on the New York City force. A desk lieutenant found DiNardo knew how to type, and for the next seventeen years DiNardo typed reports in offices in the Police Department. Because of the wave of talk about organized crime, the Chief Inspector, George Glennon, looked around headquarters one day and announced that DiNardo would be the department's expert on the Mafia.

"Why are you picking him?" The Commissioner, Michael McGrady, asked Glennon.

"Because he's a guinea," Glennon said. "He'll be able to spell the names right."

DiNardo grabbed the phone. "Organized Crime Special Attack Unit, Sergeant DiNardo speaking." Sometimes he said "Enforcement Unit," and other times he said "Investigation

Unit." It didn't matter. He was alone in his office and whatever he said was all right, as long as the names were spelled right on the records.

"This is Meyer Landsman at the *Times*. All these murders in Brooklyn. Could you tell me anything about them?"

"Like what?" DiNardo said.

"Well, take the Mangoni killing," M. E. Landsman said.

DiNardo pushed a button. It caused a file drum to rotate. DiNardo stopped the drum at M. He grabbed the folder for Joe Mangoni. "Well, Mangoni cousin married Carlo Gambino's daughter."

"I know that too," Landsman said smugly.

"Well, what else can I tell you?" DiNardo said.

"What do you think about it?" Landsman said.

"You know I can't talk," DiNardo said. "There's an investigation."

DiNardo hung up and went through a newspaper to see if there was a movie he could see that afternoon. Meyer Landsman pushed open the typewriter well on his desk and went to work. He turned his head, as he always did, while his fingers typed out: BY M. E. LANDSMAN.

His definitive story read in part:

> High police officials today are investigating a series of murders in Brooklyn to determine if they have some connection to the operations of the criminal organization known as the Cosa Nostra, or Mafia. Police officials pointed out that the murder victims, six within two months, all had police records.

The story was put on page one under a headline saying: POLICE PROBE 6 MURDERS IN BROOKLYN.

The next morning the pale sunlight came through the bare trees on the lawn outside Gracie Mansion, and the wind blew the branches, causing their shadows to flick across the newspaper the Mayor was reading at breakfast. The Mayor closed his eyes. They were red-rimmed and hot. He had been up until three a.m. unwinding after a two-hour session with 2500 angry people in a Jewish Center in Flatbush. He opened his eyes and ran them across the headlines on the *Times'* first page. There were three stories out of Washington, one out of Tel Aviv, others from Tokyo, Bombay, and Paris. The only New York story was M. E. Landsman's piece on gang murders.

"Shit!" the Mayor said. "Who the hell cares about gangsters? I mean, you'd think . . . Here I'm out all night arguing about housing, and what do they put on the first page? Gangsters. Shit!"

Harold Downing, his chief assistant, sat across from the Mayor. "He's got six murders to talk about, and he's the expert on gangsters. Maybe he'll try and stretch this out. Run one every day."

"Fuck that," the Mayor said. "There's problems in this city a little more important than gangsters. The biggest one is me getting re-elected." He picked up a phone attached to the table. "Give me Commissioner McGrady," he said.

He waited a moment, cursing under his breath. "Michael, how are you? . . . That's right, that's exactly what I'm calling about . . . Yes, yes, yes. . . . Well, you see, I couldn't care if they killed each other forever. But I have this housing bill and, shit, I can't have gangsters on the first page. You know. . . . Oh, good. All right, thanks, Michael."

Commissioner McGrady put the phone down. He stood up and walked around the immense desk Teddy Roosevelt had used when he was the city's Police Commissioner. He looked down at the thick rug for a moment. Then he pushed a buzzer. His secretary, a detective, walked in.

"Tell Gallagher to meet me at Emil's," he said.

Emil's is an old, dark-walled German restaurant a block and a half from City Hall and Police Headquarters. A corner table in the rear is always reserved for the Police Commissioner.

The place was empty. It was only 9:30. McGrady was on his second scotch by the time Gallagher walked in.

"I know what this is about," Gallagher said. "One fuckin' story in a newspaper."

"I just wanted to congratulate you on your dead guineas," McGrady said.

"Thanks," Gallagher said. "And I'd have more of them if I had my way."

"You can do two things for me," McGrady said. "First, you can have a drink. Second, you can get them to go some place else with their troubles. I had the Mayor on the phone the minute I got in this morning."

The waiter brought two shot glasses of scotch, with water on the side. "Here's how," Gallagher said. He threw a shot down, Irish style, his tongue showing as it went into the shot glass. He put the glass down. "It's this fuckin' punk Sally Palumbo," Gallagher said. "He's pushin'."

"What does Baccala have to say about that?" McGrady said.

"Well, what do you think the shootin' is about?" Gallagher said.

"Well, get on him," McGrady said.

"I'll get on that fuckin' Palumbo, that's what I'll do," Gallagher said.

"I don't care what you do, just do it," McGrady said. "Just keep the Mayor off my back."

At three a.m. the squad rooms and all the offices of the 79th Precinct were filled with detectives talking to Kid Sally Palumbo's people. Gallagher, his eyes bloodshot, walked from office to office, conferring with detectives out in the hallway.

Gallagher liked the way it was going. His men had grabbed the Palumbo outfit after midnight. By the time lawyers could drive in from Long Island and scream about civil liberties, he would have the Palumbos exhausted and bothered. Gallagher had told his detectives to abuse them. "It takes them a week to get over it when you treat them like shoeshine boys," he said. "Their guinea egos suffer."

A week would give him time. He could take it up with Baccala and see if there was a way to end it. But that was for later. Right now, all that counted was abusing everybody.

From each office, Gallagher could hear a voice saying the same thing.

"What could I tell you?" Kid Sally Palumbo was saying to two homicide detectives.

"What could I tell you?" Big Jelly was saying.

"What-a could I tell-a you?" Big Mama was saying. When she saw Gallagher, her thumb and forefinger shot out in horns.

Gallagher smiled. "Dead guineas and niggers, that's what I like," he called out. "The more I see of dead guineas and dead niggers, the better I like it."

He looked into one small office. A thin smile came onto his face and he stepped inside. "Good evening," he said.

Angela sat in a chair with a cigarette in her mouth and no make-up on her face. She inhaled and put the cigarette carefully in the ashtray. She let the smoke come out of her nose slowly.

"Get cancer," she said quietly.

"What's that?" Gallagher said.

"What could I tell you?" Angela said.

"You weren't this way the last time I saw you," Gallagher said.

The young detective talking to her was sitting on the other side of the desk. Gallagher motioned with his head for the detective to come around the desk and sit alongside her. The young detective frowned. He didn't know what Gallagher meant.

Gallagher smiled again. "Be nice to her, she's a nice college student," he said.

Angela sat and stared at the ashtray and said nothing. She was reminding herself that once you say anything except the one rote line, "What could I tell you?" you open yourself up for a slip.

The cameramen were at the bottom of the stairs, and the doors behind them were open to the morning rain. Angela held her head high and started down the stairs. She looked over their heads, at the rain in the doorway, but her eyes caught the cameras being held up. An arm in a blue rain jacket held a television floodlight high over the heads of the other cameramen. Angela was halfway down the stairs when the floodlight came on—glaring, bare light that brings up the rust on the railings and the cigarette butts and gum wrappers on the steps and the soot coating on the walls and the stale faces and the municipal smell of a police station when you are in trouble. Angela's head was high and she felt herself coming down each step and there were no more steps and the cameras were all around her and her ears became filled with the *shhhhhhh shhhhhhhhh shhhhhhh* of the cameramen shuffling backward while they kept filming her, and then there was nobody around her and she was in the morning rain on the steps of the police station. It was a winter rain. The wind blew it in gray sheets. The cold touch of the rain came through her hair and to the scalp.

"Miss Palumbo, Miss Palumbo," a woman's voice said.

Angela kept her head high and came down the steps to the sidewalk and she heard the footsteps coming alongside her.

"Miss Palumbo, are you going to your classes at college now?"

Whoever she was, she was on the left. Angela's left shoulder came up in self-protection.

"Miss Palumbo, I went to NYU myself, and I was just wondering . . ."

Angela kept walking, controlled, erect, the rain coming into her face and soaking through the shoulders of her cloth coat. She could feel the presence on her left going away. Angela's left shoulder came down.

"Artie, she won't say anything," the female voice behind her was calling out.

They had let Angela go first. It was 7:30, and she walked up to the corner and into the rush hour on an avenue in Brooklyn. The street was a wall of trailer trucks and buses with steamy windows. The sign hanging from the corner drugstore squealed while it swung in the wind and rain. A light changed, and the traffic in the street began to move. The Diesel trucks and buses shifted gears with a roar, and the squeal from the drugstore sign mixed in with the roar, and Angela walked in the heavy rain with the noise hurting her ears and her back in a little bunch against the hand she felt would touch her, a cop's hand, a cameraman's hand, somebody's hand, and nausea started in the back of her head and ran to her stomach. She swallowed against it and kept walking, controlled and erect, and people began brushing against her as they ran in the rain to the subway. She slipped into the middle of a crowd going down the steps. The train was packed and hot, and the smell of wet clothes was thick. People dressed in rainhats and raincoats stared at Angela. There had been no rain when the detectives came the night before, so she was not dressed for it. Her blue coat was dark with water, her wet stockings stuck to her legs, and her hair dripped. Angela stared out the window and was motionless all the way to Manhattan. She did not notice the stations, or the people getting on and off the trains. She thought about nothing. She was frozen. Vacantly, automatically, she got off at Second Avenue and began walking in the rain. At Mario's corner the sewer was stopped up and a puddle was spreading into the middle of the street. A cab ran through the puddle and threw a spray of water. A sheet of dirty water splashed into Angela's face. She walked through it.

Mario was in a T-shirt and his shorts when he answered the door. He said something to her, but she didn't hear it. "I'm wet," she said. She walked past him. "I just want to get dry," she said. She picked the hotel towel off the doorknob. She started into the bathroom, then went over to a chair and picked up his raincoat. In the bathroom she took off her coat and hung it on the door hook. Her plaid shift was soaked. She took it off and hung it on the shower-curtain rail. The bra felt damp. She took it off. She reached down and began to unhook her stockings, but her fingers fumbled. She peeled the girdle and stockings off at once and threw them over the rail. She put on the raincoat and started rubbing her hair with the towel. She gave a little shudder and fell on her knees and began vomiting into the toilet. Her body shook all over. When she began screaming, Mario opened the door.

He helped her to the couch and she buried her face and Mario could see her body shaking through the raincoat. He ran his hand on her back in a slow circle. She lay on her face on the couch for a half-hour and sobbed. She twisted around to look up at him. Her mouth was trembling with shock. Mario's face came down to her. He kissed her, and she was whimpering and moaning in shock and fear, and then all the trouble inside her came out in a wave of need and she had her mouth on his and her legs stretching and moving and her fingernails digging into his back while she drew in a sharp breath through clenched teeth.

She listened to the rain against the windows for a few moments. She held up her arm and squinted at the watch. It was 2:30. Mario was sitting at the easel, which he had set up in front of the windows. She put her head down and pulled the blanket up over her shoulders.

"Don't tell me you went out and bought a blanket," she said.

"People help me," Mario said. He smiled. He wished Sidney could hear that. He got the blanket one day by waiting until Sidney was stuck in the bathroom and then whisking it off Sidney's bed. Sidney heard the movement and knew he was being robbed, but he couldn't do anything about it except to scream from the bathroom, "Thief fuck!"

Angela put her head back and stretched. The police station started in her stomach. She closed her eyes against it.

"What are you doing there?" she said.

He grunted something. He had been working for five hours, using Angela's face to make up for the torn face on the painting he was copying.

"You've been working too long," she said. She shook her head against the light. He stood up and stretched. *Now all I have to do is finish this painting and find some old lady and make her buy it,* he said to himself. He had everything else he needed. He walked across to the couch.

They woke up in darkness. Angela stiffened. "My God, what time is it?" He got up and pushed the light switch. She squinted in the light from the bulb in the ceiling directly over her head. "Oh, five o'clock." She fell back. "I thought it was late, I didn't know what time it was. I have to call home. They'll be crazy if I don't call them soon." She yawned. "The light. Don't have one bulb in a room like this. Get a lamp. You'd be surprised what one lamp would do for you. We'll have to get one. But right now I'm starved." She sat up quickly. "Oh, I don't know what I have in my purse."

She pulled the blanket around her and slid off the couch and went over to the kitchen table and began going through her purse. The blanket slipped from one shoulder. Mario's eyes followed her back slanting in from the shoulder and then rolling, white, into the top of a long leg.

"I hope you have some money, because I have exactly two dollars and some change," she said.

"Nothing, I have none," he said. He swung onto the floor and went for his pants. He put them on carefully, so the change wouldn't jingle in the pocket where he had the money.

She ran a hand through her hair. "Well, what are you going to live on? I mean, you've got to eat."

"I have no money," he said. He put his hand in the pocket that had the money.

She went into the bathroom and dressed. She was running a comb through her hair when she called out, "Get dressed."

"I'll stay here," he said.

"Just get dressed," she said. "I can't leave you here like this."

"To go where?" he said.

She came out to him and kissed him. "Come home with me and get something to eat. And if anybody asks you, I met you after school."

Chapter **16**

In the City of New York, in the ninety minutes between six and seven-thirty p.m. each weekday night, there occurs the greatest flood of information directed at man in the history of the world. On the major television channels, a group of men who appear to be either studying or teaching undertaking appear on the screen with the news of the day in words and film. The film, running from talking heads in a hallway at the Board of Health to F-4 planes dropping napalm canisters into trees, comes into nearly every house, apartment, furnished room, saloon, and office in the city. And on almost every evening this television news, merely by displaying a subject, can raise the level of annoyance over a minor matter to the point where it becomes a major crisis.

Which is what was occurring around the city when, after the billboarding and commercials, the first set of straight-faced television newsmen came on camera to give all New York the lead story of the day's news.

"Good evening. Police early this morning conducted a lightning raid on a gang of Brooklyn hoodlums who were alleged to be at the bottom of the series of Cosa Nostra murders which have occurred in that borough in recent weeks. Sixty-three of the men, and two women, were brought to the 91st Precinct and questioned for several hours by homicide detectives under command of . . ."

The Mayor kicked his wastepaper basket, spilling it across the red carpeting of his office at City Hall.

"Shit!" the Mayor said.

". . . gang, which operates in Brooklyn, is said to be under the control of Salvatore (Kid Sally) Palumbo . . ."

Harold Downing stood up. He smiled. "I wish I could be the mayor, so everybody would do exactly as I tell them."

"I ask them to get rid of it for me, and what do I get?" the Mayor said. "The police running a publicity stunt for a couple of lousy gangsters."

In Baccala's office they were standing around the boss, who sat in a chair and looked at a new color set which he had set up next to the statue of Saint Anthony. On the news show there was a film clip of Angela coming down the stairs, her face set against the light glaring into her eyes.

"That's the sister," one of Baccala's black suits said.

"Who sister?" Baccala said.

"Kid Sally's sister," the Water Buffalo said.

"I make him watch while I shoot her," Baccala said.

The film now showed Kid Sally starting down the stairs. On camera, Kid Sally brought his right arm up in an elaborate movement. He was just starting to slap his left hand on the inside of his right elbow when the film clip dissolved.

"Punk!" Baccala said. His head went far back, then came forward as he spat at the television set. "Die!" He said it from deep in his throat. The Water Buffalo jumped up and spat at the television. All the black suits ran up to the set, clearing their throats to spit.

In Kid Sally Palumbo's front room, twenty of them were

crowded in and watched the show the way big football teams look at game films. "Here I go," Kid Sally said, looking at himself. Everybody groaned when the film was cut before his gesture. Big Jelly now appeared. "Watch me shine," Big Jelly said. On television he came strutting down the stairs with his tongue sticking out of the right side of his mouth. One hand was on his hip. The other hand made a fist. The fist was just starting an up-and-down motion when the film clip was dissolved.

There was a great noise in Kid Sally's front room. There was a small noise in Baccala's office. "Punk!" Baccala said again. In the office of the Mayor there was the most dangerous sound of all. Silence.

The Mayor sat immobile for several moments. He reached for an old black phone which connected him directly to the Police Commissioner's office.

"Hi. You know, I was just sitting here thinking. We're having an Urban Task Force meeting tonight, and I thought at the end of it a couple of us ought to sit down. We're a little out of sync. When? Oh, I'd say, let me see, somewhere around eleven o'clock tonight at the mansion."

At Police Headquarters, McGrady had one hand reaching for the intercom while he put down the Mayor's call. "This Protestant bastard will have me sitting up all night on account of these guineas—yeop, get me Chief Gallagher in Brooklyn South, will you please?"

The switchboard operators had left the Brooklyn District Attorney's office. The patrolman at the reception desk answered the night line. "Mr. Rogin?" The patrolman checked the list in front of him. "No, I'm sorry, he left for the day. Would you care to leave a message? Oh, excuse me. The Mayor's office. If you'll hold a minute, I'll get Mr. Goodman."

Benjamin Goodman, the chief assistant district attorney, sat hunched over his municipal green metal desk. A small round mirror, the kind women take along when traveling, was set up on top of a pile of trial minutes. Benjamin Goodman looked into the mirror while he combed his red hair.

"Mayor's office," the patrolman said.

Benjamin Goodman was on his feet in one motion. He jogged out of the office. In the hallway he began to sprint. He slid up to the phone.

"Rogin?" Goodman said to Harold Downing, "Well, yes, he's been working on this gang business. But . . ." Goodman took a deep breath. He did not need to pause. He knew what he was going to say without having to think about it. "But he's merely been assigned to it. Actually, in view of the worsening situation, I think I'd better step into the case personally. When? Gracie Mansion at eleven tonight? Of course."

In the City Room of the *Times*, a voice came over the loud-speaker. "Mr. Landsman, please report to the metropolitan desk. Mr. Landsman . . ."

M. E. Landsman walked through the long rows of desks to the front of the room, where three men in shirtsleeves, all wearing glasses, were standing in front of a television set.

"Mersh, what do you plan to do with this Palumbo business?" one of the men in shirtsleeves said. "They were just on television. God, what despicable characters."

"Oh, I'm putting up something on them," M. E. Landsman said.

"Well, we'd like to use it fairly strong, perhaps out front," the man said. "When can we see the lead?"

"Oh, I'll have it coming up right away," M. E. Landsman said.

He walked back to his desk with a sinking feeling. He had planned to write the story the next morning. Now he was going to miss his regular train home to Larchmont. He sat at his desk and took the Associated Press copy on the arrests and began to write it in different words. There was no use in trying anything else. He had nothing on Kid Sally Palumbo in his files. And he had spoken to Sergeant DiNardo earlier in the day, and DiNardo had assured him Kid Sally Palumbo was a soldier in the Mafia family in Youngstown, Ohio.

Landsman's story ran on the bottom of page one. At 10:45 p.m. the Mayor had his secretary circle it on each copy of the newspaper that was on the long conference table in the basement at Gracie Mansion. At eleven o'clock the Mayor sat down at the head of the table. He nodded to everybody and then picked up a paper. The Mayor was wearing a short-sleeved blue knit yachting shirt. This made everybody at the table think of one word: *Protestant.*

"Well, gentlemen, I want to thank you for coming," the Mayor said. "The purpose of this meeting is to further the coordination of our efforts in regard to this damnable mess in Brooklyn."

Benjamin Goodman picked up a pencil and began to scrawl on the pad in front of him. *What is this guy worrying so much about a few guinea homicides?* he thought. Idly, Goodman wrote "2%" on the pad. The Mayor, running on a Fusion ticket, had defeated the regular Democratic candidate because of a shift of 2 per cent of the Democratic voters. Goodman, like any other fifty-one-year-old clubhouse Democrat, could recite the names of party defectors.

"Look," the Mayor said, "I don't have to tell you people that if there's one thing people react to these days, it's something about crime. Hell, anything about crime. I'm up half the nights worrying about street crimes and burglaries. I couldn't care less about gangsters killing each other. But you put just one dead body in a gutter and the public reacts. It's an issue."

Goodman's pencil tapped on the pad. Goodman began drawing rows of "2%." He ripped the page off and stuffed it into his pocket. Carefully he printed a newspaper headline.

BROOKLYN DA GOODMAN MOUNTS
INTENSIVE DRIVE ON MAFIA

Goodman looked at Gallagher. The inspector's pouchy eyes returned the look. *Maybe,* Benjamin Goodman thought, *this drunken slob could help a nice alert Jewish Democrat to get 2 per cent of the vote back. Who knows? Who knows anything?*

"Am I given to understand," Goodman called out, "that Chief Gallagher will be running the Police Department's end of this?"

"Yes," McGrady said.

"With a little less noise than in the past, I would hope," the Mayor said sharply.

"Fine with me," Goodman said. "That's fine."

Later the Mayor's wife served coffee in the living quarters. Benjamin Goodman stood at the living-room windows, looking at the dark lawns that run down to the East River. The Mayor's wife was bringing Benjamin Goodman cream and sugar and she heard him muse to himself, without knowing he was saying it aloud, "This would be a helluva place for me to live."

Just before they fell asleep that night, the Mayor's wife said, "This Goodman is a slimy worm, you know."

"Why?" he asked.

"Because he's a slimy worm, that's why," she said.

Mario and Angela had come into the Palumbo apartment just as the news program started. They stood in the doorway between the kitchen and front room and watched, she in silence, Mario with little noises coming out of him when he found he was so afraid that he could not inhale. When the television announcer changed subjects, Kid Sally turned off the set. Everybody in the room looked at Mario.

"This is Mario Trantino, he is one of the boys who came here for the bike race," Angela said.

"How do you do, pleased," Kid Sally said.

"How do you do, pleased," Big Mama said.

They all reached out and shook hands with Mario, and Big Mama took him into the kitchen. "I want to change," Angela said. She went down the hall to her room. Right away, Big Jelly closed his eyes and put his head against the wall. Tony the Indian sat with both hands on top of his head. He began scratching his scalp. He knew a lot of people do this when they think, and he wanted to try it out. Big Jelly opened his eyes. When he saw Tony the Indian trying to think too, it came to him.

"That guy is a rat priest hittin' on your sister!" he snarled.

Kid Sally Palumbo picked up his head. "Who rat priest?" he said.

"Me and Tony seen him," Big Jelly said.

"Seen him where?" Kid Sally said.

"Seen him in his priest's suit," Tony the Indian said.

"By Dominic's when we was watchin' that night," Big Jelly said.

"I could of touched him . . ." Tony the Indian said.

". . . same guy . . ."

". . . rat priest . . ."

". . . I don't hafta swear, I got eyes, I could see . . ."

". . . yeah . . ."

Mario, sitting at the kitchen table, picked up a few stray words of the jumbled conversation in the front room. Therefore he knew enough to drop his chin onto his chest when Kid Sally exploded into the kitchen. With the chin down, Kid Sally could not get his hands on Mario's throat. Big Jelly grabbed

Mario by an ear in order to yank the head up so Kid Sally could do some strangling. Big Mama had a bread knife in one hand. With the other hand she tried to flatten out the fingers of Mario's right hand onto the kitchen table. Big Mama intended to saw off the thumb and forefinger of the hand. These are the fingers which are anointed when a priest is ordained. Mario made a fist so the fingers wouldn't stick out. Big Mama jabbed the tip of the knife into the fist. Mario yelped. The fingers of his hand jumped out in pain. Big Mama tried to hold them flat so she could begin sawing. Mario pulled the fingers back into a fist. Big Mama jabbed him again with the tip of the knife.

"The hell with it," Big Jelly said. He bent over and sank his teeth into Mario's ear. Mario made a loud noise.

When Angela heard Mario shriek, she tumbled out of her room. At the kitchen doorway she started to scream, but put her hands to her mouth instead and stood motionless. Centuries of Sicilian blood cause a woman to stay out of a thing like this, even if her greatest love is about to be murdered. Weep for his soul, yes. But never interfere with the necessary rite of his murder.

Beppo the Dwarf got a hand inside Mario's jacket and pulled out the picture. He turned it over and saw the writing on the back. He held the picture in front of Kid Sally's face. He turned it around so Kid Sally could see the writing.

"What's it say?" Beppo the Dwarf said.

Kid Sally's hands dropped from Mario's chin. He pushed Big Mama's knife hand away and slapped Big Jelly on the head to make him stop biting Mario's ear.

"Let's talk a bit," he said to Mario.

"I never touch!" Mario said, gesturing to Angela. "On my mother's grave, I never touch!"

"That means he touch!" Big Mama shrieked. She waved the knife. "Open his fly, I cut off!"

Kid Sally held his arm out to keep her away. He sat down across the table from Mario. "You're on the film with the priest suit?" he said. He held his hand out as if it were a boat rocking. This is the international semaphore for larceny. Mario said yes with his head. With a few more words and several hand signals, Kid Sally got the general flow of Mario's life in America.

He held up the picture. "This name on the bottom, are you *congeal* with him?"

Mario didn't understand.

"*Congeal*, he means do you know him good?" Big Jelly said.

"I don't see him yet," Mario said.

"Do you know who he is?" Kid Sally said.

Mario shook his head no.

"Dangerous old man, he finds you out, he cuts your whole head off," Kid Sally said.

Mario clutched his chest. "Then I cross out his name."

"He has money," Kid Sally said.

Mario let go of his chest. "How much money?"

"A whole roomful of money."

"Then I keep his name on the list."

"You meet him," Kid Sally said, "and we'll snatch him and get his money. I'll let you count the money while I cut his heart out." Kid Sally began to giggle. "Unless you're afraid of kidnaping an old man."

Mario closed his eyes to show fear.

Big Mama had everybody sit down for plates of spaghetti and olive oil. Nobody grumbled. They had prospects now. Angela ate in silence. She said she needed air. She and Mario went down the block to Nunzio's. An old car with dented fenders was parked a few doors up from Nunzio's. The car was parked in the wrong direction, facing the docks. Four of Kid Sally's guys, leather jackets pulled up to their cheekbones, sat in the car. Their job was to shoot at anybody or anything coming onto the street from the dock end. Another car was doing similar guard duty at the other end of the block.

Nunzio stood behind the counter, picking his silver teeth with a hunting knife. The jukebox was playing his favorite record, "Mala Femmina." The title means "Bad Woman." Nunzio always plays the record and thinks of the girl who once robbed him. While the coffee dripped from the espresso machine, Nunzio hummed and muttered his own special words to the song.

". . . whore-a basset . . ." Nunzio sang softly. As the music rose, the image of the girl who had done him wrong grew clearer in his mind. Nunzio's hand slapped down on the counter. "Rat-a whore!"

They looked out the window and did not talk. The pier was across the street from the store. The water in the slip alongside the pier was black and motionless. At the end of the pier, out in the channel, the strong night tide created ripples. Light from a slim moon splashed over the black water, and the ripples turned the light into a corrugated tray of diamonds. A tug, the running lights rigged like a necklace, moved against the tide, its snub bow throwing white water into the moonlight.

"My greenhorn," Angela said. "God knows what you *really* know." He was surprised at the tone of her voice.

"Did you bring the priest's clothes with you from Italy?" she said.

He shook his head no.

"At least," she said.

"I came here for a race and there is no race," he said. "What do I do? You know all I want to do. The painting."

"Well, that's one thing," she said.

She started to pick up the cup and stopped. The car must have been three blocks away, but it was coming so quickly its noise was clear. The car was coming from the left, racing along the deserted street in front of the piers. Nunzio stepped behind the pizza oven. Angela pulled Mario by the arm. They crouched. The car, twin exhausts booming, swept down the street along the docks and crossed Marshall Street without stopping. The four hoodlums ran from the parked car to the bundle of clothes that had been thrown from the speeding car. The bundle comprised Ezmo the Driver's new sports jacket and his slacks. Ezmo's tie was knotted around the bundle. One of the four hoodlums pulled the bundle loose. The neon from Nunzio's sign fell on the white belly of a fluke.

"They put Ezmo under the top of the water," one of the hoodlums from the car yelled.

Angela turned her head and started walking quickly. Mario caught up with her and they went along in silence. She paused for a moment in front of the house, looked up, and put her arm through his and made him keep going.

Detective Donald Jenkins, dressed in a milk-delivery uniform, sauntered out of a doorway on Columbia Avenue and followed them to the subway. As the train swayed to Manhattan, Jenkins noticed Angela taking Mario's hand and holding it tightly. He hoped they were going to a hotel. It would make surveillance easy. Twenty minutes later, when Angela and Mario went into the building on 11th Street, Jenkins watched from the corner. "I don't even know the name of the bum with her," he muttered.

In bed, Angela buried her face in Mario's chest. She shivered and tried to get the picture of the fish out of her mind. Her bare legs rubbed against Mario's. In the emptiness of the hours of the days since she had stopped going to school and begun living with slurred curses and funerals and fish in the street, Mario, simply being there, had become the only real thing in Angela's life.

Mario did not notice the softness against him. He was thinking of what it would be like to drown: thrashing in the black water, his eyes rolling wildly, his body trying to move in the chains wrapped around it, going down, down, down, realizing that he would not come up, opening his mouth to scream and immediately choking on water.

"Wa." The noise came from the bottom of Mario's throat.

"What's the matter?" Angela said. She was looking into his face.

Mario closed his eyes. Slowly, gracefully, another thought slipped into his mind. *A roomful of money.* The fear went away and he opened his eyes and smiled at her. His hands pressed on her shoulderblades and he began to come onto his side against her.

"Just remember to say that we went to an all-night movie," she whispered.

Chapter **17**

She slept late in the morning. He was up early and went right to the painting, which he kept carefully covered when Angela was around. He moved the covers from her face so he could follow the cheekbone. At 10:30 the sounds he made getting dressed woke her up. He pointed to the work under his arm. "I'll be back in one hour, two hours," he said.

She sat up. "Oh, let me look at it," she said.

He stepped away from her. "When it's finished," he said. He certainly didn't want her to see he had copied somebody else's work and tossed in only her face, or at least her cheekbones. He checked to make sure the torn original he'd been copying was under his arm too. He didn't want to leave anything around for her to see.

"I'm going to go out and get some coffee," she said.

"Uhuh."

"But I'll come right back. I don't want to be out some place and have you back here looking for me."

He walked down the staircase wondering if he wanted all this strange dependence and compliance she was showing.

He woke up Sidney again. Sidney rubbed his hands over his face to get rid of the sleep. He looked at Mario's work and let out a deep breath.

"I guess so," Sidney said.

"Yes?" Mario said. His hands were waving over Sidney's shoulder.

"I told you I guess so," Sidney said. "I don't know how the hell you did it. You got it looking like a face, not a sketch of a face."

"What should I do now?" Mario said.

"Stop breathing in my ear," Sidney said. "See Grant for anything else. The next one you do should be fast. Do ten of this thing, unload them on ten people, you'll have some sort of a living. Anyway, get the hell out of my life."

Mario was fumbling with excitement when he got to the luncheonette on his corner and dialed Dominic Laviano's number.

"Don Mario?" Laviano said. "It's good you call me. I spoke to my friend. Do you have a paper to write something down?"

Mario ripped a page out of the front of the phone book and scribbled in the white space while Dominic talked.

"Tomorrow is Wednesday. Then come Thursday. On Thursday afternoon, we see my friend. Now I have to be at the market in the Bronx. So I give you the address and you ask and get to the place yourself. I be there at three o'clock. My friend, he be there at three o'clock. So maybe you be there at three o'clock too, Don Mario?"

Dominic read off the address of a restaurant called the Della Palma on Queens Boulevard in Queens. "God bless till Thursday," Dominic said and he hung up. Mario knew he was close to money. And his art would work. Someday he would be a painter of his own. All that was in his way was a little danger.

Mario was thinking of Catanzia in the morning while he

walked back to the apartment. The smell of cow and goat urine, which hangs in every house, came into his nostrils. He thought of the white belly of the fluke in the clothes on Marshall Street. He thought of the urine smell again. It hung in his nose. He was more afraid of going back to the urine smell than he was of the fluke in the clothes.

At seven p.m. Mario took a pear from the tray on the kitchen table at Marshall Street. Casually, he took the piece of phone-book paper out of his pocket. He read out the restaurant address.

"And what time on Thursday do you meet this-a certain party?" Big Mama said.

"Three o'clock," Mario said.

Angela got up and walked out of the kitchen. She didn't want to hear. Mario put the slip of paper back into his pocket. He picked up the pear and took a deep bite.

All the years on all the streets kept running through Kid Sally's mind. He sat in the vending-machine office, rubbing his fist across his forehead, thinking slowly, step by step, of how the kidnaping and torture-death of Baccala should be done. The mistakes and missed shots and the funerals, they would all be made meaningless by one pull of a trigger. People now taking oaths on their mothers' graves to kill Kid Sally on sight would get down on one knee and kiss Kid Sally's hand if he ever got Baccala. The police would not knock on the door and bring everybody to a precinct house for questioning. Instead, they would make appointments through Kid Sally's lawyer. There would be pressure from nobody and money from everywhere.

"The truck," Kid Sally said.

"What of the truck?" Beppo the Dwarf said.

"Put a sign on it that says FISH."

A fish truck near a restaurant would seem normal.

"We need a strange car, too," Kid Sally said.

Beppo nodded. "I'll get one."

Big Mama held up her hand. "Make-a sure you throw the license plate away."

Beppo the Dwarf nodded. The art of stealing cars for purposes of murder requires, besides a stolen car, that a set of license plates must be stolen from still another car. The stolen license plates are put on the stolen car. The stolen car's plates are scaled into the river. This is because the police looking for stolen cars check license-plate numbers. And people whose license plates have been stolen never report this. They blame it on kids and go stand on line at the Motor Vehicle Bureau to get new plates. So the police are unlikely to look for any car which travels with stolen license plates. It takes at least six months for the Motor Vehicle Bureau to circulate stolen-license-plate numbers. In six months a good murderer using a stolen car in reasonable condition can cause overcrowding at a cemetery.

"We better get a couple of pieces of iron, too," Kid Sally said.

A kid named Junior and his friend, Jerry the Booster, got up and stretched. Stealing guns was their department. All shooting requires a gun that can't be traced. If you happen to shoot somebody with a gun that can be traced to your hand, jurors might happen to vote for conviction. Therefore, stolen guns are necessary.

The meeting broke up. Kid Sally, Big Jelly, Tony the Indian, and Big Lollipop went out to the car. "I got to relax a little bit so I could think clear," Kid Sally said.

The car drove off. Beppo the Dwarf went out to steal a car and license plates. And Junior and Jerry the Booster went down to the docks to steal guns and ammunition. This was one of the hardest jobs of all. Not that Junior and Jerry the Booster couldn't get onto the docks. This was easy for two tested thieves. The problem was finding the right guns and ammunition for the gang to use. The largest area of the South Brooklyn waterfront is the Brooklyn Army Terminal, a complex of gloomy gray government warehouse buildings with many piers jutting into the oily water. Large freighters load at the piers and slump through the water on the outgoing tide. They carry the basic American export. Which is why Junior and Jerry the Booster had trouble. The first pier they tried was stacked with cases of 122-mm. rockets for shipment to Haifa, Israel. On the second pier there were tarpaulin-wrapped 105-mm. howitzers addressed for shipment to Beirut, Lebanon. Junior and Jerry the Booster couldn't see how they could catch Baccala by surprise with any of this equipment. They spent the night working through crates of napalm for India and mortars for Pakistan. Finally, in an area marked for use by a United Fruit Company ship, Jerry the Booster found crates of .32 Smith and Wesson revolvers marked for Guatemala. Junior found crates of ammunition, the stencil saying it was for .32 Savage automatics.

Junior looked at the number. *Aah, .32 is .32.* "You got .32s?" he asked Jerry.

"Yop."

"I got .32s too," Junior said. He broke into the crate and began stuffing boxes of bullets into the canvas bag he was carrying.

Kid Sally and his group were taking a risk by going out. If Baccala knew about it, he would send all four hundred of his people after them. But Kid Sally was going to a place where nobody would expect him, a loud, dark discothèque named the Dream Lounge, on Bedford Avenue. To reduce the risk further, three shotguns were in the car. Kid Sally began to rock back and forth in the seat when the car pulled in front of the Dream Lounge. "This is just what I need, I need a place to think," he was saying.

Tony the Indian and Big Lollipop got out of the car first, with shotguns under their coats, and they walked into the place. Tony the Indian looked out the door and waved. Kid Sally got out of the car and smoothed his jacket. He craned his neck and fixed his tie. He put a cigarette in his mouth and lit it slowly. He hadn't felt this good in weeks. He knew that anybody looking through the door at him was looking at a real gangster. A big-league gangster. Kid Sally's shoulders swung while he walked into the place.

Big Jelly did not go directly into the Dream Lounge. He went to a drugstore on the corner. A little dark-haired man with thick glasses was behind the counter. He knew who Big Jelly was.

"Hello, baby," Big Jelly said. "How about a little something to step me up?"

"Like what," the druggist said.

"Like a fistful of red birds," Big Jelly said.

The druggist filled a small envelope with triangular-shaped red pills. He handed them to Big Jelly and then turned away to other business. He knew there was no sense in waiting to be paid even for an illegal prescription. Big Jelly ambled out and went down to the Dream Lounge. Inside, he blinked in the darkness and smoke. Tony the Indian and Big Lollipop were standing alongside the checkroom door, the shotguns bulging against their coats. They could see the street clearly. Kid Sally was on the other side of the bar. Big Jelly put two barstools together and heaved himself up on them. "One for each cheek, baby," he said to the bartender. "Now give us two glasses of water, sweetheart." Big Jelly spilled the red pills on the bar. He took three of them and swallowed them with water. Kid Sally blew smoke at the pills on the bar. He giggled and picked up three of the pills and shook them through his hand and into his mouth like peanuts.

"All right," Big Jelly said. He clapped his hands together. "Let's have a taste, sweetheart."

"What'll it be?" the bartender said.

"Double scotch and a large sauterne on the side."

Kid Sally giggled. "The same."

"Yeah!" Big Jelly said.

There was a whine from the loudspeaker system, and a four-piece band, back from a break, got set on the bandstand. The name of the band was Looey and the Birds. With a crash of electric guitars and drums, they started playing a tune whose key line was, "Your fat ass!"

The music pepped up Kid Sally. "Yeah!" he yelled out and swallowed the scotch. He banged his shot glass on the bar for more. The bartender poured scotch into the glass, then turned around and took a pencil from his ear and marked the drink down on a sheet of paper. A big sign on the register said: WE GIVE CREDIT ONLY TO A REAL CORPSE. The bartender knew enough not to bring it up. Kid Sally brought the shot glass to his mouth. He tilted his head back a little, then more, and finally, his head all the way back, his eyes looking up into the blinking psychedelic lights, he threw the scotch down and came rocking forward and slapped the shot glass on the bar with one hand and raised the sauterne with the other and threw the wine down and then he let out another shout.

"Could you see us when they hear what we done to that old greaseball?" he said to Big Jelly.

"There'd be a line-up of guys wantin' to kiss my ass that'd be longer than the two-dollar window at the track," Big Jelly said.

"Yeah!" Kid Sally said.

"And you," Big Jelly said. "They'd be lightin' candles and prayin' *to* you. You hear me? Prayin' *to* you."

"Yeah!" Kid Sally said.

"Let's have a taste, sweetheart," Big Jelly yelled to the bartender.

On the bandstand, Looey and the Birds screamed, ". . . Your fat ass! . . ." and Kid Sally and Big Jelly swallowed more scotch, and the red pills were putting glass into their eyes. A girl in a Curley McDimple wig came past the bar from the ladies' room, and Kid Sally grabbed her by the arm and pulled her to him.

"Hey," she said.

"Hey, what?" Kid Sally said.

"Buy baby a drink," she said. She chewed gum methodically and her head bounced in time to the music.

Big Jelly shook more pills onto the bar and he grabbed a couple and Kid Sally grabbed a couple and the girl looked at the remaining pills, made a face, and said, "Oh, medicine? All right, baby takes her medicine." She pushed the pills into her mouth and reached for a scotch to wash them down. Kid Sally began clapping his hands to the music. Big Jelly grabbed the bottom of her skirt and lifted it up.

"You show me yours and I'll show you mine," he said.

"Fresh," she said, hitting his hand.

"What about me, can't I show my thing to somebody?" Kid Sally said.

The three began slapping the bar and yelling for something to drink and the girl kept chewing gum and rocking to the music. Big Jelly was having trouble keeping his eyes straight, and when Kid Sally tilted his head back to throw down the double scotch, some of it ran out of the corners of his mouth and he was licking with his tongue and he kept his head tilted back, looking straight up into the maze of blinking lights, and he saw himself, very clearly, riding to Baccala's funeral in an open car, with the sidewalks of South Brooklyn lined with people clapping for the new boss of the outfit.

Mrs. Maxine Finestone was telling Mrs. Lucille Goldman, over tea and watercress sandwiches in the Plaza, that "We would never go to Lauderdale, but the boat *was* there, so you see we really had no choice. Now, to get on the boat, you had to go across this skinny little plank, just a splinter really, and in the darkness, my Lord, you could see nothing but all this water underneath you, and who knew how deep it was? So here's this little splinter of wood and do you know what Jack said? 'Maxine, you go first.' I said, 'Me? Why should *I* have to?' Jack said to me, 'I want to make sure the board won't break.' Well, dopey me, I start going out on this piece of wood. And here is my husband, standing there holding out his hand. 'Maxine, first give me the diamonds.'"

"Oh, that's your husband," Lucille Goldman said.

"You're telling me," Maxine Finestone said. "Oh, hello, isn't this nice? Grant, how *are* you?"

Grant Monroe was trying to say hello when Mario, lockstepping behind him, tripped on one of his open shoelaces and shoved Grant into Maxine Finestone's lap.

"Maxine," Grant Monroe said, "this young man is from Italy, and— Oh, Maxine! Isn't that a striking pin! Yes, this young man is from Italy. His name is Mario Trantino. This is his very first work and I was thinking to myself, *Now who could look at this?* Of course I could only think of one person."

"Why, *thank* you."

Mario bent down to kiss Maxine Finestone's hand, but because of his uncle's glasses he couldn't see and missed the hand completely. He stuck his tongue out and caught the hand with a dog lick just as his mouth went by. He swung into a chair. Grant Monroe began walking backward. Grant shook his head at Mario's paint-splattered hair. He could see Mario had twirled a paintbrush through it just before coming to the Plaza. Grant was not happy to duck away from Mario. Grant was in ecstasy.

"This painting is a very low price because it is the first I ever have done," Mario said to Maxine Finestone. "But someday, when I am very famous, this painting will be a very rich thing to have in your own house." Mario had rehearsed the line with Grant out in the lobby. It is the major line all artists have used on buyers since Michelangelo tried it on the Pope. Maxine Finestone smiled as she heard it. Her qualifications as one of the city's best-known supporters of young artists consist of a taste acquired in commercial courses at George Washington High School, a year behind the counter of her family's dairy delicatessen, and a husband named Jack, who runs a big junk business. Jack loves any painting that is explained to him in terms of an investment. For pure art, Jack Finestone will place Delco Battery posters on his walls.

"Well," Maxine Finestone said, "the face is *quite* interesting."

"Think of what this will be worth when I am famous," Mario said. Maxine Finestone nodded.

Mario tripped out of the hotel with his chest pounding. Maxine Finestone had taken the work home to her Fifth Avenue apartment. She told Mario she would have her mind made up the following afternoon. Mario almost expected to hear her say she would pay about $300 for the work. If he could put ten of the same painting on the market in a hurry, he would have the beginning of a career that one day might even become completely honest.

"So if she buys it," Angela was saying later, "that means I'll never see the first thing you ever did."

"The next one you'll see," Mario said.

"But it won't be the same thing," she said.

"It's all the same thing," he said.

He dropped the subject before it got him into trouble. They were walking into the doorway on Marshall Street, and Beppo the Dwarf stuck his head out of the vending-machine office and called Mario. Angela kept going upstairs. She did not want to hear any of it.

In the office, Kid Sally was tilted back on a chair so the rear of his head would press against the wall. This relieved some of the throbbing from the hangover the whisky and pills had left. The last thing he remembered about the night before was being in somebody's apartment and watching Big Jelly try something involving a kitchen chair and a naked girl. Big Jelly was still in the apartment.

"Now is tomorrow all right still?" Kid Sally said. Mario shook his head yes. "Then why do we got to be in suspansion all day here? Why didn't you come here early?"

"Forget. Say something important," Big Mama said. She was standing by the door. She motioned Mario to sit down.

"Let's see how we do this," Kid Sally said. His eyes, puffy, closed.

Big Mama snorted. She pointed to Mario. "You just sit in-a restaurant. When two men come in deliver the fish, you get-a you ass up and you get-a you ass out of the restaurant."

Kid Sally's eyes opened. He pointed two fingers at Mario. "Two guys with white coats on, they'll be carrying baskets of ice and fish. They'll come in like they're delivering to the kitchen. You get up like you got to go to the bat'room. Only you keep goin'."

"Where to?" Mario said.

"Right out to the subway. Go right home and stay there until you hear from one of us," Kid Sally said.

"No stop!" Big Mama said.

"If you said it, don't stop," Kid Sally said. "You just make sure you're not inside that restaurant when the two fishmen get to the table."

"Sally Kid," Beppo the Dwarf said, "when we bring this old man here, how are we goin' to get all his moneys out of him? He won't have all his moneys on him."

Kid Sally's lip came up in his sneer and he began to giggle. "We bring Baccala here, and we all say to him, 'Baccala, you nice old guinea, where you keep all your moneys hid?' "

"But he no say," Big Mama said. "But we no get mad at him. We take-a off his shoe. Rub the foot. Nice rub. Then we cut off the little toe!"

Kid Sally gazed fondly on his grandmother. "He still don't tell us. What do we do? We're stuck. The man won't talk. We tell him, 'Old man, you go home now. You look tired, old man.' But we can't let him go home like he is. He walks all crooked with the one toe off one foot. So we even up his balance. We take off his shoe and cut off the other little toe!"

"He no like that," Big Mama said.

"He tells us where he got his money," Kid Sally said. "He tells us because he got ten whole toes and he got ten whole fingers, too. We either get it in ransom or we go right to where it's hid. Whichever. But we're going to keep slicing until we get moneys."

"And then we come right back here and we cut out Baccala's heart and throw it to the lion!" Big Mama said.

Big Mama cackled. Beppo clapped his hands. Kid Sally giggled uncontrollably. The giggle became a roar.

Mario was not quite sure whether or not he actually passed out during the conversation. He did know that both his little toes had severe pains shooting through them. Dimly he heard Big Mama lecturing him about getting a night's sleep so he would be alert. He left the office and wandered up the street like a piece of frozen wash. He heard Angela running up after him and Big Mama calling to her, "Where you go?" and Angela, putting her hand on his arm, calling back, "I'm going, that's all." All the way to the subway, Mario struggled for breath. "A roomful of money," he kept repeating. He imagined Mrs. Finestone's voice on the telephone, telling him how beautiful his work was and to come up for the money any time. The two thoughts kept him on his feet until he got home. He fell onto the bed and was asleep immediately. Angela pulled the blanket over him. Exhaustion from fear made his face break into a heavy sweat while he slept.

Chapter **18**

The Della Palma Restaurant is on Queens Boulevard, in the Queens section of New York. To get there you take the Queensboro Bridge, a maze of gray spiderwork which rises out of the East Side of Manhattan and climbs across the East River. You begin the trip watching a maid cleaning the picture window of a $2000-a-month Sutton Place apartment. When you come out on the other side, there is a workman staring out of a factory window and eating a hero sandwich for lunch. Queens Boulevard starts there, amidst the el pillars and industrial slop of a place they call Long Island City. Queens Boulevard becomes a broad, crowded avenue which runs past the Irish bars of Sunnyside, grows side walls of apartments in Rego Park and Forest Hills, and comes to an end with one last apartment house, a gas station, a supermarket, and, sitting by itself, in a one-story building erected for a store, the Della Palma. Queens Boulevard then ducks down onto an expressway that goes into Kennedy Airport, two miles away. The Della Palma has always been a quiet, almost sleepy restaurant with most of its trade coming from nearby apartment houses. It became an odd-hours favorite of Baccala's because of its closeness to the airport. Big guys from out of town flew in, had shrimp and clams oreganato with Baccala, then flew out without being seen.

At ten on Thursday morning a black-haired, dark-eyed guy of about twenty-five sat in a booth against the window of the Empress Diner, three blocks from the Della Palma. He looked out at housewives talking in the bright, cold, windy morning on Queens Boulevard. Jackie Dunne is from the Horseshoe Bend section of Jersey City, which is perhaps the world's leading supplier of Irish gunmen. He is so dark that he uses Italian names, particularly the one he had chosen for the day, Vincent Scuderi. The only thing that gave Jackie Dunne away as being Irish, and you had to be Irish yourself to notice it, was the way he sat in the booth and drank his coffee. The coffee was too hot, so he spilled some of it into the saucer and picked up the saucer and began blowing on the coffee to cool it. He slurped coffee from the saucer. He did it carefully, holding the saucer far out over the table and craning his neck to it. When he set the saucer down, he ran the thumb and forefinger of each hand down the lapels of his gray suit. He began to fuss with an already immaculately knotted tie.

A probation report once devoted three full pages to Jackie Dunne's fastidiousness. The report urged he be sent to a place where young psychiatrists could study him. "He is the perfect psychopathic gunman," the report concluded. The judge, a sixty-seven-year-old product of political clubhouses, detested psychiatrists. He threw out the medical testimony and sentenced Jackie Dunne seven and a half to ten years at Attica. Jackie Dunne for three years was the star halfback of the same D Block football team on which Kid Sally Palumbo played quarterback. Jackie had seen Kid Sally off and on for the last year. Two days ago Kid Sally had sent a messenger, Joe the Sheik, over to a poolroom in Jersey City to make Jackie Dunne an offer. Kid Sally would pay $1500 for Jackie's services on Thursday. Payment would be within three days. He was to tend bar in the Della Palma Restaurant and put things in the drinks of any bodyguards Baccala came into the place with. Jackie Dunne had a face none of the Baccala people knew. When the bodyguards were out of the way, Jackie Dunne could split.

"What if the geepos with Baccala don't drink nothin'?" Jackie Dunne said.

"Hey, don't *axt* me, go axt Eisenhower," Joe the Sheik said.

Jackie Dunne thought the arrangements were sloppy, but he still took the job. For $1500, Jackie Dunne would fight tigers.

Now, right on schedule, Jackie Dunne sat in the diner booth with envelopes of chloral-hydrate crystals in his pocket and a .38 stuffed into the front of his belt, right behind the buckle.

Ten blocks down Queens Boulevard, Tony Lombardo came out of the elevator and pushed the door to the basement garage of his apartment building. Tony didn't have to be to work at the Della Palma until eleven. But he liked to get in early and dawdle over coffee and arrange the small bar so he could handle the lunchtime rush without having to keep reaching for bottles left in the wrong places. Tony liked the job at the Della Palma. The lunch hour was busy, but it tailed off sharply at two, and the restaurant was usually totally empty until five.

Tony Lombardo had the door open and he was walking into the garage when somebody put a gun to his left ear.

"You're dead," Big Jelly said to him. "Take a deep breath and you're dead."

A few minutes later a blue fish truck came slowly past the Empress Diner on Queens Boulevard. Beppo the Dwarf began waving out the window of the truck. Jackie Dunne, sitting at the diner window, nodded.

Big Jelly was wiping his forehead while he drove the truck. "I should of gone to the Turkish bath," he told Beppo the

Dwarf. "I'm still shot from the other night." In the back of the truck Tony Lombardo was tied up like a chicken. He was so frightened that he fell asleep.

One of the waiters in the Della Palma was fixing up the tables in the front, so he answered the phone when it rang. "This is Sailor, the agent for Local Fifteen," a voice, Kid Sally Palumbo's, said. "Your regular bartender, Tony, he won't make it today. Guy's sick. He called in a half-hour ago. So we're sending a very good man down to you. Name of Scuderi. He should be there ten, fifteen minutes from now."

The waiter said he guessed it was all right and hung up. He walked back to the kitchen and told Nick, the owner. Nick said he hoped Tony was all right. Ten minutes later, exactly, Jackie Dunne walked into the restaurant. "You got coffee made yet?" he asked a waiter. Jackie hung his jacket in the checkroom and put on the red bartender's jacket that was on the hook. He checked to make sure the jacket came down far enough to cover the pistol in his belt. He went behind the bar and moved his shoulders around inside the red jacket. This was, he told himself, going to be the easiest $1500 he ever earned.

On one side, the Della Palma is separated from the supermarket by a large parking lot. On the other side of the restaurant there is an empty lot. The restaurant is in a long, narrow building. You enter a small vestibule which has a cigarette machine and two pay telephones on the wall. You step to the left and come into the bar area. Used mainly for service, it is a small bar, which faces you as you come out of the vestibule. At one end the bar stops at the storefront plate-glass window half covered with drapes. Opposite the bar is the checkroom and a staircase going down to the men's and ladies' rooms. The bar area ends at a breakfront. Behind it is the long, narrow restaurant, running back to the kitchen. Deliveries to the restaurant are made through the front door, to save the deliverymen the trouble of slogging to the back of the store. There is no room behind the Della Palma for anything to park. The Della Palma keeps its back door locked and barred. Which is another reason why Baccala always liked the restaurant.

At 10:30 Mario and Angela sat next to each other in a booth in the coffee shop on the corner near his flat. The windows of the shop were frosted in the cold and the wind. Brightness from the unseen sun flooded through the frosted windows and spilled onto the aluminum and formica of the coffee shop. Angela tucked her legs under her on the seat and leaned against Mario. She spooned grape jelly onto a half-piece of toast and held the toast up to Mario. He took a bite of it. They smiled at each other. Mario sat and drank coffee with the steady, gentle weight of her body against him.

It was nearly 2:15 p.m. when the waiters in the Della Palma moved through the dining room, changing tablecloths and putting out water glasses and silverware shining from the dishwasher. Three salesmen, sitting over espresso, were the last customers in the restaurant. One of the men picked up the espresso pot and tilted it over his cup. A small black trickle ran out of the thin spout. He put the pot down and asked the men with him if he should order another pot. They shook their heads no. The man waved for a check. When the three salesmen took their coats out of the checkroom and walked past the bar to go out, Jackie Dunne slipped a hand under his jacket and patted the gun stuck into his belt. *I'm on next*, he said to himself.

Dominic Laviano walked in at a quarter to three. He nodded to Jackie Dunne and stood at the breakfront until a waiter came and helped him out of his coat. "There be three or four of us," Dominic said. The waiter led him to a table in the middle of the room.

Ten minutes later a black Cadillac pulled in front of the restaurant. Two black suits got out of it and came into the restaurant. They waved to Dominic Laviano and went back out to the car. Baccala, flanked by black suits, paraded into the Della Palma. He walked past the bar without looking at Jackie Dunne. He took no notice of the waiter helping him out of his coat. If royalty were to acknowledge each chambermaid, royalty would become painfully common.

Baccala went to the table. The two black suits took up posts at the bar.

"Help you fellas?" Jackie Dunne said.

"Gimme dimes for the meter," one of them said. He put a dollar on the bar.

"Somethin' to drink too?" Jackie said.

"I said gimme dimes for the meter, that's all I said," the black suit said.

Jackie gave him ten dimes. The black suits walked out to the car. The Water Buffalo had already eaten lunch. He did not care to sit through a conversation with some priest. If Baccala wanted to talk and buy his way into heaven, that was fine. But the Water Buffalo was not interested. "I'm going to take a ride aroun' for a half-hour or so," the Water Buffalo said. The black suits asked him for the dimes back. The Water Buffalo spat at them and started the car up.

"What am I, a dope? He beats me for a whole dollar," one of them said. The black suits came back and sat at the bar and kept looking out the window to check the street. Jackie Dunne could see the outlines of the pistols in shoulder holsters under their suits.

Mario's knees buckled when he came through the door. The two black suits jumped up, hands inside their jackets. Mario threw open the raincoat to show the priest's collar. Dominic Laviano, who had been watching for Mario, waved to him. Mario walked to the table, torn by a tremendous fear of what was behind him and a tremendous greed for the man in front of him. Baccala had been breaking off pieces of bread to chew on with his wine. He had the tablecloth and the floor around his feet covered with brown breadcrust. Dominic Laviano presented Don Mario Trantino to Baccala. Baccala grunted. For a cardinal, perhaps, Baccala would extend a hand and rise.

"Now I bless this table and all who eat at it," Mario said.

"*Grazie*," Baccala mumbled.

Mario's right hand rose. He murmured in Latin.

"You say one more prayer?" Baccala said.

"Certainly," Mario said.

"Say a prayer that all people who don't like Baccala will get cancer."

Mario pretended not to hear this.

Dominic Laviano waved for a waiter. The waiters were all in the kitchen, reading newspapers and listening to a radio. None of them got up. Dominic sat with his hand waving over his head like he was a helicopter.

Baccala took a breath. "Hey!" he shouted.

Waiters spilled out of the kitchen, the napkins over their arms flapping as they ran to the table.

Mario looked at the menu. He was about to talk to the waiter when Dominic Laviano nudged him into silence.

"You like-a shrimp and clams oreganato?" Baccala said to Dominic.

"Yes."

"You like-a?" he said to Mario. Dominic nudged again.

"Yes."

Baccala smiled. "Then we have spaghetti alla Carbonara, right?"

"Right," Dominic said.

"And veal alla marsala."

"Good," Dominic said. He nudged Mario again. Mario smiled that it was fine.

Mario waited until Baccala finished mopping a piece of bread through the last gravy from the shrimps and clams before bringing out the picture. He handed it to Baccala.

"When did you leave Catanzia?" he asked Baccala.

"I come from Sicilia," Baccala said.

Mario's throat stuck together. Baccala studied the picture. He turned it over and read the note. He went back to the picture again.

"*Che peccat'*," Dominic Laviano said. "And the people from Catanzia who are here, they don't have so much money."

Baccala looked at the picture. He seemed indifferent. He put it down and leaned forward.

"You hear my-a confess'?"

"Yes," Mario said.

"And when you hear this-a confess', you give the absolution?"

"Oh, of course," Mario said.

"You guarantee I go to heaven?"

Mario nodded vigorously.

Baccala leaned back in his chair. He pursed his lips. "Now, what if I no tell you everything in this confess'? You still put me heaven?"

"How could a man of such bearing as yourself not tell the truth?" Mario said.

"I no lie," Baccala said. "I just no tell."

"If you don't tell me a thing in confession, why, it means you just forget to tell it," Mario said. "This does not mean you lie, or you hide something. You just forget."

Baccala poked Dominic Laviano. "Young priests, they the best of the best. These old geepos, they sit there and they say, 'Baccala, go 'way.'"

Baccala leaned forward with his chin almost touching the table. He whispered.

"Besides, I only peek up the little girl's dress. I no touch."

"Oh, you are a man of honor," Mario said.

Baccala raised his wineglass. "*Salut!*"

At the bar, Jackie Dunne was getting a little nervous. The two black suits had ordered nothing. Jackie fingered the chloral hydrate in his pocket.

"Time for a drink, fellas," he said.

"Screwdrivers," one of the black suits said. Jackie's eye caught the fish truck pulling up outside.

Big Jelly pulled the truck into the same space the Water Buffalo had pulled out of. Kid Sally sat alongside him. Both were wearing long white deliverymen's coats, gray truck-driver's caps, and big round sunglasses.

"Don't look, but the two bums is right there in the window," Big Jelly said.

"What the hell is Jackie doin' in there?" Kid Sally said.

"We'll just have to wait, what can I tell you," Big Jelly said.

Beppo the Dwarf crouched in the back of the truck. Two baskets of chopped ice and codfish were on the floor by the doors. Tony Lombardo was asleep with his head against one of the baskets. The ice water seeped out of the basket and went into his hair. Tony shivered in his sleep. He was dreaming that he was in Antarctica. Beppo sat with coils of nylon rope, four sets of handcuffs, and Johnson & Johnson five-inch adhesive tape. He had to be ready for fast moving. The plan was to load Baccala onto the truck, kick Tony Lombardo off it, then truss up Baccala while the truck sped away.

He had one other thing to do. He reached into a paper bag and brought out three of the stolen blue-black Savage automatics. He opened a box of the stolen bullets. He had a little trouble loading the automatics.

"Here you go," Beppo said. He held out two loaded automatics. Kid Sally took them. Beppo stuffed the third into his belt.

Just up from the Della Palma, in front of the supermarket, Mrs. Rosalind Seneca Wiggins, who is known to her friends as Roz, sauntered along in her brand new size-46 blue-gray Meter Maid uniform. Roz was big enough to be listed in *Jane's Fighting Ships*. Rox had been on the job for three days. She was hired at a salary of $75 a week by the City of New York. Her job was to patrol a six-block stretch of Queens Boulevard and put tickets on all vehicles that were illegally parked. Illegal parking includes all those cars parked in front of meters which have a red flag showing to indicate the half-hour has expired.

Roz loved her new job. Instead of scrubbing floors for white people, she could walk along and give them $15 tickets. She stopped in front of the supermarket for a moment. She had a few more meters to check; then she could start on the opposite side of the boulevard. She glanced at the clock in the supermarket. It was almost 3:30. Roz quit at four.

From the window by the bar, the two black suits were unable to make out who was sitting in the front seat of the fish truck. They began muttering about the truck being parked and nobody coming out of it. Jackie Dunne heard this and picked up two glasses and began grabbing ice cubes, swirling orange juice and vodka bottles around. He made two drinks and put them on the sink under the bar. He went to his pocket for the chloral hydrate. The crystals dissolved into the orange juice. They dissolved into a heavy smell of chlorine, a stronger smell than a swimming pool gives off. Jackie let the drinks stand for a moment. He hoped the smell would go away. He was becoming very nervous now. He had never used knockout drops before. All he had ever done was hear about them. Just put them in a drink, everybody said, and the other guy never knows the difference and the next thing you know, he's on the floor. Like most of these things, it was nonsense. Jackie Dunne bent over and sniffed the drinks again. His stomach turned. The odor was even heavier now. Nobody sane would touch a drink like this. Jackie draped a towel over his hand and went to his belt for the pistol. He kept the gun hand down. He put the drinks on the bar with the other.

"Fellas," he said.

The two black suits turned around. They picked up the glasses. The smell hit their noses at once.

Jackie's hand brought up the pistol under the towel. "Right there," Jackie said. The hands were tense and shook a little. They stayed motionless holding the drinks, but Jackie knew he had only a few seconds to keep them under control.

Jackie made sure the gun did not move a fraction of an inch. One show of motion, even tiny motion, would send both these guys flopping to the floor and pulling out their guns. Jackie could feel his weight automatically come back on the heels so he could pull away if one of them threw a glass.

"Very slow, bring your mouth down to the glass. Down, not up." They bent over, their eyes glaring up at him the way a dog does when he has a bone in his mouth. *Look out, look out, or here they go,* Jackie said to himself.

"Now drink the whole thing," he said quickly.

In the tension and fear, the two black suits knew the smell was there, but they didn't really notice it. The word "poison" ran through their minds.

Jackie Dunne pushed the gun at them and their bodies jumped. "Drink!" he said.

Each of them took a small gulp.

"I said drink!" Jackie said. His nerves were beginning to take over his voice and his body. His voice was tight, and the gun waved quickly.

The black suits, still looking at him, began swallowing.

When they got near the bottom, Jackie waved the gun at them again.

"All right. Slow. Glasses down. Both hands on the bar. Slow."

The two stood hunched over the bar and Jackie held the gun on them. Three pairs of hands were twitching, and three sets of lips were trembling. Jackie knew it was going to start any fraction of a second. His finger was wet on the trigger.

One of the black suits felt his insides falling into his pants. He put a hand over his mouth and threw up into it. The other black suit exploded from every opening in his body except his ears.

They were coughing and retching and Jackie went inside their jackets and pulled out the guns. He dropped them into the sink. He stuffed his own pistol back into his belt. With a deep, free breath he came out from behind the bar and took each of them by the arm and tugged them to the stairs leading to the men's room. Jackie glanced into the dining room. Through the breakfront, he could see the three at the table busy talking. He pushed the two black suits onto the stairs. Throwing up, gagging, coming out of both ends, the black suits staggered down the steps.

Jackie stepped into the checkroom. He took off the red jacket, grabbed his suit jacket, and swung out of the checkroom. He was out on the street in two steps, heading for the subway.

Kid Sally jumped. "That's it," he said. He fumbled with the door and tumbled out of the truck onto the street side. Big Jelly, wiping the hangover sweat from his face, came onto the sidewalk. He felt himself bumping into something while he was heading for the back of the truck.

"Please watch where you goin'," Roz said. She was standing with her Meter Maid book open, standing right in front of the meter the fish truck was parked at, the meter with the red flag showing.

In the back of the truck, Kid Sally and Big Jelly were grabbing the baskets of fish from Beppo the Dwarf. They each put a basket on a shoulder and started for the restaurant.

"What's this?" Kid Sally said. Roz was copying down the license-plate number from the front of the truck.

"Get rid of her," Kid Sally said. He kept walking to the door.

"Come on, lady," Big Jelly said to Roz.

"Just as soon as I finish my job," Roz said.

Kid Sally was in the Della Palma vestibule now, leaning against the cigarette machine. The ice water was running out of the fish basket and down his arm and onto his hand. He was afraid the hand would be slippery when he held the gun. *Come on, Jelly,* he said to himself.

Big Jelly was standing chest to chest with Roz. "Hey, lady, we're workin', go bother somebody else," he said.

"When I finish," Roz said. She said it slowly and without looking up from the pad on which she was writing.

"Come on," Big Jelly said.

Roz did not answer.

"Oh come on, you fuckin' nigger," Big Jelly said.

Roz put the top back on her pen.

"Black cunt," Big Jelly said.

Roz put the pen back into the breast pocket of her uniform.

"Old nigger cunt."

Roz tore off the parking ticket from her pad. She was careful to tear it on the perforated line.

"I'll piss on your leg, you fuckin' nigger."

Roz walked over to the truck and began to stick the ticket to the windshield-wiper.

"Fuckin' nigger cunt."

"You know," Roz said very softly and very offhandedly, "you know, you should of been a cop. Yes, you should of been a cop. Because your father was a police dog, you fat motherfucker."

Big Jelly held the basket of fish over his head like he was King Kong. He brought it down onto Roz's head. He threw a kick at Roz's legs. Roz twisted away, and the kick missed. She pulled the basket off her head with one hand. The other was out in front of her, reaching and pawing and finding Big Jelly's fat cheek. Big Jelly threw a wild left hand onto the side of Roz's head. Mrs. Rosalind Seneca Wiggins, who has a head that has broken a thousand bottles, took the punch, blinked, and reached for Big Jelly's private parts. She had to dig hard through the apron, but she got them. A scream went up from Big Jelly's mouth. His left knee came up to his chest.

Kid Sally banged his head against the cigarette machine. He dropped the basket onto the floor and pulled out the automatic. Now there was no plan and no time. Now he could only do one thing: go inside and kill Baccala cowboy-style and come running for his life. Kid Sally's lip came up in a sneer. He began to giggle. The gun out, giggling, the giggle becoming very loud, he came into the Della Palma Restaurant for a shooting that would go down in gangland history, go down with the killing of Albert Anastasia in the barber chair and Vincent Coll in the phone booth and Willie Moretti in a clam bar.

The waiter and Mario saw Kid Sally at the same time. The waiter was coming out of the kitchen with a pan of spaghetti alla Carbonara to serve the table. The spaghetti alla Carbonara went into the air and the waiter belly-whopped under a table. Mario saw Kid Sally because for the last fifteen minutes Mario had been watching the door out of one corner of his eye so he could run the moment the fish deliverymen came in.

Now, when Mario saw Kid Sally coming in with the gun out, a roar filled his ears. He came out of his chair with his hands out and a scream.

"Gesù!"

Dominic Laviano dove to the left. Baccala, mouth open, eyes wide, tried to get off the chair. He could not move.

Kid Sally brushed through two tables, giggling, the gun coming out farther. Mario fell over him.

"Gesù!"

Kid Sally's left hand pushed against Mario. The giggle now turned into a shriek. Kid Sally jammed the gun against Baccala's temple. Baccala's eyes closed. His face twisted. Kid Sally could hear Big Mama in his mind, Big Mama shouting at him, "No miss!" Kid Sally pulled the trigger, and the explosion filled the room and Baccala tumbled from his chair. Kid Sally had wanted to empty the automatic into Baccala's head, but he could not do this because the wrong-sized ammunition blew up the gun right away. In one flash Kid Sally's hand was shredded and his dreams and chances were gone and he was in shock, with blood from his hand running all over him. He turned and did not remember running out of the place and into the brightness and the wind and the cold and Big Jelly screaming on the sidewalk.

The side of Baccala's head burned. He could feel the huge hole in his head. He closed his eyes tighter. He was afraid to open them and have to look at the Sacred Heart. His heart pounded so hard that he heard nothing else. Then his leg began to ache from being doubled under him. Baccala's heart slowed. Why should his leg hurt him when he was dead? Baccala opened his eyes. He saw the floor of the Della Palma and Dominic Laviano's ass. Slowly Baccala's hand reached for the hole in the side of his head. There was no hole. His fingers touched the hair over his ear, which had been singed by the powder burn. His fingers ran over the entire side of his face. There wasn't even blood.

Baccala got up from the floor. He looked into Mario's eyes. Baccala bowed his head. He clasped his hands.

"*Mirac'*," Baccala said softly.

He looked up into Mario's eyes. "*Mirac'*," he said to Mario.

Baccala looked up at the ceiling and shouted it. "*Mirac'.*" Baccala came around the table and jumped into Mario's arms and began licking Mario's face with his tongue. "*Mirac'*," he kept slobbering.

Chapter **19**

The Water Buffalo turned the corner slowly and came back onto Queens Boulevard. As he was thinking quite hard about women's underwear, the full impact of what was happening did not reach him all at once. First his eyes focused, and, three-quarters of a second later, his mind registered on Beppo the Dwarf tumbling out of the back of the panel truck in front of the restaurant. "Germ!" the Water Buffalo's mind shouted. His foot came down on the gas. The car shot toward the dwarf. Beppo darted for the sidewalk. The Water Buffalo had to swerve the car and hit the brakes. The Water Buffalo's head nearly went through the windshield. When the Water Buffalo righted himself, he saw Kid Sally Palumbo, hands pressed to his midsection, hopping around in front of the restaurant like a chicken. The Water Buffalo did not see Big Jelly, who was pounding both his hands on top of Roz's head. This was being done in order to force her teeth to slip loose from their tight grip on Big Jelly's left ear. Big Jelly was also bleeding from the nose. Roz had bitten him there first.

So the Water Buffalo jackknifed over the car seat and began fishing for the shotgun on the floor in the back and he was figuring only on Kid Sally Palumbo and he never saw Big Jelly reel up to the car. Big Jelly reached through the driver's window and put his pistol into the back of the Water Buffalo's neck. Beppo the Dwarf opened the back door, grabbed the shotgun away from the Water Buffalo, and pressed an automatic into the Water Buffalo's cheek. Kid Sally Palumbo, trying to wring the pain from his bleeding hand, pushed into the back seat. He was closing the door with his good hand while Big Jelly got the car going. Big Jelly had Baccala's limousine up to 65 by the time it hit the corner. The Water Buffalo sat in a daze in the back seat. Kid Sally Palumbo, giggling through the pain, held the shotgun muzzle right under the Water Buffalo's chin.

There was so much traffic on the parkway going to Brooklyn that Kid Sally and Big Jelly agreed it would be foolish to kill the Water Buffalo and throw him out of the car. "Besides, I want to have some fun with this punk," Kid Sally said. He slapped the Water Buffalo in the mouth with the shotgun muzzle. At Marshall Street, they pushed the Water Buffalo into the vending-machine office. Beppo went into the desk and came out with a pair of handcuffs and a roll of his Johnson and Johnson five-inch tape. They handcuffed the Water Buffalo's hands behind his back, slapped tape over his mouth, and used most of the roll to bind his ankles. Beppo opened the cellar door, and Big Jelly half lifted and half kicked the Water Buffalo down the stairs.

"Get me some rope," Kid Sally said to Beppo.

Beppo clapped his hands. "Geez, a garrote!"

"I'm gonna get somethin' out of this freakin' day," Kid Sally said.

The Water Buffalo tumbled down the cellar stairs in the darkness. Right away, his nostrils flared in the urine smell. The Water Buffalo rolled onto his stomach on the floor at the foot of the cellar stairs. He heard a rustle off to one side. His eyes darted around. Five or six steps away, framed in the half-light from a cellar window, was an apparition, a tousle-haired lion. The Water Buffalo slipped into mild shock. He exploded out of the shock when the apparition began moving. The Water Buffalo started rolling to get away from the lion. This had the same effect on the lion that a rolling spool of thread does on a cat. The lion leaped. The lion then pounced on the Water Buffalo. The Water Buffalo was in the face-down section of his roll when the lion landed. As the Water Buffalo came face up, he was looking straight up into the lion's face. It was the last thing the Water Buffalo ever saw. He did not go into mild shock this time. He went into straight heart failure and was dead in a moment.

"Come on, come on," Kid Sally Palumbo was saying a few minutes later. He pinched the Water Buffalo's cheek. There was no response. He began twisting the cheek. Nothing happened. Kid Sally bent over and looked closely.

"The freakin' rat lion killed him!" he shouted. He jumped up and went for the lion. The lion scuttled into a hole in the piles of junk in the cellar.

"Just when we were going to say somethin'," Big Jelly said.

"This rat bastard," Beppo said. He kicked the Water Buffalo. "This guy never was no fun in his whole life. He just proved it."

"We got to split out of here right away," Kid Sally said. "When the cops get here they'll stay for breakfast they'll be here so long."

Big Jelly slapped the cinderblock wall. He went to the toolbox under the stairs and pulled out a sledgehammer and chisel.

At 5:45 the three of them came out into the early winter darkness with the Water Buffalo's body, which had a cinderblock tied to the ankles and another tied to the neck. The vending-machine office was crowded.

"What you hang here for?" Kid Sally said as he struggled out the door. "You know how many cops is going to make it here?"

"Will the cops shoot us?" one of the crowd said.

"No, but—"

"Then we stay here," the guy cut in.

They threw the body into the back of Baccala's car. Big Jelly drove. They had hours to kill before the street emptied and they could get rid of a body without having an audience. Big Jelly drove to Dr. Lambert's office. Lambert was trembling. He had received rumors, and now, looking at Kid Sally's hand, he knew he was seeing direct evidence. He cleaned the hand and put in seven stitches. With each stitch, he shook a bit more. By the time he got to Big Jelly, Lambert was an epileptic. Roz the Meter Maid's worst bite had been on Big Jelly's nose. Lambert slipped, bit his tongue, tried again, and, accompanied by a long wolf howl from Big Jelly, succeeded in stitching Big Jelly's nostrils together. Big Jelly came out of the office with his nose covered with tape and his mouth hanging open so he could breathe. Kid Sally's hand was wrapped in bandages, but the trigger finger was usable. Beppo the Dwarf opened the car door for them and they drove off.

A mile away, in the Brooklyn Municipal Building, Benjamin Goodman was sitting in his office with Inspector Gallagher and a detective from the 103rd Squad in Queens, which had caught the trouble at the Della Palma.

"All right now, let me see if I have this," Goodman said. "Inside there was Baccala, a man named Laviano, and a priest."

"That's as far as we know. Plus the help."

"All right. And outside there was who, now?"

"Catalano . . ."

"Is he the fat slob?" Goodman asked.

"Yes. And the dwarf, and we're pretty sure there was one or two others in a getaway car some place but they never showed. They must of panicked."

"And Kid Sally, of course," Goodman said.

"What else?" Gallagher said.

"And you have Baccala, Laviano, and the priest here now?"

"Well, they just come with me," Gallagher said. "I mean, we got no reason to, you know . . ."

Goodman smiled. "I know all about it. You can tell Mr. Baccala he can take his priest with him and go home and pray that he's still alive. We're not interested in him. Then come back here and let's sit down and we'll give this Mr. Palumbo something to think about for a couple of years."

Gallagher had one of his people take Baccala out the back way so he wouldn't have to pass the news people in the outer lobby. Baccala held tightly onto Mario's arm. Dominic Laviano walked behind them.

"Is this your first *mirac'*?" Baccala whispered.

"It is the first time I have been this blessed," Mario said.

Detective Donald Jenkins was sitting on a wooden bench by the door leading to the staircase. The floor around his feet was littered with cigarette butts. For three hours now, Jenkins had been waiting for Inspector Gallagher to come out and tell him what to do.

Jenkins decided to throw the stare at Baccala. *It's the most they'll ever do to this freakin' old guinea,* Jenkins told himself. Jenkins clenched his teeth on his cigarette. His eyes flashed steadily at Baccala. When Baccala wouldn't look at him, and kept talking to this fellow walking down the hall alongside him, Jenkins became irritated. He glanced at the one Baccala was with. Jenkins' hand went right away to the cigarette gripped in his teeth. He pulled the cigarette out and held it away from his face so there would be no smoke in his eyes while he looked at this priest. The same priest he had seen in civilian clothes taking Angela Palumbo in the subway over to 11th Street in Manhattan.

Jenkins came off the bench and walked very quickly down to Benjamin Goodman's office and knocked on the door.

Big Jelly and Kid Sally drove through the streets of Brooklyn, listening to the radio. Big Jelly drove with his right hand on the wheel and his head hanging out the window like a police dog's, so the wind would rush up any tiny passageway in his nose left by the stitches. At midnight, there still was no news of the Della Palma incident. The police were keeping the lid on it. There was no news of Red D'Orio yet, either. This was not because of any official reluctance. The delay was merely the result of slow typing in Brooklyn South Homicide.

Early in the evening Red D'Orio had become bored hanging around the vending-machine office. He decided to go out for a drink. "I'll be a moving target," he said. Which he was. He had four scotches in Esposito's on Carroll Street. He promptly swung over to Busceglia's in Williamsburg. He had four scotches in Busceglia's and whisked across town to the Caprice on Fourth Avenue. An hour later he was in the Showboat Bar on Atlantic Avenue. "Beautiful," Red D'Orio complimented himself. "How could they get me when they never see me? Just keep walkin' and talkin'." He held his glass out for another drink. Nothing happened. Blearily, Red D'Orio looked down the bar. There was no bartender. This was because the bartender had just received a phone call telling him to get into the men's room or stand a chance of getting shot too. The rest of the place was empty. "Where did all the guys go?" Red said. The door to the Showboat opened. Red D'Orio brightened. He needed company. He turned to the door. "Hi, guys," he said. "Hi," one of them said. The other two did not talk. They were too busy shooting.

Rain began to fall at midnight. It rapidly turned into heavy rain, with the cold wind blowing it in sheets. The rain emptied the streets. Kid Sally, sitting in the front seat of the car, began hitting himself on the forehead. It was time to think of a good place to dump the body. He decided on the weed-fringed industrial slop of the bay on the far side of Staten Island. No human being would be in the vicinity on a night like this. Big Jelly drove onto the parkway that goes to the Verrazano Bridge. The bridge runs across the Narrows of New York Harbor to Staten Island. As they came up the approach ramp, the rain was so heavy that Big Jelly had to drive slowly. The windshield was covered with running water. The reflection of the bridge lights on the running water made Big Jelly blink. The car crept onto the wide, brilliantly lit bridge runway. Kid Sally was staring moodily out the window on his side. He rolled the window down and put his head out into the rain. He looked ahead. He turned his head and squinted to see behind the car.

"Nobody's on the whole bridge," he said.

"Everybody must of got smart and pulled off the road," Big Jelly said.

Kid Sally giggled. "Stop the car in the middle," he said.

"The middle?" Big Jelly said.

"Just stop the car in the middle," Kid Sally said. His lip curled into a sneer. He began giggling.

Big Jelly pulled the car to the side of the bridge and rolled to a stop.

"The greatest." Kid Sally giggled.

"What greatest?" Big Jelly said.

"Just let's go," Kid Sally said. He opened the car door.

"Go what?" Beppo said.

"Go to watch the first man ever to come off of the bridge," Kid Sally said.

"Wow!" Beppo said.

"That's different," Big Jelly said. "Whyn't you tell me?" He pushed his door open.

Kid Sally stood in the rain, tugging the Water Buffalo by the shoulders out of the back seat. Beppo stood in the back and kicked the body. Big Jelly reached for the legs. Grunting against the weight of the body and the cinderblocks, the rain washing their hair into their faces and soaking through their clothes, the three of them staggered with the body to the low battleship-gray wall on the side of the roadway. High above them, on the towers and cables, the bridge lights were strung out in a burning necklace that can be seen for thirty miles. Stright out, and below them, there was only blackness with rain whipping out of it. They heaved the Water Buffalo's body on top of the wall. The three of them went back a couple of steps. "Now!" Kid Sally said. They rushed forward, arms straight out in what football people refer to as a forearm shiver. They hit the Water Buffalo's body and sent it out into the blackness. Under the roadway, a great steel beam protrudes. The cinderblocks hit the lip of the beam and bounced off into the black air. The Water Buffalo's body followed. The bridge is 228 feet in the air. The rushing water below it is 180 feet deep. The initial airdrafts caused the cinderblocks and the body to wiggle a bit, as bombs do when they begin falling. The wiggling stopped, and the Water Buffalo and cinderblocks fell straight and true through the black air.

The three of them dove back into the car. They were laughing and hitting themselves while Big Jelly got the car going.

In the harbor water under the bridge at this time was the tugboat *Grace Moran,* pushing against the tide on its way to a scow-hauling job at Erie Basin. Also, the Greek freighter *Olympic Zenith,* which was sliding on the tide to the ocean. The *Olympic Zenith,* Theodore Kritzalis commanding, was carrying a cargo of steam turbines for Athens and also letter mail and printed matter for Lisbon, Naples, Piraeus, and Cyprus. The entire ship seemed to shake when the Water Buffalo hit the front hatch.

One crewman on duty at the bow, Peter Chingos, fainted. Captain Kritzalis, brought up under German dive bombing, instinctively fell to the bridge deck. When there was no immediate explosion, Captain Kritzalis crawled to the intercom and ordered the crew to run to the stern of the ship. Captain Kritzalis had seen these delayed fuses before. The American harbor pilot, George Edmundson, tried to speak, but his voice failed to come out. He scribbled on a sheet of paper, "Raise Coast Guard!" A mate rushed the paper to the radio shack.

Within minutes the Coast Guard cutter *Lawson* was streaming down the harbor toward the *Olympic Zenith*. Also converging on the freighter were the New York City Fire Department boat *John F. Kennedy* and New York City Police Department Harbor Launch No. 7. The *Olympic Zenith* lay dead in the water and searchlights poked through rain and fell on the bow. The searchlights intensified the light cast by the worklights on the winches over the front hatch. And now, through the heavy rain and blackness, the damage could be seen. Sticking up from the hatch cover, which had been smashed almost completely through, were the Water Buffalo's still magnificent $110 alligator Bostonians. The rest of the Water Buffalo was dangling in the air in the front hold.

Preliminary reports reached all responsible parties.

Louis Samuels, night man in the Mayor's office at City Hall, scribbled quickly on a yellow legal pad while the communications man from Police Headquarters read off the report.

"Uhuh," Samuels said. He flicked the call off and then pressed down another key on the small monitor board and began to flick it up and down rapidly.

"What?" The Mayor's voice was husky with sleep.

"Mr. Mayor, the police say that a gangster was thrown off the Verrazano Bridge and the body landed on a Greek freighter."

Samuels' ear was filled with the hollow sound of the Mayor's phone falling from the night table and dangling in the air. He could hear a rustle and the phone being picked up again.

"Hello," the Mayor's wife said. "I don't know what it is, but he'll have to call you back. He just had to go to the bathroom."

In Brooklyn, Benjamin Goodman leaned over a sink in one corner of his crowded office. Goodman ran cold water and slapped it over his red-rimmed eyes. He took a paper towel and dried himself. His face felt a little better now.

"All right," he called out to the crowd of detectives. "Now let's go over this again. I want the timing checked out step by step. I want to have this thing come off smooth, and I don't want to miss one of these animals."

It was eight a.m. in London. Georges Pappajohn, a silk robe wrapped around his 5-foot-4, 265-pound body, stood at the living-room window of his suite in the Dorchester. He looked down at the morning traffic in Hyde Park and muttered impatiently while the overseas operator put his call through to Washington. Pappajohn, seventy-one, is known as the Floating Greek because of all the ships he owns.

"Come on, come on," Georges Pappajohn snarled at the operator. "I buy your company and fire you."

"What's the matter, Georgie?" His wife, Rona, almost eighteen, stood in the doorway in a Baby Doll nightgown.

"I'm busy, can't you see?" Pappajohn said.

"Oh, Georgie, always business." Rona Pappajohn pouted. "And you promised."

"Hello, operator!"

"Georgie, you promised to buy little Rony a bracelet today so she won't be mad at you for running out of ink in your pen."

"Allo, allo," Pappajohn said. "Ah, Meester Assistant Secretary of State. How are you, Meester Assistant Secretary? I don't like to wake you up at this hour, but I have a question to ask of you. Meester Assistant Secretary of State, what is this *bullshit* with my ship?"

In Washington, in his house in Georgetown, MacGregor Wallingford of State listened glumly while the world's biggest shipping magnate screamed about an accident in Brooklyn involving gangsters. Wallingford didn't know what it was about. When Pappajohn hung up, Wallingford clicked the phone and told the State Department operator to get the Attorney General at his home.

Chapter 20

In the morning after the rain, the breezes coming down the street did not cause the usual swirl of soot to rise from the sidewalk on 11th Street. The streets seemed washed, and the air was clean and cold and sparkling in the sun. At the subway station, the lightshafts coming down the subway stairs made even the dingy change booth seem pleasant.

Angela and Mario were holding hands while they came down the stairs. They stopped in the pool of light in front of the change booth.

"I'll be back soon," he said.

"Well, I don't know, I have to be home," she said.

"Why go there?"

"Because I have to."

He let go of her hand and thought for a moment. He pulled out the key to his apartment.

"Go back and wait, it won't be long," he said.

"I have to see. I'm afraid there's so much trouble."

"Don't go home any more. I don't want you near the trouble."

"I just don't know." She bit her lip.

She took the key from his hand and lifted her face and kissed him. He took her hand.

"I just have to see the woman about my painting and come back," he said. He took out twenty dollars. He felt strange when he held it out to her. He had never given away anything in his life. "Buy something if you need something," he said.

She gave him another quick kiss. He went up to the change booth. She spun and went up the stairs with her legs kicking freely. She had her head down and was humming something to herself and she didn't see the two men at the top of the stairs until one of them reached out and took her by the arm. The other pulled a warrant out of his jacket pocket.

Mario got to the fountain in front of the Plaza Hotel at 11:15. His date with Maxine Finestone was at noon. Over the phone the night before she had told him her husband was excited about the painting. That meant money, Mario knew. He sat down on one of the benches around the fountain. He was shaky, as are all veterans immediately after a battle. But the proximity of success soothed him. The woman would pay for the painting, and Baccala, between kisses, had given him a private phone number. He would be able to raise so many thousands out of Baccala that a subsidy for an art career, and also a good start toward building an orphanage in Catanzia, seemed assured. Mario thought it was so good that he would have to steal only one-third of the money for Father Marsalano, instead of half. He bent down and pulled his shoelaces apart. He reached into his pocket and took out his uncle's eyeglasses. He got up and began stumbling over to the steps of the Plaza.

Detective Donald Jenkins came off the bench on the other side of the fountain.

"Now where is he going?" Jenkins said.

"Look at the walk," a detective with him said.

"He's a pisser," Jenkins said.

"What the hell is he doing?" the detective said.

"I don't know," Jenkins said. "One day he's a priest, and now he's blind, I guess. The hell with it, let's start finding out right now what this son-of-a-bitch does."

They came onto Mario from each side. They guided him to a black Plymouth which had pulled up in front of the hotel a few minutes before.

The raid on Marshall Street took place at 10:15. It would have been much earlier, but Benjamin Goodman, in making calls to news desks, found that two of the local television channels did not have camera crews scheduled to work before nine a.m., and there was no way to get them in earlier. Goodman postponed the raid until the crews reported for work, picked up announcers, and drove to Brooklyn. The raid itself went off smoothly. Cops hit the block in battalion strength. No resistance was offered. They arrested Kid Sally Palumbo and fifty-nine others without incident. The day's only accident came when Benjamin Goodman, charging the vending-machine office for the television cameras, pulled open the cellar door and the lion flew out at him. This caused Benjamin Goodman to faint, but his reputation for fearlessness was saved by television cameramen who fled when they saw the lion.

The bridge man in Part I, Brooklyn Criminal Court, needed cough drops near the end of the afternoon to finish calling out the various charges against the sixty defendants. The charges began with homicide and attempted homicide and ran through conspiracy to commit homicide, felonious assault, possession of automatic weapons, unlawful possession of a lion, and, as the last line on Big Jelly's warrant, illegal possession of narcotics.

"It was only marijuana, I'm allowed to have that," Big Jelly said.

"What do you mean by that?" the judge snapped.

"I'm a high-school student," Big Jelly said.

There were sixty people in the courtroom. Bail was set at $100,000 each. The total came to $6,000,000, highest bail figure ever heard in a courtroom anywhere. Benjamin Goodman rushed into the men's room and began combing his hair. He came out into the television lights and gave interviews for an hour. It was after six when he got back into his office. Gallagher was tapping Mario's passport against the desk.

"What are we supposed to do with the girl?" Goodman said.

"Do what we're supposed to do," Gallagher said.

"What am I going to hold her on?" Goodman said.

"What you got now is good enough. Material witness."

"Where does that take us?"

"Right to here," Gallagher said. He slapped the passport against the desk. "He gets us everything we need."

"All right. Put the girl up in a hotel, like any other material witness," Goodman said. "Then let's bring this wop of yours in here and have a talk with him."

"How do you want to work it with him?" Gallagher said.

"Put him into the grand jury with immunity, and when he's through, your lovely Italian girl is no longer a material witness. She's a defendant. And I've got myself a good witness as a little insurance policy in case the rest of these bums try to go to trial with this."

Jenkins had been sitting with Mario in a dingy room at the end of the hall. Now he brought Mario into Goodman's office.

"Did you advise him of his rights?" Goodman said.

Jenkins shook his head yes.

"All right, you can go," Goodman said.

He leaned back in his chair. "Want a lawyer?" he said to Mario.

"I don't know one," Mario said.

"You better get one, you're in a lot of trouble," Goodman said.

"You're going to jail," Gallagher said.

"Have you ever been locked up with fags?" Goodman said.

Mario didn't understand the slang.

Goodman smiled. "A man of the world like you doesn't know what fags do to you in jail?"

"I don't know what they do in Italy, but in this country they make a big line in jail and they all rape you," Gallagher said.

Mario clutched his chest. But he said nothing.

Goodman leafed through the passport. "Pretty serious matter," he said. "Impersonating a priest, conspiracy to commit murder." He shook his head. "Why did you come to this country?"

"I think the big question is, how does he like it here?" Gallagher said. "Would he like to stay here, or would he like to get sent home right away?"

Mario picked him up on it. Now they were telling him what they had on their minds.

"What do I have to do?" he said.

Goodman and Gallagher smiled at each other. "You know, you're pretty cute," Goodman said to him.

"You're going into a room where nobody can see you," Gallagher said, "and you're going to tell a jury, a private jury we call a grand jury, you're going to tell them what you've seen and heard."

"Nobody can see me?" Mario said.

"Nobody."

"Who will know what I say?"

"Nobody," Goodman said. "I'll be there, you'll be there, and the jury will be there. Nobody else. You understand? Nobody else. Grand-jury testimony is secret."

"What do I have to say?"

"Just what you've seen and heard."

Mario nodded.

"If you don't, you get sent home. Bingo. Home to sunny Italy. Right to the town you came here from."

"All right," Mario said.

"Did the girl use to sit down with them and talk about what they were going to do?" Gallagher said softly.

Mario took a sharp breath.

"Didn't she?" Gallagher said.

Mario looked carefully at their faces. "Does she get in trouble?"

"You get sent straight home to Italy," Gallagher said.

"I never said that," Goodman said. "I never said we'd forgo criminal charges before deportation."

It was a very easy thing for Mario to do. He simply nodded yes, and he stood up, and this detective, Jenkins, came and took him out of the building and they drove to a new motel overlooking fishing piers in Sheepshead Bay. They ate in the room and sat and watched television, and Mario felt nothing.

All the next morning Mario sat in Benjamin Goodman's office and went over what he was to say in front of the grand jury.

"And who came into the restaurant?" Goodman said.

"Kid Sally Palumbo," Mario said.

"And what did Mr. Palumbo have in his hand?"

"A gun."

"All right," Goodman said. "Now, let's go back. When you sat in the kitchen at fifty-one Marshall Street, with whom did you sit?"

"The grandmother, the brother, the little man you call dwarf, and the fat one, Jelly, and the sister."

"The sister's name is?"

"Angela."

"And during the conversation did Angela Palumbo contribute anything?"

"Contribute?"

"Yes, say anything. Did she say anything?"

"Yes."

"What did she say?"

"She said, 'Don't forget to steal license plates for the truck.'"

Goodman sat back. Gallagher smiled. "Accessory before an attempted homicide," Goodman said.

"All right, tomorrow is your big day," he said to Mario.

Mario felt good the next morning. One of the detectives had bought him a new shirt. Mario whistled while he buttoned the shirt. All he had to do was walk into this room where nobody could see him, say what he had been told to say, then walk out of the room and go back to the apartment on 11th Street. When he thought of the apartment, Mario could feel Angela next to him. He reached for his tie and began knotting it. Maybe, he thought, it was better that he hadn't met Mrs. Finestone at the Plaza yesterday. It would make him seem more independent, like a real artist.

The hallways at the District Attorney's office were crowded in the morning with assistants coming in and out of their offices and going down to the courtrooms. Jenkins took Mario to Goodman's office and Goodman, leafing through a briefcase, told Jenkins to take Mario down to the grand-jury room. He would follow. Jenkins led Mario down the hallway toward the rear elevators. A policewoman was standing in a doorway near the end of the hall.

"Hi," she said to Jenkins.

"Who's that?" Jenkins said.

"You know," the policewoman said. She glanced into the office.

"Hey!" Jenkins said. He put his arm out to stop Mario. The policewoman tried to step inside the office and close the door. But Mario was even with the doorway and he could see Angela sitting inside. She was in a chair by the window. She had her coat on, and her hands were in her coat pockets. Her face was very white, and she looked very small and very young. He was looking at her, with no expression on his face, and Jenkins' hand pressed against his back and moved him on down the hall. While he waited for the elevator, Mario wondered if Mrs. Finestone would pay more than $300 for the painting.

The twenty-three people on the grand jury shifted around in red leather chairs when Mario came in. He sat facing them. Goodman walked in, carrying a bundle of yellow legal pads and crinkly onionskin paper covered with smeared typing. He put the bundle on the desk and began going through it. Mario sat in the chair and looked around. Fluorescent lights played on the brown walnut paneling of the room. There were no windows. The people on the grand jury were men, old men mostly, with chicken skin hanging over their collarbuttons. Most of them wore these dark ties with tiny dots.

"Good morning, gentlemen," Goodman said. The light played on his red hair.

He turned to Mario. "All right, now would you please tell these gentlemen if you know an Angela Palumbo."

"Parlo solo Italiano," Mario said.

Goodman smiled. "No, no, just relax. Answer the question in English."

"Parlo solo Italiano."

"What are you saying to me?" Goodman said.

"Io no sache."

"Can't he speak English?" the foreman of the grand jury, a retired bank official named Everett Cashman, said.

"*Tu pari ca ti chiavi a mammata,*" * Mario said to the foreman.

"What's that?" the foreman said.

"One of the words was your mother, I know that," a man sitting next to Cashman said.

Mario smiled and nodded in agreement. "*Sorita sa appaura di te la notta,*" ** he said.

Benjamin Goodman's eyes widened. His lips pursed. His finger shot out at Mario. "Now you listen to me . . ."

Mario stood up, made a courtly little bow, and came out of the bow with the middle finger of his right hand held up.

"*A foongool a bep!*"

Mario never did stop to think about what he had done. He just sat in one office while everybody screamed and cursed at him, and then went with the detectives over to another building, the Federal Court Building, and two other men who looked like detectives put him in an office and somebody brought him a sandwich and cup of coffee. Late in the day he was brought into a huge paneled courtroom. A man from the Italian consulate was there. Mario heard discussions about whether he wanted a hearing and when the judge glanced at him, Mario said, "*Tu si nu porco grasso.*" †

The man from the consulate spoke to Mario in Italian. He said Mario could have an immigration hearing at a future date, but he would have to stay in jail while awaiting it. And there would be a chance he would have to face criminal charges. Or Mario could just sign a waiver and be sent back to Italy immediately. Mario shrugged. Anything but jail. At dusk

---

* "You look like you have sex with your mother."
** "Your sister must be afraid of you at night."
† "You fat pig."

two men who looked like detectives drove Mario through the heavy traffic to Kennedy Airport. At the Alitalia terminal they were ushered into a small cinderblock office.

"You've got about two hours before the plane leaves," one of the men with Mario said.

Mario folded his arms and closed his eyes. He wondered if Mrs. Finestone would have paid $350 for his painting.

At the Brooklyn District Attorney's office there had been so much shouting and commotion in the hallway that the police-woman was afraid to put her head out and ask for anything. Finally, when the office was getting dark and she had to put on the light, she decided to look outside and ask.

"Hey," she said to a detective, "what do I do with her?"

"With who?"

"I've got Palumbo's sister in here. Been here all day. No-body told me what to do with her."

"Stay there and I'll find out," the detective said.

He walked down to Goodman's office. Goodman ran a hand over his eyes.

"I don't have time to start on her," he said.

"Well, the policewoman wants to know what to do with her."

"Throw her out of here," Goodman said. "I got no use for her now."

"Just send her home?" the detective said.

"I don't care where she flops, just throw her out of here without me seeing her," Goodman said. "And this old broad the grandmother, too. She's in detention. Release her. I can't hold her now. Just make sure I don't see them walking out of here."

"You can go home," the policewoman said to Angela.

Angela was still sitting motionless, hands in her pockets, by the window. She looked up.

"Home?"

"That's right, dear, you can go home."

Angela got up slowly. The policewoman held the door open.

"If I were you, just between us girls, I'd go right home and write your boy friend a thank-you note."

"A note?" Angela said.

"Yes, dearie, I think you'll find your wonderful boy friend has just had his ass thrown out of the country."

"Out?"

"Today. Bang! Out on his ass."

"When did he go?"

"Don't ask me. Just get yourself together and leave so I can go home too. I didn't even get lunch here today."

In the hallway, Angela asked a detective if he knew about Mario Trantino.

"Who?" the guy said.

She looked around at the faces walking past her in the hall, and she left the office. She came running out of the lobby into the start of the night and her arm was up to call for a cab but two lawyers edged in front of her and took it. She stood on the crowded downtown Brooklyn street, waving her arm. All the cabs were filled. After fifteen minutes, she turned and ran into the subway.

The train went to New Lots Avenue station in the East New York section, which is close to Kennedy Airport. Angela wedged into the car and rode with a musty-smelling workman's jacket pushing into her face. The train made every stop and people wedged their shoulders to get out each time. Some of them got stuck in the doors while the doors were closing, and the conductor had to reopen the doors and try to close them again. At Kingston Throop Station a man stood with his shoulder blocking the doors. He wouldn't move. The train did not move while the door was still partially open. After what seemed like five minutes, the conductor walked down and pushed the man's shoulder into the car so the doors would close. The conductor walked back to his position between cars and pressed a buzzer. The train started slowly.

Angela came up onto the street at New Lots Avenue at 6:40 p.m. There were three cabs sitting at the corner. The drive to Kennedy took twenty minutes.

"What airline?" the driver said as he came into the maze of purple and blue and winking yellow lights of the terminal section.

The first terminal building handling overseas flights was the Pan American. Angela got out into the glare of lights and uniformed baggage-handlers and trim blond passenger aides. She ran into the crowded terminal and started one way and she saw the information sign and doubled back. A man in line in front of her wanted information on a flight to Karachi. The girl behind the counter patiently went through folders. Another girl was free and she nodded to Angela.

"Rome?" the girl said. "Flight 101 departing at 8:30 p.m."

Angela gave her the name. She picked up a white telephone and dialed a number.

"Hello, on flight 101. Passenger Trantino, Mario. Is he on the list? Hmmmmm. All right."

She put down the phone. "No, he isn't. Are you sure he was on this flight?"

"No, I'm not," Angela said.

"Alitalia has a 7:40."

Angela ran out of the terminal and down the circular driveway. She ran over a plot of dead grass and onto the driveway of the next terminal and then onto the long, crowded, brightly lit sidewalk running in front of the international terminal. The Alitalia terminal was halfway down the long building.

"Trantino?" the clerk said. He looked at a typewritten sheet. He looked up at Angela.

"Just a moment," he said. The clerk stepped away from the counter and went through a door.

One of the United States Naturalization and Immigration agents sitting with Mario got up and answered the knocking on the door to the cinderblock office.

"Yeah?" he said to the clerk.

The clerk whispered to the agent.

The agent shook his head. "Fuck that," he said. "No."

The door shut and the clerk came back into the space behind the counters. He was walking over to Angela when a man at a desk reached for his arm and handed him the phone. The clerk took the phone and began talking over it. He talked for minutes. People were pushing into the lobby, and a family escorting a priest wedged past Angela to the counter. When the clerk got off the phone and came back to the counter he had his head down and he was looking for something and a man in the family was pushing the priest's airline ticket at the clerk and the pink pages were flapping in the light and the loudspeaker called for boarding and people were pushing and Angela was trying to step through and now she spat out a word and slashed at the crowd with her hands. People looked at her in surprise and stepped away.

The clerk bent over the counter. "I'm sorry, I'm sorry, I got so busy all of a sudden." He paused. "Why don't you go up to the observation deck? It is straight up the stairs here." He glanced up at the clock. "Don't say I said anything."

The observation deck at Kennedy Airport is one flight over the planes. There is a railing on it and you can lean over the railing and look down at the people walking onto the plane and call to them and wave to them. It is crowded in the summer, but few people stand on it in the winter. They say good-by inside the terminals.

Angela was the only person on the observation deck over

the green-striped Alitalia plane. She stood with her hands gripping the railing and her eyes burning on the foot of the staircase leading to the plane. A mechanic in white coveralls and a blue baseball cap walked down the staircase. An airlines official in a navy-blue uniform and white hat stood at the foot of the ramp. A slow whine came from one of the engines. A blue tractor drove away from the nose of the plane, pulling empty baggage carts with it. Another whine started in another engine. The sound was very loud now.

Very quickly, with two men flanking him, Mario walked out into the whine. The two men held him by the elbows. Mario trotted up the steps and he was at the top and through the doorway and into the lighted cabin. The two men with him stood in the doorway for a moment. They stepped back and the airlines man in the uniform came up the steps and tugged on the plane door and slammed it shut.

The plane was parked at an angle to the observation deck so that when your eye tried to sweep along the egg-shaped lighted windows, the windows seemed to run together. Angela was trying to see into each window, and her eyes were smarting and she could not see Mario, and the whine of all four engines became loud and stabbed into her ears. Her hair began to blow in the kerosene fumes of the jet exhaust. The engines made more noise and her hair was whipping and the bottom of her coat was blowing and the plane was moving and Angela Palumbo put her hands over her ears and screamed into the noise of the plane and the fumes whipping into her and the lights and the night beyond them.

Two months later, after considerable legal maneuvering, the Kid Sally Palumbo mob, in toto, agreed to plead guilty to charges of conspiring to kill approximately every citizen in the borough of Brooklyn. For this chance to get sixty hoodlums off the street without the expense of a trial, the state agreed to one-year sentences for all. A year does not sound like a lot in print, but it is a very long time in jail. All authorities agreed it would be long enough to end the great gang war and take much of the ambition for any future trouble out of nearly all the Palumbo gang members.

There was only one small hitch to the deal. Just before sentencing, with all sixty crowded in front of the bench, Kid Sally Palumbo looked around and saw his sister and grandmother. He whispered to the lawyer. The lawyer asked for a very short recess before sentencing. Kid Sally waved to his sister and she came up to the railing and he called out something to her. She looked up at the ceiling. Her lips moved in a short prayer. She ducked out of the courtroom. She returned in five minutes, holding a paper bag from the chain drugstore down the block from the court building.

"What's that you got there?" a court attendant said.

"He forgot a toothbrush," she said.

At 11:30 a.m., out in Beachhaven, Long Island, Mrs. Baccala started the car. When the car did not blow up from a bomb, Baccala got up from the kitchen floor and walked out into the driveway, patted Mrs. Baccala on the head as she came out of the car, got in, and backed down the driveway to start another day as a major American organized-crime overlord.